214

BURN
FOR ME

D0971417

DON'T MISS

The Fallen
AVENGING ANGEL

ANGEL BETRAYED

ANGEL IN CHAINS

ANGEL OF DARKNESS

NEVER CRY WOLF

IMMORTAL DANGER

MIDNIGHT'S MASTER

MIDNIGHT SINS

And read more from Cynthia Eden in these collections!

HOWL FOR IT

THE NAUGHTY LIST

BELONG TO THE NIGHT

WHEN HE WAS BAD

EVERLASTING BAD BOYS

BURN FOR ME

CYNTHIA EDEN

BRAVA

KENSINGTON PUBLISHING CORP.
www.kensingtonbooks.com

BRAVA BOOKS are published by

Kensington Publishing Corp.
119 West 40th Street
New York, NY 10018

All Kensington titles, imprints, and distributed lines are available at special quantity discounts for bulk purchases for sales promotions, premiums, fund-raising, educational, or institutional use.

Special book excerpts or customized printings can also be created to fit specific needs. For details, write or phone the office of the Kensington special sales manager: Kensington Publishing Corp., 119 West 40th Street, New York, NY 10018, attn: Special Sales Department; phone: 1-800-221-2647.

BRAVA and the B logo are Reg. U.S. Pat. & TM Off.

ISBN-13: 978-0-7582-8404-4
ISBN-10: 0-7582-8404-7

First Kensington Trade Paperback Printing: February 2014

10 9 8 7 6 5 4 3 2 1

Printed in the United States of America

First Electronic Edition: February 2014

ISBN-13: 978-0-7582-8406-8
ISBN-10: 0-7582-8406-3

ACKNOWLEDGMENTS

I need to offer a round of thanks to so many people.

First, my readers—thank you for all the support that you have given to me. You are absolutely incredible.

To Eden's Agents—what would I do without you? You're all amazing!

For my fabulous editor, Esi Sogah—thank you for your wonderful editorial insight. Working with you has been a pleasure.

Happy reading!

CHAPTER ONE

The first time Eve Bradley saw Subject Thirteen, he was in chains.

She froze in front of the glass wall that separated her from him—a wall that, to Subject Thirteen, would look just like a mirror. The two-way mirror let the doctors and observers watch his every move. Not that the guy could do much moving when he was chained to the wall.

"I-I thought . . ." Eve tried to fight the tremble in her voice. She was supposed to look like she belonged here. Like she fit in with all the other researchers who were so eager to experiment on the test subjects. "I thought everyone was here voluntarily."

Dr. Richard Wyatt turned to face her, his white lab coat brushing against her. "The chains are for his safety." His tone implied she should have realized that obvious fact.

Yeah, right.

Was she really supposed to buy that line? Being chained up—that equaled safety in what mixed-up world?

"Dr. Bradley . . ." Wyatt's dark eyebrows lifted as he studied her with an assessing gaze. "You do realize that all the subjects here are far, far from human, correct?"

She knew the spiel. "Yes, of course, I do. They're supernaturals. Here to take part in experiments that will help the U.S. military." So all the fancy guys in suits had told the media when the Genesis group started their recruitment program last fall.

Not that she believed their story. It had taken her months, *months,* to set up this cover and get inside the research facility.

If she'd been on her own, she never would have passed clearance. But, luckily, Eve had managed to make a few powerful friends over the years.

Friends who wanted to know the truth about this place as much as she did. They all had an interest in Genesis.

Some reporters really could smell a story. Right now, Eve's nose was twitching.

She glanced back at Subject Thirteen. Everyone knew paranormals were out there, living in the midst of humans. About ten years ago, the first supernaturals had made themselves known. They'd come out of their paranormal closets. And why not? Why should they have been forced to keep hiding? Always hiding in the shadows had to suck. Maybe they'd just gotten tired of living a lie and decided to force the humans to see what was right in front of them— or what was living right beside them.

Since the big revelation, things had changed for the paranormals. Some were hunted. Some turned into instant celebrities. The reaction from the humans, well, that was mixed, too.

Some humans hated the supernaturals. Some feared them. Some really enjoyed fucking them.

Eve didn't necessarily fall into any of those categories.

Subject Thirteen was staring right at her. A small shiver slid over Eve's body.

His eyes were dark. They looked almost black—as black as the thick hair that hung a little too long as it brushed over his broad shoulders. Thirteen was a handsome man, strong, muscled—*definitely muscled*—and with the sculpted bone structure that had probably caught plenty of attention from the ladies.

High cheeks. Square jaw. Lips that were hard, a little thin, but still sexy . . . though she could have sworn that mouth held a cruel curve.

Her heartbeat began to pound faster. Thirteen's eyes were sweeping over her body. A slow, deliberate glance. "Can he—can he see through the mirror?" His gaze felt like a hot touch on her skin.

"Of course not" was Dr. Wyatt's instant response. The doc sounded annoyed with her.

Her shoulders relaxed.

Subject Thirteen smiled.

Damn. Her shoulders tensed right back up again.

Wyatt checked his notes and then told her, "Go check his vitals before we begin the procedure for today."

Right. Vitals check. Her job. Eve nodded. She'd done two years of med school before realizing the gig wasn't for her, so she could pass muster with these guys, no problem. Only part of her résumé was fake.

The good part.

Eve walked slowly toward the metal door that was the only entrance and exit to Thirteen's holding room. A guard opened the door for her. An *armed* guard—which brought up the next question. *Why did volunteers have to be guarded?*

Oh, jeez, but this place was creeping her out. *Volunteers, my ass.*

Sure, she'd seen a couple other subjects during her time at the Genesis facility. Not many, though. Her clearance wasn't high enough to get her past level one. Or it hadn't been . . . until today.

Until she'd been told that Dr. Wyatt needed her services for his latest experiment. Dr. Richard Wyatt *was* Genesis.

A former kid genius, the guy had a couple fists full of degrees, and currently was the leading expert in the field of paranormal genetics.

He was also a hard-ass who gave her the creeps when his cold green eyes locked on her. Maybe he was a fairly attractive guy, but something about him made her blood ice.

The guard waved his hand, indicating that it was clear for Eve to proceed. When she walked into Thirteen's holding room, Eve saw the slight flare of the man's nostrils. Then his head turned toward her slowly, the move almost like a snake's as he sized her up.

He didn't speak, but his powerful hands clenched.

Eve opened her small black bag. "Hello." Her voice came out too high-pitched. She drew in a steadying breath. The guy was chained. It wasn't like anything could happen to her. She needed to get a grip and do her job. "I'm just here to run a few quick checks on you." No machines were hooked up to him. No monitors. Wyatt wanted these checks done the old-fashioned way—hell if she knew why. Eve pulled out her stethoscope and stopped a foot away from Thirteen. "I-I'll need to listen to your heartbeat."

Still nothing. Okay. Eve swallowed and offered a weak smile. Obviously, she wasn't dealing with a chatty fellow.

Eve slid closer to him. Her gaze darted to the chains. They held his arms trapped at his sides. Even if he'd wanted to grab her—*don't grab me, don't!*—he couldn't move.

What if Wyatt was setting her up? The guy was chained and that had to mean he was dangerous, right? Those were some seriously thick chains. They looked like something right out of a medieval torture chamber.

"I won't hurt you."

She jumped at the sound of his voice; and what a dark, rumbling voice it was. When the big, bad wolf from that old fairy tale talked, Eve bet the beast had sounded just like Subject Thirteen.

She exhaled and hoped she didn't look rattled. "I didn't think you would."

His lips twisted in the faintest of smiles—one that called her a liar.

Eve put the stethoscope over his heart. She adjusted the equipment, listened, and glanced up at him in surprise. "Is your heartbeat always this fast?" Grabbing his chart, she scanned through the notes. Fast, but not *this* fast. His heart was galloping like a racehorse.

Eve put her hand against his forehead and hissed out a breath. The guy was hot. Not warm, not feverish, *hot*.

And she was so close to him that her breasts brushed his arm.

Subject Thirteen's heartbeat grew even faster.

Oh . . . just . . . *oh*. Hell. She hurried backward a bit.

"I need to draw a sample of your blood." She also wanted to take his temperature because the guy had to be scorching. Just what was he? Not a vampire, those guys could never heat up this much. A shifter? Maybe. She'd seen one of those subjects on her first day. But the shifter had been in a cozy dorm-type room.

He hadn't been shackled.

Eve put up the stethoscope and reached for a needle. She eased closer to Thirteen once more and rose onto her toes. The guy was big, at least six three, maybe six four, so she couldn't quite reach his ear as she whispered, "Are you here willingly?"

Eve began to draw his blood. Thirteen didn't even flinch as the needle slid into his arm.

But he did give a small, negative shake of his head.

Shit. She eased back down and tried to figure out just how she could help him.

"I'm Eve." She licked her lips. His gaze followed the movement. The darkness in his stare seemed to heat. Everything about the guy was hot. "I-I can help you."

He laughed then, and the sound chilled her. "No," he said in that deep rumble of a voice, "you can't."

Eve realized she was standing between his legs. His unsecured legs. His thighs brushed against hers, and she flinched.

The smile on his face was as cold as his laughter. She'd been correct when she thought she saw a cruel edge to his lips. She could see that hardness right then. "You should be afraid," he told her.

Yes, she was definitely getting that clue.

Eve pulled out the needle. Swabbed some alcohol over a wound she couldn't even see. Then she stepped back, as quickly as she could.

"Don't come back in here," he told her, eyes narrowing. A warning.

Or a threat?

Eve turned away.

"You smell like fucking candy . . ."

She stilled. Now her heartbeat was the one racing too fast.

"You make me . . ." His voice dropped, but she caught the ragged growl of "hungry."

And he made her afraid. Eve slammed her hand onto the metal door. "Guard!" Her own voice was too high. "We're done!"

The door opened and she all but fell out of the room. Even though she was afraid, she risked one last look back. Thirteen was staring after her, his jaw locked tight. He did look hungry. Only not for food.

For me.

The door slid shut and she remembered how to breathe. She sucked in a deep breath as she looked up—right into Dr. Wyatt's too sharp green gaze.

"Problem?" He asked softly, the barest hint of a southern drawl sliding beneath his words. Since the Genesis facility was hidden away in the Blue Ridge Mountains, many of the folks working there had a slight drawl that spoke of roots in the South.

The guards, anyway. Thirteen hadn't possessed any accent that she could hear.

Yanking back her control, Eve shook her head and pushed Thirteen's chart toward him. "No problem at all, sir."

Liar, Liar.

She could still feel Subject Thirteen's stare on her body. Worse, she could feel *him.*

"Good," Wyatt said, "because it's time to begin."

Uh, begin? She'd rather thought her job was done.

He motioned to the guard. She'd already learned that guy's name. Mitchell. Barnes Mitchell. As Eve watched, he pulled out his gun and checked the clip.

"The first shot shouldn't be to the heart," Wyatt instructed as he cocked his head to the side and pursed his lips. "We want a comparison shot. Wound him first," he said with a nod, "then go for the heart."

What?

But Barnes just nodded and headed back into Thirteen's room with his gun ready.

Eve lost the breath she'd taken as horror nearly choked her.

Cain O'Connor drew in a deep breath. The air smelled of her. A light, sweet scent. He could almost taste the woman—and he wanted more of her. So much more.

What were the bastards thinking? Sending in a little morsel like her. Didn't they know what he could do to her? What he wanted to do? After all these months . . .

Maybe they'd wanted to tempt him. He pulled on the chains, testing their strength. They weren't made of any metal he'd ever come across. Reinforced with who the hell knew what. The Genesis pricks thought they were so smart with their inventions. "Supernatural-proof" as that ass Wyatt had gloatingly told him when he'd asked about the chains.

The chains wouldn't hold him forever. This prison would end. *Their* nightmare would begin.

Soon.

The door of his cell opened. He caught a glimpse of her—Eve—as she glanced back at him. Her blue eyes were wide, afraid. She should be afraid. She should run as fast as she could from this place. Before it was too late for her.

It was already too late for the others. He'd marked them for death. Especially that bastard Wyatt. The doctor got off on torture.

How will you like it when you're the one screaming, Wyatt? Will it be so much fun then?

The guard stepped inside. He smelled of sweat and cigarettes. The door closed behind him. No more Eve.

But Cain could hear her footsteps. Hers and Wyatt's. His senses were far more acute than he'd let on. Why give the enemy any advantage?

Why give them any fucking thing at all?

The guard, a stocky bastard with shifty eyes and a definite taste for torture, had his weapon out. Cain's jaw locked. He knew what the gun meant. This time, they were going to try old-fashioned bullets.

Would they take a heart shot? Or a head? Maybe the guard would shoot him right between the eyes and blow his brains out.

"What are you doing?" Eve's voice. Drifting lightly to his ears like a whisper. They thought they'd soundproofed his room.

They were wrong. He couldn't hear the voices perfectly, but he caught the whispers. Knew so much more than the not-so-good doctor realized.

Cain glanced toward the mirror. He saw right through

the reflection and into the room. All it took was a little focus, a slight push of power . . .

There she was.

Her dark hair was pinned at the base of her neck. Her face—so damn pretty. Glass-sharp cheekbones, red, plump lips that made him think of sin and sheets.

And her eyes . . . fucking lethal.

Perhaps one of the few things that could be lethal to him.

"Why does the guard have his gun out?" Eve demanded, and he heard the fear shaking in her words.

He didn't like the sound of fear in her voice. Didn't like the smell of it on her, either. When Eve had gotten close to him, she'd been afraid.

Poor Eve. She probably didn't know who she should fear more . . . him or Wyatt.

Cain looked at the gun that Barnes held. "Hardly seems fair," Cain muttered, "shooting me when I'm chained."

"You're gonna let the guard shoot him?" was Eve's immediate cry.

Ah, she was definitely not like the others. That could be a problem. When hell came calling, and it would be calling soon, he'd have to make sure she didn't get burned.

Not too much, anyway.

The intercom clicked on. "Proceed with the test," Wyatt's annoying drawl ordered as it drifted through the speakers and into Cain's cell.

Dammit. Cain tightened his muscles. He hated for the woman to watch this, but perhaps she needed to see just what these bastards were capable of doing. She'd signed on for this, so she should understand just how psychotic her boss truly was.

"He can't proceed—" Eve shouted, her words tumbling through the intercom—

Just as the guard fired.

The bullet drove right into Cain's side. Tore through flesh and muscle. Blood spattered. Agony had his body shuddering.

But he didn't make a sound. That was a pleasure he wouldn't give the sadistic bastard watching.

"Silver bullets can pierce the subject's flesh," Wyatt's cool voice rattled off as if the guy were talking about the weather.

Cain's hands clenched into fists. The next shot would be to a vital organ. He knew the drill. Wyatt liked to play at first. *Torturing SOB—*

"Stop!"

Cain glanced up. Eve was pounding on the glass. The mirror was shaking beneath the force of her fists. "Guard, get away from him!" she yelled, the desperate words echoing through the intercom system. "Drop the weapon!"

Not like the others.

Wyatt grabbed her by the shoulders and pulled her back. Anger pulsed in Cain's blood. The doctor shouldn't be touching her.

"Proceed." Wyatt's order.

Eve shrieked and twisted in Wyatt's arms.

Cain saw her break away from the doctor. She ran for the cell door. Yanked it open.

"Proceed." Ah, now Wyatt sounded pissed.

Eve was rushing inside. "Get away from him!" she yelled at the guard. "Drop your weapon and just—"

The guard fired.

The bullet drove right into Cain's heart. He heard the *thud* as it tunneled into his flesh. Felt the sharp tear as it ripped through his heart. One instant of time. Two.

His gaze met Eve's. Her eyes—so blue—widened and her lips parted in a scream he didn't hear.

Too late. Cain was already dead.

★ ★ ★

Blood bloomed on Thirteen's chest. The bullet had blasted right into him—straight into his heart.

Eve ran toward him, ignoring the gun that the guard was slowly lowering. *Fucking killer.* Shooting a chained man. Yeah, that was fair.

Thirteen's legs had given way, but the chains had stopped him from crashing onto the floor. His head sagged forward, hanging limply.

Her hands slid under his jaw, and she tilted his head back. *Oh, damn.* His eyes were closed, his lashes casting heavy shadows on his cheeks. Her breath whispered over him. "I'm sorry." She should have moved faster. Knocked out the guard. Done *something* to save this man.

Instead, she'd just watched him die.

"You need to step away from the test subject, Dr. Bradley," Wyatt said, his voice not on the intercom, but coming from behind her.

Eve stiffened. "You just murdered a man in cold blood." She'd never expected to discover this. Experiments were one thing. Murder was a whole damn other sin.

One that wouldn't be forgiven.

Her fingers brushed lightly through Thirteen's hair. She'd said she would help him.

"He's not a man." Wyatt sounded amused. "You know that. No humans are test subjects in this facility. Genesis only recruits paranormals."

Fury had her shaking. "Human or supernatural . . . you *killed* him." She glanced back at Wyatt and the guard. Both were standing a good ten feet away from her.

Wyatt shrugged. "It's part of the experiment."

What?

He huffed out a frustrated breath. "You really should step away. If you don't, well, I'm sorry, but I can't guarantee your safety."

Insane. The doc was a mental case, and as soon as she got

out of this joint, she'd blast her story loud and proud to every media outlet in the country. She'd shut down this hellhole if it was the last thing she ever did.

Sure, some folks were hesitant about the supernaturals, but no one was going to accept a killing facility. No one would—

Thirteen moved, just a bit, beneath her touch.

"Step back, Doctor Bradley."

Was that fear in Wyatt's voice? Eve couldn't tell, and since she wasn't looking at him, there was no way to read the emotion that might be on his face. Her attention was on Thirteen because . . . she could've sworn that she'd just felt him take a breath.

Impossible.

Sure, vampires could survive an assortment of attacks, but this guy was no vampire. Eve would bet her life on that. She'd seen him *die.* It was—

His lashes lifted. His eyes locked on her. Only his eyes weren't black anymore. They were red, burning like flames. Burning so bright—burning, *burning* . . .

Hard hands yanked Eve back. She fell onto the floor, dragging Wyatt and the guard down with her. *Their* hands were on her. They were the ones pulling her away from Thirteen.

But almost instantly, Wyatt and Mitchell were back on their feet, and hauling her across the room with them.

Eve let them drag her away, but she couldn't take her gaze off Thirteen. Smoke was rising from his flesh, as if he were burning from the inside. That gaze—it looked like she was staring straight into hell. A man's eyes shouldn't flicker with fire.

His did.

The smoke rising from his body began to thicken.

"Out!" Wyatt's bark. The guard grabbed one of her hands. Wyatt grabbed the other. They all stumbled out into the hallway. Wyatt closed the door and quickly punched in a security code to lock the room down.

Eve memorized that code. Because what locked a man in . . . might just be able to let him out.

Then they all were racing back to that two-way mirror. Because it wasn't just smoke rising from Thirteen's body any longer. Flames were covering him.

"Oh, my God." The stunned whisper slipped from her.

Thirteen's head turned. Through the flames, he gazed at her.

Every muscle in her body tightened with pure terror. She'd never seen anything like this before. How? How could he be standing? He was *standing* now. Not on his knees any longer. Not hanging from the chains. *Standing.*

The flames slowly died. They'd melted his clothes away. Ash drifted around him. Thirteen stood there, naked, strong, his body absolutely perfect.

No sign of the bullet wound that had ended his life.

Only . . . his life hadn't really ended, and he was still watching her.

"W-what is he?" Eve managed to ask.

Thirteen pulled on the chains that still bound him. Chains that had to be impervious to fire.

"I don't know . . ." Wyatt told her, and there was no missing the excitement that hummed in his words, "but I'm going to find out."

Thirteen's gaze cut to the doctor.

He sees us. She didn't know how, but the man who should have been dead could see right through that protective glass.

"Another successful experiment." Wyatt turned away from the observation mirror and headed toward the corridor that lead back to his office. "Tomorrow, we'll try drowning. It will be interesting to see if the test subject's flames burn through the water . . ."

Eve didn't move. She couldn't.

Tomorrow, we'll try drowning.

Dr. Richard Wyatt was some kind of seriously messed-up Frankenstein scientist. She put her hand to the glass. She didn't know what Thirteen was, but she couldn't let Wyatt keep torturing him.

"I'll stop him," she whispered.

But Thirteen shook his head. Then he mouthed two simple words: *I will.*

Richard Wyatt glanced over his shoulder just in time to see Eve put her hand to the glass—as if she were trying to touch the test subject. She should have been terrified, desperate to get away after what she'd just witnessed.

The others had been.

But, no, she was still there, staring in fascination at Subject Thirteen. Just as the subject was staring back at her.

How absolutely perfect. The experiment had been even more productive than he could have hoped. This new development could open up a whole world of unexpected possibilities.

A perfect killing machine. An immortal assassin.

One that only he could control.

The experiment had been a definite success. He could hardly wait for tomorrow's show to start.

Those flames were so beautiful. Would they burn Eve's delicate skin? Or would Thirteen finally start to show his true strength?

For her sake, Thirteen had better hold on to his control. Because the lovely Eve wouldn't just be an observer for tomorrow's event.

She'd be a participant.

CHAPTER TWO

Eve slipped silently down the corridor that led to Subject Thirteen's holding room. The facility was dead quiet—nearly everyone had retired for the night and the place was on lockdown.

She'd pretended to retire, too. Gone inside the staff dorms and made a big show of shutting down for the night. Then at 2:00 A.M., she'd known it was time to make her move.

Staff dorms—all the research personnel were given rooms at the facility. Once you took the job, you didn't leave.

And how creepy was that?

Wyatt had said the lodging requirement was to keep his research protected. That all personnel would be well compensated for the time they spent at Genesis. But . . .

But she'd found a hidden camera in her dorm. Since when was it okay to video employees in their private rooms?

She crept around the corner. Thirteen's room was just a few feet away. No guard at the door. Perfect. She'd go in, not get too close—*didn't want to burn, after all*—and get his side of the story.

Then she'd see about getting them both out of there before anyone else knew what was happening.

They'd shot him. Actually freaking shot the guy. Why? Just to watch him die?

Wyatt was a twisted jerk, and she was getting this story to the press as fast as she could.

Her fingers trembled as she hurriedly punched in Wyatt's security code. She'd always been good at memorization. One of her little quirks.

The lock slid open with a soft hiss. Fingers trembling, Eve pushed open the heavy metal door. The interior of Thirteen's room was pitch black. The place reminded her of a tomb—she hated tombs.

No sound from inside reached her, and her breathing seemed far too ragged in that thick silence. But Eve tiptoed inside and made sure to seal the door behind her.

"Ah . . . hello?" she whispered as she crept into the room. "Can you—"

Rough hands grabbed her—one locking tight around her waist, one circling her throat—as she was hauled back against a rock-hard body.

A body that *wasn't* still chained to the back wall.

She grabbed at the hand around her throat, struggling to suck in the breath he'd taken from her. "P-please . . ."

"*Candy.*" His growl. In the next instant, he'd spun her around and shoved her against a wall. Her eyes fought to adjust to the darkness, and, finally, she saw the dark image of Thirteen appear before her. A big, thick shadow that seemed to surround her as his arms caged her to the wall.

Wait, he *was* still chained. Only the chains stretched much longer now. Long enough for the guy to be strolling around the room and grabbing good Samaritans who were only trying to help him.

And he still had his hand around her throat. But he wasn't trying to strangle her anymore. His fingers seemed to almost be . . . caressing her.

"L-let me go." Better he not touch her at all. When a

guy could do a serious flame-on, those hands of his needed to stay away from her person.

But he didn't let her go. Crap. Eve held herself perfectly still and said, "Please. I'm here to help you."

"If you're one of them . . ." His voice was a grating whisper, such a threat in the dark, "then you're just here for the latest game of torture."

Eve shook her head. Wait. He could see that, couldn't he? He'd seen through the two-way mirror. Surely he could see in the darkness.

"I . . . tried to stop them." She had. Like it had done much good. But her words sounded weak. *Should have tried harder.*

He grunted. Okay, she could understand him not being grateful, particularly since he'd gotten shot in the heart and her help had done zero good.

"What are you?" The question slipped out. She couldn't help it. Curiosity had always been a weakness for her—and one of the reasons she was a reporter.

Thirteen let his hand fall away. The chain slipped over his skin and rattled softly. "I'm someone you don't want to piss off."

Check. She got that. She'd actually gotten that part the minute the guy had burst into flames. "You said . . . you said you weren't here willingly."

He took a step back, distancing his body from hers. "Do they know you're in here with me?"

"No." Though she wasn't sure how much longer that would last, so they needed to cut through some of the chit-chat. "By the time they do, we'll both be gone."

He laughed then, a rough bark of sound.

Being alone with him in the dark was too intimate. Her senses were hyperaware of every move that he made. Every time the chain rattled, her body tensed.

"Just where do you think we're going?" Thirteen wanted

to know. "In case you didn't notice, they've got me on a fucking leash."

A leash that they obviously lengthened when they weren't getting ready to shoot him. Interesting. She figured the chain must be able to lengthen or shorten from its feed in the wall. Eve exhaled slowly and tried to calm her heartbeat. *No dice.* "Wyatt is planning to . . . to drown you tomorrow." Just saying the words had her stomach clenching.

He grunted. "Tell me something I don't know."

Uh, okay. "How about I'm damn good at picking locks?" She reached into her pocket and pulled out her penlight. She flashed it on, and the light hit his chest. A bare chest. Rippling with muscles. Whoever—whatever—Thirteen was, the guy was seriously built.

She lowered the light to the chain that connected to his right wrist. "I can get you out of those."

Silence.

"Don't you *want* to get out?" Eve pressed because it wasn't exactly the reaction she'd been expecting. "Or am I wrong? You said you didn't volunteer—"

"I was *sold* into the program."

That gave her pause. "Sold? What do you—"

"A soon-to-be-dead shifter named Jimmy Vance is making deals with Wyatt. Setting up paranormals for the bastard to collect and cashing in when we get caged."

Her heart raced faster. "You're saying there are others who aren't here voluntarily, too?" That was what she'd suspected—why she'd risked so much to get inside Genesis.

"I'm saying the real experiments, the ones that Wyatt won't let the world see . . . they're all performed on those of us who are being kept prisoners." He yanked on the chains and the metal groaned. "Tell me, do I really look like I'm here fucking voluntarily?"

"You're so strong . . ." She wasn't just talking about the

he-man muscles. That fire-light show had been impressive. "Why can't you just break out?"

"Fireproof." He growled the words. "The walls are reinforced with steel and titanium and some damn other mix he created, and Wyatt made sure my own private hell could withstand any heat I sent at it."

From what she'd seen, he could send plenty of heat.

She inched toward him and eased her lock-picking set from her pocket. Eve knew how to be prepared—though she'd never been a Girl Scout. More of a juvenile delinquent. "I want your promise that you won't hurt me." This was a risk, she knew that. Trusting him could be insanity.

But I'm not going to let Wyatt drown the guy. No way. They were getting out now, long before Wyatt had a chance to hurt this man again.

Thirteen's hand reached for her. She almost flinched away. Almost.

But Eve had learned it was best to face the monsters in the dark with a brave face. She wasn't new to the monster world. Sure, most folks had been shocked ten years ago when the first vamps appeared, but she hadn't been surprised. She'd known about monsters since before she could even walk.

His fingers weren't rough against her skin. Eve had expected them to be. The gentleness made her feel . . . strange. He touched her cheek. Her lips. "Would you trust what I say?" he asked, voice quiet.

Did she have much choice? "Tell me your name," she breathed the words against his hand.

Her light cast darker shadows on his face. "Cain." He touched her lips again, then pulled his hand back. "Cain O'Connor."

I'm hungry. Why, oh, why, did she have to remember those particular words right then?

Her heart double-timed inside her chest. "Cain, I think we have to trust each other here." She dropped to her knees beside him and shined the light on the links of metal that circled his wrists. There was a locking mechanism there. Her fingers brushed over the soft fabric of his jogging pants. Well, at least the guy wasn't naked anymore.

But he'd sure stiffened at her touch.

"It will only take a few moments," Eve told him as she began to position her tools. "It will—"

"We don't have a few moments."

That was the only warning she got. In the next instant, the lights flooded on in Cain's room. He grabbed her, yanked her to her feet, and put her body right in front of his as they faced the two-way mirror.

"Dr. Bradley . . ." Wyatt's drawling voice floated to them. "I don't remember giving you permission to visit Subject Thirteen tonight."

Shit, shit, shit.

And, um, why was Cain's hand around her throat again? "I-I was worried about him." True. "After what happened . . ." She let the words trail off and tried to look suitably pitiful and lost. Not overly hard at that exact moment. "I just wanted to . . . check on him."

She'd already shoved her lock pick back into her pocket. Her penlight had fallen to the floor.

And Cain was still caging her against him.

"Unlock the chains!" Cain called out. His voice was a lethal snarl. "Or I'll kill her."

Wow. Wait, that *hadn't* been part of the deal. Eve yanked against him. He didn't budge. But his left hand skimmed lightly down her side. Like he was trying to soothe her.

Since he'd just threatened to kill her, Eve didn't feel particularly soothed.

"Unlock the chains!" Cain demanded. "Or watch her die."

When there was no response, his next words cut like

a knife. "I can guarantee you, Wyatt, she won't come back."

No, she wouldn't.

"She can be replaced," was Wyatt's calm-as-you please response. "You can't."

Eve kicked back, knocking right into Cain's shins. The guy didn't so much as grunt.

"Unlock the chains." Cain's fingers tightened around her throat.

So much for trust. So much for it being them against Wyatt. So much for—

A faint hiss began to fill the room.

"Fuck," Cain growled.

She looked up, trying to track that hiss. There were small vents near the top of the ceiling. Was—was air coming in? No, not air, *gas.*

"You remember our second experiment, don't you?" Wyatt's voice asked. So mellow. So . . . emotionless as his words drifted over the intercom. "I wanted to see if you could revive from poisonous gas."

Eve began to choke. She shoved her fingers into her pocket, pulled them back out, and began to claw at the hand around her throat—and that tight lock that surrounded Cain's wrist.

"The longer you hold her, the more *you* ensure she dies," Wyatt promised. "Because you're the one who's making her inhale the poison."

Cain spun her around. She kept clawing at the chain. Only . . . she wasn't really clawing. She was doing her damnedest to pick the lock without Wyatt realizing what she was up to.

Unfortunately, she was starting to lose control of her fingers. They were fumbling, the coordination slipping from her as the poison filled her lungs. She was trying not to breathe, but . . .

Her knees began to buckle.

Cain caught her. Lifted her into his arms.

"Do you want her to die?" Wyatt asked.

Cain stared down at her. Such a hard face. She'd wanted to help him. Needed to.

There were more than enough sins on her soul. One good deed. One person saved. It wouldn't have tipped the scales, but it would have counted for something.

Cain kissed her.

It was the last thing Eve expected, but his lips, warm, firm, came down on hers, and—he blew lightly into her mouth. Just a small breath of air, but it seemed to push back the growing cobwebs in her mind.

Her fingers started to work faster on that lock.

He kept kissing her. Lightly moving his mouth against hers. Sharing his breath with her.

She felt the give in the lock. One wrist would be free. One . . .

The hissing grew louder.

More gas.

Cain lifted his head. "I knew that I'd like the way you taste."

She was only upright because of his grip on her body.

His eyes narrowed. "I'll want more."

His fingers caught hers. It looked like he was holding her. But . . . he was taking the lock pick from her.

Then he lifted her up against his chest. One arm looped under her knees. One slipped under her head.

"Don't die on me." His order. So soft she might have imagined it. He got as close as he could to the door. The chain stretched behind him, stopping him from taking any more steps. "Get her out!"

The door didn't open.

"Get. Her. Out!"

Her lungs were burning, her whole body aching.

"Now I think we understand each other better . . ." Wyatt said, and even with her thoughts getting hazy, there was no missing the guy's smug satisfaction.

The door slid open. Hands reached for Eve. Yanked her out. She glanced back and managed to lock her eyes on Cain.

She saw the rage on his face. The wild fury.

Then the door closed.

Eve tried to suck in air as quickly and deeply as she could. Her mind seemed foggy, her movements too slow, but she had to say . . . "T-turn off . . . gas . . ." They'd left it running. There was no need now, no . . .

Wyatt crouched before her. "I'm sorry, but that's not possible." The faint smirk on his lips belied the false sorrow. "Once the system activates, there's no way to stop the gas."

No way—she grabbed him and smashed his perfect white shirt in her fists. *"Help . . . him . . ."* She choked a bit as she fought to drag in clear oxygen.

Two guards pulled her off him.

Wyatt straightened his shirt. "Don't worry. We already know the gas only kills Thirteen for a little while."

She jerked against the guards. Her mind was clearing, her body growing strong again, but the hands holding her just tightened. They led her back to the observation area. Back to that damn two-way mirror.

More gas pumped in. More. Cain stood in the middle of the room, shoulders back, and his eyes—his eyes were focused only on her.

I'm sorry. This time, she was the one to silently offer the words. Her lips moved, but no sound emerged.

A muscle jerked in his jaw.

"He's withstanding the gas for a longer period of time. He should have been on his knees by this point." Wyatt sounded so damn clinical.

"You're a . . . sick asshole . . ." she managed. Her body

wasn't back to normal, not yet, and talking required some serious effort.

He smiled. "And you're not who you claim to be, *Dr. Bradley.*"

Screw him. Like she had to explain herself to him.

"But I knew you weren't the real deal from the first moment you stepped into the facility."

How had he known that? Her cover should have been perfect. She'd sweat blood making that cover.

Eve pulled her gaze off Cain and glared at the doctor. "Then why . . . let me stay? Why show . . . me—"

"Subject Thirteen?"

"His name's . . . Cain!" Not just a number, dammit.

"Because I knew once you came to Genesis, you wouldn't be leaving." He inclined his head toward the guards. "And I'd hoped to be able to use you."

Use her?

"It looks like you'll be more beneficial than I ever hoped."

The guards began to pull her away from the observation mirror.

She dug in her heels, fighting. Cain—he was dropping to his knees. His head sagging.

"I'm surprised he didn't kill you." The psychotic doc appeared puzzled. "Especially so soon after a change."

Cain's body hit the floor.

No.

She didn't realize she'd screamed until Wyatt heaved out a sigh. "Don't be so dramatic. I told you . . . the gas won't kill him for long."

But it *had* killed him.

The guards dragged her away and her scream seemed to bounce off the walls of her new hell.

★　★　★

The fire consumed his flesh, burning him from the inside out. Cain sucked in a breath and tasted the ash on his tongue. The changes were coming faster now, harder, hotter, and with each change . . .

He felt the darkness inside him growing.

Kill. Destroy.

The whispers were there—coming from the beast he'd tried hard to keep locked away for so many years.

Death brought the darkness closer. Made him lose more of the man he'd once been.

Turned him into the beast that destiny had designed him to become.

He put his hands on the floor. Pushed up. Saw the fire slide across the hard stone of his room, then die away.

Rising, he sucked in more breaths. He didn't want the taste of ash on his tongue, he wanted her. *Eve.*

The beast snarled, and the flames flared higher. He stared through the window. They were watching. Always watching.

They didn't realize what they'd unleashed. Their fucking games. Each death only made him stronger. More dangerous.

As the man faded and the beast quickened within him . . . *more fucking dangerous.*

The echo of the woman's screams pierced his ears. She'd tried to help him.

Why?

"The woman is secure." That damn voice. Driving him insane. "Don't worry," the voice continued, "we'll take good care of her."

The flames began to die away. He had to swallow back the fire, again and again, before he could manage speech. "I don't give a shit what you do to her."

Soft laughter. "Yes, you do."

He didn't move. He knew his eyes would still be burning with fire, and he wanted one of those assholes to come inside. To just come close enough to touch . . .

"You still remember her." The voice—*Wyatt*—sounded pleased. "You remember who you are . . . after our fifth experiment, you couldn't remember anything, not for days."

Because the beast had taken over. Too much darkness. Wyatt and his army of lab coats didn't get it. They weren't just playing with fire when it came to him. They were playing with hell.

When the beast broke free—*can't hold him back much longer*—there would be no stopping him. He'd destroy everyone and everything around him.

Even her.

Sometimes, the risings were harder than others. Sometimes, he lost hold of what little humanity he had because he *wanted* that darkness and fire. He wanted to kill and destroy.

This time . . . this time, it had been different. He'd held on. . . .

Why?

For . . . her?

Cain shook his head, lost, body aching, beast clawing him from the inside. "Wyatt, this is your last chance . . ." Because he was done holding back. His control wasn't strong enough to last through another death. He couldn't do it. There just wasn't enough power left within him. *Can't hold back the beast.* "Let me go or watch everyone here burn."

The doctor stepped back from the mirror. Because he was afraid. Hiding behind his experiments, acting like he didn't get off on causing pain to others.

Eve. Her name whispered through Cain's mind.

Wyatt's chin lifted. "You burn us, then you burn her."

Arrogant dick. "I don't care about her." Cain had just met her. Why should he—

"Then you would have let her die in the gas. You would have snapped her neck." Satisfaction all but purred in Wyatt's voice. "But you let her live."

Mistake. The doctor always watched him too closely. He should have known . . . Eve was just another experiment.

"Yeah, well," Cain turned away from that two-way mirror. "Maybe I just wanted a fuck and she was the first good-looking woman I'd seen since you threw my ass in here." How long ago? He couldn't even remember.

If he'd been imprisoned by normal steel, he would have escaped easily.

There was nothing normal about his imprisonment. The chains that bound him were made of some experimental metal that even his enhanced strength couldn't break. But Eve had loosened one lock for him.

He glanced down. The fire had incinerated the pick set.

But one lock was open . . .

He could work with that.

Cain smiled and knew that the doctor didn't see his grin. Good . . . better for Wyatt to be surprised when hell came for him.

Would the prick still be smiling when the flames began to eat his flesh?

It was twelve hours before Cain's cell door opened again. A few moments before the door opened, the length of his chains had retracted, the way they usually did right before a guard came inside.

They pulled back the leash so he wouldn't attack.

He expected a guard to come in first. Maybe Wyatt.

But Eve entered the room.

She was pale, paler than before, and still wearing the tight jeans and loose top she'd had on during the night. Her gaze swept over him, lingering a moment on the locks near his wrists.

Wyatt gave her a push, and she stepped fully into the room. "I've brought a present," he announced.

Eve's eyes narrowed. "I'm not a damn present."

Wyatt just laughed. Why didn't his superiors see that the guy was a nut job? Or did they just not care? As long as he got the job done, maybe it didn't matter how ass-crazy he was.

Wyatt was doing one killer job of breaking the supernaturals. Of experimenting on them, slicing them up. Finding out just what made them tick.

So he could try to splice their genetics and make a whole new breed of monsters. Unstoppable soldiers who truly fed on fear and blood. Cain had been held captive long enough to figure out exactly what was going on in that place. And it wasn't like Wyatt had tried to keep things secret from him. Hell, at first, he'd even thought that Cain should appreciate the damn genius of his plans.

Genius?

Insanity.

Wyatt's laughter faded as his gaze swept back to Eve. "What you are, Ms. Bradley, is a reporter, which is something altogether . . . annoying."

A reporter? Hell. Cain kept his expression blank as he waited to see what game the doc would play next.

But Eve straightened her shoulders. "Damn straight I'm a reporter, and that means I can't just vanish. People know I'm here. They'll be looking for me."

"There might not be anything left for them to find," Wyatt told her, shrugging, and not appearing the slightest bit concerned. "Wouldn't that be a crying shame?"

"Fuck off," Eve snapped.

That was when Cain noticed the gun. The guard—Barnes again, that jerk just loved being Wyatt's lackey—had his weapon trained right on Eve.

Wyatt laughed. "Actually, my dear, that's why you're here."

Eve blinked.

"I think Subject Thirteen—"

"Cain," Eve spat the name at him. She was a feisty one. Cain rather liked that. "The guy has a name. It's Cain. Try using it."

Wyatt waved his hand. "I think Subject Thirteen wants to fuck you."

Her jaw dropped.

Cain didn't move. *I do.* But he had his control. He had—

"Anger rouses his fire." Wyatt was walking around the room. Studying Cain with his head tilted to the side and his fingers drumming against his chin. "So I'm curious to see if passion will do the same."

Come closer, bastard. Just a little closer . . .

One touch, and this could all be over.

Wyatt pointed at Cain. "I'm figuring you out."

Doubtful.

"I think I even know what you are."

Was he supposed to be worried?

"All that power . . ." Wyatt shook his head and his hand fell to his side. "We're going to change the world."

Screw that. "When I break out of here, I'm killing you." A promise.

Eve tried to edge back toward the door. The guard stopped her.

"You're not leaving us, Ms. Bradley. You're the one who begged me to postpone the drowning experiment for the day." Wyatt straightened his lab coat. Like the thing hadn't already been straight. The guy and his control—he was always so perfectly controlled. "Because I'm feeling charitable, I'll defer to your wishes this time."

Lying jerk. This was all part of his plan, one of his sick games.

Wyatt continued, "Since I can't enjoy that particular experiment, I'll just have to substitute it for another."

"I'm human," she gritted out. "I'm not part of any *experiment* that you—"

"Today, you *are* the experiment."

Cain would enjoy frying him.

Wyatt sent him an assessing stare. "I told you, I really did come offering a present today." He paused. "You wanted her. She's yours . . . for the next hour."

"What?" Eve's shriek. "Uh, yeah, I'm not some kind of—"

"Stay with him . . . or you can spend the next hour in the cell with the vampire I haven't fed for six weeks."

Cain saw her flinch.

A starving vampire? Her delicate neck? Hell, *no*.

Eve cleared her throat. "I think—I think I'll just be choosing option A, if you don't mind. Vamps and me—we don't exactly get along."

She shouldn't have told that to the doctor. Wyatt would just use that information against her later on. He loved to know what his experiments feared and what they craved.

The doctor turned and began to brush by Eve.

She stumbled into him, hard enough that they both nearly fell to the ground. "Don't," Eve said, voice high. "*Don't* leave me with him. You know what he can do. He'll burn me!"

Cain didn't move.

The guard and Wyatt pried her hands loose. When she tried to hold on, Barnes shoved the butt of his gun into her side.

Cain snarled.

Barnes froze, then turned his head very slowly and looked at Cain.

You're dead.

Eve was on the floor. Not begging anymore. Not moving.

Wyatt smiled. "Have fun." Then he left. Barnes followed him and pulled the door shut. Cain heard the click of the lock sliding into place as the cell was secured. Eve remained crouched on the floor, one arm curled protectively over her body.

Her scent began to fill the air. The woman truly did smell like candy . . . and he'd so enjoyed the treat. He could still feel her mouth on his.

He could also feel the other eyes on them. Wyatt. Watching. Enjoying another insane experiment.

"I-I have a boyfriend." Eve sounded scared. Probably because she had to be fucking terrified. "So, um, whatever you think is going to happen here"—she glanced back at the two-way mirror—"it's not. My cop boyfriend is going to hunt me down and kick your asses!"

Ah, now she wasn't sounding afraid. The bite in her words almost made him want to smile.

"Be more accommodating . . ." Wyatt's voice ordered as the intercom crackled on. "Or you'll be feeding the vampire."

She rose to her feet. Her arm still curved over her body. "Whoring me out . . . nice touch, *Doctor* Wyatt. Classy."

Cain didn't move. Just watched her. Waited. Wyatt had read him well. He did want her, but he had to be careful.

He didn't want to hurt her.

But she was coming closer to him. Bringing her sweet scent and staring at him with—with *no* fear in her eyes. Her back was to the mirror now, and a faint smile curved her lips.

This woman didn't look scared. Didn't look angry. She looked damned pleased with herself.

"But I guess . . ." she said, voice carrying, "if there's no choice . . ."

Her arms wrapped around him. Slightly cool, her touch nonetheless blazed right through him. "If there's no choice," she said again, voice softer for just him, "then I guess we have to do whatever's necessary to survive."

She pressed her lips to his.

CHAPTER THREE

Eve knew the role that she had to play, and she was willing to do her part, up to a point. So she rose onto her tiptoes and pressed her mouth against Cain's.

Even as her hand unfurled against his, she pressed the keys to his chains into his palm.

Yeah, she hadn't been some pathetic, hopeless weeping machine for nothing. She'd used that time to get close to Wyatt. While he'd been trying to pry her loose, she'd been relieving him of his keys.

That summer of pickpocketing didn't feel quite so shameful right then.

Her lips moved softly on Cain's. Just pretending. Just keeping up appearances until he could unlock those cuffs.

Then he'd better get them the hell out of there.

Only . . . only Cain wasn't using the keys to break loose. His arms were wrapping around her, pulling her tighter against him. His mouth hardened on hers, became rougher. More demanding.

She brought her hand up between them. He was *hot* to the touch. "Cain—"

"They're watching." His voice was an almost soundless whisper. "Not yet . . ."

Oh. She stopped pushing against him. Forced her body to relax.

He was just so damned . . . big.

"Let me in . . ."

A shiver slipped over her, and because they had to make this look good, look . . . real . . . she opened her mouth.

Who was she kidding?

I want to kiss him.

His tongue pushed into her mouth. She kept standing on her toes to better meet the kiss because, oh yes, her pyro could sure kiss. His tongue thrust against hers, licked the curve of her lip, and a moan rose in her throat.

Even as she felt a very distinct part of his anatomy rising against her.

Her left hand was still between them. Still against his naked chest. She'd never touched anyone who felt as hot as he did. It was like he was burning with a fever.

Eve tore her lips from his. Cain's eyes blazed down at her, not with the fire she'd seen before, but with lust. Need.

Before she could speak, he spun her around and pushed her against the wall behind him, caging her body. No, not caging her, blocking her with his body.

"Open the lock." He pressed the keys back against her hand.

Oh, okay. The lock on his right wrist still *looked* like it was secured, even though she knew he could pop free of it at any moment.

His lips slid over her throat. "Do it."

He was covering her while she freed him. Check. Not about sex. Not about . . .

He licked her neck, his tongue sliding over the spot that always made her knees go weak. Then he . . . bit her.

Her breath heaved out even as she slid the key into the lock.

★   ★   ★

Wyatt stared through the glass, grim satisfaction filling him. He'd finally done it. Finally found a way to break Subject Thirteen.

Who would have thought the reporter would come in so handy?

Thirteen could withstand any torture. Any pain. But . . . he wouldn't be able to hold out against her. She'd be the key Wyatt needed.

Once Thirteen broke, there'd be no stopping the next stage of the project's development.

He turned away from the test subjects. After all these years, all the time and blood he'd poured into Genesis, he was finally close to a breakthrough.

Subject Thirteen would be that breakthrough.

A being that couldn't truly die. One that could withstand gunshots, poison, dismemberment . . . because he'd tried them all. Each time Thirteen died, he just burned, and rose up again. Stronger than before.

Just like a mythical phoenix.

Only . . . clearly that story hadn't been merely a myth.

The guard's eyes widened. Barnes licked his lips. The guy was obviously enjoying the show.

That had to mean that things were getting hot in there. Just what Thirteen needed.

Wyatt glanced down at his watch. They'd barely had ten minutes of the promised hour. He'd let Thirteen enjoy himself for a little while longer . . .

Until the flames started.

The lock snicked open, but Cain moved quickly, twisting his wrist so that the mechanism still appeared to be closed. If those watching saw that he was loose, they'd turn on the gas again.

Cain needed Wyatt to open the door for him. If that door would just open . . .

He'd unleash hell.

He brought his lips close to Eve's small ear. "We have to make this look real."

She shuddered against him. Fear. Had to be in fear. She'd seen what he could do. She had to be terrified that he'd hurt her.

He wouldn't.

Cain had his control gripped as tightly as he could. He just had to hold on for an hour. Then the fire could rip free.

One hour . . .

At least fifteen minutes had passed already. Had to have.

He grabbed her hips, lifted her up against him. Held her easily.

Her breath caught as her hands curled around his shoulders. To the men watching, it would look like he was pinning her to the wall and driving his aroused flesh against her.

Because . . . he was.

She just felt so *good*. Soft. Silken. Her taste filled his mouth and her body trembled against his.

It would be easy to strip her clothes away. To thrust into her. To let go.

Her hands lifted and sank into his hair with surprising strength. "It can look real." Her lips skimmed over his jaw. "But it won't be."

His lips curled. *Maybe it will be.*

Then he heard the door slide open behind them. Metal grated. In an instant, he spun around, putting his body in front of Eve's.

He expected Wyatt. Instead, Barnes stood smirking at them. "Change of plans."

"I have an hour!" Cain's voice thundered out.

Barnes backed up a step. "That was before the vamp started convulsing. He needs fresh blood—and guess who's gonna be his donor?"

The hell she was.

"Now come on, lady." Barnes lifted his gun and pointed it at Cain's chest. "We're leaving."

"No." Cain stalked forward. One step. Another. More, a few more feet . . . and the chains weren't supposed to let him advance any farther.

His leash stretched taut behind him.

The guard was sweating. Sweating, but still looking too confident.

If those chains had been locked, the guard would have possessed the power.

Would . . .

"You shouldn't have hit her with your gun." Cain kept his eyes down. Barnes couldn't be allowed to see what was coming, not yet.

The guard's feet shifted on the floor.

Eve stayed pressed against the back wall. Smart woman.

Cain flexed his hands. One lunge, and the chains would fall away. He had to be fast. Fast enough to get through that open door.

"And you *really* shouldn't have fucking cut out my heart in your third experiment . . ." That shit had hurt.

The bastard guard had *laughed* while he cut into Cain's chest.

Cain glanced up. Barnes wasn't laughing now.

He'd never laugh again.

Cain lunged forward. He shoved his hand into Barnes's chest and threw the asshole back through the doorway.

Barnes screamed, calling out for help. Help wouldn't come in time.

Cain cleared the doorway. No more locks. No more chains. He felt the power swelling inside him. Building higher and higher.

Barnes was on the floor. Shooting at him. The bullets were like bee stings on his flesh.

Eve screamed behind him. Cain didn't stop advancing. He grabbed the gun. The metal melted in his hand. Then he grabbed Barnes.

Flames erupted, burning so bright. . . .

The shriek of the alarm froze Wyatt as he entered his private office.

He turned to the right and pulled up the security feed.

Sector Three. Subject Thirteen. He stared at the monitor. Thirteen stood before a pile of ash. *Outside* his holding cell.

Dammit. They had to tranq him. Had to knock him out before—

Thirteen looked up at the security camera and smiled.

Wyatt could see the flames burning in Thirteen's eyes. The beast was out, and he was ready to destroy.

"Stop him," Wyatt whispered into the intercom. His message would feed into the earpieces of every security guard in the facility. "Use the SP-tranq." It was their all-purpose drug to take out the supernaturals. Sure, the weaker ones never woke up after getting an injection, and the stronger ones, well, it didn't keep them out for long. . . .

But they didn't need too long, just—

Thirteen wasn't on the monitor anymore. Shouts and gunfire echoed through the facility, and Wyatt could smell smoke. Thirteen was leaving a path of fire in his wake.

He wasn't just escaping. He was keeping his promise.

Sending us all to hell.

Wyatt wasn't ready for hell. Not yet.

He sealed the door to his office.

Not yet.

There was too much work to do first.

★   ★   ★

Cain had just . . . incinerated the guard. Eve stared in horror at the pile of ash at her feet. He had touched Barnes and in the next second, flames had consumed the man.

Cain raced down the hallway, and fire seemed to be taking over the facility. Eating at the walls. Snaking up to the ceiling. Burning everything.

Eve jumped back, away from the flames.

"Run."

Her head lifted and she found herself staring into Cain's eyes. He'd turned back to look at her. Only . . . fire was in his eyes. She could actually see the flames burning right in his gaze.

"Run . . . or die," he told her, the words more growl than anything else.

When he put it that way . . . Eve ran. The facility was going down, burning around her—some guards were fighting, shooting at Cain. But the guards weren't the only ones in the facility.

If this place went up in flames, and it sure looked like it would, then all the other test subjects would die.

The corridor sprinklers burst on from overhead. About freaking time. They drenched her clothes and fought the fire. Some of the flames died. Some grew stronger.

Chaos reigned.

She grabbed a white lab coat from a storage closet. Yanked it on. Tried to blend with the other researchers who were running for the exits.

Only . . . Eve didn't head for the nearest exit. She raced for the stairs that would take her down to the next level of the facility. The level she'd never accessed.

More test subjects waited down there.

She shoved her hand against the stairwell door. The alarm blared constantly, driving her crazy. She hurried, nearly fell, but caught herself as she staggered down the steps.

She opened the next door—and came face-to-face with an armed guard.

"What are you—" he began.

Eve hit him. Just punched him right in the face. She guessed that she hadn't looked particularly threatening, because he sure seemed caught by surprise. She grabbed his gun when he stumbled back. "Now get the hell out of here!" she told him. Screams reached her from upstairs. "Before you burn."

His eyes bulged, but then he ran up the stairs.

He was smarter than he appeared.

She hurried toward the guard station. Heard some order on the intercom system about using something called an SP-tranq. Whatever. She got down on her knees as she yanked open the drawers, shoving her hands in. She found key cards—had to be for the cells—grabbed them, and jumped to her feet.

More guards rushed by her, but she just tucked the gun down next to her leg, and they barely glanced her way. They were too busy fleeing to pay her much attention. No, they were hauling ass.

And leaving the paranormals as prisoners. *Not on my watch.* The test subjects weren't just going to be left to die.

She found the first room down a twisting hallway. A two-way mirror let her see into his room. A man. Tall. Muscled. Pacing back and forth. Back and—

He whirled to face her, and Eve caught sight of his gleaming fangs.

Hell.

"Fresh blood . . ." he whispered.

Okay. Eve hesitated. Maybe freeing him wasn't the—

Smoke drifted toward her. The vamp's head snapped up. He wasn't looking right at her, not the way Cain had, but the vamp sure seemed to be . . . smelling her. "Fire."

Yeah, his sense of smell was working just fine.

And even though he was a vampire . . . *I can't leave him.* Vampires were just like humans—some good, some bad. She just had to keep reminding herself of that. *He doesn't have to be bad.*

Eve rushed around the corner. Flipped through the key cards and tried to find the one that would give her access to his cell. This holding room didn't have a manual code, not like Cain's. The door looked thicker, heavier, and—

The third card she swiped had the lights near the door's handle flashing green. She brought her gun up in an instant even as the door flew open.

"Don't bite me!" Her quick yell.

The blond vampire had already lunged forward, but he froze at her yell—or maybe he froze at the sight of her gun. Didn't really matter why to Eve.

Freezing was good. Better than biting. "I'm here to help you."

His eyes narrowed. "Says the woman with the gun aimed at my chest." His fangs were way too sharp.

"Look, that's just to—"

He ripped the gun from her hand in a lightning-fast move. Grabbed her. Shoved her back against the door and yanked her head to the side.

"Hungry . . ." Cain had said something like that, too, only he hadn't raked his fangs against her skin the way Dracula was doing.

"I'm . . . helping . . ." Eve muttered. *"Trying* . . . to . . . help . . ." Damn the vampires. Always biting the hands— or the necks—of those who helped.

"Need . . . you . . ." the vampire rasped.

Then he was the one being yanked away. The vampire's body hit the wall with a thud. "Too fucking bad," Cain snarled at him. "Cause I saw her first."

Uh, what?

Cain offered her his hand. Eve glanced at his open palm,

then back at his blazing eyes. She didn't move toward him. Right then she wasn't sure who was safer—the guy who'd almost torn out her throat, or the man who was destroying the whole building.

"You have to get out of here," Cain told her, a muscle flexing along his jaw.

The vampire rose slowly to his feet.

"Touch her again"—Cain's deadly focus was on the vamp—"and I'll turn you to dust."

A very real threat. Vampires and fire didn't mix so well.

Cain stopped waiting on her to take his hand. He grabbed her wrist and hauled her to his side. "Come on."

Every instinct she had screamed for her to run from the fire, but . . . "There are others. They're trapped and—"

An explosion shook the building. A fierce detonation that had the walls shuddering and thick cracks breaking across the ceiling.

The vampire stared at Cain for an instant, then when the screams started—screams that seemed to come from everywhere—the vamp shoved past Cain and Eve and raced away.

So many screams . . . and more explosions.

"He's not letting us out." Cain's grip was unbreakable. "The fucking bastard . . . Wyatt is gonna kill everyone before he lets his experiments get away."

Wyatt was blowing up the lab? She shook her head. This wasn't supposed to happen. *None* of this should have happened. "We have to help the others!"

A chunk of ceiling fell down, barely missing her leg. Cain pulled her down the hallway. She fought him, dragging in her heels. "No, the others—"

She choked on the smoke.

They were almost at the stairwell.

"Please . . ."

The one word stopped him.

"They'll die." Unless they were like Cain, and that was highly doubtful. She'd never met anyone else quite like him.

He grabbed the key cards from her hand. "Then *I'll* get them out." A push sent her into the stairwell. "You get that sweet ass out of this place."

Another explosion rocked Genesis, and Cain left her—rushing back down the winding hallway even as the building began to collapse.

The smoke was thicker than Seattle fog as Eve fought her way down the corridor toward Wyatt's office. The coldhearted bastard was trying to kill everyone, even his own research teams. The detonations had gone off with near perfect timing. Sealing doorways. Destroying equipment.

Burying evidence.

He wasn't going to get away with this. She wouldn't let him. People deserved to know the truth—and the truth was that vampires and shifters weren't the only monsters.

Some humans could be the worst monsters out there.

Her lungs burned as she shoved against his office door. Locked. Sealed tight from the inside. Eve snarled as she pushed against that door. Just—

The door opened with a hiss, and she fell inside. The place was perfect. Freaking pristine, while hell stalked the hallways outside.

She stumbled to Wyatt's desk and yanked up the laptop that looked like it had been waiting for her.

"I was wondering when you'd come my way."

She whirled around. The bookcase to the left wasn't a real bookcase. Wyatt had rigged the place, all right. Given himself the perfect exit, one hidden so easily.

"There's no data there." He inclined his head toward her and the laptop. "I erased those files."

More screams. Cries for help.

Eve shifted forward, moving onto the balls of her feet, then she went completely still when she saw the gun in his hand.

"You really fucked things up for me." Wyatt sighed. "And to think, I had such hopes for you."

What? Hopes to do what—torture and maim her? *Freak.* "It's over, Wyatt. Your facility is burning. Your people are dying—*it's over.*"

Wyatt shook his head. "I'll take my data. Go forward, but you . . ." That gun didn't waver. "You're not going anywhere." His clinical façade was cracking right before her eyes as the rage swept through him.

"Why?" The question tore from her. "Why are you doing this to them?"

"Because they don't deserve to be the ones with the power." Disgust tightened his mouth. "They won't be the strong ones. They won't destroy us!"

Sounded like the doc had some personal issues going on. She could understand. Seeing as how vampires had killed her family, she wasn't exactly warm and tingly when it came to all the supernaturals. But killing them?

Torturing them?

No.

"We don't get to play God." She edged behind his desk. The laptop was clutched in front of her. Like it would stop a bullet.

"Some of us do." Wyatt's response, arrogant and so cold, drifted across the room.

Her eyes narrowed. "You're gonna blame all of this"— her free hand waved toward the smoke filling the room— "on them, aren't you?" He was setting up the explosions to make it look like the paranormals were the ones who'd attacked. *I bet he blames everything on Cain.*

Wyatt smiled. Sometimes, it was easy to see madness. Sometimes, it was harder to see evil.

Wyatt kept the gun up as he said, "When no one walks away but me . . . there will be no other story to believe."

"Cain . . . Cain will walk away." The fire wouldn't stop him. Not when he could control the flames so easily. "You know he'll live, you know—"

Wyatt laughed. "Cain's the worst monster there is. You think I'm bad? You don't even know what he's done."

Then he shot her. Not in the heart or head, as she'd expected. But in the stomach. She fell down, gasping at the pain. The laptop fell from her fingers.

"You will, though," he promised her. "You will."

He stepped back into the small opening made by the bookshelf. His perfect exit strategy. He'd planned so well—and now the jerk was going to get away.

"No!" She couldn't stand. Her whole body felt heavy, weighted. She tried to crawl to him. "You can't—"

The bookshelf closed, sealing him inside. No, sealing *her* inside the room and letting him get wherever the hell he wanted to go.

"Help!" She yelled, crawling a bit more. She'd find something. Something she could use to help her and she'd get out. She'd—

Fire raced into the room.

Fire . . . and Cain.

"Help me," she begged him, staring up—and looking right into his eyes. Into the fire.

He's worse than me.

Cain lifted her into his arms. Held her against his chest. Fire blocked the door. Blazed down the hall.

"Can you . . ." The smoke was choking her. Dammit, if they didn't move, that would be what killed her. Not the fire.

Never the fire.

She'd lied to Wyatt. To Cain. To just about everyone. She had plenty of secrets that no one knew, not even those who were supposed to be her closest friends.

"Can you . . . get through . . . the fire?" she asked him. It was getting hard to speak. Hard to focus. Wyatt hadn't shot her with a regular bullet. More like some kind of drug, a tranq that was making her numb.

Cain nodded. "I can." His face was grim. "You can't."

The drug was making her hallucinate. Why else would she think that the guy's voice had sounded all gruff and sad? "I . . . can. Trust . . . m-me."

But he wasn't moving. Just standing there.

What? Waiting for death?

"I . . . lied." She could barely whisper the words.

Fire caught the bottom of his jogging pants. Burned higher. He tried to yank her away from the flames.

Eve reached out and touched them. The flames slid right over her skin. She could feel the heat, but there was no burn.

For her, there never had been.

"I'm not . . . exactly . . . human."

His eyes widened, but he didn't speak. Not then. Just held her tight—and raced through the fire.

As the drug pushed through her body, everything slowly faded away. The last thing she saw was the fire.

Burning so bright.

CHAPTER FOUR

Genesis burned faster than he'd thought it would. Screams filled the night, mixing with the crackle of the flames as the fire raged.

And Cain just stood back and watched the hellhole burn.

Humans were fleeing. Shouting. Some tried to put out the fire. Fools. That fire wasn't dying.

The paranormals escaping the blaze didn't even glance back. They fled into the woods. Ran fast. A few stopped to beat the hell out of some guards hanging around.

Interesting.

He'd freed the paranormals trapped on the lower level. He could have let them burn, maybe he *should* have, but . . .

Cain's gaze lowered to Eve's face. Her eyes were closed. Ash stained her cheek. The drug had knocked her out, and he'd carried her right through the blaze.

A blaze that hadn't even blistered her skin.

He'd saved those paranormals because he'd given his word to her. He'd stared into her blue eyes and hadn't been able to refuse her. Not then.

Want her.

She wasn't like the others. She was something special.

His gaze swept over her delicate form. She was something damn dangerous. To him, she was lethal.

"Let her go."

The voice came from the shadows. It was a rough voice, male, desperate.

Hungry.

The vampire.

Cain glanced up at him. His hold on Eve tightened. "I knew letting you live was a mistake."

Blood dripped down the vampire's chin. He'd fed, probably on the screaming guards. The man stalked toward Cain with fangs bared and fists clenched.

He really should turn the dumbass to dust.

"She . . . saved me," the vampire gritted out. "I won't let you hurt her."

Did it look like he was hurting her? And since when did a vampire play hero for anyone or anything? From what Cain had witnessed, those bloodsuckers were good for only one thing—killing.

Cain stared at the vampire and knew that the fire of his power would burn in his eyes. "You don't want to tangle with me." He'd watched the destruction. Made sure that Wyatt hadn't crawled out of the chaos.

It was time to leave.

And he was taking Eve with him.

Why can't I have what I want? This one time . . .

"She's human," the vampire said with a hard shake of his head. "I don't know what the hell you are, and—"

"She's not." Her lie. She was far more than human, and he just had to figure out what she was.

"Doesn't matter," the vamp growled back at him as the guy took a step forward. "I won't let you hurt her."

"I wasn't the one trying to eat her."

"No, you're just the one who wants to fuck her."

Cain's eyes narrowed. It was true, but the words still pissed him off. It wouldn't take very long to kill the parasite. Just a few seconds.

But time was already running out for them. The smoke

was rising high into the sky. Others would see the blaze. More humans would come. Cain wanted to be long gone before their arrival.

He knew some of the Genesis personnel kept their vehicles in the garage to the east. He'd take one of those cars.

The vampire was blocking his path. He'd give the guy fair warning, then he'd attack. "If you don't move, you're dead."

The vamp's eyes narrowed. "You can't—"

The fire was raging inside Cain. That blaze might not hurt Eve, but he could incinerate this jerk. And the vampire *had* been ready to bite Eve before.

Didn't that mean he deserved to get singed? Even if he was trying to do some lame-ass white knight bit? *You don't fool me.*

The vamp wasn't leaving. No, the guy was actually coming closer.

Cain let the fire rip from his hand. It flew right at the vamp, tumbling end over end in a deadly ball. The vamp yelled and threw his body to the side. Cain let the fire circle the ground around the vampire, trapping him within the blaze.

Cain walked right by him. The flames would keep the vamp contained, for now. But he left him with a warning. "If you ever come at her again, you'll feel the full force of my fire." Cain would make sure of it. "And you won't have time to scream then. You'll just die."

While the vamp froze within his temporary prison of fire, Cain made his way to that garage. He wasn't the only paranormal with the plan to steal a getaway vehicle. That was obvious. Only two trucks and a motorcycle were left, and some guy with red hair was making his way toward the nearest truck.

"Don't even think about it." Cain shifted Eve so that she lay over his left shoulder. Probably not the most comfortable position for her, but he had to be ready to attack. His left arm curled around her legs as he lifted his right hand. He let the man see the flames he carried. "Unless you're in the mood to burn."

The guy shook his head and frantically backed up. *Ah, smarter than the vamp.* Then he jumped on the motorcycle and roared out of there.

Some folks were so afraid of the fire.

Cain eased Eve inside the truck. He pulled the seat belt over her, and she seemed to stir, just a bit. But her eyes didn't open.

He figured she'd been dosed with the SP-tranq. He'd seen that tranq kill a weak paranormal once. His fingers slid to her throat. Felt the faint pulse. "You *aren't* dying on me." An order.

But . . . it was one she couldn't hear.

Her breath whispered out.

Hell.

More paranormals were rushing their way. Shouts and screams filled the air.

Cain jumped in the truck. Some helpful human had left the keys under the dash, so no hot-wiring necessary. The engine revved to life, and he jerked the vehicle into reverse, making several of the paranormals leap out of the way.

If they hadn't moved, he would have happily gone through them.

"C-Cain?" The softest rasp of Eve's voice.

His hands tightened on the wheel. Her lashes were fluttering.

The SP-tranq never kept the most powerful paranormals out for long. It had only kept him unconscious for a few minutes.

She'd been out about fifteen minutes. Not long . . .

"You're safe," he told her. Wasn't that all she needed to know right now? He yanked the wheel to the right. He knew this area. Another mistake for the Genesis assholes. They were playing in his backyard. He'd just needed to get away from the facility and those chains, and, now that he was out, he'd be able to vanish almost instantly.

He drove them down a twisted, dirt road. Turned to the left. The right.

The blaze behind them vanished, but the smoke still thickened the air.

"What's . . . burning?" Eve's voice. Soft. So lost.

Everything. He felt a grim smile curl his lips. Genesis was dead—and it was about fucking time.

The cabin was easy to find only if you knew where to go. The Blue Ridge Mountains held plenty of secrets, and this safe house was one that Cain hadn't shared with anyone else. Trust wasn't exactly easy for him.

And when he was betrayed, as he'd been betrayed by that worthless shifter Jimmy Vance, Cain always made sure to seek his vengeance. Jimmy wouldn't get away with selling him out.

The deception would prove to be a fatal mistake for the shifter. A fatal and oh so painful mistake.

"W-where are we?"

Cain killed the engine at the sound of Eve's voice. Her eyes were open, but the blue of her gaze looked cloudy, and the faint line between her brows showed her confusion.

At least she was back with him. For a little bit, he'd almost . . . worried.

As a rule, he didn't give a shit about anyone.

"A safe house," he told her. The place would do, for now. They needed to hide out until the fire died. Those flames would bring more humans—humans who wanted to investigate. They'd stay hidden until the flames and the smoke vanished.

Her breath rushed out. "You . . . saved me." Shock coated the words.

He shoved open his door. Stalked around the truck and paused near the passenger side of the vehicle. She frowned at him and fumbled, trying to open the door. Eve couldn't seem to get the lock to disengage.

He yanked open the door, shattering the lock, and pulled her into his arms. Why the hell did she seem to fit against him so well?

His whole body tensed as he lifted her against his chest. "I can . . . walk." She sounded disgruntled.

Would a little thank-you have killed the woman? He had hauled her ass out of a nightmare and gotten her to safety. But if the woman wanted to walk . . .

Jaw locking, Cain eased her onto her feet and backed up.

Her dark hair fell around her face, but he saw her shoulders straighten. Then she took a step forward.

He caught her before she slammed, face-first, into the dirt. The little growl of frustration that she gave shouldn't have sounded sexy.

But every damn thing about her was sexy to him.

She can stand the heat.

He lifted her right back against his chest. Her head eased onto his shoulder, and her hair brushed lightly against him. She should have smelled like smoke and ash. They'd gone through hell.

But she still smelled like candy to him. Sweet. Light. Delicious.

I want a bite.

He'd be taking that bite before he let her go. Cain carried her inside the cabin. Set the security system. Turned on the lights. The cabin wasn't big. Not fancy, but the place had a bed. Four walls. Food.

What more did they really need right then? Just a place to lay low.

He headed toward the bed.

Eve's body stiffened in his arms. "Um . . . wait . . . what—"

Carefully, he put her down on top of the covers. She looked right in his bed. She'd look even better naked. The woman *did* need to get out of those burned clothes. "Genesis is gone." Did she remember that part? The flames? The screams?

Her eyes widened. She glanced down at her clothes. Had to see the ash. The fire had burned part of her clothing, but the flames hadn't marred her flesh. "You . . . took me out." Her voice was stronger. Still husky. Still like a hot stroke right over his groin. "Got me out of the flames after . . ." She sat up slowly, sliding over the covers with a hiss of sound. "After that bastard *shot* me."

Anger sharpened her words. But who wouldn't be pissed after getting shot?

He reached for her.

She flinched away from him.

Cain's jaw clenched. Right. Just because he'd *saved* her, just because she could handle the flames, didn't mean her opinion of him would be any different from anybody else's. She'd still look at him and see the freak who could burn.

The man who touched hell.

"I'm just checking your wound," he snapped. Like she hadn't been kissing him before. Rubbing her body against his. Acting like she wanted him.

But they'd had an audience then, and maybe every moan, every stroke of her body against his had been nothing more than an act.

The woman is one fine actress. He'd have to remember that. She'd just been playing a role.

When he'd been fucking desperate to take her. To finally be with someone who could handle his power.

Her hand lifted slowly and slid over her stomach. The

bottom of the shirt had been burned away. The tranq had caught her in the stomach, he knew that, but her hand slid over smooth, unblemished skin.

Not that the tranq ever left much of a mark, anyway. Wyatt had designed it to be a subtle but painful attack. Easier to take out prey and then deny any action later.

"What was it?" she asked as her fingers pressed against her stomach. Smooth flesh. Pale.

Lickable.

"A tranq." His voice sounded like ragged gravel, so he cleared his throat and tried again. "A special mix Wyatt made. It can knock out even the strongest paranormals." *And kill the weakest.*

Good thing she hadn't been weak.

What was she?

"Can you create the fire?" he asked because maybe—his heart raced faster—maybe she was just like him. He'd always been an outcast in the paranormal world. A freak, even among the monsters. But if she was like him, if he wasn't alone . . .

She shook her head. "N-no." Her gaze darted around the room. "What happened to Wyatt?"

"He burned."

Another flinch from her.

Why wasn't she looking at him? Cain caught her chin in his hand and made her focus on him. "Forget him. He deserved a fast trip to hell." Did she have any idea how many paranormals that bastard had tortured? Cain had heard their screams. He knew.

"What about the others?" Eve asked. "Did they get out? Did they—"

"A lot of them did." Not everyone, not all the paranormals and not all the humans. Those explosions had been timed too perfectly.

Wyatt hadn't minded killing his lab rats or his own research teams.

And the guy thought Cain was the monster? Wyatt was as sadistic and twisted as any killer could possibly be.

Her breath rushed out. "I have to—I have to call this story in—I need to tell—"

He remembered what Wyatt had said about her. Eve wasn't another scientist out to poke and prod her prey. She was a reporter. A woman after a story. *I won't be her story.* "You're not telling anyone anything."

She pulled away from him.

"Not yet," he said, trying to soften his words. "Not until it's safer." Not until he'd had his fill of her.

She's afraid of me. So what? Everyone is. He could work past her fear. He had to.

He'd been held captive for too damn long.

And he wanted her too much.

"You can stand the fire," he whispered.

Her gaze came back to his. Still laced with fear, but . . . was that a flash of awareness in her eyes? "Yes."

His stare dropped to her lips. He wanted to taste her again. Cain leaned forward, bringing his mouth closer to hers. Eve didn't pull back.

Did she—hell, did she lean toward him? He sure thought that she did.

He pressed his lips against hers. He wanted to ravage her mouth. To take and taste and hear her moan. But he touched her lightly with his lips, carefully . . . at first.

Don't scare her any more. Not yet.

His control was razor thin. He needed to woo her while he could.

Her lips parted beneath his. *Still not pulling away.* Then her tongue came out and licked against his.

Fuck.

That control got even thinner. "I want you." Guttural. His cock was so full and aching—from one damn kiss— that he hurt.

He couldn't remember his last lover. He couldn't picture her in his mind. The lovers he'd taken before hadn't mattered to him. He hadn't let them matter. They couldn't get close to him. Couldn't find out what he really was.

Bodies in the dark. Pleasure. Sex.

That was all his past had been.

The light of dawn streaked through the cabin. It wouldn't be sex in the shadows. Eve wouldn't be a woman that he forgot.

Her gaze held his.

"If you don't want me, you'd better tell me to stop now." While he could still stop. Because in a few more seconds . . .

Take her.

There'd be no turning back.

Her lips were red. Slick. Her breath came faster. But . . .

But she shook her head.

He pulled away from her, every move so painful that he wanted to rage.

"Your eyes . . ." Her whisper.

And he knew that his control was breaking. He'd used too much power back at Genesis. He couldn't let the beast out and expect to instantly shove him back in the cage.

Want her. Need her. She could soothe him. Make him forget hell.

Except she was pulling away from him. Rising. Stumbling toward the door on the right. The bathroom.

Leaving him aching. Hungry. Aroused.

Saying *no.*

When the door shut behind her, the beast broke free.

★ ★ ★

What in the world was happening?

Eve stared at herself in the mirror. Was she really about to have sex with Cain? A man she barely knew?

A man who'd made her wet with just a kiss.

She twisted the faucet and sent a burst of cold water pouring into the sink. She cupped her hands and threw a cold spray on her face. The water rinsed off the ash and who the hell knew what else from her skin. She tossed away her clothes. They were ruined anyway, and if she was doing this, then she was damn well doing it right.

Adrenaline pumped through her blood. She could remember the fire. That jerkoff Wyatt. Screams and death.

And Cain. He'd held her. Gotten her out of that nightmare.

She'd wanted him before he'd saved her.

She still wanted him.

They were in the middle of nowhere. Alone. With a big bed just waiting for them.

Why couldn't she want him? Why *shouldn't* she want him?

She kicked away her clothes. Took a minute to survey herself in the mirror.

There was no sound from the other room. He'd better not have changed his mind. A girl just needed a little time to try and get sexy after an all-out hell battle. Was that such a bad thing? Not like it was a crazy urge.

Because . . . he mattered. She wanted it to be right. Special.

He'd be grand lover number four in her life. Didn't that deserve special fanfare? Eve figured the situation at least called for some non-singed clothes and a non-ash-covered body.

She turned back toward the door. Put her hand on the wood. The drug wasn't making her body feel limp anymore. No, limp was the last thing she felt right then.

Her nipples were tight. Her sex quivering.

Because Cain was waiting on her.

She opened the door. Naked, she walked to him.

Cain whirled around when the door squeaked open. His face was hard, more menacing than she'd seen it before, and his strong jaw had locked.

But she wasn't about to lose her nerve. Eve lifted her chin, licked her lips. "I . . . want you, Cain."

His eyes blazed. Literally blazed with fire. Not dark anymore. Burning bright.

She liked them that way.

Two steps, and he had her. He rushed toward her, took her mouth. Not softly, not lightly anymore. Good. She hadn't wanted that. Maybe it was the drug leaving her system. Maybe it was the adrenaline. Maybe it was just *him.*

But she didn't want easy and soft. She'd had that with the other men. Men who were careful with their touches and too hesitant in the dark. Right then, she wanted passion and she wanted fire.

The real world would intrude soon enough. She got that. For the moment, though, . . . *screw off, real world.*

She put her arms around him. His chest was bare. He wore a pair of loose jogging pants, pants that had been burned and ripped, and those pants did nothing to conceal the thick length of his arousal.

He pushed her back against the wall. Caged her. He was so . . . *hot.*

She loved the feel of his hot flesh against her. Actually, she wanted more. A lot more. Even as she kissed him back, matching the wildness of his mouth, her hand slid down his body. Over those rock-hard abs—*damn*—down to the waistband of his pants. Eve shoved them down. Touched the cock that pushed toward her. Hot silk over leashed power.

So sexy.

What would he taste like?

She stroked him and wanted to find out.

But he was kissing his way down her neck. Oh, his mouth felt good on her. Then he used the edge of his teeth, and her whole body shuddered. "Cain!" She pumped him harder with her hand. Faster.

He pulled away.

What?

His chest heaving, he stared down at her with those burning eyes. In that fire, she just saw need. Raw desire.

Lust.

"On the bed." His words were thick with the same lust that lit his eyes.

Her knees wanted to tremble as she walked toward the bed. Would sex against the wall have been so bad? She'd never tried that before, maybe—

He didn't let her make it to the bed. Two more steps, and he pounced. The room spun around her. She blinked, then found herself flat on the mattress. Her legs were parted, dangling over the edge of the bed, and Cain was between them.

"Need to taste . . . have to . . ."

He put his mouth against her. A mouth that was just as warm as the rest of him. Not burning. Heated just . . . *right*. His tongue licked over her clit. His fingers slid into her. He tasted.

She came.

But he didn't stop. His fingers plunged inside her, again and again, and he kept licking her. Sucking her flesh. Her body twisted on the bed. Her nipples were aching, and she wanted him to touch them. Wanted him to keep his mouth on her. Wanted—

Another orgasm hit her. She screamed because it snapped right through her, hard enough to steal her breath even as the pleasure crashed over her body.

Then he was rising up. Staring at her with a face that

could have been carved from stone. He positioned his cock between her legs. Took her hands. Twined his fingers with hers.

"I've been waiting for you . . ."

She blinked, then shook her head, sure that she'd misunderstood. He couldn't have just said those words. They didn't make any sense but . . .

I feel like I've been waiting for him, too.

"No diseases," he growled. "I can't . . . get . . ."

No, he wouldn't. From what she'd seen, the guy healed from everything when he burned and rose once more. She was on birth control, so pregnancy wasn't an issue for her.

Want him.

"Eve?"

"Yes . . ." Her whisper. "Cain, *come in* . . ."

He thrust into her and she forgot everything else. Her legs wrapped around his hips. Eve arched up against him. She'd never been filled this way before. Completely. Totally. This wasn't just sex.

Possession.

Heat.

Need.

Pleasure.

Every stroke had the sensitive inner muscles of her sex clenching. Aftershocks of release still hummed through her, and the withdrawal and thrust of his aroused flesh just made those aftershocks feel stronger.

Deeper, harder, he thrust.

Her heels dug into his ass. "More." Her greedy gasp.

He gave her more. The bed jerked beneath then. The headboard rammed into the wall.

He kept giving her more.

Her sex was slick and eager, and Cain slid in deeper. She couldn't come again—wait, was she still coming? Eve couldn't tell. There was too much pleasure. Pleasure that didn't end. It rippled through her body, spiking and rolling, and she cried out his name.

And felt him erupt inside her. His eyes were on her when he came, and those eyes—the flames flared brighter. The heat from his body raged.

Then he kissed her.

The pleasure just kept coming.

So did she.

Eve slept beside him, her slender body naked, pale in the growing light.

Carefully, Cain began to inspect her flesh. He couldn't remember enough of what had happened—there'd only been a storm of need inside him. Lust that had broken free.

He'd never let his control shatter like that before.

Once, so long ago, he'd seen what had happened to a human when his power flared too hot during sex. The woman with him had screamed when blisters appeared on her arms.

His touch had been too hot.

He'd been too hot.

She'd screamed and shoved away from him, but he'd been so horrified by what he'd done he had leaped back. He'd seen the red imprints on her flesh. The perfect match to his fingertips.

He'd been so careful after that. Holding tight to his control. Never letting go. Surviving on sips of pleasure only.

Not with Eve.

He'd known she could handle any fire he sent her way, and he'd taken every last bit of pleasure that he could.

Her skin was flawless. No blisters. No burns.

But then, he'd seen the flames come toward her at Genesis. They'd burned over her flesh, but never actually hurt her.

What are you?

She'd said she couldn't create fire, but was that another lie? He couldn't trust her, wouldn't.

But he sure as hellfire wanted her again.

He could easily grow addicted to Eve Bradley, and that addiction would be a very dangerous thing.

For him.

Especially for her. She didn't seem to understand just how dangerous it was for him to want her. His desire could be deadly.

His fingers slid down the curve of her back. She wasn't warm like him. Slightly cool to the touch, her flesh was so silken and smooth. Touching her seemed to . . . soothe him.

He wasn't the type to want soothing.

He pulled away from her when his instincts told him to pull her closer. He dressed, yanking on extra clothes that he kept stored at the cabin.

Then he headed toward the door and didn't look back.

CHAPTER FIVE

He'd left her. Eve had realized that fun fact about, oh, four hours ago. When she'd woken up alone, naked, and cold.

He'd given her a good orgasm—or three. Four? Showing a girl a good time did not mean that the guy could just waltz out the door when she shut her eyes for a minute. Talk about being an inconsiderate jackass.

When she got her hands on him . . .

The door to the cabin flew open. She whirled around. Weapon! She needed a—

Cain stood in the doorway.

Her eyes narrowed to slits. She *still* needed a weapon. Maybe a lamp to throw at his thick head so he'd get that a guy wasn't supposed to desert a lady right after mind-blowing sex.

Even paranormals could do some pillow talk.

"Where were you?" Eve demanded then realized she sounded like some really angry girlfriend. Crap.

Wow. Not me. She'd never done the angry scene before. She guessed there was a first time for everything. *Jack. Ass.*

Cain lifted the object he was holding. "I went back for this. Thought you might want it. You were sure clinging to it tight enough back in Wyatt's office."

Wyatt's laptop. Eve flew across the room and grabbed it.

Okay, so it was black with soot and ash, kinda dinged up, but it didn't look *too* bad. No, actually, it looked so good and sweet—*evidence!*—that she almost kissed it.

She rushed away from him, and sat down at the small table, and opened the laptop. Yes, yes, the power hummed right on and then—

"You're welcome," Cain drawled from behind her.

She heard the door shut. Her cheeks flushed, and she glanced over her shoulder at him. He stood in front of the door with his hands crossed over his chest. Sometimes, she got a little too carried away with things. *He'd gone back for the laptop.* That was rather . . . awesome. And kinda sweet. Eve forced herself to turn away from the laptop and rise slowly to face Cain. "Thank you." She needed that laptop. It was proof. Well, it was her proof, and so was Cain. Living, breathing, talking proof.

His gaze dropped to her mouth. "Thank me with a kiss."

She could feel her flush getting deeper.

"It wasn't easy to get it, either. Local cops are swarming that place, and I had to crawl through the rubble left behind in order to find it." He took a step toward her. One. Then another. Stalking her. His gaze was on her face as he said, "I figure a kiss is the least I deserve for that little prize."

Kissing him wasn't exactly a hardship for her. She wet her lips. His eyes weren't blazing—a good thing—they were back to being dark and intense. But she could still see the lust in his stare.

Her heart began to race faster. "A kiss . . . seems fair to me." If he had been there when she woke up, she would have given him a whole lot more than just a kiss good morning.

Since he'd left to retrieve the laptop for her, Eve figured she could forgive the guy. The laptop was way more important than pillow talk.

She had her priorities. Most days.

So she was the one that closed the distance between them. The one to lift her hands and curl them around his neck. He was still warm to the touch, but not as hot as he'd been before. Eve rose onto her toes as his head lowered toward her.

The kiss was easy, light. Exploring.

At first.

Then she caught his lower lip between her teeth. Tugged gently. Nipped.

He shuddered against her.

The kiss stopped being so easy and light.

His tongue thrust into her mouth. His hands settled on her ass and lifted her right up against his cock. Ah, he was *definitely* responding to the kiss. So was she. Her nipples were getting tight and heavy. She'd wanted his mouth on them last night. Maybe now he could—

Cain's head lifted. "How do you smell so good?"

What? She blinked at him.

"Sweet, light," he said, eyes narrowing as they swept over. "Like candy."

Oh. Ahem. She cleared her throat. "That's the soap I use." Soap. Shampoo. Body lotion. She'd gotten some big kit last Christmas, and she used it all the time. Eve couldn't remember the name, something like peppermint dreams or—

"It makes me want to lick you all over."

That didn't sound like such a bad plan to her. "Will I get a turn?" Her voice lowered as she asked. Licking him would be pretty damn fantastic.

But he stiffened and pushed her away. Eve's brows lowered, and she shook her head. In her limited experience, guys didn't turn down offers like the one she'd just made. Guys *jumped* on those offers. "Cain?"

He'd spun away from her and was at the window, peeking out through the thin curtains. "Company."

She didn't hear anything, but she still hurried to his side. Okay, she didn't see anything, either. "Are you sure?"

"Two cars. Police. They're searching the area. I thought we'd have more time . . ." He grabbed her arm and pulled her away from the window. "We're leaving. *Now.*"

So in addition to being a literal firepower, the guy had super senses, too. She'd known that he'd heard her and Wyatt through that so-called soundproof glass, but now he was just being extra impressive.

Eve hurried over to the laptop. A new screen was up— one that asked for a password. Like a password request would stop her. She knew people—or rather, one very smart guy in particular—who could work around pretty much any tech code out there.

"Hurry, Eve."

She turned back to him. She was wearing an old shirt that she'd found in his closet, one that she'd belted to make look like a rather unstylish dress. She had on her shoes, and after a shower, she looked semi—

"*Eve.*"

Right. Screw beauty. She hurried after him. They jumped into the truck and rushed down a dirt road. She looked back behind them as Cain hauled ass, but still didn't see anyone. "If Genesis is dead, why are we running?"

"Because cops and I damn well don't mix." He was flooring the truck, sending it bouncing along the road and hurtling down the mountain.

She yanked on her seat belt. "We're the innocent ones here. Wyatt was the one who—"

His cold laughter stopped her. "Baby, I've never been innocent a day in my life."

Eve could believe that. Actually, she wasn't sure that she wanted to know about all the things he'd done.

"When you do your big report on Genesis and that prick Wyatt, do me one favor . . ." Cain slanted a fast glance her way even as he punched the gas harder. "Leave my name out of it."

"But—but what he did to you . . ." She'd seen it with her own eyes. "They *killed* you. Tortured you." He deserved justice for that. People should know his story.

"Not like it's the first time for any of that." Cain's voice was growing colder, but the truck was still going just as fast. "So tell your story, but leave me the hell out of it. The last thing I want is any attention from the media—or the humans."

Her hand tightened around the seat belt strap that crossed her shoulder. "Okay." She figured he deserved that protection. He'd hauled her butt out of the fire. She'd keep his name out of her story. Subject Thirteen. That was all he'd be to the people who read about the nightmare of Genesis.

Except . . .

"I'd like to know, though," Eve told him. His profile was so strong. Hard. Had he really burned for her just minutes before? No, she'd burned for *him*. She was still aroused. Aching. She was very worried Cain might be ruining her for other men. "What are you?"

He didn't answer at first, and she didn't think that he would. But after a time, he said, "I'm the devil."

A chill skated down her spine because he sounded so . . . serious. She shook her head. "No, you're not. You're just—" *Trying to scare me.* But she didn't say those words.

In this world, anything could be possible, Eve knew that. If vamps could live forever, was there really a limit to what other beings could exist?

"I've killed," he told her in a voice devoid of emotion. "Tortured far worse than Wyatt ever could."

That chill got worse. She didn't want to hear this. She'd wanted him to be the good guy.

"I'm not some damn hero, no matter what you think."

She *had* thought that, and barely controlled her wince. "I'm the monster in the dark. The big, fucking bad wolf. I've seen hell, and I've brought hell to earth."

He wasn't looking at her. Maybe that was a good thing.

"And I'll do it again and again," Cain promised in his growling voice. "That's who I am—*what I am*. I bring death. I bring hell."

The breath in her lungs seemed to have frozen. He was wrong, she knew it. But Eve didn't know what to say to him and as they headed down that mountain—so fast—the silence in the vehicle deepened.

He'd frightened her.

Cain braked the truck at the edge of Atlanta. They'd driven for hours, heading fast to get away from the remains of Genesis. He'd asked Eve where she needed to go. Where she'd be safe. After only the smallest of hesitations, she'd named the city. As he'd driven, the miles had passed in heavy silence.

He'd felt Eve's stare on him so many times during that long drive, but she hadn't spoken. What was she supposed to say? How did a woman respond when she'd learned that she'd just fucked a killer?

She didn't. She just ran away. That was what all the others had done, and he knew that was exactly what Eve planned to do. You didn't stay with the devil forever, not if you wanted to keep your soul.

His gaze scanned the lot. There were big rigs at the truck stop. A handful of them. Exhaust fumes drifted up into the dark sky.

"What happens now?" Eve asked, finally speaking. Her voice was husky, soft.

What happens . . . he wanted to keep her with him. To find a motel room. To strip her and take her all over again until the pleasure left them both weak and tired. Until he couldn't move and she didn't want to.

But he had a target to take down. Genesis had burned, but his vengeance wasn't complete, not yet. He still owed the traitor who'd gotten him locked in that pit.

"It's the end of the line." He tossed the keys to her. "You keep the truck." He'd find another ride. Easy enough.

He jumped out of the vehicle. Slammed the door shut behind him. Left her. He'd never been one for the good-bye scene, and telling *her* good-bye—no. Not what he wanted to do. Better to just walk away and not see her—

A door slammed behind him. "Wait!" Eve's voice. Not so husky anymore. Sharp. Angry.

He stilled.

Then her hand was on his shoulder, jerking him around to face her. For someone so small, she had a pretty strong grip. "You're *leaving* me?" Her eyes were wide with a combination of shock and fury.

What had she expected? "You said you had friends in this city." He'd gotten her to talk only one time during the ride. Good thing she'd said Atlanta was where she needed to be . . . it was exactly where he'd be finding his target, too.

The more dangerous paranormals liked the big cities. With all the humans running around, there was plenty of prey for them. Since their coming-out party, the paranormals had actually done a good job of taking over the big cities in the U.S. There was strength in numbers, usually.

That's why Genesis was afraid of us. They knew how powerful we were becoming. If the paranormals took over, then what happened to the humans?

They get on the endangered species list.

Eve's fingers dug into his shoulder. "You're just walking away? After what happened between us?"

His hand rose. His fingers slid over her cheek. She didn't

seem to realize it, but he was trying to protect her. *From myself.* If he stayed with her . . . *I'll never let go.*

Because he already craved her.

She was a weakness to him. The only one he had. She could be too dangerous.

Cain's hand slid away and he stepped back, making her hand fall. "I've got a shifter to kill." *Jimmy Vance.*

"W-what?" She obviously hadn't expected his response.

"He won't sell out any more paranormals. He won't sell *me* out ever again." He wouldn't be able to . . . kinda hard to sell out folks when you were rotting in the ground.

"You can't just—just kill him!"

He'd told her the truth about himself, but she still didn't seem to get it. *Not the good guy.* "Sure I can." He closed his eyes. Summoned up the power that was always inside him. Let it swell. Let it grow. Let the dark edges seep past his control. When his eyes opened again, he knew that she'd see the fire in his eyes. "I can do anything I want."

No one would stop him. His guard wouldn't be lowered again. Wyatt was dead. Fried to ash.

Soon Jimmy would be, too.

Paranormals had died in that facility, and, unlike him, they hadn't been able to regenerate and come back. He'd heard their screams. Their last desperate cries.

They deserved their vengeance, too. He'd give it to them. He turned away from her again. Began walking.

"Don't." Her soft voice behind him.

But he didn't stop. He didn't look back. He had a shifter to kill, and Eve, with her big, blue eyes and her trembling, red lips, wasn't going to stop him.

No one was.

He'd left her. The jerk had actually dumped her at a truck stop. Just . . . walked away. Okay, he'd left the truck with her, so she hadn't exactly been stranded, but . . .

He'd still ditched her.

And gone off to kill.

No, you're not doing it. She wasn't just going to stand back while some shifter was slaughtered.

Even if he deserved that death?

She jumped out of the truck. Slammed the door and raced the rest of the way up the graveled drive. She'd told Cain the truth when she'd said that she had friends in this city. This particular friend was loaded—and that was why he had a giant house on twenty private acres in Atlanta.

She pounded on the door. *Hurry, hurry* . . .

The door opened. Trace Frost glared down at her, wearing a pair of pajama pants and looking severely irritated. His eyes were narrowed, the faint lines around his eyes tight.

"It's two-thirty in the morning, Eve," he growled. "Two damn thirty. Unless you're here to have sex, then—"

"Someone's about to die."

Her words cut him off.

Trace blinked at her, his green eyes waking up very quickly. The guy was built, muscled, freakishly smart.

He was also a shifter.

So Trace usually kept tabs on any other shifters in his town. It was the whole keep your friends close, and your enemies closer bit. His motto was keep the shifters close . . . and be ready to defend your fucking territory from friends *and* enemies.

He raked a hand over his face. "You would be coming about something like that."

She pushed the laptop against his chest. He'd be the one cracking that pass code for her later. The guy owed her. Seriously owed her since she'd risked her life for him more than once. "Jimmy Vance."

Trace whistled as he rocked back on his heels. "You don't want to mess with that guy." His native Texas rolled faintly beneath the words. Trace gave a quick shake of his head. "Vance would sell out his own mother for—"

"If I don't find him soon, he's dead." She didn't want Vance dead because, well, one, killing the guy was *wrong*. You couldn't just go up and torch a shifter. Cain would find his own ass hunted if he did that. And, two, she needed Vance. Eve wanted to break the Genesis story wide open, and if Jimmy Vance had been dealing with Wyatt, then she wanted to talk to him.

Preferably while he was still breathing. Otherwise, it would be rather difficult to accomplish.

"I don't know if his death would be such a loss," Trace muttered as he lifted up the laptop. "You didn't have to bring me a present." The porch light glinted off his tousled, blond hair.

"You're getting me into that system," she told him, putting her hands on her hips, "*after* you take me to Vance."

Trace's gaze came back to her. Then that stare slowly swept over her body. He winced. "Fine, but, seriously, if we're hunting shifters tonight, you have to change. You won't get into a fight looking like that."

Whoa, hold up. "A fight?" She followed him into the house.

He tucked the laptop under one arm and shut the door behind her. The alarm beeped. "Vance—and the shifters like him—always head to the cage fights on Saturday nights."

Her stomach clenched. "You're not talking about a normal cage fight, are you?"

Trace shook his head. "Just to get in that fight, one of us will have to bleed."

Dammit. Why does everything with the paranormals always have to be about blood?

Jimmy Vance had better be freaking grateful when she saved his butt.

★ ★ ★

No, no, this was definitely *not* a normal cage fight. Eve had seen cage fights on TV. Even done an interview or two at fights back when she'd worked in Texas.

This was different. And, yeah, they'd had to bleed to get inside.

Apparently, no one got in without signing up for a fight. She'd come with Trace, and he'd been the one to agree to enter the cage. If she'd come alone, well, she never would have made it past the hulks at the door.

Eve's eyes were locked on the cage as Trace swiped out with his claws and cut into his opponent's stomach.

More blood pooled on the already slick cage floor.

If I'd come alone, I'd probably be dead.

She couldn't fight a shifter. No way. Not even in her nightmares.

The crowd around her was cheering. Yelling, screaming. Throwing fists and claws in the air as they placed wagers on who would be walking out of that cage.

And who wouldn't.

Horror had Eve's mouth hanging open. She'd never expected . . . *this.* But Trace—he'd known exactly where to go. Down the twisting, dark back streets of Atlanta. Inside the old warehouse that had looked abandoned to her.

A trick. The place had been packed inside. Once they'd cleared the first level of the warehouse, she'd started to hear the yells—and to smell the blood.

Trace had flashed fang and claws, shifter-style, when they saw the bouncers. One of the bouncers had even greeted him by name.

Not Trace's first trip into the cage.

The place reeked of blood and violence. Men and women jostled her as they fought to get closer to the cage. The floor of the cage had to be about ten feet wide, and the walls—okay, the caged fencing—stretched all the way to the ceiling.

A loud cheer erupted from the crowd. Eve's gaze jerked back to the fighters. One man was down, moaning.

That man wasn't Trace.

Trace had his claws in the air. Sweat glinted off his body, and the guy was . . . smiling.

Her back teeth clenched. She hadn't realized just how much he would enjoy the violence.

The cage opened and Trace stalked out. Someone else dragged his bleeding opponent toward one of the back rooms. More money exchanged hands. The smoke in the area deepened.

Beers were tossed around.

The blood pooled in the cage.

Eve shoved her way through the crowd around Trace. He was getting slapped on the back. Figured. Shifters and violence. They went together too well.

And she *knew* Trace had a dark side. Taking the guy there hadn't been her best plan ever.

She grabbed his arm. "Where's Vance?" They weren't there so Trace could rip and claw his way through the fighters. They had a job to do.

Trace glanced her way. Blood dripped from his mouth. "I talked to the organizer . . ."

Wait, there was an organizer?

The cage door was being opened again.

"Vance is fighting now." Trace wrapped his arm around her shoulders and turned her to face the cage. "Provided he survives this fight, you can talk to Vance all you want—*after.*"

She stared at the man entering the cage with an arrogant swagger. His head was shaved, and his eyes, small, angry, swept over the crowd. A tattoo of a giant snake covered his bare chest and an old pair of faded jeans hung low on his hips.

"No weapons," Trace murmured in her ear as he leaned

in close to her. "Except the ones God gave you. Those are the cage rules."

Jimmy opened his mouth and the light glinted off the too sharp and far too long teeth on each side of his mouth.

That just was seriously scary. She'd never seen teeth quite like those before, not even on vamps. "W-what kind of shifter is he?"

"Snake."

Hell. The tattoo made sense then, and so did the sharp, thin fangs. Fangs that curved a bit, just like a snake's.

Snake shifters were supposed to be devious. She'd heard rumors about them, but tonight was her first shot at an up-close look at the real deal.

Jimmy lifted his hands and the people watching and drinking roared.

Trace's hold tightened on her. "It seems that Vance is a crowd favorite."

Looked that way. She glanced over at Trace. She'd seen him shift once, that was how they'd met. She'd found him hurt, far too close to death, on a lonely stretch of Texas highway.

She'd thought about leaving the bloody wolf when he snarled at her with his bared fangs, but she hadn't been able to walk away.

Not even when the wolf had become a man.

"How long have you been coming here?" On top of everything else that was happening, she had to deal with this, too.

Her best friend, sliding right back into that dark pool of violence and blood that had stalked him before they'd met.

Trace didn't answer her and that alone was answer enough. She knew he had to feel the tension in her body.

His gaze was on the cage when he said, "If I hadn't come here, you wouldn't have found Vance tonight."

Right. One problem at a time. She edged back toward the cage with Trace at her side. She'd managed to find clothes at Trace's place—mostly because Trace had far too many female friends who left their shit behind—so she was wearing a miniskirt, one that was a little too short, and a top that was a little too loose. It kept slipping off her shoulder. The heels were high, ridiculously so, but the clothes made her fit in with the other women there, and that was the point, right? Blending in was a necessity with the supernaturals.

"Vance!" She yelled his name, but he didn't glance her way. The crowd was roaring so loudly that she knew he hadn't heard her. She tried again, yelling louder this time, "You're in danger!"

He needed to slither his butt out of that cage and get over to her.

Eve didn't know how much of a lead she had on Cain, and she sure didn't want to waste any lead time while Vance enjoyed getting bloody by beating the hell out of some other shifter.

"We're not hurting any humans," Trace told her, voice gruff.

Oh, what? Was he starting to feel guilty for keeping this secret from her?

"That's why we come here. You know the beasts need to fight. Here, we can face off against each other."

Face off—until what point? Until only one shifter could claim dominance on a bloodstained floor?

The cage door opened.

The crowd didn't cheer when the next fighter entered the ring. There wasn't any sound from them at all. Her head turned toward the fighter because she wanted to see why everyone had gone so deadly quiet.

"He doesn't smell like a shifter," Trace said, lifting his head. "And I haven't seen that guy before."

The guy had a dark hood over his head, a hood that connected with the loose sweatshirt he wore. His shoulders were broad, his legs braced apart.

Vance frowned at him and . . . backed up a step? Eve caught the flash of fear on Vance's face.

The new fighter shoved the hood off his head. The bright, almost glaring lights hit the stark lines of his face. It was a face she knew too well.

"Cain," Eve whispered.

And she knew that she'd arrived too late.

CHAPTER SIX

"Cain!" Eve screamed his name even as the crowd chanted for Vance. No, no, they didn't realize what was happening. They had no idea just how screwed they could all be.

The whole place could go up in flames.

"You know him?" Trace demanded as his hand curled over her arm.

She glanced at him. She'd tried to brief Trace as much as possible on Genesis as they rushed to the fight, but, sure, she'd skimmed over a few details. *Like the sex. Like Cain leaving me at the truck stop.* Some details you didn't tell your best friend. Especially when that friend had a serious overprotective streak. "He's . . . Subject Thirteen." She'd told him that part. Told him that she'd helped Thirteen escape from Genesis.

Trace was still staring up at Cain. "He's not like any shifter I've seen before."

Vance was curling his hands into fists.

Cain stood, smiling faintly at him. Definitely a chilling smile—so why wasn't Vance running the hell out of there? The guy should be trying to claw open the side of the cage and get to safety.

But he wasn't.

"Get out," she whispered. Vance had to know what Cain was capable of doing.

"No one can leave, not until a body hits the floor," Trace told her, voice grim.

That wasn't good.

She elbowed a lady out of her way. When the lady turned with a hiss, Trace stepped in to make sure Eve didn't get clawed. Eve muttered her apology and tried to make sure she didn't elbow anyone else.

Don't want a beating right now. Don't.

She was at the cage, curling her fingers tight around the heavy wiring. "Cain! Cain, stop!"

His head snapped toward her. Their eyes locked.

"Don't do this," she screamed. "Please, don't—"

Vance attacked, leaping at Cain while his attention was on Eve. The two men were almost the same size, and Vance hurtled right at him, knocking Cain to the floor.

Then Vance—bit Cain?

"Shit. Snake venom." Trace was at her back again. "Your Thirteen's about to go out. That stuff's fucking poison."

Vance sure seemed to think so. He was jumping off Cain's body. Heading back toward the other side of the cage. Distancing himself, while he waited for his enemy to fall. He waved his hands in the air, encouraging the shouts from the crowd.

Venom. Venom. Venom.

Now she understood what they had been screaming for so long. The crowd had wanted to see the snake bite.

They'd gotten their wish.

Eve couldn't move. She'd distracted Cain. She hadn't wanted him to kill Vance, but she sure hadn't wanted Cain to suffer, either.

Cain was still crouched on the floor. His head was down. The crowd was going wild. They were screaming for another bite. They wanted blood. They wanted violence.

Cain's head tilted up. His gaze met hers once more.

They were going to get it.

She saw the fire lighting his eyes.

Her head turned toward Trace. "You should . . ." She cleared her throat because her voice had gone hoarse. Fear could do that. Fear could steal her voice. She tried again. "You should run."

Because she knew an attack was coming.

Who the fuck was that blond jerk beside Eve? With his hand on her? The fool needed to step back.

The venom pumped through Cain's blood, making the burn inside him hotter. Jimmy was a fool. His venom might work on the weaker shifters, but it wasn't going to incapacitate Cain. It wasn't doing anything but making his fury deepen.

"You shouldn't have come after me, man!" Jimmy snarled at him. "Always thinking you were so big and bad. *Who's bad now?*" Jimmy threw his arms into the air and spun to face the crowd.

Eve was whispering something to the blond dick beside her. She looked back at Cain and he saw her lips form, "No!" but there was no stopping him. Jimmy was begging for death.

Cain rose to his feet. Lifted his hand. Let the flames dance above his palm.

The cries died from the crowd. Fear—ah, he could smell it.

Jimmy froze with his hands still in the air. Maybe he smelled the fear, too.

"You sold me out," Cain told him, his voice carrying easily. "Me and a dozen other paranormals."

Murmurs came from the crowd. Some folks—the smart ones—started heading for the door. Eve didn't leave. Neither did the blond with the death wish.

Jimmy's hands lowered. He turned back to face Cain and his face had whitened. "N-no, I—"

Cain wasn't in the mood for his lies. "You let the humans cut into us. Torture us." For days. Weeks. Some paranormals hadn't lasted more than a few hours. Some had screamed until they'd lost their voices.

The crowd wasn't cheering for Jimmy anymore. It looked like he'd lost his bloodthirsty fans. Selling out your own kind could make you hated.

And targeted.

If I don't kill him tonight, others will. In the paranormal world, you didn't sell out your own kind, not to the humans. That was the one rule that shouldn't be broken.

"I didn't sell nobody out!" Jimmy yelled. His gaze darted around the cage. Looking for a way out. Unless the guy shifted, there was no way for him to escape, and Cain wasn't about to give him time for a shift.

"Yes," Cain said flatly, "you did." It was his turn to leap forward. His turn to attack. Jimmy tried to slip away, but that snake just wasn't fast enough. Cain slammed his hand and his fire right into Jimmy's chest. The shifter screamed and the scent of burning flesh filled his nostrils.

"Sonofabitch." Trace yanked Eve away from the cage. "We're getting out of here, now."

They weren't the only ones looking to flee. Everyone seemed to be running away from the cage.

Animals were often afraid of fire, and the animals inside the shifters were never very far from the surface.

But while the others were screaming and running— those flames weren't even that high yet—Eve dug in her heels. She'd come to that warehouse for a reason. She wasn't leaving without Vance—or Cain. "Go," she told Trace and yanked away from him.

He never held her too tightly. When it came to women, he was always conscious of his strength. With his past, he couldn't be any other way.

"I'll meet you back at your place." She didn't wait for his response. She lunged through the crowd and headed for the entrance to the cage. Okay, maybe those flames *were* getting pretty high in there.

But Vance wasn't dead. He'd rolled and put out the flames on his chest. His flesh was blistered, charred, and the snake tattoo had sure gotten scorched. The flames scattered around him, licking at the floor and at the edges of the cage.

Cain stood in the middle of that chaos. His hands were at his sides and his gaze was on Vance.

She grabbed for the cage door.

"Oh no, sweet thing," a hard voice told her.

And just that fast, Eve found herself in a grip that *hurt*. A man held her arms. A big, burly guy with lots of piercings and slicked-back red hair. "I want to see how this one ends. Got me two grand riding on the snake."

She twisted and kicked, but the guy didn't let her go. Crap. "You're . . . gonna lose that money . . ." Eve gasped out as she fought to break free.

If he didn't let her go and get out of there before those flames got much higher, he might just wind up losing his life, too.

Jimmy lifted his hands. "D-don't kill me!"

The first blast hadn't been meant to kill. Only to hurt. To show the snake just what it felt like to be tortured.

"Weeks," Cain snapped out as he stalked his prey. Smoke rose in the air, heavy and thick, and Jimmy started to cough.

"For weeks, they kept me chained up. They cut into me. Sliced me apart. Drugged me."

Jimmy's back was pressed against the side of the cage. The guy actually whimpered.

This was the tough SOB that the crowd had cheered for? The guy looked like he was about to piss his pants.

Some paranormals liked to give pain, but they just couldn't take it.

Some . . . like soon-to-be-dead Jimmy.

"How much?" Cain demanded, a foot away from Jimmy. One more touch, and he'd incinerate the guy. Just one. "How much was my life worth to you?"

Jimmy's gaze darted to the left. To the right. And—wait, did a faint smile curve his thin lips?

Cain tensed. Jimmy shouldn't be smiling. Begging, yes. Smiling, no.

Jimmy's shoulders straightened and his chin shoved out. "You were worth more than the others. Twenty thousand"—Jimmy paused—"*then.*" His small smile widened to show his curving fangs. "The price is double now."

The price is double now. Cain's body stiffened

"It's a two-for-one deal this time," Jimmy said, voice strengthening. Definitely turning into a cocky bastard once more. "Genesis doesn't just want you—they want the pretty girl you escaped with. The same girl who's fighting to get in this cage. To get to you."

Cain's head whipped to the right. Eve *was* fighting some giant jerk, twisting and punching in his hands and he was—

The bastard hit her back.

Cain roared his fury.

Then he heard the thunder of . . . gunshots.

"Dumbass, I figured you'd show tonight. I knew you'd want my blood." Jimmy scrambled back against the cage wall. "But guess what? They want yours, too. And you're not escapin' tonight. Wyatt's getting you and you won't ever escape again."

The thunder of more bullets. Exploding. Firing.

Cain leaped to the side as those bullets tore through the cage.

He'd hit her so hard that her head snapped back. Everything went dim for a moment and then Eve could have sworn she heard fireworks popping.

"Sonofabitch."

A familiar snarl. Trace. Hadn't she told him to leave? Twice? She dug her nails into the giant's arms and got ready to head butt him.

But the giant dropped her. Mostly because Trace had just clawed the guy's side open.

"You should"—Trace snarled as he sliced again—"treat women with more *respect.*"

The giant scrambled back, tripped in his own blood, and—

And a bullet tore into the guy's head.

Eve screamed. That hadn't been fireworks. That sound had been the thunder of bullets. Her gaze flew around the area. Armed men were storming in. Men who wore all black and were covered with heavy, bulletproof vests. Men who were shooting at the paranormals. Taking them out with cold precision.

"Time to *go,*" Trace said, voice flat.

"Not without Cain! I—"

A barrage of bullets slammed into the cage.

"No!"

The bullets didn't hit Cain. They thudded into a smiling Vance . . . who stopped smiling once his blood splattered around him. When he hit the floor, his face had locked in lines of stunned horror.

Cain . . . wasn't in the cage. The left side of the cage hung open. He'd *burned* his way out.

He was attacking the armed men. Using his fire. Fighting back.

Heading for her with eyes that blazed.

"Before that crazy hoss gets here, we're leaving," Trace snapped. Sprinklers burst on from overhead and the water soaked them. A shrill alarm cut through the room. "Come on!"

With the bullets and the blood and the growing fire around her, Eve went with him.

She couldn't afford to be caught again. And Cain—she *knew* the armed men wouldn't catch him. He was too strong for them.

Already, the fire was thickening. The sprinklers and the gushing water couldn't stop Cain's fire. It was hard to see through the smoke and flames. But Trace knew the way out—through some back door that took them up a narrow flight of stairs and spit them out into the waning night.

Trace sucked in a deep, heaving breath, his hold on her never loosening. Her gaze swept to the left, and—

The building was surrounded. Police cruisers with blazing blue lights had circled the warehouse.

"Put your hands up!" a voice blared from behind the line of cruisers. "Step away from the woman!"

Trace swore and stepped in front of her. Figured he'd do something like that. He stepped in front of her and lifted his hands. No claws sprang from his fingers, not yet. Eve knew they could appear in an instant.

Did the cops know who they were dealing with? The armed guys inside had known, but these local cops—Eve wasn't so sure.

"I'm a reporter," Eve called out, trying to defuse the situation. "People are being hurt inside and—"

A bullet blasted from a policeman's gun and slammed into Trace's shoulder.

People are being hurt out here, too.

"Screw this," Trace growled. He turned, grabbed Eve, and tossed her over his shoulder. Her head slammed into his back and before she could suck in a strong breath, he was running. That shifter could run *fast*. She bounced along his shoulder, holding on as best she could. Bullets were flying, and the white-hot burn of one grazed the skin of her leg.

Then they were leaping through the air, clearing one of the parked police cars in one jump—because yeah, some shifters could do that.

And some could run freakishly fast, even in human form. Trace had always been one of the strongest shifters Eve had ever met, and the guy certainly wasn't disappointing her.

She held tight to Trace and managed to glance back one final time . . . just as the warehouse exploded and all the cops scrambled away, screaming.

"Do you think he's dead?"

Eve glanced up at Trace's voice. They'd made it back to his house easily enough. The blaze had stopped the cops dead in their tracks.

Why had cops been attacking? Jeez, she'd thought the cops had vowed to protect and serve everyone. Not just the humans.

"Subject Thirteen," Trace said as he walked into the bedroom he'd given her for the night. "Do you think he made it out?"

"Fire wouldn't hurt him." She'd changed into an old T-shirt and a pair of loose jeans. Trace had bandaged her leg, and she'd dug the bullet out of his shoulder.

Just like old times. Almost.

The wooden floor creaked beneath his footsteps. "You didn't mention that the new boyfriend was a serious pyro."

New boyfriend. She glanced up from the story she'd been working on. A story that included tortured paranormals, rogue scientists, and crooked cops. The sooner she got this story to a media outlet, the better. She had a great connection at the *Atlanta Daily.* The paper could have this story on their Web edition first thing, then it could hit print and—

"Before anything else happens, I think you might need to back up a bit and tell me a little more about Thirteen." Trace leaned his hip against the desk and stared down at her.

Eve lifted one brow. "Did you crack the password for me?"

"Uh, yeah. In about two seconds."

Perfect—that was the proof she'd need to take to the editor and—

"But you're not getting that laptop, not until you answer a few questions for me."

Seriously? Did she look like she needed this hard time right then?

"Want to tell me why Thirteen seemed like he was ready to rip my head off?"

Um, she'd missed that part. She'd been a bit distracted by other things. "The guy has some anger issues." Understatement. From what she'd seen, Cain had more than a few issues. In the interest of keeping Trace unscathed, she added, "If you see him, you'd be safer if you didn't get within touching distance."

His shoulders straightened. "I'm not exactly easy prey here."

No, he wasn't, but they weren't just talking about your average paranormal predator, either. "I've seen him burn men alive. Don't let him touch you."

Silence.

Trace's eyes weighed her. "And what happens when he touches you?"

Eve's heart raced faster in her chest. *I burn.* Only the fire simmered inside her, igniting a hungry lust that she could barely control. "It doesn't matter. I'm working on a story, doing my job." Stopping other paranormals from being exploited. Hurt. Killed. "He's long gone now and—"

Trace's head cocked to the side. "I'd guess again," he murmured, taking a step away from her, heading toward the door.

"What?" He'd lost her. Then she heard the sound of breaking glass, and Trace's alarm system began to beep.

"Company's calling," he threw the words over his shoulder as he hurried from the room.

Company? Cain? No, he wouldn't follow her. He'd *left* her at that truck stop, not the other way around. She hadn't been the one to ditch their new partnership.

But Eve rushed out of that room because whoever was breaking in, well, she wasn't leaving Trace to handle them alone.

He was already down the stairs and—

Arms wrapped around her. Strong. Hard. She was hauled back against a body that, yes, dammit, she already recognized by touch. Rather hard to mistake those abs. They left quite the impression on a girl's memory.

"Cain."

The alarm stopped beeping. She heard footsteps coming back toward her. Trace would know exactly where the intruder was. That shifter nose of his would lead him right back to them.

And, sure enough, she saw Trace's blond head appear at the bottom of the stairs. He stared up at them, eyes angry, intense.

Trace wasn't attacking, not yet, but his jaw was locked tight as he ordered, "Let her go."

She could feel the tension running through Cain's body. The scent of smoke clung to him. His face was near the side of her head, and when he spoke, his breath blew over the shell of her ear, sending a shiver through her.

"You're not safe," he whispered.

Eve swallowed. Her body fit against his too well. "Is that why you decided to do some breaking and entering?" She turned easily in his arms. His hold hadn't been meant to keep her immobile, but . . . to do what? Pull her close? "The last time I saw you, the bullets were flying. Seems to me, you're the one who isn't safe."

"We're being hunted." His gaze narrowed on her jaw and then he caught her chin and carefully lifted it up, swearing when he saw the tender mark on her flesh. "That fucking asshole bruised you."

Yeah, well, when a bear swung at you, that hit tended to leave a mark. The graze on her leg hurt worse, but she wasn't about to point that injury out to him.

"Don't worry," Trace said as he headed up the stairs. "I damn near gutted him."

She glanced back over her shoulder and found Trace staring up at Cain with icy eyes. "And I can do the same to you . . ."

Okay, now she swung back around and deliberately planted her body between the two men. Seeing those two battle wasn't exactly her idea of a fun time.

Trace was the only family she had. And Cain—

Cain could seriously hurt Trace. Burn him.

She didn't want him killing her only family. So when Trace charged up those last few steps, she shoved one hand on his chest and one hand on Cain's. *"Stop."* They weren't enemies.

You're being hunted.

She had the bullet wound to prove it.

"Is this the cop?" Cain demanded in a voice that vibrated with a leashed fury. "The one you told me about?"

Her gaze swung between the two men.

Trace kept glowering. Right. As if he'd ever be confused with a cop. He'd spent too much time behind bars for that to happen.

When he'd been sixteen, Trace had killed a man. That had been the day his claws had first broken free.

"Trace isn't a cop," she said, proud of the way she kept her voice steady. And really, what was Cain even rambling about? She hadn't told him about any cop.

"Then where's the boyfriend?" Cain wanted to know. "The big, tough-cop-badass you told me about when we were back at Genesis?"

Eve's face flushed as she finally figured out what he was rambling about. When Wyatt had thrown her at Cain, she'd told him about her fictional lover. *My cop boyfriend is going to hunt me down and kick your asses!*

That had just been for show. If she'd really had a badass boyfriend, she wouldn't have been screwing around with Cain. Just what kind of girl did he think she was?

The easy kind.

Obviously. Jerk.

She shoved against his chest. Hard. "There's no boyfriend," she gritted out. "That was a lie, okay? It was kind of a desperate moment."

His lashes flickered. She could have sworn that some of the tension seemed to ease from his clenched jaw.

"As fun as this shit isn't," Trace said, bringing her attention right back to him, "wanna tell me why you just broke into my house?"

"I'm here for her." Cain's voice was flat. "I came back for Eve."

Like she was some kind of package he needed to pick up. She dropped her hands and headed back to the bedroom. "La di damn da. Isn't that fantastic?" She was pretty sure no violence was about to wreck the stairs, so she felt safe walking away.

She paused at the threshold of her bedroom and told him, "In case you didn't know, I have a life—and a story to write. One very big, important story. I was going to talk to Vance tonight and get more material, but then you—"

Cain tackled her. Her body slammed into the floor even as the window near the bed exploded and glass flew into the room. Glass . . . and smoke.

"Are you all right?" Cain's voice.

She blinked and managed to open her eyes. She wanted to talk and say that, yeah, except for having a two-hundred-pound male crushing her, she was fine.

Only . . . she couldn't talk.

And she wasn't fine. And that wasn't smoke filling the room. It was some kind of gas. Choking her. Making her body feel limp and dizzy and . . . dammit, she remembered this feeling from Genesis! They were trying to drug her again.

She coughed and pushed at Cain's chest.

"Get her out of there!" Trace yelled.

Cain already had her up. He pulled her with him and back toward the stairs.

"Told you," Cain growled. More glass exploded—she could hear it shattering all through the house. "You're being . . . hunted."

Cain had followed her back to Trace's house. Either he'd lead the hunters to her . . . they'd followed him or . . .

Or they followed me and Trace when we left the warehouse. We got away too easily. They followed us and they waited for Cain to show up.

If her throat weren't burning so much, she could say

this . . . but *no*, she couldn't manage so much as a word right then.

"They're coming in. They want us alive." Cain was talking to Trace now.

What? Were they suddenly buddy-buddy? A little hell could do that to guys.

"Well, they want her alive anyway. They'll either kill you or take you in."

"I'm not going in a cage." The fury in Trace's voice chilled her. He'd been in a cage as a teen—trapped in prison. He'd sworn never to go back.

The cage hurt his beast too much.

Hurt *him* too much.

Trace needed to leave her. He could run so fast.

Without her, Eve knew he'd be able to get away from the hunters coming. "L-leave . . ." The word was a raw whisper in her throat. Why wasn't the gas affecting them as much?

Trace staggered and fell down three steps. The gas *was* hitting him.

Her chest ached.

"I've got her," Cain said. "Get out of here!"

But was it too late? Eve could hear the thud of footsteps racing inside Trace's house. The hunters were coming for them.

Why?

Wyatt was dead. Genesis had burned. They should be safe.

"Hurt her"—Trace snarled—"and I'll . . . kill you."

She saw the beast shining in his eyes. His shift was coming.

"You can try," Cain told him, not sounding too concerned, "but I can't promise I'll stay dead."

The gas must've had the smallest impact on him. He still sounded normal. Was still walking and—

No, he was running. Running right down the stairs, dragging her with him, and fire was flowing from the fingers of his right hand. Fire that raced toward the men with guns. They shot their bullets, aiming at him. Eve heard Cain grunt, but he didn't slow down.

The fire blew open the front door. She was behind him, stumbling, holding on to him as best she could as he faced the shooters. His fire swept out, forming a wall that shoved the others back, even as Cain pulled her toward a motorcycle that waited near the edge of the property.

The fresh air slid into her lungs, making her stronger. The light of dawn was a red streak across the sky as she climbed onto the motorcycle. She heard a wolf howl and saw a dark shadow race into the trees.

Trace. He'd gotten away. He was safe. Eve sucked in a deep breath of that fresh, mind-clearing air. Trace was safe . . .

And his house was being gutted.

The motorcycle roared to life. Cain had jumped on behind her, his body curved around hers. Eve gripped the handlebars and she drove that bike the hell out of there. She knew her motorcycles. Knew exactly how to handle them.

A hail of bullets rained down on them.

Eve swore and tried to steer the motorcycle in as much of a serpentine style as she could in order to avoid the bullets.

Cain's fingers wrapped around hers. Held tight. Helped her to keep steering and to get them away from the hunters.

Then the bullets were distant echoes, whispers of thunder floating on the wind. The shooters were too far away to hit them. They'd have to give chase, have to keep hunting them, so she needed to get away as fast as possible.

Good thing she knew this area.

And the perfect safe house.

"Faster," Cain whispered behind her.

The wind whipped her hair back and seemed to bite right through her clothes.

But she drove faster and held on to the handlebars as tightly as she could.

With rage building within him, Richard Wyatt watched the motorcycle disappear into the darkness.

"Sorry, sir," one of the hunters said to him, shaking his head. "We weren't expecting that much power and—"

Excuses. He'd warned them just how powerful Cain could be. "How many bullets did you put into Subject Thirteen?"

That had been his real goal. Killing Thirteen. Capture would have been good, but this way . . . this way he got to experiment a bit more. Every time Thirteen died, Richard learned so much more about his test subject.

The human swallowed and glanced away, his gaze heading toward the small patch of road that Eve had used when she escaped. "We hit him . . . hell, at least four times. The guy just didn't go down."

He would. With four bullets in his body, Thirteen would be going down. Sooner or later.

Richard tapped his chin and then gave the order. "Follow them."

"And the wolf?"

That big, snarling beast that had rushed into the woods? "Forget him." Wolves were a dime a dozen. But Thirteen and Eve Bradley, they were special.

The guard turned away to carry out Wyatt's orders. Richard didn't move, not at first. He stared down that twisting road. *Hit four times.* Wonderful.

If the bullets didn't kill Thirteen, then the blood loss probably would.

And what would happen to Eve when Cain burned . . . and rose? Did she have any idea how dangerous the beast was when he first rose?

Probably not. Sometimes, Cain was able to hold on to some of his sanity when he rose.

Sometimes . . .

But on other risings, the beast took total control. Fire. Hell. Fury. Death.

Eve was about to learn a whole lot more about her new lover. She just might not survive her discoveries.

CHAPTER SEVEN

Cain couldn't move his feet. They hung limply, scraping over the road.

Did Eve realize what a deadweight he was on her?

That last bullet had lodged low in his spine. His fingers were working—barely—but he couldn't feel his legs.

And the blood had already soaked his clothes. Too many bullets. Too many injuries.

He knew when death was coming.

Fuck. Eve needed to get away from him. But he couldn't tell her. Couldn't do anything but slump over her and try to hold on.

I'm sorry.

For what would come next.

She'd taken the motorcycle over so many roads, then *off* the roads. They were on a long, lonely field in the middle of nowhere. The engine growled softly, the only sound that Cain could hear.

When he saw the small, stark cabin rising before him, Cain knew Eve had thought to bring them to a safe house. Pity, no house would be safe enough for them.

Just a few feet from the house, she turned off the motorcycle. Tried to push him back. "We'll be . . . ah . . . safe here. This place has been empty"—she gave another push back against him—"ever since—*Cain!*"

He'd fallen off the motorcycle. He barely felt the crash onto the ground. He was too far gone.

Eve was beside him. She rolled him over and stroked his face. "Cain?" Her voice was soft with worry and fear.

He tried to speak, but blood was choking him. *Go. Run. When I come back, don't let me touch you.*

Because when he came back, the darkness inside him would be even stronger.

After a rising, sometimes he couldn't even remember his name. Sometimes . . . he didn't care—about anything or anyone. He just wanted the rush of fury. Of rage.

Every rising pushed him closer and closer to the edge. And with each death, he wondered . . . *will this time be it?* This time, would he rise as the monster he'd always feared? The one that lived and breathed inside him?

"Cain!"

He realized she'd been yelling his name. He hadn't heard her. Couldn't speak still, so it didn't matter.

Her hands were sweeping over him and finding all the injuries. Too many. He'd shielded her as best he could and taken all the hits.

Cain knew that he could come back from death. But if Eve had been hit—she wouldn't have been able to rise. Coming back from death wasn't a luxury that she had.

Not a luxury. It's a fucking curse.

His eyes found hers.

"You took the bullets," Eve whispered. It almost looked like she was crying.

No one had ever cried for him before. His chest began to ache.

She slammed her fist right into his heart. "You took the bullets! Damn you!"

What? Had she wanted to die? Death wasn't a nice easy ride. It was a fucking bitch.

Or maybe that was just hell.

"You're dying on me . . ." Anger rumbled in her words. "And, what? I just have to sit back and watch?"

Yes.

She grabbed his jaw and turned his face toward hers. When had he looked away?

"You're coming back." Her words were a demand.

He couldn't speak.

"You're coming back." Then she put her mouth against his. Sweet. Death had never tasted so sweet. "You have to come back."

He could feel the fire building inside him. She had to feel the growing heat, too, but she still kept her hands on his face. Kept her lips so close to his.

"Come back," she told him once more. "Don't leave me."

The flames were going to burst free. He knew it, but first—first he had to die.

His heart stopped beating. The blood choked him. His eyes stayed open, on her.

Eve's lips trembled. Her hands rose slowly, so slowly, and she closed his eyelids.

"Come back." A final whisper from her. Her fingers brushed over his cheek. Then she pulled away.

Death took him.

The fire burst over his flesh, so bright that it lit up the sky. A giant blaze that burned so hot the ground was singed about five feet in every direction.

Eve stood back, watching. Not because she was afraid of the flames, but because she was afraid any move she made might stop the fire.

Cain wasn't back yet, not fully. But . . .

Soon.

Her knees pushed into the dirt as she knelt and watched him. She'd tried to get them away from the city. She hadn't even realized that he'd been hurt. Not this bad.

Bad enough to die.

He won't stay dead. He hadn't before. He'd come back. She knew he would return to her. He had to.

The fire raged hotter. She could barely see his body. The flames actually seemed to be roaring.

No. That wasn't the flames.

That was Cain.

Because those flames were rising, *he* was rising. Standing up, spreading his arms out by his sides, and roaring his fury to the world.

She didn't move.

The heat blasted around her and . . .

He turned to look at her. As the flames began to fade away, vanishing and leaving his golden, tanned flesh behind, unmarred, perfect, he stared at her.

His eyes still burned. She could see the flames flickering there.

What are you?

His hands were at his sides, his feet braced apart. The clothing had burned from his body, and her gaze swept over him. No more bullet wounds.

Only strong, hard flesh.

Her breath rasped out. "I knew you'd be okay." Knew, hoped—same thing.

He took a step toward her. The flames in his eyes eased back into the normal darkness of his stare.

She offered him a smile and hoped that it didn't look as desperate as it felt. "You scared me, though." Her legs weren't quite working yet, which was why she still knelt on the ground as he approached. "I don't exactly like it when people die right in front of me."

His death had brought back too many memories of the family she hadn't been able to save. Of the flames and the fire that had taken them, but left her behind.

Don't leave me. Daddy, Daddy, don't leave!

But in the end, they'd all left her. She'd been so alone.

Eve took another deep breath and straightened her shoulders. "Well, now that you're back, what are we going to—"

He pulled her off the ground and right up into his arms. Her words ended in a yelp as she lost her breath. He held her above the ground with his too-hot touch, letting her feet dangle a good foot in the air.

His gaze stared hard into her own. A faint furrow appeared between his brows, and the guy actually stared at her as if he had no clue who she was.

And that scared her. A lot. Because she'd seen what he did to the folks he considered his enemies.

"C-Cain?"

His head jerked at the sound of her voice.

"You're hurting me," she said, but the words weren't quite the truth. His hold was strong, but not bruising. Didn't matter though. She wanted down. There was something about his stare that chilled her.

And Cain wasn't the chilling kind.

That furrow between his brows deepened, but he slowly lowered her to the ground once more. Then his head leaned toward her and he—had he just sniffed her?

She put her hands on his chest. "We need to go inside. It's not safe out here." They were in the middle of nowhere, so she was hoping no one had seen that blaze light the night, but if their pursuers were close enough . . .

We could be screwed.

"Who are you?"

Those words, stilted, flat, had her own eyes widening.

She realized that there was no recognition in Cain's gaze. Just . . . darkness.

"I'm Eve," she whispered as she stepped back. She swallowed, glanced down, and forced herself to reach for his hand. *It's Cain. He just needs a few minutes. Give him time.*

He'd risen before and still known her. He'd remember her this time, too. He just needed—hell, she wasn't sure what. *Time.* "We have to go inside. It's not safe here," she said again.

"Why not?" Still flat. No emotion.

How long would it take before his memory came back? A few minutes? A few hours? If only she'd had the chance to read Wyatt's notes on Cain. "We're not safe because there are men after us. They want to kill me."

That got no response. Not even a blink.

"And they want to kill you," she added.

He shrugged. "I can't die." He smiled, and it was a smile with an edge of evil. "I'm sure they can die. I'll just kill them and listen to them beg and scream."

This wasn't the guy she knew. Goose bumps rose on her arms. "Cain?"

Something was off. He was off.

He glanced toward her. "Scared?"

Hell, yes. "No. Of course not." She straightened her shoulders. "Now come on. It'll be light soon. Let's get inside and figure out what we're supposed to do next."

She tugged his hand and he actually followed her into the small home. It was a bit dusty inside. Since seventy-two-year-old John Monroe had gone hitchhiking across the U.S. last June, no one had been there—which made the place perfect for hiding.

"Maybe we can find you some clothes and—"

He yanked her back against him. "I like the way you smell."

Um, okay. "Cain, I—"

He kissed her. Deep and hard, driving his tongue into her mouth and locking his hands tightly around her. The kiss was wild, wicked, and dominant. He didn't seduce her with his lips and tongue.

He took.

Her nails sank into his shoulders, and she turned her head away from him. The last time she'd had sex with him, it had turned into slam-bam-good-bye ma'am. He might be having some issues right then, but she wasn't just going to offer herself up again.

Even if the sex had been fantastic.

He was kissing her throat. Licking her. Lightly nipping the flesh. "I remember"—his voice was a growl—"your taste."

She wouldn't ever be able to forget his. "Let me go."

He didn't speak, but pressed another kiss to the curve of her neck. Damn, but that was a weak spot for her. One lick there and she was already arching her hips against him.

Down girl. "Let me go," she said again, the words harder. She'd give him ten more seconds, then she'd start punching.

His head lifted. He stared at her. Had his eyes always been so dark? Like midnight with no stars or moon—total darkness. His breath came out, ragged, and he said, "I can't."

Then he kissed her again.

She tasted the desperation in his kiss. The wild lust. And knew . . .

Something was very, very wrong with Cain.

Eve didn't shove him away. Maybe she should have. But . . . she was afraid. Not of him. His fire didn't scare her at all.

She was just terrified for him.

Her hands slid over his shoulders. Held him. Her mouth met his, but she fought to gentle the kiss. Her lips brushed over his. Her tongue stroked his.

Cain shuddered against her and his hold tightened even more.

Then he spun her around and pressed her back against the wall, caging her with his body.

His very aroused body.

His tongue slid over hers. The guy could really do some amazing things with that tongue and—

Cain's head lifted. His eyes were still so dark. *Lost.* He stared down at her. "I remember your taste."

That was, ah, something, right?

"Eve." His voice was so low and rough.

She nodded.

His eyes squeezed shut and he turned his head away from her. "This . . . *I'm trying to stop.*"

He sounded like he was hurting. So bad.

Her hands were on his shoulders. Stroking his too-hot skin. "What's happening to you?"

He flinched at her voice even as he seemed to turn in to her touch.

"Cain? You . . . you know me." He hadn't appeared to recognize her moments before. He'd just looked at her and lusted. Sometimes, a girl could enjoy being the focus of all that raw need.

Sometimes, she needed more.

His gaze met hers, and she saw the danger in his stare. "Even hell can't make me forget some things." His hand rose to her mouth. "I came back . . . wanting your taste again."

Eve swallowed. "Cain?"

"I opened my eyes"—he pulled away from her and stood with his back to her—"saw you and thought . . ."

What? What had he thought?

"Mine," Cain growled out the one word.

Her heart was about to race right out of her chest.

"You should leave. Run away from me." Still in that dark, rough voice. One that sent shivers sliding over her because it was . . . sexy.

Danger had always been sexy to her.

Cain was definitely dangerous.

She wasn't leaving. He'd helped her. She'd helped him. Didn't he get it? They were a team.

Until this mess was over.

"I'm not going anyplace," Eve told him and was rather proud of the firm sound of her own voice.

His back tensed. "You don't know . . . how thin my control is right now." He glanced back at her, and she saw the stark hunger etched on his face. "When I come back . . . I'm not the same . . . I *need*."

She was getting that.

She was also thinking . . . *He isn't the only one who needs.* "You're not leaving me alone this time."

He frowned at her. Still looked lost and angry and wild.

Eve licked her lips and his jaw locked. Her breath whispered out and she said, "This time, you don't dump me at a truck stop and never look back."

"Eve . . ."

She stepped toward him. Lifted her chin. "I want you, too." The stark truth. Pride wasn't going to hold her back. He needed. She needed.

Screw pride.

"If you dump me like that again, I will hunt your ass down."

He was shaking his head. "This is your chance . . . *go*."

Simply, she said, "No."

And he took her. Pounced. Had her in his arms and pushed right back up against the wall behind her. She could almost hear the shredding of his control, and Eve didn't care. She wanted his wildness. Wanted the lust and the fury and the pleasure.

Wanted everything.

When you'd had nothing for so long, you were greedy for every emotion.

The adrenaline still pumped through her body, heightening her sensitivity to his every touch. They fought, both trying to yank off her shirt, and then it was on the ground.

He shoved her bra out of the way and his mouth closed over one nipple. Licking. Sucking. Scoring the tight peak lightly with his teeth.

Her hand sank into his hair even as she moaned his name.

His fingers slid down her body as he licked her. Cain pushed down her jeans. She kicked away her shoes. Then his fingers were between her legs.

And she was already wet for him. Slick, hot, so ready. His fingers slid inside, thrusting knuckles deep.

"Can't . . . wait . . ." A growl against her skin.

Then he lifted her up. She wrapped her legs around him. Needed. Wanted—

Cain drove into her, sinking deep in a thrust that had her gasping. Her shoulders slammed back against the wall. He withdrew. Plunged deep. No easy ride. No tender touches.

Everything was just . . . wild.

Rough. Hard. Fast. He drove into her again and again. Her sex closed around him, holding tight, and his cock seemed to swell more inside her, stretching her with delicious pleasure.

His hands were on her hips. Holding her. Lifting her. Getting her to take more of him. More.

The climax hit her, slamming through her, and Eve screamed.

He kept thrusting. Deeper. Harder. As if he couldn't get enough of her.

His eyes were on hers. Such darkness. How could there be so much need in one man's stare?

"Not . . . enough . . ." He bit the words off and then he was turning, carrying her, holding her tight. Her sex trembled and clenched around him as the contractions of her climax sent sensual aftershocks racing through her body.

They entered another room. Dark. Two more steps and they fell on the bed. He caught her legs. Lifted them up higher, pushing them so that he could thrust deeper inside her. The angle sent his cock sliding over her clit with every stroke of his body. Her flesh was already too sensitive and that touch . . .

She lost her breath.

Her nails dug into his skin. She arched her hips against him. Wanted more. Everything.

Every. Damn. Thing.

His mouth was on her throat. Licking. Biting. That perfect spot. This time, she didn't just climax.

She erupted.

So did he. Eve felt Cain's climax jet inside her as his body stiffened. He shuddered and his head lifted. His eyes had gone blind from the pleasure, a pleasure that was hitting her with the same wild intensity.

When the release finally ended, her breath was heaving in ragged gasps. Her hands slid off his shoulders, falling limply aside, and her legs eased back down to the bed.

Cain pushed up on his arms so that his weight wasn't on her. He stared into her eyes. Didn't speak.

She found she didn't know what to say right then, either.

So when he rolled to his side and pulled her close, she just let her heartbeat slow down.

And wondered what would happen next.

He had to tell her.

Cain sat up when Eve walked out of the shower. Her hair was wet, falling over her shoulders. Her skin was shining and soft—

Beautiful.

He fucking had to tell her.

Easing up in bed, he studied her for a moment in silence. When he'd come back after the last death and the fire had raged, he hadn't been in control. When he rose, his control could be shattered. The fire was too strong. The beast he carried too powerful.

But he'd known her.

Not her name, not at first. He'd looked at her and just thought . . .

Mine.

Dangerous. To her and to him.

He couldn't afford any attachments. Attachments would make him weak. Vulnerable.

That was why Wyatt wanted her. The bastard had figured out that Eve was a tool he could use. *To control me.*

"Is it always like that?" Her voice came softly as she turned the force of her gaze on him.

Cain knew he should apologize. He'd been too rough, too wild. He just stared back at her.

"At the lab, I didn't think . . . you seemed different when you rose this time."

He had been different. She deserved a warning. "Each rising is different. There are times when I come back . . . times when I don't even know my own damn name." Then there were what he thought of as the lucky times—though those were few and far between—when he could come back, like he had at the lab, and his memories were fresh. Crisp.

It just seemed like, more and more . . . the man had to fight the beast within in order to get back those memories.

"When I rise, I'm at my most dangerous. I can kill . . . without meaning to." Because he knew only fury and fire.

Her tongue slid over her lower lip. "You didn't kill me."

No, he'd just fucked her like a desperate man.

"I think you might have more control that you realize."

He didn't. He tried to warn her. "Next time, just get as far from me as you can."

"How about we just don't have a next time? How about you just stay alive?"

Easier said than done.

Eve exhaled heavily as she turned from him. Her delicate shoulders rolled, then sagged a bit. "Any idea why those jerkoffs are after us?" she asked as she pushed back the curtain of her hair. "I thought with Wyatt gone we'd—"

Ah, more bad news that Cain had to share. *Tell her.* "He isn't."

She glanced over her shoulder at him. "What?"

His breath eased out. She needed to understand that the battle wasn't over. It was just starting. "Last night, Jimmy told me that Wyatt had put a price on my head." He paused and wondered why he was even hesitating. "He put a price on yours, too."

She turned to face him. "Wyatt's dead. You told me—"

"I never saw him come out of Genesis. I thought he'd died." He'd thought wrong. "But the bastard must have had an escape route mapped out, one that took him away from the fire."

Her eyes were wide.

"He's alive, and he's after us."

She shook her head. "This can't happen."

Yeah, it could.

"I'm not just some random human on the street! He can't hunt me down, shoot me."

Human. No, she wasn't quite human. "I think they want you alive." Him it didn't matter so much. They knew he'd just come back if they killed him. So they'd use as much force as necessary to take him down. But for her . . . "Wyatt must have seen me take you through the fire, Eve. He knows you're not human."

Her breath rushed out. He saw fear flicker in the depths

of her stare, but she controlled the emotion quickly. Too quickly.

She would be smart to be afraid. "He wants to experiment on you, just like he did with the others at Genesis." Actually, Cain thought the bastard wanted more than that, but he'd already said enough. For now.

"No." She spun away. Marched into the other room.

Cain followed. He'd found a pair of old jeans that fit with the aid of a belt and some beaten boots that would do. The T-shirt he wore was old and faded, but he didn't exactly have a lot of options.

She was pacing in front of the main door. "This isn't going to happen." Back and forth, she paced. "It's *not*."

Paranormals disappeared every day. Didn't she realize that? Since they'd come out to the world, they'd become the experiment of choice for Uncle Sam.

And for every other government out there.

Everyone wanted to have the biggest, strongest military. You didn't get stronger than the paranormals.

We should have stayed in the fucking dark. He'd never wanted the world to know his secret. Humans were better off not knowing.

When they found out the truth, most of them just freaked the hell out and stared at him like they thought he was going to eat their kids.

He was on a no-kid diet.

"I'm going to the press. I might not have the laptop anymore"—she whirled around and pointed at him—"but I've got you. We'll tell our story. They'll listen. I'll *make* them listen."

A big reveal to the media was the last thing he wanted. "You don't think they're waiting for you there?"

She blinked.

"Wyatt knows you're a reporter. He's probably staked out every media outlet you've ever worked for in your life.

And he's got the cops in this area in his pocket. The government hired him. Shit, baby, there's no place you can go that he won't be waiting."

Her shoulders straightened. "He wasn't waiting here."

Cain shook his head, knowing she didn't understand. "He let us get away."

"Bull. He—"

"He knew I was dying, and he probably wanted to find out what would happen if you were left alone with me when I rose." Cain headed toward the window. "He could be out there right now, watching and waiting to see what we do."

"W-what would happen if we were left alone?" she repeated, frowning. "Just what did he think would happen?"

Cain knew that he might as well tell her. "That I'd kill you." He looked back at her. "Usually when I rise, I kill." Wyatt had learned that lesson soon enough. So after each rising, Cain had been kept chained tightly to the wall.

Until his control came back.

Then Wyatt had loosened the leash, just a bit.

Some days, the control could come back within thirty minutes. Other days . . . it could take hours for sanity to reign once more.

Her lips parted, and he heard the faint whistle as she sucked in a deep breath. "But you—"

"I fucked you instead." Because he hadn't risen and looked at her as an enemy.

She was something more.

Damn you, Wyatt. You won't use her against me.

"When he sees that you survived my rising, he'll want you in his lab. He'll want to know what you are." Just as Cain wanted to know.

Did she even realize how powerful she could truly be? How deadly?

To me.

"I'm going to the media." Her hands fisted at her sides. "I'm not—I won't be hunted. I'll break this story. Wyatt will be the one who runs. Not me."

She turned away. Yanked open the front door. Sunlight poured into the small cabin.

"Eve . . ."

Glancing back over her shoulder, she hesitated.

"The minute you call one of your contacts, Wyatt will have you. The minute you show up at a news station or paper, you'll vanish." She had to realize this.

Eve shook her head. "You're giving him too much power. He won't be in a hurry to attract attention. He's not going to try and grab me when others are around."

Wyatt wouldn't give a damn who was around. With enough money and power, anyone could vanish. "He's got connections you can't begin to imagine."

"I can imagine a hell of a lot."

The woman just wasn't getting it. "The only way to stop him is to kill him."

She turned back toward the sunlight. "I don't kill as easily as you do."

He took the shot—it was true. Few could kill as easily as he did. "It was harder once." He hadn't meant to say that.

A small shiver slid over her body. "How old were you?" *The first time you killed.*

He wouldn't tell her. "Doesn't matter." The only thing that mattered was stopping Wyatt. "I'm gonna find the bastard, and I will stop him."

"No." She stared into the sunlight. He'd never noticed the red highlights hidden in her dark hair before. Almost like fire. "*We're* going to stop him because I'll be damned if I let that bastard take my life away."

The way he'd taken so many others?

"Maybe it's time we became the hunters," she said and stepped into that light. "Maybe it's time we taught him to fear."

A lesson Cain would happily teach.

Only he wouldn't stop with fear. He wouldn't stop at all, not until Richard Wyatt was nothing but ash floating away in the sunlight.

CHAPTER EIGHT

The *Atlanta Daily* building stood stark and strong in the middle of the downtown business district. Eve had been to that building hundreds of times before. She'd worked as a freelance reporter, and she'd damn well brought in top-notch stories for Gloria Long, the paper's editor in chief.

When it came to stories, Gloria was a bulldog. She never backed away from anything or anyone.

Gloria would believe her. She'd help to bust Genesis and their work wide open. The paranormals wouldn't have to fear being snatched away and locked in a lab, not anymore.

"This is a mistake," Cain told her. He stood right behind her on the busy street corner, gazing up at the building.

Her shoulders stiffened. "So you've told me about ten times already." But he was still with her. He'd said that he'd stay by her side until they stopped Wyatt.

Her own pyro bodyguard. What else did a girl need?

They hadn't talked about what had happened—the hot sex, the wild pleasure—the whole dark-side thing that he had going on.

One problem at a time. Problem one for her right then—Wyatt. Making sure that his thugs weren't about to go ballistic on her again.

She'd known this story was big. She hadn't known that it could possibly destroy her life.

Eve grabbed a copy of the *Atlanta Daily* from the nearby newsstand. She held it up, checking for—

"Oh, shit." The words slipped from her. She'd made headlines before with her stories, sure, but . . .

But she'd never *been* the headline before.

In big, thick block letters, the headline screamed ROGUE REPORTER TORCHES CLUB.

Um, rogue reporter? And she hadn't torched any damn club—that had been Wyatt!

Her gaze scanned the story. *Dammit.* It said she'd torched that warehouse. That she'd attacked police officers. That she was fleeing with known felon Cain O'Connor—and that they were both armed and dangerous.

"I am dangerous," Cain murmured as he read over her shoulder.

Her fingers fisted the paper. "He attacked first." He'd beaten her to the press. Started a smear campaign so that no one would believe her. So that the public would believe—

Only him.

"I told you," Cain said as he tossed the paper. "You're not quite understanding his power."

"He's not understanding me," she snapped right back. Her gaze went to the *Atlanta Daily* building once more. She knew this routine. *Knew it.* So maybe Wyatt and his goons were inside, waiting for her to show.

Eve eased back, hiding in the shadows of the nearby restaurant. She didn't have to go in that big, imposing building. She knew Gloria's habits, and Gloria would be heading out of the *Atlanta Daily* on her usual chocolate run in five, four, three . . .

A woman with short blond hair and long, confident strides pushed through the *Atlanta Daily's* glass doors. Ah, Gloria. She could never make it through a full day without getting her fix.

Georgio's Chocolates was just one block over.

"Come on," Eve told Cain as she gave chase. No way should Gloria have printed that piece. The woman *knew* her. Gloria had integrity, she had—

Gloria had stopped in front of Georgio's. She appeared to be staring at her reflection in the glass.

Eve moved beside her and simply said, "What the hell?"

Gloria bent over as if inspecting the chocolate displayed in the window. "You need to get out of town. Get out and don't ever come back."

Cain hung back just a few steps.

"You need to print the truth," Eve fired back.

Gloria laughed, but the sound was weak and sad. "The truth? The truth is that our government knows about Wyatt's experiments . . . and they don't want them to stop. They're giving him more power, not less." She tapped the glass. "You know he's promised them an immortal soldier? One that can rise again and again, no matter how many times he dies? His heart can stop"—her hand slapped at the glass—"then boom, he's right back."

Hell. Wyatt was promising them Cain.

"The soldier won't need blood like a vampire. He won't be weak in sunlight. He'll be strong all the time. He'll be the perfect weapon of death."

Was that truly what Cain was? Eve swallowed. "Richard Wyatt is feeding the government a line of bullshit. Nothing—no one—like that exists."

Gloria straightened, but still didn't glance her way. "Wyatt knows about me."

Eve knew her secret, too.

Not human.

"If I don't play ball with him, I could wind up in a lab." Fear—an emotion Eve had never heard in Gloria's voice—hummed beneath the words.

Eve could only stare at the other woman. Gloria had

been in more wars that Eve could count. She'd faced terrorists. Murderers. Never flinched. Until now. "So you sold me out because you were afraid?" Fear could make anyone desperate. She got that.

Gloria gave a short, sad shake of her head. "I ran the article because I was scared to death. I came here to warn you because you're my friend."

Gloria had been her friend.

But Gloria turned away from her. "Don't try to talk to me again. Just . . . get out of here and don't look back."

"I don't run, Gloria."

Gloria glanced back at her too briefly. "Then you'll die, Eve."

Her friend strode into the chocolate shop. The bell that hung over the door gave a happy little jingle.

In the next instant, the shop exploded.

The force of the blast threw Eve back and she screamed, then lost her breath as she slammed into the ground.

"Eve!" Cain was there, turning her over and staring down at her with a face gone white.

She was bleeding. Her hands and her legs were cut and bleeding and she hurt everywhere . . . and . . . Gloria was dead.

Eve's eyes were on the burning building. Or what was left of it.

Cain lifted her into his arms. Sirens were screaming from someplace and a crowd was gathering on the street.

"I'm a doctor," a Good Samaritan in a blue shirt and running shorts said. "Let me look at her, I can help—"

"Step the fuck back," Cain snarled at him and held her carefully.

The Good Samaritan stepped the fuck back.

The pain began to slip away. Eve stared at the fire. Cain had tried to warn her.

He'd warned her.

Brakes squealed near them. She caught the stench of burning rubber.

Gloria died because of me. Eve realized she was crying.

There'd better be a special place in hell waiting for Wyatt.

"Get in!"

Wait. That voice was familiar. That snarl—it was Trace's voice.

She turned her head and saw that he'd been the one squealing to a stop. He was in a black SUV, his hands tightly gripping the wheel.

"Get. *In!*"

Cain put her in the back of the vehicle. Climbed in beside her. Her blood was on his hands.

Only fair. Gloria's was on hers.

The SUV roared away, racing right past a line of fire trucks heading for the burning remains of the chocolate shop.

Those fire trucks sure had gotten to the scene fast. *Too fast.*

I wasn't the only one who knew Gloria's routine. The bomb had been planted, the authorities tipped off.

And Gloria had died.

"You were right," Eve spoke through numb lips. "I should have stayed away." Cain had warned her, but she hadn't listened. She'd been so sure that she could approach Gloria quietly, that she could get her story out there.

Cain turned over her hands. Eve's palms were shredded. She'd thrown up her hands to cover her face when she went flying into the street, and when she'd hit, her palms had slammed into the asphalt.

"The paper said . . . the story said I torched that warehouse, the club with the people inside . . ." She licked her lips. Tasted the fire. "People will say I did the same here. That I killed her."

You did. A dark voice whispered in her mind. It was the voice of her own guilt. Gloria shouldn't have died for her.

Trace cursed from the front seat and sent the SUV careening around a curve.

"Slow down," Cain snapped, but his fingers softly stroked Eve's hands. "You want to blend in now, not stick out."

But Eve shook her head, knowing blending in wasn't an option. Eyes had been watching them. Cameras had probably been stationed on that shop, recording their every move. "They'll have seen the SUV. Gotten the plates . . ."

"On it," Trace muttered and pulled them into the winding entrance of a parking garage. "We're ditching this ride and getting the hell out of here."

"He's setting me up," she whispered, her heart like lead in her chest. "Wyatt is making me look like a criminal so no one will believe anything I say."

Cain just stared at her. A muscle jerked in his jaw. His hand lifted and brushed over her cheek. More blood smeared his fingers. She hadn't even realized that her cheek was bleeding.

"Attack first," Trace said from the front. The SUV braked to a jarring stop. "Give your enemy no time to run or rest. Fucking smart strategy."

No one had ever said Doctor Richard Wyatt wasn't smart.

Cain shoved open the back door, but after he jumped out, he turned back to gently help her out of the SUV.

"There." Trace was already heading toward another vehicle—a pickup truck. One with an extended cab and lots of room in the rear. "You two get back there and stay down."

He had the truck hot-wired in ten seconds flat. She'd taught him that particular skill, one long ago day. Eve slid down in the back, and Cain came down on top of her. Their bodies were pressed together. So close.

She turned her head away. She didn't want him this close. This close, he'd be able to see it when she cried.

I'm sorry, Gloria.

"I'll stop him," Cain promised her.

The lump in her throat was choking her. Eve tried to swallow. Once. Twice.

Then she felt Cain's lips on her cheek. He was . . . kissing away her tears.

"I'll kill him." So soft. Such a deadly vow.

She knew that Cain would keep his word.

If they didn't stop Wyatt, he'd keep coming. More innocent people would die. Wyatt didn't care. The blood on the streets didn't make a damn difference to him.

He'd keep coming.

Until they burned his ass and sent him to hell.

Wyatt surveyed the smoking remains before him. A good warning. Now Eve would understand just who she was facing.

Had she truly thought he'd fear being exposed in the media?

That would never happen. It couldn't. His experiments were too important.

Firemen were rushing onto the scene. No survivors would be inside. How could they possibly be? Those in that shop weren't like Cain . . . or Eve.

Such a surprise. He never would have known about her special skills if she hadn't come right to him.

Her mistake.

He'd had the chance to conduct two experiments in the field. Two very rewarding experiments.

Cain hadn't killed Eve once he'd risen. He'd been able to maintain his control with her. Interesting. If the chains hadn't bound him at Genesis, Cain would have destroyed everyone around him after some of his risings. He'd been too out of control. Too wild.

But he hadn't needed chains to stop him from hurting the lovely Eve.

And even a very powerful blast—one that had taken place just inches away from Eve's own face—hadn't been able to kill her.

Wyatt had been watching her when that building exploded. He'd seen exactly what she'd done.

Eve had thrown up her hands, and, for an instant, the flames had washed right over her skin. The force of those flames—and the blast—had tossed her through the air. She'd been bruised and bloody when she rose again, but the injuries had come from her slamming into the pavement.

The fire had never hurt her. The flames had burned right over her flesh, but the fire hadn't so much as blistered her skin.

Eve held great power over the fire.

He had been watching her every move through his binoculars. He'd seen the blood dripping from her wounds. Seen the way Cain cradled her. While the fire might not be able to hurt Eve, she was still very, very vulnerable. Eve *could* be hurt. Just not with fire.

The drugs he'd used at Genesis—and again last night— had a definite effect on her. And her skin cut open all too easily.

But she was immune to the flames.

Interesting.

A puzzle . . . and he did love a good puzzle. Once he got Eve in his lab, strapped to his table, he'd learn every one of her secrets.

She'd beg to tell them to him.

★ ★ ★

"Was that place rigged?" Trace asked quietly as he faced Cain, "or did you start the fire?"

They'd gotten out of Atlanta. Driven a few hours, crossed the South Carolina border, and kept going. They'd finally stopped at a small motel on the outskirts of Charlotte. Water from the shower pounded steadily, muffled slightly by the closed bathroom door.

Cain had been left alone with the shifter while Eve washed the blood away.

Trace raised a brow as he studied Cain. "She's not here—and she doesn't have shifter hearing, so just talk straight with me. Drop the bullshit, man."

Cain didn't like the wolf.

"I know what you are, and I know exactly what you can do," Trace told him.

I doubt that. In Cain's experience, few people actually knew what he was—and even fewer understood just how powerful he was. He stared steadily back at Trace. He'd washed Eve's blood off his hands, but he could almost still feel that blood coating his fingertips. "And you think I would hurt her?"

"I think you've got a monster inside, one that you can't control." Flat, hard words.

Cain held that cold stare. "I guess you'd know all about having a beast inside." He didn't like this bastard. Just what was his relationship with Eve? They were far too close.

Too close.

Jealousy burned in Cain's gut.

Trace bared his growing fangs. "Yeah, I fucking would know." He dropped his arms and stalked toward Cain. "She helped you, so now do her a favor . . ."

If Trace really knew what he was, then the wolf should be backing away, not coming closer. Unless he just wanted an ass-kicking.

The knot of jealousy spread within Cain.

"Get the hell away from Eve," Trace told him bluntly. "Before she's hurt again."

The guy had him confused with someone who gave a shit about what he had to say. "She wants me close," Cain murmured, not about to back down. Time to clear the air here. "So I'm not going anyplace."

"Even if you put her at risk?"

Were the shifter's claws starting to come out? They were. Fool. Fire trumped claws any day of the week. "I'm the one who can keep her safe." The only one.

"Because you're the big, tough, nightmare-myth, right?"

Myth. The word almost surprised him. It appeared that Trace *did* have a clue about just what Cain was. "Myths aren't real." Monsters were.

"Before my house—the house I damn well loved—got torched, I hacked into Wyatt's computer." Trace's eyes showed only his cold rage as he studied Cain. "I read the files on you. I know what he did."

"Good for you." Cain tried not to let any emotion show on his face. He didn't want to think about those days at Genesis.

"He killed you at least a dozen times."

More. But Cain had stopped counting after a while. What had been the point?

"And each time you died, you rose back up. You burned and you rose."

The shower had stopped. He could barely hear the faint drip, drip of the water.

"Silver bullets. Dismemberment." Trace was rattling off a brutal list, and with every word he spoke, the memories flashed through Cain's mind.

I was alive when they started dismembering me.

The bathroom's wooden door opened. Eve stood there, dressed in the jeans and T-shirt that they'd picked up from a thrift store down the road. Her hair was wet, and her eyes were on Cain.

Trace locked his jaw and stopped talking. Finally.

Eve shook her head. "I want to hear this." She was still pale, but she didn't look as shell-shocked. Had she cried in the shower? Dammit, he hated that she hurt.

Wyatt would think nothing about the bombing at that shop. The people who'd died would just be collateral damage. Necessary sacrifices to achieve the big picture. Wyatt was all about the big picture.

Trace glanced at Eve. "You think you already know about him, don't you?"

Her gaze lingered on Cain. "I know he didn't set that shop on fire."

"How do you know?" Trace demanded instantly. "Fire is his bitch to control, it's—"

"His fire feels different." She walked past the two men. Peeked out of the faded curtains, then turned back to face them. "That was a planned explosion. A bomb." Her lips twisted. "Humans at work."

Trace headed toward her and caught her wrist. Cain tensed. He didn't like the handsy shifter. Not a fucking bit.

"He's trouble, okay?" Trace said, leaning too close to Eve. Cain's hands clenched as the werewolf continued, "Any being that can't die—you don't want to be around him."

Eve's gaze darted to Trace's hand, then back to his face. "When you've got an army of trigger-happy jerks and a mad scientist after you, an unstoppable immortal is *exactly* who you need at your side."

Her words slid over Cain like a warm caress, and he straightened his shoulders. The words weren't the exact truth, though. He wasn't immortal. He could be killed. Not by much, granted, but with the right weapon—

Her.

—he could taste his last death.

"Phoenix." Trace tossed the word out like a curse. Maybe because that was what it was. "They're not supposed to actually exist. But he"—Trace inclined his head toward Cain—"is real. And he's one of the most dangerous monsters that I've ever met."

Not *one* of the most. *The* most. The wolf needed to get his facts straight. And he needed to get his hands *off* Eve.

"He burns and he rises," Eve said softly, her eyes on Cain.

"And ashes are left in his fucking wake," Trace cut in. "Eve, shit, this is too dangerous for you. He's too dangerous. Let's get out of here and get you someplace safe."

The wolf was pissing off Cain. Maybe it was time to singe some of that asshole's fur—

"No." Eve's voice. Sharp. Demanding. "Don't even think about hurting him, Cain."

"What?" Trace snarled and he swung around, claws out. "Oh, come on, pyro, you just—"

"*Stop!*" Eve held up her hands. The hands that were still scratched and red. "In case you two jerks missed it, we're all being hunted. We don't have time for this alpha crap."

It wouldn't take much time. Cain was sure he'd have the wolf fleeing in about, oh, five seconds.

Maybe even three.

"We have to stop Wyatt," Eve said, rubbing her forehead, "before he hurts anyone else."

Cain would lay odds that the guy was undoubtedly out hurting someone else right then.

"His prey got away. Genesis was destroyed." She swallowed. "So he's probably looking for new test subjects."

"Yeah," Trace drawled, "and you're one of them, sweetheart."

Cain's eyes narrowed as he took a step forward. The

wolf was far too damn familiar with Eve. Touching. Using endearments. *Sweetheart—my ass.* Trace needed to back the hell off.

Cain had cut the shifter some slack since he'd been there with that getaway vehicle in the city, but that slack—yeah, it was ending.

"I can't be the only one," Eve argued. "He's not going to stop his experiments. Wyatt will be out looking for more paranormals."

And Jimmy Vance wouldn't be supplying that "more" any longer.

"I'm not just going to wait for him to come and find me again. He wants a hunt?" Eve demanded. "Then I'll give him a hunt. *I'll* hunt that bastard."

The exact plan that Cain wanted to follow. Only he wasn't just planning a hunt.

I'm going to kill you, Wyatt. He'd watch the bastard burn to ash. There'd be no escape for him.

"How are you gonna do that?" Trace wanted to know. The werewolf shook his head. "You're not a paranormal, Eve, you're not strong enough to—"

Cain laughed. The wolf really didn't know her that well. "Guess again," he murmured.

Trace frowned.

Eve's gaze lowered to the floor.

"Eve?" Trace said her name with uncertainty. "What's going on?"

She's not human. She's not your fucking sweetheart. How about you choke on that?

But Eve wasn't talking. Fine. He'd help her out. Cain took his time walking to her side. He lifted his hand and let the fire rise above his fingers.

"What the hell are you doing?" Trace shouted and then he charged at Cain.

Too late. The fire was already sliding toward Eve. The

fire whispered over her arm, right over the flesh, then vanished in a puff of smoke.

Trace shoved him to the ground. Lifted his claws—

"The fire can't hurt me," Eve said. Her soft voice seemed loud in the quiet room.

Trace froze. Then he looked up at her. He shook his head . . . twice. "Eve . . . how?"

Because he'd been wanting to do it, Cain punched the wolf in the jaw. Trace's head snapped back as he fell to the side. Cain lifted his hand, eager for another swing.

But Trace wasn't fighting back. He just stared up at Eve and looked lost. "Why didn't you tell me?"

"Because there wasn't a lot to tell!" Her voice rose even as her body tensed. "Fire doesn't hurt me. I don't know why. It just . . . doesn't." Her gaze flew between them. "And I don't know what I am, okay? When you don't know what the hell you are, then what are you supposed to say?"

"You say *something* to your friends. You knew all my secrets," Trace gritted out, rising slowly to his feet.

Cain shadowed his moves.

He didn't like the wolf's tone and positioned his body near Eve's. "Back off." They had others to attack. "My fire can't hurt her. She's safe with me, got it?" That was all the guy needed to know.

The anger in Trace's eyes—anger directed at Eve—the wolf needed to dial that shit back. Or Cain would dial it back for him.

"We can't afford to waste the dark," Eve said. She was right. The night was coming. Hunts were always easier in the dark. "We need to get out there and start hunting him. Every second we waste just gives Wyatt more time to collect new subjects and more time to come for us."

Cain had never a fan of sitting back and waiting—for anything—and surely not for some bastard hunters to come and attack him.

But Trace was shaking his head. "It's too dangerous, you need—"

"I know what I need," Eve told him. Damn, but she was sexy. Fierce. Determined. "I need to keep my friends alive. I need to make sure that no one else dies because of me."

Trace didn't argue. Maybe he was getting smarter.

"So I'm hunting." She threw the words out, and they sounded like a dare. "And I'm taking that bastard down."

Vampire bars always smelled of blood and death. They also always sported a long line of eager humans, all dressed in Goth black, who were eager to get inside and play victims to the bloodsuckers.

Charlotte, North Carolina, had two vamp bars. One on each side of the city, because the vamps were extremely territorial. From what Eve had seen over the years, those parasites just didn't share well.

Trace had taken the bar to the north, and Eve and Cain were headed to the one down south—the pit called Blood Bath. Nice name—if you were into getting your body drained and tossed away like garbage. Judging from the winding line of humans, it looked like a lot of folks *were* into that scene. Some people just begged for death. Eve didn't get it.

They'd be meeting up with Trace the next day, after they'd all had time to do some recon work. They'd picked a meeting spot and scheduled the rendezvous for the afternoon. Hopefully, they'd have good intel by then.

Eve paused across the street from the club. Her heart was pounding too fast. She'd bandaged up her hands before she left the motel, a useless precaution. Even with the bandages, the vamps would be able to smell her blood.

They always closed in when they smelled fresh prey. They were like sharks that way.

"You sure you want to start with the vamps?" Cain asked as his arm pressed against her.

No, she didn't want to start with them. The vampires were the last creatures she wanted to face, but . . . "Wyatt had a vampire at Genesis. If he lost one, he'll want another." What better place to pick up a new specimen? Vamps gorged at these bars. Got drunk on blood and the alcohol in their prey's bodies and often passed out.

Snatching a vamp from a place like this would be child's play for Wyatt.

She inhaled a deep breath. Could almost taste the blood in the air. "Let's do this."

But Cain stopped her. He blocked her path and stared down into her eyes. "Why do you fear them so much?"

"Uh, because they're bloodsuckers with super sharp teeth and an unquenchable thirst for death?" What sane person wouldn't fear them?

He shook his head. "Try again."

Her jaw dropped. Her line had seemed perfectly believable. Well, most folks would have bought the line, anyway. Now wasn't the time for a little heart-to-heart. She *hated* those talks. She'd already managed to make Trace angry by not telling him her secrets, and now Cain thought she'd just cut her soul open and reveal all to him on this crowded street?

Not gonna happen. "We have a club of vampires waiting about fifteen feet away." Give or take a bit. "We don't have time to pore over my *issues* with them right now." The issues didn't matter. She'd managed to control her fear plenty over the years, and Eve wasn't about to break down. "I'll keep it together, all right?"

His stare told her it wasn't. "You don't trust me."

No, she didn't.

His fingers brushed down her cheek. She barely controlled a shiver. The guy seemed to like touching her, sliding his fingers over her skin.

She liked it, too.

"Don't worry," Cain told her in that deep, rumbling voice that always made her knees want to jiggle—even when she was standing in front of a vampire bar. "I won't let them get close to you."

Promise? She clamped her lips together to hold that bit back. She didn't want to look weak right then. Or ever.

Cain led her across the street. He didn't get in that long line of eager humans. He headed right for the door. The bouncer glanced at him, baring fangs—but whatever he saw in Cain's gaze had the guy stepping back.

Probably the flames. She could feel Cain's body heating up beside her.

He shoved open the bar's door, and the scent of blood grew even stronger. Music pounded. Humans moaned.

Vamps fed.

Lights flashed inside in a sickening whirl. Illuminating, then concealing. She saw the flash of fangs. Blood dripping down a woman's throat.

The vamps had been the ones to start the paranormal coming-out party. They'd wanted an all-you-can-eat-buffet.

They'd gotten it.

She tried to see through the darkness. Vamps and prey. None of Wyatt's hunters but . . .

Someone bumped her. "I like the way you smell," a male voice whispered near her ear.

She stiffened. *She smells so innocent . . . let me have a bite.* The words were an echo from her nightmares. The ones that never stopped.

A hand was on her arm. Sliding over her skin. The fingers pressing against her were so cold. "You're already bleeding," the man murmured. "Want to give me a lick?"

"No, she fucking doesn't," Cain snarled and threw the vampire back a good ten feet.

The lights kept flashing around them.

But in those flashes, she saw that the vampires were moving. Rising. Closing in on them. Uh-oh.

"Cain . . ."

Vampires had closed in on her before. Only they hadn't been hidden in the darkness. Fire had raged. Burned. Those flames had driven the vampires back right before their fangs could sink into her.

Let 'em all fucking burn. The words from her nightmares came again. The dark voice that she'd never forget. The vampire—he'd left her to the fire. Left her to die.

She'd screamed, but the vampires had run away and given her to the flames.

She'd been four years old. She'd screamed and screamed and screamed.

Blood and fire were a terrible mix.

"Someone's scared," a vampire whispered. When the lights flashed again, a big, tall, dark-haired vamp was two feet from her. Smiling. "Fear can taste so sweet."

Cain pushed her behind him. "Know what doesn't taste sweet? *Fire.*"

His fire blasted right at the vampire, who screamed and fell to the floor, rolling to put out the flames that were racing over his flesh.

The guy had to hurry . . . fire could kill a vampire. No stake to the heart needed.

The other vamps started to lunge forward.

But Cain just let more fire burn. He created a line of fire that separated him and Eve from the vampires. "Listen up!" he called out, voice clear and strong. "Unless you want this whole club to burn, some of you are gonna start talking."

That wasn't exactly the approach she'd planned to use. Eve had been hoping to talk quietly with some of the vamps, to ask some sly questions and broker some deals in the back of Blood Bath. She wanted a low profile.

She obviously wasn't getting what she wanted.

"I want to know about a prick named Richard Wyatt!" Cain's voice carried to every corner of the bar. "A bastard who's been hunting your kind."

The vampires were silent and they were damn well staying behind that line of fire.

"Tell me what you know about him," Cain demanded, voice rumbling. *"Tell me."*

A more subtle approach might have worked best, but . . .

"Come with me." A male's voice. Rising above the flames. A voice that seemed familiar.

The lights flashed again. Again. Eve saw the vampire who'd moved too close to the fire. A vampire with blond hair, wide shoulders, and a face that she knew.

The vampire from Genesis.

Her fingers curled around Cain's shoulder. "Let's talk to him."

The flames died.

A few smart humans ran out the door. The rest offered their necks again. Vamps went back to feeding. Business as usual. Guess it took more than a little fire to rattle those guys.

The blond vampire headed toward them with his hands up. His eyes were on her. "I owe you."

She forced herself to breathe. The last time she'd gotten close to this guy, he'd tried to take a bite out of her.

"You've got to work on that fear," he told her with a shake of his head. "It's like an aphrodisiac to every vamp in the room. Don't you know"—he gave a small pause—"we get off on fear?"

"And here I thought it was just the blood," she muttered with a glare.

Cain was beside her, and, yeah, she was sure grateful for his strength. Without him, would she have been able to go into the vamp bar? She would have tried, but the stark truth was . . . vampires terrified her. When they'd closed in . . .

She forced her muscles to unlock. "We need to talk. Privately." Not in the middle of that chaos. Preferably in a room with a lot fewer vampires.

The blond vamp pointed to the left. She couldn't see anything that way, but she followed the vamp and Cain. They headed down a hallway and slid inside another pitch-black room.

The vamp's hand hit the wall, and lights flooded on. The brightness had her blinking as spots danced before her eyes.

When the spots vanished, the vampire was staring at her.

"I'm Ryder Duncan." He offered a faint smile, one that showed the sharp edge of a fang. "I didn't get to introduce myself the last time we met."

No, he'd been too busy trying to bite her—while she'd been fighting to save him.

Ryder's gaze swept over to Cain. "I see you're still playing guard. Haven't let her get away yet, have you?"

Uh, what?

Cain glared back at him. "Where's Wyatt?"

"Seems we'd both like to know that," Ryder said, face hardening. "That bastard has something I want, something I *need,* and I will be getting it back."

Great for him. "Did you see Wyatt that night? Did you see him escape?" Eve needed to know.

Ryder shook his head. "Not then. I thought the guy burned. It wasn't until the next day that I started to hear the stories."

Cain stepped toward him. "Just what stories did you hear?"

"Some of those who escaped . . . they said Wyatt retreated to his second lab."

A second lab? Eve's stomach knotted. There were more paranormals being held out there? Being tortured?

She'd tried so hard to research Genesis before she'd gone in, but the place was surrounded by miles and miles of red tape. She'd bribed her way to some security files and learned what she could.

The original Genesis Foundation had been created over forty years ago, by Richard Wyatt's father Jeremiah. After his death, Richard had taken over the family business.

What a twisted, bloody business it was.

Two labs.

"Wyatt's got a bounty on you both." Ryder's gaze—a sharp, cold green—went from Cain back to Eve. "Seems he wants you two very, very badly."

"Badly enough to kill," Eve said.

Ryder nodded. "And he's got plenty of firepower behind him."

Yes, she knew that part. Cops at his beck and call. Guards armed to the teeth. So what? Richard Wyatt would still go down. She'd make sure of it.

"Do you know where he is?" The question was Cain's.

Ryder hesitated, then shook his head.

"Then what good are you?" Cain asked him as he lifted his hands.

Ryder took a fast step back. "Easy, *easy.* Shit. I'm not looking for you to send your flames at me again."

When had Cain done that?

Ryder exhaled on a hard breath. "I don't know where he is, but I know how to get the guy to come to us, okay? I know how to bring the bastard right out into the open so we can take him."

Now that was sounding promising. "And how do we do

that?" Eve wanted to know. The sooner they took Wyatt out, the better.

Ryder's attention focused on her. "We give him what he wants. We give him . . . you."

CHAPTER NINE

In the next instant, Cain had slammed Ryder back against the wall. The thud of the vamp's head hitting that brick wall made him smile. "No deal," Cain growled.

Give Eve up to that guy? Hell, no.

"Wait, listen. *Listen!*" Ryder's teeth flashed, but he didn't fight Cain's hold. "We just need bait."

Cain had to step back. It was either step back or burn the vamp. "Eve's not bait." No one would use her.

"No," Eve muttered from behind him. "I'm not. If that's the best idea you had, vampy, then, sorry, time for a new plan."

"He wants you *alive!*"

The vamp needed to shut the hell up.

But the guy just kept talking. "Wyatt wouldn't hurt you. He'd take you back to the lab—wherever that second lab is hidden. We could follow you there, get you out, and *end* Wyatt."

While they were doing all that ending . . . "Let me guess," Cain muttered. "You get to retrieve that 'something' that Wyatt took of yours, right?"

A grim nod from the vamp. "It's in the second lab. Has to be. And if I have to, I'll tear that place to the ground in order to find it."

The vampire's features were tense. Stark. Had the guy

been feeding? Because it looked like he could sure use more blood.

The vampire's gaze dropped to Eve's throat.

"Don't even think it," Cain snarled at him.

That gaze flew back to Cain. "Then help me find what was taken. *Help me . . .* and I'll help you."

Eve laughed, a cold sound. "Doesn't sound like much help to me. Sounds like you're just trading me in order to get what you want."

Sounded the same way to Cain. He caught Eve's hand. Led her back toward the door. "No deal, vamp."

Ryder didn't follow them. "You're making a mistake. If we work together, I can *help* you."

No, he couldn't.

Cain yanked open the door. Music still pounded. Too damn loud. Voices whispered. Vampires gulped blood. He could hear all those sounds. All of them and—*more.*

The lights flashed around him, but he could see perfectly in the dark—or in that blinding light.

The room Ryder had taken them inside—the walls had been too thick. *Soundproofed.* Reinforced one hell of a lot more than the rooms had been at Genesis. He'd been so focused on the vamp that he hadn't even noticed the quiet that surrounded him.

My mistake. Cain knew the mistake could prove fatal. He hadn't realized the threat that was growing around them. Hadn't realized just how close the hunters were.

He could hear their footsteps now. Could smell their sweat. *Moving in for the kill.*

"Eve!" Ryder shouted her name even as Cain shoved her behind him.

The gunfire came then, erupting in a lightning-fast burst. The bullets thudded into his chest. Again and again.

The hunters had come in nice and close. Good. When he rose, it would make killing them so much easier.

Eve's scream echoed in his ears, and he fought to stay up. Fought to keep blocking those bullets.

But Cain knew that he'd be dying soon.

"No!" Eve screamed and leaped forward, but Cain pushed her back. His body jerked as the bullets slammed into him, one after the other in fast succession. The bullets were perfectly aimed for maximum, up-close impact.

Then . . .

Silence.

Cain's body slumped to the floor. She grabbed for him, aware of the others stalking forward. "Cain?"

His eyes were open. Staring at nothing.

Blood soaked her knees. His blood. All around her.

"You'd better run," she said, not looking up at the men. She kept her hold on Cain. "Because when he rises, you're gonna die." Not a threat. A promise.

Hard hands reached for her. She fought those hands. Punching. Kicking.

They were too strong. She was too weak. She could stop fire, but couldn't stop them. Her gaze flew around, looking for help. From someone.

Ryder was gone. He'd left them. Set them up—and left.

Cain wasn't moving.

"Leave him. Just get her out of here."

She knew that voice with the hint of the South sliding beneath the words. She *knew*—

"Hello, Eve," Richard Wyatt said as he stepped from the shadows. "So nice to see you again."

She tried claw her way to him, but one of the hunters holding her lifted his gun and slammed it into the side of her head.

After that, she didn't see anything else.

Screams echoed in his ears. Cain smelled ash. Burning flesh. Death.

The fire was around him. In him. Burning hotter every second. Consuming. Destroying.

There was pain. More agony than most could ever imagine. There was a price for life. A price for death.

He'd never been able to stop the pain as it burned him alive and then seemed to mold him back together. The fire—it was all he knew.

Power. Fury. Fire.

His eyes opened. The flames were around him, streaking up walls, sliding down some dark corridor.

People ran away, screaming. He liked the screams. He let the fire flare higher.

His mind was torn, fragmented, the way it so often was after the fire. He stared at those around him and thought only . . .

Burn.

Shouldn't everyone feel the same burn that he did? Shouldn't everyone suffer?

It only seemed fair.

He lifted his hand and let the fire leap away at his touch.

Destroy.

"They took her!" someone screamed.

He didn't care. Cain began to head down the hallway. The fire spread in his wake.

"Dammit, stop!" A man stood before him, just beyond the reach of the fire. Fool. He must have thought he was safe. Didn't he realize the fire could go anywhere? He'd show the man. He'd—

"Eve's gone! We have to follow them!"

Eve. The name slid past the flames. Past the beast. Cain screamed his fury and the fire raged higher.

The one who'd said her name—a blond male with a face too pale—leaped back. Even as the fire ripped forward.

More screams.

Eve.

Someone was shooting at Cain. The bullets never made it past the flames, and the fire licked out at his attacker.

No more bullets.

Only ash.

Eve.

His fire blew a hole in the wall nearest him and he walked out into the night. Black vans and SUVs waited. More men with guns. Their bullets came at him even as one van sped away.

Eve.

The fire erupted. The men stopped shooting. They ran. As fast and as far as they could.

His gaze turned back to the van. To the one that was racing away so quickly.

"Pull it back!" It was the blond male again. Perhaps Cain should know him. But he knew only fury. "Pull it back before you hurt an innocent!"

There were no innocents in the world. There hadn't been, not for a very long time. Only monsters and killers and men who wanted more than they should ever possess.

"Pull it back . . . or Eve will die!"

Eve. She was the one link to sanity that he still had. The only link.

He sucked in a breath. Another. Tasted the ash and the fire. But the fire began to flicker around him. The flames turned back in on themselves.

The van's taillights were gone. He couldn't see them anymore.

"Eve." Her name was a rasp from his throat as he shoved the beast back inside his cage.

The woman they'd taken—that was his Eve.

His eyes squeezed shut and he fought to regain his sanity. She was Eve. He was Cain.

Not a monster.

Yes, I am.

He was both—beast and man. Killer and—

Lover? *Eve's lover.*

"Come on!" the guy beside him said. A vampire. Cain knew him. Ryder. He'd . . . wanted to use Eve as bait.

He *had* used her as bait.

"We'll follow them," Ryder said, the words coming fast. "We'll get her back and stop Wyatt and we'll—"

Cain grabbed the guy and hurled him back toward the burning building. "You set her up."

He turned away. The vampire could fight the flames. Cain had a battle of his own—he had to find Eve. Had to get her back.

Because if he didn't, he wasn't sure how long his sanity would last.

No, no, dammit, this *wasn't* happening. Eve yanked at her handcuffs, twisting and jerking. The assholes had cuffed her hands and shackled her feet, then tossed her in the back of a van.

"Let me go!" she yelled.

The guard next to her pushed her harder against the van's floor. "Settle down. Wyatt wants you to—"

She slammed her feet into his stomach. The guy swore and grabbed at her, but she rammed her head right into his face as hard as she could. Bones crunched and she knew she'd broken his nose. Savage satisfaction filled her. She wasn't making this easy on them. No way.

She hit him again with her head, harder, barely feeling the pain that swept over her at the blows. She had to get out of the van. If they took her to Wyatt's other lab . . .

I won't get out. He'd experiment on her. Cut her up. Kill her.

The guard's body slumped beside her. *One down.*

"What the hell's going on back there?" a voice demanded from the front of the vehicle.

Panting, Eve searched through the unconscious guard's pockets. Keys. *Keys.* They had to be there. They'd been dumb enough to leave only one guard with her in the back, and that guy had been the one to handcuff her in the first place.

He had to be the one with the keys.

Her fingers closed around the metal keys. *Yes.* Twisting her wrists, she managed to shove the key into the lock binding her left hand.

Click.

Eve froze. That sound hadn't been the lock snicking open.

"Wyatt wanted you brought in alive." It was the same voice that had called out minutes before. The guy who *should* have still been in the front of the van. He wasn't up in front any longer.

Eve looked up and found a gun barrel pressed into her forehead. "But if you fight too much and I have to *contain* you, well, then I guess Wyatt will just have to enjoy playing with your dead body."

Her legs were still shackled. She couldn't get out like this.

And of course, the guard she'd taken out would choose that moment to groan and shift beside her. "Bitch," he muttered.

She wanted to punch him again.

Instead, he raised his fist to punch her. She braced, knowing this was going to hurt and—

"Stand down, Martinez." The order came from the guy with the gun.

Wait. He'd just offered to casually kill her, but he was telling his buddy to ease up? What the hell?

Martinez hesitated, then he snatched the keys from Eve's fingers. "I hope Wyatt cuts you into a hundred damn pieces."

He probably would.

"Go up front," the guy with the gun ordered Martinez.
Martinez crawled past her. He made sure to kick her in the gut on his way. She grunted at the impact.

The other guard tensed. *"Martinez."*

She wanted to kick Martinez's ass. Oh, wait. She'd just done it. She'd like to do it again. But with a gun on her, it wasn't the best moment for another attack.

Eve waited for him to haul his bleeding carcass into the front. Then she focused on the man with the gun.

It was too dark for her to see much about him. He was big. Strong. Holding a gun.

Did she need to know a lot more?

Cain would have risen already, right? He'd chase after her. She *hoped* he would but . . .

Why would he risk himself for me?

It was the question that wouldn't leave her alone. Deep inside, she worried that Cain would just cut his losses. He'd leave her.

She needed to get herself out of this mess. She couldn't count on Cain. She wanted to trust that he'd help her but . . .

"Just settle down," the guard told her. "No more fighting."

He had no idea who he was talking to. Maybe she didn't think Cain was coming for her, but this guy didn't know that. "He's going to kill you all." She'd always been good at bluffing.

The gun didn't waver. "I don't see anyone else here, ma'am."

"He'll follow me. He'll track me down, and Cain will make sure that anyone who took me *dies.*" Did that sound good and dramatic enough? She rather thought so.

The gun stayed pointed at her head.

"The plan is for him to follow," the guard told her quietly. "But nobody on my team will die. We're gonna be ready for him."

So not what she wanted to hear.

Why did everyone want to use her as bait? This sucked.

"Your boyfriend needs to be contained. He's too dangerous to be left out with the humans."

Damn right he was dangerous—to Wyatt and this team of jerkoffs. "Want to move that gun, you know, before we hit a pothole and you accidentally blow my brains out?"

The gun eased away. He even put the safety back on. Wasn't he a gem?

"It won't be long now." There was no accent at all in his voice. "So you just stay calm and do what you're told."

Not about to happen. He'd lowered the gun. Did he realize that she'd managed to get one cuff unlocked? "So where's Wyatt? He up in the front, too?"

She'd seen that bastard. Just for an instant. He'd left in a hurry—probably because he'd been afraid Cain would rise and torch his ass.

He will.

The guard didn't speak. So now he got quiet? The guy had sure seemed chatty enough earlier.

"He's crazy, you know." She had plenty to say. They were the ones who hadn't been smart enough to gag her. "The humans who died at Genesis—"

"Your *boyfriend* killed them." Ah, he was talking again. And sounding good and pissed.

She shook her head. Kept the cuffs in her lap so he wouldn't see that she was easing her left wrist free. "No, the bombs that Wyatt set off did that. The guy giving you the orders is a psychotic freak who'll kill you if you become any kind of hindrance to him. You won't be anything more than collateral damage." *Just like Gloria.*

Eve's breath rushed out. Maybe if she kept talking, she

could convince the guard to listen to her. If he thought his life was in danger . . .

The van braked to a stop.

Hell.

"We're here," he said.

Eve's body tensed. With her ankles shackled, she wouldn't be able to run. She wasn't sure exactly where "here" was—Wyatt's second lab? Some other fun little pit of hell? She didn't think they'd driven far enough to actually leave North Carolina.

"So why don't you just snap that cuff back in place," he added, "before someone gets hurt."

The back of the van opened. Bright light hit her. They were inside a big parking garage.

She could hear distant sounds from a city. *Definitely not the second lab.* Wyatt liked his privacy too much to put the lab near too many other people. So this had to be some kind of temporary holding facility. With Wyatt's power and reach, he probably had places like this scattered over half the East Coast.

The guard snapped her cuff back into place, then hauled her out of the van. She wobbled on her feet, nearly falling as she tried to find balance in the shackles. He put a hand on her side, steadying her.

She turned her head toward him. This guy kept helping her. She might be able to work him and—

Thin, white scars slid down the right side of his face. Scars that looked just like claw marks.

No wonder he wasn't exactly pro paranormal.

But she still had to try. "He's going to kill me." There was no need to add a tremulous quiver to her voice. It was already there. "Wyatt will—"

The guard just picked her up. Hoisted her over his shoulder and carried her. She tried to fight her way free— *not happening.* The man's grip was unbreakable and so strong that Eve started to wonder if the guy was human or something more.

A door creaked open. Then she was inside yet another room. He put her down, and her gaze flew around the area. Heavy, metal-looking walls. A clear-glass window located right next to the door. Not on an exterior wall. Interior. One glance and she knew exactly what that window was for. *Observation.* Wyatt always liked to have a good view of his subjects, and she knew he'd watch her through that glass while she was tortured.

The guard freed her wrists and feet, but before she could try to rush him, he had his gun pointed at her again. "Stay in this room." He began to back toward the door. Her gaze darted to his gun, and her eyes narrowed on the tattoo that she saw peeking back from his wrist. *Wolves.*

Eve pulled her gaze away and studied the room even as she rocked forward on the balls of her feet. There were vents on the floor. Sprinklers on the ceiling. No, no, *no.*

The guard was almost at the door.

"Please." The whisper came from her. No faking. No acting. "I'm a reporter. I'm just trying to stop Wyatt from hurting anyone else."

The guard shook his head. "Wyatt's trying to save lives."

Brainwashed bastard. "No, he isn't." She swallowed back the lump in her throat. "When you see what he does to me, you'll understand."

Only by then, it would be too late.

Tracking Eve was the easy part. Cain took out one of the hunters left behind at the vampire club, and he stole the asshole's clothes—the black uniform. The gun. And, since the fellow wouldn't be needing it, Cain borrowed the jerk's ride, too.

He followed behind the dark van, and when the group drove down a ramp into a thick, squat building, he headed right in after them. No Trespassing signs were posted all around the perimeter and guards patrolled the entrance.

He drove right past the guards. Damn idiots. The vehicle's tinted windows hid him from view, and they thought he was one of them.

Never.

Good thing their security sucked. It would make taking them all out so much easier.

Once inside the building, Cain tapped his fingers against the wheel, waiting a moment until he was certain that the coast was clear. The occupants of the van had already cleared out before he parked. They sure hadn't wasted any time. Cain eased out of the SUV. No other vehicles would be following him. He'd made sure of it. Disabling the others back at Blood Bath had been child's play for him.

Find Eve. She was his priority. He studied the area around him. Where the hell would they take her in this place? It was too big. Hulking and—

"The bitch broke my nose."

Cain turned at the angry snarl. The words had come from the left. From some whiny prick. Cain crept closer to the voice, making sure to keep to the shadows as much as possible. Once the other men got a good look at his face, they'd know he didn't belong.

"She'll pay. She'll *bleed.*"

Cain could see the guy. Another idiot in black. This idiot had blood streaming down his face, and his nose was obviously broken.

The bloody one was talking to another one of Wyatt's goons. The second man was smaller, with light red hair. "I think she's gonna burn before she bleeds." Laughter.

Burn before she bleeds.

Cain rushed toward them. "The hell she is." He slammed their heads together, and before their bodies hit the floor, he was already racing down the hallway.

★ ★ ★

The temperature in the room was rising. Heat seemed to be coming from the vents in the floor.

Eve kicked at the door. It had sealed as soon as the guard cleared the threshold. There was no doorknob on her side. Nothing to grab and yank. Dammit.

She moved toward the glass window. The guard watched her. His brown gaze steady, intense. Determined.

Sweat coated her skin, and that slickness wasn't just from heat . . . but from fear, too.

"We're almost ready now, Eve" Wyatt's voice drifted into the room over some kind of intercom. She'd noticed the speaker located above the door.

Eve swallowed back her fear. "Ready for what?" she demanded, trying not to let her fear show. The room was wired. She could hear him, he could hear her. But she couldn't see him because the bastard was hanging back.

"I have to make sure you're the one," Wyatt said.

She slammed her palm against the glass. The glass didn't so much as crack. "The one what?" She kept her eyes on the guard. *Help me,* she mouthed.

The guard didn't move.

"The one who can kill him," Wyatt told her.

There was a faint hum, then tapping. *Strokes on a keyboard.* She'd thought Wyatt would come in for an up-close view, but it looked like the guard was going to be the only one who saw her suffer in person.

Wyatt's voice continued, droning on. "I have to be sure."

She didn't have any idea what the crazy psycho was talking about. "Kill who?"

"O'Connor, of course." Irritation hummed in the words.

Kill Cain? Her heart shoved against her chest. "You killed him." Another slam of her hand against the glass. *Break.* It was so damn hot in there. "You've killed him over and over."

"But you can truly make him die." Wyatt's cool voice. The irritation was gone. He was back to sounding clinical again. "If you're what I think, then, Eve, you alone will have the power to make certain that Cain can die—and never rise again."

What I think . . . His words echoed in Eve's head. *What,* not *who.* The guy wasn't even seeing her as a person any longer.

The guard's eyes were on her. *Please. Help me.*

A muscle jerked in his jaw. She could see the struggle on his face.

Maybe he wanted to help her, but the guy wasn't moving.

She kept her own face desperate, afraid. Not hard to do because she *was* desperate and freaking terrified.

"We have to see how much heat you can handle." Wyatt's voice seemed emotionless, but she knew the truth. He was enjoying what he was doing. He'd enjoy her screams. "So we must get the fire to burn as hot as possible. Maximum temperature levels are necessary."

"It's necessary for you to kiss my ass!" Eve snarled. Her hands fisted, and she pounded them into the glass. Nothing. She hit the window again. Again.

Nothing.

"Help me!" Eve screamed at the guard.

His eyes were wide. Wide and—

Fire was rising from the floor. From every vent. Shooting toward her, burning so hot that her clothes melted, that the floor hurt her feet, that she screamed—

And was swallowed by the fire.

Another damn guard. The guy was yanking at some door, swearing, trying so hard to get inside the room that waited before him.

"Stop!" he screamed. He pulled out his gun. Shot at the glass window near him. "Fucking *stop!*"

Cain rushed the guard, swung him around and—

"*Help her,*" the guard said. His eyes were wild. "There's a woman in there—Wyatt's fucking *burning her alive.*"

A woman—Eve. Cain's gaze rose to the window. He'd smelled the flames. They'd led him this way. The fire was raging inside that room, burning hot and bright. He couldn't see her. Just the fire.

But she could handle the fire, couldn't she? Eve could handle his heat.

The flames died away as he watched, seeming to vanish right back into the room's floor.

And there was Eve. Naked, with her arms wrapped around her body. Shivering. Her gaze found his. Her mouth opened. She was screaming, but through that sound-proofed wall, her words came to him as a whisper . . .

Cain, help me. Make it stop.

It was fucking stopping.

He tossed the guard away. Kicked open that damn door, knocking down half the surrounding wall.

Eve hadn't moved. Her arms were still around her body, and she was shaking so much. He went toward her, seeing ash float in the room around them.

Cain reached out to her. She flinched.

"Eve?"

"He was watching," she whispered. Her voice was hollow. "I couldn't stop it. The fire was everywhere."

The floor below them was heating up again. Shit. Cain snatched off his stolen shirt and put it over her. It hung low, falling past her knees. "Come on." He couldn't stand to see her look that way. So . . . broken.

She was shaking her head. "They wanted to lure you in. They wanted you to come . . ."

Cain's fingers locked with hers. "Screw 'em and what they want. I'm getting you out of here."

She didn't move. "Wyatt's here." A faint line appeared between her brows. "I heard him. We can find him." Her words came faster. "We can stop him."

She wasn't moving. Fine. He'd move her. Cain lifted her into his arms and carried her the hell out of that place.

"But Wyatt—"

"He's not here." The guard had vanished. He'd damn well better stay gone. Actually, the whole place looked empty as Cain headed back for the garage. No guards. No bodies. The place was as quiet as a tomb. But he was catching dozens of scents in the air, scents that told them just what Wyatt planned next. "This place is about to explode. It's wired—I can smell the damn explosives."

The bastard was still experimenting. Probably watching with video cameras to see just how much fire Eve could handle.

An alarm was beeping somewhere. Understanding hit. No, that wasn't an alarm.

It was a countdown.

His hold tightened on her, and he raced down the corridor. No guards—they'd sure cleared out fast.

The SUV waited for them, just where he'd left it. Only the gate leading back outside had been locked, trapping them inside.

"Cain?" Eve's worried voice.

He flashed her a smile. "We're getting out."

He could smell the fire again. The smoke. Wyatt's latest fire had already started.

He put her in the passenger side. Rushed around the vehicle. Jumped in and gunned the engine. "Hold on." He jerked the vehicle into reverse.

For an instant, Cain stared at that heavy gate. Then he smiled. His hand lifted, hanging outside of the driver's window, and he tossed a ball of flames right in the middle of that gate, weakening it. Then he pushed the gas pedal all the way down to the floorboard. The SUV lurched backward and crashed right through the gate.

They made it outside with a scream of metal and tires. Cain spun the car forward and didn't slow down, not for an instant. He kept the gas pinned to the floor and drove as fast as he could.

Right then, Wyatt didn't matter. Nothing mattered but getting Eve away from there.

Cain knew exactly why the freak scientist had been testing her. He knew what Wyatt wanted her to do.

You just had to see how much fire she could handle, didn't you?

Wyatt had wanted to make sure that Eve was strong enough for a deadly job.

She'd survived the flames. Come away without even a mild burn. And Wyatt had seen it. He'd seen everything.

Wyatt had just proved to himself—and to Cain—that Eve could be a very, very dangerous woman.

A woman who could kill a phoenix.

CHAPTER TEN

"I . . . didn't expect you to come after me." Eve's voice. Soft. Hesitant.

Cain turned away from the window and glanced back at her. This time, he'd picked the hiding spot. No more holes-in-the-wall. He hated those places. Instead, they were inside a luxury cabin on the top of the mountain—one that would let him see when any unwanted guests were coming. They'd driven hell-fast and hard to get to this refuge. Normally, the drive would've taken three hours. They'd made it to the place in less than two.

It was a cabin that he owned. This one and half a dozen others, scattered all around the Southeast. He liked to keep his options open.

And he liked to have a safe place to crash when necessary. The cabins couldn't be traced back to him. He'd made sure of that.

Eve rocked forward on her heels. "Wyatt was counting on you coming. He wanted to trap you." Her laugh was weak. Rough. "I was his bait, too. Seems everyone wants me to be bait."

"That's not what I want."

She stared into his eyes. "What do you want?"

You. He hadn't gotten her out of his system yet, not even close. But he looked away from her. Showing her how hungry he was for her . . . was one bad idea. She already had enough power over him. "I want to make Wyatt pay for what he's done." Death for death. Wasn't that a fair enough exchange?

It was in Cain's book.

"Cain . . . how can—how can you die?"

The question was the last he'd expected from her, and every muscle in his body tightened as he went on full alert. "I can't die." A lie. "Not really." He forced a smile as he walked toward her. She was still just wearing the shirt he'd given her. She smelled of smoke and fear and woman. "I just come back, again and again."

Her gaze searched his. Then she took a deep breath. "If you're going to keep lying to me, how am I ever supposed to trust you?" Eve turned away and headed for the stairs. "Everything and everyone can die."

True enough. The trick was to strike at the right time, and in the right way.

She was halfway up the stairs, and after all she'd been through, he shouldn't have his eyes glued to the bare expanse of her legs.

He did, though. The woman's legs were perfect. Sexy. Long.

Eve paused and her fingers trailed over the banister. "Sometimes I see you looking at me"—her shoulders fell—"and I can't tell if you want to make love to me or if . . ."

She didn't say more.

Helpless, he walked toward the stairs. Toward her. "Or if what?" A grandfather clock ticked slowly in the other room. Too loud in the silence that fell between them.

Her head bent. She studied the banister like it held the secrets to the universe. It didn't. "If I were all-powerful, able to come back again and again—come back stronger with each death—I wouldn't fear anything or anyone."

He didn't. He didn't fear a damn thing.

"But even Superman had his Kryptonite," she said, voice sad. "No matter how strong . . . everyone has a weakness."

She was hitting too close to the truth for him.

"Weaknesses can make a person angry. So angry . . ." Eve glanced over her shoulder at him. Her bright gaze caught his. "And sometimes, when you look at me, I see that anger."

Cain forced himself to speak. "The fury that I carry isn't about you. It's not *for* you." There was just too much rage inside his beast. He'd never be able to fully control it.

Did he even want to?

"Wyatt was testing me."

Yeah, Cain fucking knew that. Sick prick.

"He wanted to see how much heat I could handle."

Cain saw the whisper of fear cross her face.

"I'd never . . . I'd never been in fire that hot. When the flames came at me, I thought I was going to die."

Why was his chest aching? Cain pressed a palm over the spot, pressing back against the burn.

"You're doing it again," she whispered with a small shake of her head. "Staring at me like you don't know . . . do you want me?"

Hell, yes.

"Or do you hate me?"

He cleared his throat. "Why would I hate you?" She'd never done anything to him. Never tried—

"Because according to Wyatt, I can kill you." Her lips twisted, and her smile made the ache deepen in his chest. "I don't think he was talking about the kind of death that just stops you for a few moments."

No, Wyatt hadn't been.

"He tested me to see if I was strong enough to handle the hottest fire that can burn from you. He tested me"— her hair brushed over her shoulders as she tilted her head to the right and stared at him—"because he wants me to kill you."

Cain stared back at her. "Wyatt is a sociopathic prick who gets off on torturing people in the name of science." He raised his brows. "I wouldn't believe anything he has to say."

She kept her gaze on him. "Can I kill you, Cain?"

"Anyone can—"

One of her hands impatiently waved that away. "A *real* death. One that doesn't let you come back—come back from wherever it is that you go."

Her stare was too bright. Too intense. But why hide the truth? She already knew anyway, thanks to Wyatt. "Yes, you can."

A slow nod. "So that's why you look at me that way."

He looked at her with lust in his eyes because he wanted her so much he wanted to damn near eat her alive.

"You want me," Eve said, "but you also want to get as far from me as you can."

Because she could destroy him.

Or he could destroy her.

"So why did you save me? Why come after me at all?"

Because the thing that could kill him was the thing he needed more than breath.

But Eve had turned away. Her steps were slow as she climbed up the stairs. Cain didn't stop her. Didn't call out to her.

He heard the soft click of the door shutting a few seconds later, then the shower came on with a rattle of the pipes.

Why did you save me?

He hadn't hesitated when she'd vanished. He'd known that he had to get to her as soon as possible.

She'd saved him. He'd saved her. They were even now. Right?

His gaze rose to the top of the stairs.

He'd wanted to get her back before Wyatt ran any more experiments, but he'd been too late. Wyatt had proof of what she could do, and the bastard wouldn't ever let her vanish.

He'd want to do more tests. On Eve. On Cain.

And in the end, Cain knew that Wyatt would use Eve against him. It was just a matter of time.

The one thing he wanted . . . was the one thing that could cost him everything.

Richard Wyatt stared at the video screens. He'd watched the feed over and over, zooming in to catch every single shot. That fire had been glorious. So beautiful. And when it came at Eve—

She'd been afraid.

The woman didn't understand her own power. Maybe because she didn't realize what she was.

He'd set up his cameras outside the testing room. If they'd been inside, they would have melted almost as fast as Eve's clothes.

The fire had burned her clothes, burned everywhere around Eve, but the flames hadn't been able to hurt her flesh. Not her fingernails. Not even her hair. The fire couldn't damage any part of her body.

"You ever seen anything like that before?" his assistant asked.

He didn't bother glancing at Keith Ridgeway. The guy had so much to learn. Richard had pulled the geneticist from his ivory tower, just like he'd pulled a dozen others. But Ridgeway didn't understand the paranormals. The fool had actually thought vampires and shifters were the only supernaturals on the streets.

They were just the ones that got the most attention.

"If we could replicate her skin," Ridgeway said, excitement in his voice, "it would help so many—"

"I haven't seen another like her before . . . but I've read reports. . . . My father had a test subject similar to her." Richard's words cut through the other doctor's fast speech as he finally glanced at the younger man.

"Your . . . your father?" Ridgeway pushed his glasses higher on his nose. "A subject with the exact capabilities?"

"No. The first test subject could do even more." Richard frowned, remembering. His father had spent so many years researching paranormals, conducting his painstaking experiments. Richard's hands clenched into fists. Even before the paranormals had publicly made themselves known, his father had discovered them and started his research.

Jeremiah Wyatt had always been a very thorough man.

Richard exhaled slowly. "Unfortunately, the test subject objected to the experiments." His father had noted that tidbit in his journal. His father wouldn't have cared about the objections. *He never did.* "She escaped from the facility and attacked a number of guards."

Ridgeway's eyes widened. "What did she do to them?"

That part he remembered perfectly. "She burned every bit of skin off their bodies."

Ridgeway weaved a bit. "W-what?"

"That subject wasn't just immune to the fire. She could control it. Could send it out at specified targets." He tapped his chin, remembering, "But that was only when she shifted."

Ridgeway stared at him, eyes still too wide. "What could she become?"

"A beast of enormous power and strength." A beast that his father had never expected. "You know those old stories about dragons attacking castles and burning knights?"

A quick nod.

"Those stories were based on truth. Dragon shifters existed once, but they were hunted to near extinction." His father had thought they *were* extinct after the unfortunate death of his test subject but . . . Richard's gaze turned back to the screen. Back to Eve Bradley. "But it seems we may have one left, after all."

Silence. Then . . . "Uh, Doctor Wyatt, that woman doesn't look like a dragon to me."

No, she didn't. And she should have shifted when the fire hit her. She would have shifted, *if* she'd been a full-blooded shifter.

Are you like your mother, Eve?

"There weren't any of her kind left," Richard murmured, still staring at that screen. "So she had to find a human to take as her mate. "

His father had said that his test subject found sanctuary with humans. That she'd been hiding, using them for cover. Of course, Jeremiah must not have realized the truth. *The test subject mated with a human.*

If he had realized that important fact, then Richard figured that his father wouldn't have told the soldiers to kill them all.

His father's order. He'd wanted to cover his tracks. The test subject couldn't be controlled, so she'd had to be eliminated. Jeremiah had wanted to make sure no witnesses were left behind.

The humans had needed to die.

Pity.

But . . . his father had kept meticulous research. Blood samples, hair, tissue—all of those still remained from the dragon shifter. It would be easy enough to discover if his own suspicions were true.

And if Eve did turn out to be the child of a dragon shifter . . .

Then he would be able to take his father's research to the

next level. He smiled. He'd finish what the old man started. *Prove I'm better, stronger.* He would be the one with the perfect killing machine. And his father could fucking choke on his success.

The water poured over her, ice cold because she needed the chill. Every time that Eve closed her eyes, she saw the fire.

But . . . it wasn't just the flames that Wyatt had sent out at her.

It was another time. Another place.

Memories that haunted her.

Mommy! Mommy! The fire had been everywhere. Fire and blood and the flash of vampire fangs.

Bet you taste good. Kids always fuckin' do.

Her eyes squeezed closed tighter as she pushed her head under the water. It should have cooled her down. It didn't. It just made her feel hotter.

Her mother had died in that long-ago fire. Her father . . . he'd been dead before the flames hit him. The vampires had ripped out his throat.

Eve shuddered. *I hate vampires.*

Every time she turned around, a vampire was attacking— or selling her out. *Thanks, Ryder.* She'd be sure to pay him back.

If it hadn't been for me, you would have burned at Genesis.

He'd returned her solid favor by tossing her right at Wyatt. What a prince.

She turned off the water with a yank of her hand. Stood in the shower, with her forehead pressed against the tiled wall.

"Eve."

She'd known that Cain was there, so she didn't jump or rush to cover herself. What would be the point? He had already seen all of her.

She turned. The glass door hadn't steamed beside her and she could see right through to him. He watched her with eyes that were so hungry. Full of need.

Right then, she could only see the lust in his stare.

What happened when she saw more?

He walked toward her slowly, never taking his eyes from her. Drops of water were sliding down her body. Her nipples were tight from the cold water.

He opened the shower door and stared down at her. "I'd . . . never hurt you."

He hadn't. "But what if I hurt you?" Her fear. She knew Wyatt must have a plan. He'd tested her because he wanted to use her.

To hurt Cain? To kill him?

His hand lifted. Traced the curve of one breast. "You won't."

She couldn't be so sure of that, but right then, she just wanted to stop thinking. To stop remembering fire and death. "Make it stop," she whispered to him.

Frowning, he glanced back up at her.

"The fire," Eve told him, her voice a bare breath. "The blood. I don't want to think about it anymore."

She didn't want to see death.

Her eyes closed once more.

His lips feathered over hers. Soft. Gentle.

"No." She turned her head away from him. Gentleness wasn't what she needed at that moment. She was tearing apart from the inside out. She wanted to scream. To fight. To rage.

"Eve?"

Her eyes opened. "Wild." That was what she needed, the way she felt inside. Too many emotions were splitting her in two. She had to stop the rush of feeling.

She needed . . . him.

Eve pushed him back and stepped out of the shower. He was still dressed, or at least, still wearing pants. She eased to her knees on the plush bathroom rug. She'd make him as wild as she felt. She could do it. She might not have been able to push her other lovers past the point of no control, but she hadn't wanted them the way she wanted Cain.

She'd never wanted anyone this much.

His zipper eased down and the heavy length of his cock—fully aroused—pushed into her hands. She bent toward him, licking her lips. She'd nearly touched death.

Time to taste life.

She put her mouth on him. His breath hissed out as his hands clamped down on her shoulders. But he wasn't pushing her away. No, he was urging her closer. Closer was exactly where she wanted to be.

Her lips opened wider. She licked him. Sucked. Tasted. Wanted more.

Her hand curled around the base of his shaft as she pumped him into her mouth. His taste was rich, salty, good. She licked the head of his cock, then took him deeper into her mouth. So deep she could feel him in the back of her throat.

"Enough."

No, no, it wasn't. He could still talk. She could still feel. They had to go further. Push more. She licked him. Sucked around his length.

And found herself pulled away. Pulled up into his arms.

"Cain—"

His mouth locked onto hers even as he carried her toward the bed. Then they were falling together. Crashing into the bed.

Her nails raked down his back. Hard. She opened her legs, wanting him to thrust in deep. "Lose control," was her whisper to him. A desperate order. She couldn't be the only one feeling this way.

He stilled. Cain stared down at her with the gaze she should fear. Too bright. Too hot. "You don't want that."

Yes, she did. It was the thing she needed most.

"Lose control," she said again.

His hands were on her thighs. Pushing them farther apart. Then his fingers were on her sex. Stroking over her clit, pushing inside her. Deeper.

It wasn't enough for her.

She grabbed his head. Kissed him with all the passion she felt. He still had his control. Why couldn't it break?

She was breaking. Shattering on the inside.

Blood.

Her eyes were closed. Her body shaking.

Fire.

"No." His growl. "Stay with me." Then his fingers were gone from her body. His cock pushed against her. Her gaze flew to meet his.

"Stay with me," he said again and drove into her. In that one moment, as she stared into his eyes, she saw the man's control rip away.

And only the beast was left.

Eve smiled even as she held onto him as tightly as she could. His thrusts were deep, driving, plunging into her. The rhythm was fast and frantic. He held her hands down against the sheets. Pounded into her again and again and she loved it.

The rush of pleasure built fast. No gentle peak. A tidal wave that flooded over her and took her breath.

It didn't stop. He didn't stop. More. More. He rolled her over on the bed. Lifted her onto her knees. Surrounded her with his body and his heat and his power and—

Took.

Deeper. Harder. Her hands fisted in the sheets. She yanked, pulling the sheets toward her even as she arched her hips back against him.

The release hadn't stopped. The pleasure pounded through her. Again and again and the scent of sex filled the air around her.

He was so big, filling her completely. His mouth was on her shoulder. Licking. Biting. She couldn't suck in a deep breath. Couldn't do anything but feel.

The pleasure hit her again, hollowing her out, leaving her shaking and weak.

He came inside her, exploding with a growl as his hold tightened around her. He held her so close. Held her so tight.

Right there, with him, death seemed so far away.

But she knew . . . the monsters were coming for her. Soon, they'd be at the door.

Her scream woke him at dawn. Eve was thrashing in the covers, struggling to escape.

Cain reached for her. "Eve?"

Her eyes opened, and she screamed.

What the hell? He pulled her close.

She was shaking. "V-vampire . . ."

"There aren't any vampires here, baby." Just a nightmare. So why was his heart racing so fast? "You're okay. I've got you."

"Blood . . ." She sounded lost. Her eyes were open, but was she seeing him?

Cain didn't think so. "There isn't any blood."

"I hate . . . fire."

His body tensed. "There's no fire." His fingers tightened on her. She felt too cold in his hands. Trembles shook her body, and she didn't sound like his Eve.

I don't want her lost.

He pressed a kiss to her lips. "Wake up."

Her breath came in low pants.

"Eve, wake—"

"Vampires are coming," she whispered. Her voice was as cold as her body. "We have to stop them."

Cain shook his head. "There aren't any vamps here. You're safe. You're—"

He heard it. A thud from downstairs, at the door. His head whipped to the right as tension tightened his muscles. Wyatt and his men? Already? No way should they already be at the cabin. The place was *secure.*

He leaped from the bed, but Eve grabbed his hand. "Stop the vampires."

It wasn't the vampires. Vamps didn't attack during the day. That wasn't the way they operated. Most of them holed up underground during the daylight hours.

He went to the window. Searched below. Saw no one. But that just meant his prey was good at hiding. "Stay here," he told Eve.

She was sitting up in bed, frowning. Her gaze didn't look lost and when she said, "Cain?" he knew that she was back with him.

"We've got company." And he was never a good host. He yanked on a pair of jeans and headed down the stairs. He heard the squeak of the hardwood floor behind him and knew that Eve was following.

Figured.

He eased open the front door. Listened for every sound and whisper. No cars had approached. He would have heard them. Their guest had to have come in on foot.

Cain inhaled, taking in all the scents. He focused his hearing, narrowed it down until he heard . . .

The creak of hardwood floor. One step. Two.

Eve, coming after him.

Another creak. And the smell of fresh blood.

Cain whirled around. The threat wasn't outside, not any longer. He lunged for the stairs, his heart racing. Eve was heading toward him and she didn't even realize . . .

A vampire stood two steps behind her.

CHAPTER ELEVEN

Eve saw Cain's eyes widen as he lunged forward. The air seemed to rush against her skin, and, before she could turn around, she felt hard arms wrap around her waist. She was yanked back against someone—a male—and she felt something sharp press against her throat.

"Stand down, phoenix."

At the vamp's words, Cain froze. "Ryder, you're begging to feel the fire."

Ryder? The vamp who'd sold her out? Her teeth ground together as her nails sank into his arm. She arched her neck and tried to pull away from him. No dice. That vamp's grip was hard—and painful.

"Where is she?" he snarled into her ear.

Um, she was standing right there. Standing there, and feeling lost. Ryder had *known* that Cain was a phoenix? All along?

First Trace, now Ryder. She was feeling left behind on the whole paranormal-knowledge bit. Did everyone else know that the ancient phoenix myth was real?

Her breath heaved out and her eyes found Cain's.

"Where?" So much fury as Ryder nearly screamed the word.

Those were claws at her throat. So much for the scratches that she was leaving on his arm. The guy was about to cut her throat open. Eve stopped fighting, for the moment. With her struggles, she was just making his claws press harder against her skin.

"You're dead," Cain promised him.

Ryder just laughed and the sound was wild. "Don't you think I fucking know that? Without her, I'm dying. Day by damn day." He spun Eve to face him. "You saw her, didn't you? When Wyatt took you, I know you saw her."

Okay, she was dealing with a psycho vampire and she didn't have a weapon. But she had something better. She had Cain.

"She's still alive, isn't she?" Ryder asked, shaking Eve. "She's—"

Eve kneed him in the groin as hard as she could. She didn't know if the move actually hurt him or just caught him by surprise, but either way, his grip eased and his claws—two-inch long, razor-sharp claws—pulled away from her throat.

That instant was all she needed. She stumbled back. Cain leaped forward.

"You're dying, asshole," Cain snarled and put his hand on Ryder's chest. Flames were already rising from Cain's fingers. Eve scrambled back. Vampires burned fast. She'd seen it happen once before.

Twice.

Ryder would go up like a firecracker and—

He was laughing.

Not burning, *laughing.*

How was that even possible?

Cain tried to pull back. Ryder grabbed Cain's hand and shoved it harder against his own chest. The fire burned between them, melting away Ryder's shirt, but the vamp wasn't dying.

He's like me.

"See what she did?" Ryder demanded. "Do you see what her blood did to me? Didn't realize it . . . not until I had to escape your fire at Genesis. It didn't burn me. The fire doesn't . . . not any more. . . ."

Cain yanked his hand away from the vamp and punched Ryder. The vampire hurtled over the side of the staircase and crashed to the floor. Cain jumped over the banister and landed in a crouch beside him. Ryder wasn't rising. He'd fallen on the wooden table and a huge chunk of wood burst from his chest.

Fire might not kill him, but a good, old-fashioned stake to the heart would.

Eve rushed down the rest of the stairs and hurried to Cain's side. Only . . . Cain wasn't finishing the vamp. Cain just stared at Ryder with his hands clenched.

"I crave her," Ryder said as blood dripped from his mouth. "Every damn moment . . . I need her." His eyes locked on Eve. *"Tell me where she is!"*

Eve grabbed a piece of broken wood. She just had to take out the bastard's heart. She could do this. Cain had been right. They never should have rescued Ryder from Genesis. Some monsters couldn't be saved. She needed to stop trying.

Eve pushed forward with her weapon ready, but . . . Cain stopped her. He grabbed her and yanked the stake from her hands.

"No." Cain's voice. Firm. Flat.

What? She could still feel Ryder's claws at her throat. Her blood had spilled onto her shirt. He'd cut her. Would have killed her.

The kids always taste so good. The voice from her past whispered through her mind. Eve wanted to slap her hands over her ears, but she knew that wouldn't do any good. The voice was on the inside. It would be with her forever.

Ryder was rising and yanking the wood from his chest. Blood had pooled beneath him.

Mommy! Another echo from the past. the echo of her own scream.

Ryder reached for her, but Cain stepped between them. His hand wrapped around the vampire's throat and lifted Ryder into the air. "Control yourself . . . or I'll kill you right now."

Ryder's fangs flashed.

Cain tightened his hold. "I'll snap your neck, and while your body tries to recover from that injury, I'll shove a stake in your heart."

Ryder wasn't fighting. His breath came out ragged, panting.

"I know crazy," Cain said, voice a snarl. "Trust me, I fucking know it."

Eve picked up the shattered piece of wood. A foot long. Jagged on both ends. It would be a perfect stake.

"Get that crazy under control," Cain ordered, "and tell me what the hell you're talking about, vampire."

Eve shook her head. This was a mistake. "He led them to us again." Didn't Cain realize that? "He's sold us out, just like he did before."

Cain stared at Ryder. "You're talking about a woman, aren't you? The thing that Wyatt took. The thing you want so badly . . . it's her."

Her who?

Ryder nodded. Cain dropped him to the floor. The vampire scrambled back and then rose slowly to his feet.

Eve kept her fingers curled around the wood. If he came at her, she'd stake him. She'd already tried to play the Girl Scout with him and that bit hadn't worked.

The guy probably ate Girl Scouts for breakfast.

"She's . . . like you," Ryder said as he stared at Cain. "She burns, then comes back."

Eve's gaze darted between them.

"Just like you did in that bar," Ryder added. "I saw you."

"How do you know she's like me? How can you be sure?" Cain demanded. His voice had lowered, hardened.

Ryder hung his head as if in shame. "Because I killed her, and she came back."

A muscle jerked in Cain's jaw. The air around his body seemed to heat up.

"Wyatt starved me," Ryder said. His eyes were on Cain, but Eve could see the emotion flooding his gaze. Pain. Rage. "I wasn't there for just a few months—it was a whole fucking year. A year kept in his cage. Trapped. I was so hungry, and then he brought her to me."

Wyatt had told Eve about the starving vampire. He'd threatened to feed her to him. Goose bumps rose on her arms and pity stirred in her heart for the woman she didn't even know.

"Her blood—it was different. Tasted different from anything I'd ever had before. I didn't know what I was doing. I *couldn't stop.* I tried and I tried, but I couldn't. . . ." Ryder's eyes squeezed shut, but there was no missing the torment on his face. "Then she was still, and I couldn't get her to open her eyes."

"You drained her," Cain said. His legs were braced apart. His hands loose at his sides.

Eve couldn't tell if he was about to attack the vampire—or give the guy a free pass out of the cabin.

No free pass. Eve still had her weapon ready.

Ryder's eyes opened. Darted to her, then back to Cain. "I called for the guards. Begged them to help, but they wouldn't touch her."

Eve bet that had been on Wyatt's orders. The doctor had been waiting, probably eager to see what would happen next.

"Then she burned." The quiet words came from Cain.

Ryder nodded stiffly. "I was fighting the guards, trying to get back to her. I thought . . . I thought I could try to turn her."

Turn her. Eve felt nausea rise in her throat. No matter what else happened to her in this life, she never wanted to become a vampire. Not that most people survived the brutal turning, anyway. If they did, the vamps would have taken over the world long ago.

Ryder jerked a hand through his hair. "Then I smelled the smoke. The fire was everywhere. Wyatt was in the hallway, watching her, smiling. *Smiling* when she burned, and—"

"When she came back," Eve said, cutting into his words. She'd seen the same thing with Cain. Wyatt, standing back in his pristine lab coat. Studying the death scene with a steady gaze, then smiling when the fire brought his subject back to life.

"I have to get her out of there." Ryder's gaze was on Eve again. Pleading. Demanding. "You saw her, I know you did. When Wyatt took you, *you saw her.*"

Eve shook her head. "There were only guards. I didn't see anyone else."

Ryder lurched back. "You're lying." Anger flashed in his eyes and his claws rose up. "Tell me where she is!"

Eve's hold tightened on the chunk of wood. Why did she have to get stuck with the crazies?

"You need to feed." Cain's voice was quiet, calm, such a contrast to the vampire's frantic words.

Ryder impatiently shook his head. "He did . . . something to me. I can drink other blood. I fucking have. Over and over. But it doesn't quench the thirst. It just makes me crave her more. *Wyatt did something.*"

Yes, but with Wyatt, there was no telling exactly what he'd done. Anything was possible with Dr. Frankenstein.

"He wanted me addicted to her." A hard rush of breath escaped Ryder. "I am. And I'm getting her out of there. I'm not going to let Wyatt keep hurting her!"

"How do you know she wasn't at Genesis when it burned?" Eve asked him. *How do you know Wyatt still has her?* Maybe the woman had escaped—from Wyatt and from the vampire who'd killed her.

But Ryder was adamant. "He had two labs. I know he did. I heard him talking . . . he was transferring her to the second lab for more study."

Study or torture? Eve figured they were the same thing in Wyatt's twisted mind.

"He wants you," Ryder said, focusing on her with a sudden intensity that made her breath catch. "He'll keep coming after you. He won't stop. Once he gets you, we can follow him back to the second lab and—"

Cain punched him in the jaw. The vampire flew a good five feet back and slammed into the side of the fireplace. Two bricks fell to the ground.

"She's not bait." Cain's deadly growl.

No, she wasn't. The vamp needed to get that bit clear, yesterday.

"He's *hurting* her," Ryder snarled back at him. He pushed to his feet then, voice ragged, said, "*I* hurt her. I owe her. I have to get her out of that hell."

Eve knew the vamp would be willing to trade her life in an instant, if it meant he could get his phoenix back. He was like a drug addict, desperate for his next hit of magic blood.

"You aren't using Eve," Cain snapped at him. "Think of another plan, because she isn't your ticket inside Wyatt's lab, got it?"

The vamp had better get it.

Ryder's gaze darted between them. "You're just gonna leave her with him? She's like you! She's one of yours!"

Yours? Eve stiffened a bit and glanced at Cain from the corner of her eye.

Cain was staring at her. "Did you know he had another phoenix?"

She didn't like the suspicion in his gaze. She'd been the one helping his ass the whole time. So why was he looking at her like she might be the enemy? Some trust wouldn't kill him. *Nothing really does.* "I didn't even know *you* were a phoenix!" Being in the dark sucked. "When I first found you in Genesis, I didn't know what the hell you were." She still didn't fully understand it. Was he a shifter at his core? With a beast that transformed at his death? Or was he both . . . a blend of man and myth?

She shook her head. Was she supposed to be the all-knowing Oz? Jeez. "I knew there were shifters and a vamp at the facility, okay? I didn't have intel on anyone or anything else." Cain had come as a total shock to her. When he'd burned the first time, she'd flipped out. She figured that was a pretty normal response.

Cain just kept staring at her.

Eve straightened her shoulders. "I tried to get everyone out when the explosions started. I was trying to help as many people as I could!" He shouldn't need the reminder. He'd been there. He'd seen her fighting to save those paranormals.

But her efforts hadn't been enough. People had died. Wyatt had escaped. And she still hadn't been able to break her story.

Because she hadn't broken Wyatt. The asshole was stronger than her, moving freaking pieces on a chessboard while the world went to hell around him.

"Help her," Ryder demanded, voice ragged.

Cain finally glanced back at the vamp. "You sold us out to Wyatt."

Ryder shrugged, apparently unconcerned with that not-so-little issue. "You're both still alive, aren't you?"

Eve lunged for him, but Cain grabbed her, wrapping his arms around her stomach and hauling her back against him. "You asshole!" Eve screamed at the vamp. "He burned me! He locked me a damn room and he *burned me!*"

The vamp's eyelids flickered. His gaze swept over her. "Yet you look surprisingly . . . unharmed."

Cain tensed behind her. "Get out of here," he ordered, voice clipped. "Get the fuck out of here now, or you're dead."

Some of the desperation had faded from the vampire's eyes. Eve didn't like the way he was looking at her. His stare was too similar to Wyatt's. "Interesting." Ryder smiled, but backed toward the door.

Why were they letting him get away? She still had her stake ready.

"I guess you don't need to save my phoenix"—a trace of cold bitterness had entered the vamp's voice—"when you have your own."

What? Eve frowned. "I'm no—"

Cain's hold tightened on her and she shut up.

"Your mistake," the vampire whispered. Hate hardened his eyes and his face. "One I'll make sure you never forget."

Then he was just . . . gone.

Crazy. That guy was in-freaking-sane. Eve blinked, chest heaving. She'd been holding her breath at the thick tension in the room. But one minute, the vamp was there, the next—magic act time.

"He's old," Cain murmured. He didn't release her. If anything, his hands pulled her closer against him. "Powerful."

Eve had made it a policy to learn as much as she could about vampires. *Know your enemy.* The older a vampire was, the stronger he was. Vamps didn't usually move at human speed. More like amped-up superhero speed. In a blink, they could run a mile. They could crush steel with their hands. Rip the heart right out of their prey.

Be general nightmares to the human population.

Ryder was a nightmare, no getting around it.

He was also their enemy.

A second lab.

She turned, as much as Cain's hands would allow, and gazed up into his eyes. No fear there. Just a steady darkness that stared back at her.

How did he feel, knowing another phoenix was out there? *One of yours . . .*

He didn't exactly look overwhelmed by the news.

"Cain, did you know?"

He shook his head. "I thought that was the only lab. Not like Wyatt let me out to see—"

"No." She shook her head and her hair brushed over his chest. "About the woman. Did you know Wyatt had captured others like you?"

His gaze drifted behind her. He tilted his head as if listening. *To see if the vampire was still close by?* But after a moment, his eyes turned back to her. "I thought I was the only one left alive."

Simple. Hollow. Cold.

She shivered. What would it be like to think you were the last of your kind? The only one left on the whole earth? *Lonely.*

But the vamp had said there was another like Cain. A phoenix female.

A muscle flexed in his jaw. "I'll have to kill her."

Shock rippled through Eve. "Why?" His response was the last thing she expected.

"There's a reason there haven't been many of my kind in this world." His hands fell away from her as he headed toward the open door. Sunlight fell inside, but the light just made the angles and planes of his face appear even harder. "Who else knows our weaknesses?" Cain murmured. "Who better to attack . . ."

She rubbed her arms. "You're telling me that the reason there aren't a lot of . . . of phoenixes running around is because you guys kill each other off?"

He didn't glance at her. "Only the strong survive."

That didn't make any sense to her. Even vamps didn't hunt each other to extinction. "What about the old phrase that there's strength in numbers? I mean, come on, Cain. It's not like you killed your own mother or anything, right?"

His shoulders stiffened. "My mother wasn't a phoenix." Slowly, he shut the door and turned back to face her. "And I didn't have to kill her. My father eliminated her when I was a boy."

Eliminated her. His words were cold. Callous. Was her face supposed to be feeling so icy? "*Why?*"

"Because the beasts within us have two drives."

She didn't speak. Just waited. *Beasts within* . . . the phoenix was a type of shifter. A beast held inside the body of a man. Trapped inside—until the beast broke free.

The fire frees him.

"To mate," Cain said.

Her breath heaved in her chest.

"And to kill."

"You kill what you love?" she asked through lips that seemed numb.

He shook his head. "We don't love."

So certain. So chilling. Did he hear the too-fast beating of her heart?

He gave her a smile, and she knew that he did hear that telling beat. "Didn't you realize it, baby? I truly am a monster . . . the worst one walking the earth."

He wanted to scare her. He'd succeeded. But Eve made herself walk toward him. One foot in front of the other. He could probably smell the fear rolling off her, but she didn't care.

"If you are so evil"—as he kept telling her—"why'd you come for me? Why not leave me to die with Wyatt?"

"Wyatt wasn't going to kill you. Death would have been too easy."

She flinched. She'd never thought of death as particularly easy.

Cain moved toward her, stopping less than a foot away. His hand lifted and curved around her cheek. "When we rise, we're at our most dangerous."

Eve believed that. She'd seen the beast stare back at her when he rose.

"My mother tried to kill my father when she learned that he . . . wasn't human. She attacked him. Stabbed him in the heart."

That wouldn't have been enough.

"When he rose, the beast had power. The beast was in control."

Cain kept talking about a beast and she was understanding that . . . well, despite all his power and fire, maybe deep down he was just another type of shifter. A very, very deadly type.

Trace had often talked about his beast as if he and the wolf were two different beings. Maybe it was the same for Cain. Maybe there was the man. And there was the phoenix. The one she'd seen staring back at her from eyes that burned.

"My mother tried to attack again." His voice roughed. "She realized that I was like my father, and she tried to kill me."

A child? Her own child?

"Humans can't love monsters," he said, frowning at Eve

as if she should understand that fact. "Not even the ones they bring into the world."

"Cain . . ."

"She didn't move fast enough," he said and shrugged.

Shrugged?

"My father's fire killed her."

There were chill bumps on Eve's arm. The fire had never hurt her, but she felt cold all too well. She was freezing, but the cold seemed to be coming from inside her. "What happened to him?"

"Another phoenix ended him about a century later."

"A century?" she repeated, stunned.

Cain had turned away from her. "The vampire is out there, either selling us out to Wyatt right now or planning to attack and separate us."

She grabbed his arm. "Hold on!" Eve forced him to look at her.

"We need to leave. If we don't, Wyatt's men will surround the cabin. They'll try to take you. I'll kill them all." One dark brow rose. "I have no problem killing them, but you seem to get upset when others die."

He was playing the unfeeling bastard, but he wasn't like that.

Softly, Eve said, "I know you."

That brow stayed up. "Do you." Not a question.

He'd revealed a bit of his past to her, and now the guy was shutting down. She shook her head again. It wasn't going to work like that. "You won't scare me away from you."

He laughed at that. Actually laughed. A deep, husky laugh that made her feel strange. He'd never laughed before, had he? His lips were still curved in a smile. "Oh, Eve, I already know the truth about you. . . ."

No, he didn't. She had a few secrets of her own.

"You're fucking terrified of me." His hand pressed against

her chest. Over the swell of her breast and over the heart that raced too fast. His head lowered to her. His lips brushed over her ear. "But part of you *likes* that fear, don't you?"

"No," she gritted out. He didn't understand her at all.

"Then why do you want me to fuck you, even now, even with all I've said . . ."

Two drives . . .

To mate.

To kill.

His breath blew lightly on her ear.

She wasn't going to deny that she wanted him. It was like her body was tuned to his. One touch, and she needed. But the guy was seriously mistaken about her motives. "I don't like the fear." She felt it. Wouldn't lie. "But I want you"—Eve's lashes lifted, and she stared into his eyes—"in spite of that, not because of it."

He blinked, and for an instant, seemed lost.

"So remember that," she muttered and grabbed his head. She pulled him down toward her and pressed her lips against his. The kiss was fast, hard, frantic, and meant to prove a point.

Fear doesn't make me want you less.

She slipped her tongue into his mouth. Tasted him. Felt the press of his fingers against her ass. She let the kiss linger, savoring for an instant, but . . . Eve pulled her lips from his. "All humans aren't the same." It was a lesson he needed to learn. "I'm not going to come at you with a knife in my hand."

Another smile from him, but this one . . . this one made her heart hurt. "Yes, you will." He pulled away and headed for the stairs.

Eve stared after him. She'd thought that she was the one with the trust issues. It looked like they both had to learn how to deal—fast.

Cain's hand was on the banister. "We'll leave in ten minutes."

Looked like sharing time was definitely over. "Where are we going?"

Another step. "You're going to a safe house. You're out of the game."

She wasn't going to rush after him. "This *isn't* a game."

"I'll take care of Wyatt."

While she what? Sat in the corner like a good little girl? He obviously had her confused with someone else. Wyatt had come after *her*. He'd killed *her* friend. She wasn't walking away from that guy. "I can *help* you."

"You can get captured again. Tortured." Cain turned back to her. "The fire doesn't hurt you, but from what I can tell, everything else out there does."

She swallowed. He was right.

His gaze raked her. "You know what I am. I didn't keep that secret."

No, he hadn't.

"But baby, what the fuck are you?"

Eve stiffened. That *hurt*.

"If you die, will you burn and come back?" he asked her. "Are you like me?"

A phoenix. She lifted her chin. "If I am, does that mean you'll want to kill me, too?"

He didn't answer. Maybe that *was* an answer.

She tried to sound calm. "I'm not a threat to you, Cain."

"Yes," he bit out, "you are."

"Why?"

"Because a phoenix can only die—truly die—in that one moment when the fire rises and pulls us from the ashes. When we're coming back and the flames surround us . . . we're vulnerable."

But those flames burned so hot.

"Most can't touch us then. Most . . ."

Eve understood. Other phoenixes would be able to reach through the fire.

"In that one instant," Cain said, "we can truly die. And not come back."

A vulnerability. He shouldn't be telling her this. Why was he telling her this?

"That's why we kill our own kind. Phoenixes . . . we're the only ones who can stand the fire. The only ones who can reach through the flames to kill."

But . . . but she could reach through the fire, too.

"Are you like me?" he asked again, staring down at her. "If you die, Eve, will you rise again?"

She could only shake her head. *I don't know.* She'd never known what she was. Maybe that was why she spent so much time looking for the truth about others.

I can't find it for myself.

Cain said, "You can't help me fight Wyatt. You'll just slow me down."

Well, crap, the guy sure wasn't pulling any punches. But she had an ace up her sleeve. "Before you go tossing me into some safe house, there's one thing you should know."

"And what's that?"

Eve offered him a smile that showed lots of teeth. "I wasn't totally honest with the vampire." *So sue me.* "Thanks to my little abduction last night, I know how to find Wyatt." She kept her expression determined. "As soon as we rendezvous with Trace, I'll tell you both everything I know."

The wolf shifter wasn't at the meeting point in Charlotte. Cain's fingers tapped on the steering wheel. Eve was curiously still beside him. The woman had never been this quiet before, not for so long.

They'd been waiting twenty minutes already. There was no sign of the wolf.

Cain cranked the engine.

Her hand flew out, and her fingers wrapped around his. "We *aren't* leaving," she told him, her voice almost a growl.

He turned his head toward her. Met that bright blue stare. "Yeah, we are." He was definite on this. The longer they stayed there, the more danger they could face.

She had to see the writing on the wall. She had to. Trace wasn't meeting them because the wolf *couldn't* meet them.

Eve hadn't been the only one taken last night, but she had been the only one rescued.

Two vamp bars. Two traps. One missing wolf.

Cain frowned. He should have known that Wyatt would have a backup plan in place.

They'd picked the old park as a meeting point because it was isolated. Private. But it looked like the meeting wasn't going to happen.

Cain eased the vehicle—another stolen ride—away from the curb.

"Take me to the bar," Eve whispered.

From the corner of his eye, Cain saw her hands clench in her lap. He knew which bar she meant.

Thirty minutes later, they were in front of Bite—the vamp bar that Trace had visited the night before.

There wasn't much left of the place. Charred bricks. Ash. The shell of a wall in the back. Humans—probably arson investigators—were combing through the wreckage and yellow lines of tape marked off the area, keeping the gawkers back.

Hell.

"Wyatt has him," Eve said. There was no emotion in her voice.

Cain kept driving past the bar. Nice and slow. Their windows were tinted so no one would get a good look at him and Eve, and he sure wasn't doing anything to attract attention to them, not yet.

He also didn't respond to Eve's comment. Wyatt could have the wolf shifter—

Or Trace could be dead. If the wolf had fought back, death was a strong possibility. Cain knew other paranormals who hadn't been taken alive. Wyatt just burned their bodies and moved on to his next target.

"You said that you knew how to find Wyatt," Cain said instead, trying to keep her focused and away from the wall of worry he could almost feel growing around her. As soon as he learned what she knew, he would be dropping Eve off with a supernatural who owed him more than a few favors. The guy would keep her safe—until Cain made sure Wyatt wasn't coming after any of them ever again.

"He wasn't supposed to take Trace."

A red light flashed. He slowed the car. Glanced in the rearview mirror. No sign of a tail. Yet. "He did." Maybe the words were too cold, but Cain didn't know any other way to be.

He heard the sharp rasp of her breath, then she said, "Turn right."

He did.

"Left." The word was clipped. Eve was worried about her shifter, but she was holding herself together. The woman was strong. Far stronger than Cain had initially realized. "Head straight for two miles," she told him, "then turn at the federal building."

He followed her instructions without question, wondering what Eve had planned next.

She had him stop in front of a small tattoo shop called Death Ink. The lights were off, and the place looked abandoned.

"Last night, while I was fighting that guard who locked me in that room to burn"—she exhaled on a heavy breath—"I saw a tat on his arm."

"Wyatt has a shitload of military guys working for him."

Or ex-military assholes who'd been kicked out because they were psychotic. "Most of 'em are probably sporting ink."

"Not like this. *Not like this.*" She shoved open the door and headed for the small shop.

Death Ink was located right in the middle of a bar strip. Since it was early afternoon, those bars were shut down tight. Cain's gaze scanned the street. He didn't see another person anywhere around. He eased from the car. Watched the nice sway of Eve's ass as she headed for Death Ink. Her ass truly was fine.

It was such a pity the woman could be so lethal.

She slammed her hand on the glass door. "Dru, open the hell up!"

There was no sound from inside. No rustle of movement. No footsteps.

Cain sauntered toward her. She was a wanted woman, her face splashed on the news. Maybe she shouldn't be screaming so loudly—deserted street or not. "I don't think anyone's home," he murmured.

"Yeah, she is. She's always here during the day. Dru's just trying to ignore me." Eve obviously wasn't in the mood to be ignored. She lifted her foot and kicked at the door. Glass broke in a long, thin crack. She swore and kicked again. Harder. Again.

It was going to take forever her way.

Cain cleared his throat. She kept kicking. He picked her up, scooted her back, then rammed his fist through the glass. One nice, clean punch. The glass rained down on the ground around them.

"Supernatural show-off," Eve said, but there was an edge of appreciation in her words.

Cain caught himself smiling. It wasn't the time or the place. But Eve . . . kept sliding under his guard. *Dangerous.*

He reached inside and jerked the lock, opening the door.

When he stepped inside the shop, the scent of incense and oils burned his nose. But he still didn't hear anyone. Didn't see anyone, either. "Told you," he said as he turned back to glance at her. "No one's—"

The floor creaked a few feet away from him. Cain whirled to face the threat—and a baseball bat slammed into his head.

CHAPTER TWELVE

When the bat came swinging at him again, Cain was ready. He caught the bat in his left hand. "Don't fucking think so," he said as he snatched the bat out of his attacker's grip, ready to take a swing of his own.

"No!" Eve grabbed the bat. She tried—and failed—to pull it from his grip. "Don't hurt her. We *need* her."

He got a good look at his attacker. All five feet nothing of her. Deceptively delicate, the woman stood mostly in the shadows of the shop. Her eyes were dark and slanted, her skin a light mocha. Her hair was cut short, almost brutally so, as if she'd wanted to look tough.

The cut just made her look more . . . delicate.

"Who the hell is he, Eve?" the slugger asked, jutting up her pointed chin. "And why'd you trash my door?"

"Because you weren't answering my knock," Eve fired back even as she kept pulling on the baseball bat. "I need to talk to you, Dru. I had to come inside."

This is Dru? Cain let Eve take the bat from him.

She tossed it into a corner and faced off against Dru.

Dru's hot glare swept over Eve. "Do you know how many cops are looking for you right now? You need to be getting your ass out of Dodge."

Eve shook her head. "No, what I need to be doing is clearing my name, and you're going to help me."

But Dru was backing up—very, very fast. "No, I'm not."

Cain frowned, studying her. She was just a few feet from him, but he couldn't smell her. Couldn't hear her heartbeat. If the floor beneath her hadn't creaked when she'd moved, this Dru could have bashed his head in without any warning.

"Stop looking at me like that," she snapped at him as she rolled her shoulders. "*I'm* not the freak in the room."

"Why can't I smell you?" He inhaled deeply, but still got nothing.

"'Cause I don't stink?" she threw right back at him and edged closer to the back wall.

He suspected she was looking for a new weapon. Interesting. His head cocked to the side as he studied her. "I don't hear your heart beating." Even vampires had beating hearts, despite the myths about them being the walking dead.

Dru waved that away. "Trust me, it's beating. So fast my chest hurts." She jumped behind the counter and came back up with a handgun. "Eve, get your ass out of my shop."

The sight of the gun had Eve tensing, but she said, "I will, but I want information first."

Dru raised her gun. "Um, do you want a bullet in your head?"

It was Cain's turn to step forward. He positioned himself between Eve and the barrel of the gun. "Fire if you want to," he invited softly, "but then you should probably run."

Her nostrils flared as if she were trying to get his scent. "You smell"—Dru whispered—"like blood and fire."

He stared back at her. "And you smell like a woman who's been using witchcraft." A woman with no scent. The witches could do that. They could make a brew to cloak scents.

She laughed then. A deep, rumbling laugh that he hadn't expected from such a small package. "I don't mess with any crazy witches"—she leaned forward—"but I do know how to mix some herbs for a little protection."

Protection that could mask her smell? Yes, he'd heard of that, but . . . "Why doesn't your heart beat?" When he focused just on her, he should be able to hear it.

He couldn't.

The laughter faded from her face. "Maybe I lied before. Maybe I just don't have a heart."

Eve sighed from behind him. "And maybe you're just bullshitting." She shoved Cain aside. "She wears a special vest under her clothes, okay? One that mutes the sound so that no one else can hear it."

Dru gave a little shrug. "An unfortunate encounter with a vampire a few years ago. Even though he's rotting in the ground, it's made me a bit . . . obsessive . . . about a few things."

"Yeah," Eve muttered, "but maybe instead of worrying so much about your scent and heartbeat, you should look into investing in a new door and store alarm." She cleared her throat and slapped her hand on the counter. "But right now, I need you to help me."

"And I should because . . . ?"

"Because it was my story that put your freak of a stepfather on death row." Eve bared her teeth. "You're welcome. Now pay me back, and I'll get my butt out of your shop."

Dru's hand tightened around the gun, but she slowly lowered the weapon to the countertop. "What do you want?"

Eve backed up and hit the lights. When the illumination flooded on, Cain saw the sketches and photographs that lined the wall behind Dru's head.

"No one inks wolves quite like you." Eve's voice was flat.

Cain frowned and searched the pictures. He saw half a

dozen wolves scattered in the images. Some were hunting. Howling. Running.

"Even when they're supposed to look like monsters, the eyes give them away. Your eyes are always different."

Cain's own eyes narrowed. He could see what Eve was talking about. The lines drawn for the wolves' eyes . . . were distinctive. Not an animal. A human gaze.

"It's like a fingerprint. I saw your fingerprint last night." Eve's voice came faster. "I saw your fingerprint on the right inner wrist of a man who locked me in a room and watched while I burned."

Dru swallowed.

"He was military, don't know if he was current or discharged, but the guy moved like Special Ops. Controlled. Dangerous. He was six foot two, about two hundred twenty pounds, with dark hair and scars that cut across the right side of his face—"

Dru held up her hand. "You should have started with the scars." She bent beneath the counter. Pulled out a heavy, black book, and began flipping through the sketches. She stopped and her finger tapped on the image of two wolves.

One wolf had just killed the other. The victor stared back, fangs glinting. Eyes shining.

"He hated the way I did the eyes," Dru said and her lips pulled down in a frown. "Asshole thought he'd get his money back because I made the wolf look like he had a soul."

And monsters weren't supposed to have souls.

"The guy's a Ranger." Dru flipped the book around so Eve could scan the notes she'd jotted next to the image. "Name's Damon Tyler. And I even have his address for you."

An address Cain had already memorized. He knew this town pretty well, and he knew where to find that street.

"Now are we done?" Dru demanded. "Does this square us up?"

Eve nodded and backed up. "Thank you." She turned away and Cain followed at her back.

"I should thank you. . . ." Dru's voice was soft. Far more subdued.

Cain paused when Eve glanced over her shoulder at the other woman.

A grim smile lifted Dru's lips. "My stepfather really was a freak—and I'm counting down the days until the needle goes into his arm." Her lips tightened. "But you might want to move faster, Eve, 'cause I set off my alarm as soon as you kicked my door, and the cops are gonna be here any minute."

Eve's face tensed. "Don't tell them I was here."

Dru nodded.

Eve took Cain's hand, and the move surprised him so much that he let her drag him from the shop. A few moments later, they were in the vehicle, driving away. Not too fast—why look guilty? He was heading straight for the Ranger who damn well would take them to Wyatt.

"Told you I could find him," Eve said, staring out the window. "Guess I'm not so useless after all."

He stiffened. Had he called her that? He hadn't meant . . .

"We find Damon, we find Wyatt. The bastard won't see us coming until it's too late. He'll be the hunted one now."

Cain drove in silence, then he had to know. "What did her stepfather do?"

"He liked to cut up girls. The younger, the better." She pulled in a rough breath. "Dru . . . had a little sister. She went missing, just like two other girls had in her neighborhood."

His fingers tightened around the steering wheel. A needle in the arm was too good for the prick. "You knew it was him?"

"Dru did. She came to me because I was the only reporter in town who'd listen to her." A sad laugh. "Maybe because I was the newest one then?"

No, he thought it was more than her just being the new kid on the block who'd been hungry for a story.

"She'd tried going to the cops, but Leon was too good at playing the grieving father. He was also very good at not leaving evidence behind."

"How'd you catch him?" Cain drove easily, but his attention was on Eve.

"Humans couldn't find his tracks. Supernaturals could." A brief pause. "I used a shifter to sniff him out . . . and to help me find the bodies." Silence, then . . . "I never want to see graves that small ever again."

Cain's gaze cut to her.

Her lips trembled. But then she shook her head as if trying to shake off the memory. "I took the cops to the bodies. Said I'd had a source call me. There was enough DNA left behind that we could tie the bastard to the killings. He's been on death row for five years, and it's time for him to go to hell."

"Dru knew you used a shifter to help you."

"That's why she can't ever make wolves look like the monsters most people think they are. To Dru, the shifters were the heroes."

And she always showed that in their eyes.

Cain slowed the car as he neared the small, ranch-style house located at the end of Branchline Road.

Eve cleared her throat. "So . . . who gets to play good cop when we go inside?"

He killed the engine. Turned his head to slowly glance her way. "I've never been good."

She nodded. A ghost of a smile lifted her lips as she reached for her door handle. "Right, then I'll—"

Cain caught her hand. "You'll stay behind me." The guy

was a Ranger, trained to kill in more ways than most humans could count. Tyler wasn't getting close to Eve. "If he's here, then I'll be the one to face him."

"And I'll—"

"Stand back and not get hurt."

She stared at him.

"The price of being human," he murmured.

Her eyes narrowed. "We both know I'm not."

"We don't know *what* you are." It was eating him up inside, wondering if she was like him.

Eve glanced back at the house. Cain had parked a little ways down the street, but they had a perfect view of 2808 Branchline. "If he's not home, we'll search his house," she said. "We might be able to find intel that we can use."

The searching part she could handle. He'd do the attacking.

They climbed from the vehicle. Instead of keeping to the shadows of the trees, Cain headed for the guy's front door.

Eve grabbed his arm. "Uh, have you heard of the subtle approach?"

"I'm more familiar with the ass-kicking approach." No neighbors were around. Probably all at work. Good. Cain slammed his fist into the door. Heard no sound from inside.

"Here," he told her, backing up a bit, "I'll try your routine."

"Cain, wait—"

His foot drove into the door. His kick was far more effective than hers had been at Death Ink. The wood splintered, and the door flew open.

The human didn't rush out to attack, but Cain heard a faint groan from inside the house.

He entered the small foyer, then spun to the left and

rushed toward that sound. With every step, the scent of blood filled his nose.

Dammit.

He ran into the kitchen and found a human male on the floor, soaked in blood. The man's hands were spread out beside him, palms up, and the dark tattoo stared back up at Cain.

"I guess someone else wanted him dead, too," Cain said quietly.

Eve pushed past him and fell to her knees. She put her hands on the man, one hand on his chest, one hand on his neck. "He's not dead yet."

With that much blood, he would be. Soon.

Eve grabbed a towel off the counter and shoved it against Damon's wounds. "He's been shot, looks like two times." She leaned over the man. *"Damon! Open your eyes. Look at me!"*

Cain could already smell death coming. She had to smell it, too. He backed up, prowling around the house. Making sure the shooter wasn't still close by.

"Missed his heart . . ." Eve's voice floated toward Cain as she muttered. "Bullet's still in. Has to get out . . . *Cain, call an ambulance!*"

He was supposed to help the bastard who'd watched her burn?

Slowly, Cain made his way back to the kitchen. Blood was on Eve's hands. What the hell had she been doing? Why was she doing it?

"Damon, *Damon,* look at me!"

The man's eyes flickered, then opened.

"You're gonna be okay . . ."

Why was she lying to him? Cain frowned. Death was there, hovering so close.

"Who did this to you?" Eve asked him.

The bleeding male's lips curved. The guy was smiling. At death? Cain looked at the human with new interest.

"Can't . . . trust . . . anyone . . ." Damon gasped. More blood came from his lips.

"Where's Wyatt?" Eve demanded as she put pressure on his wounds. "Where is he?"

More blood. Grunts.

Eve glanced up at Cain. *"Call the ambulance."*

Cain didn't move. "Why? They'd never make it here in time."

She stared at him in shock. "C-Cain?"

He didn't move toward the phone. "He's gonna be dead long before any help can arrive."

Air wheezed from the man's lips. His eyes were wide open, and he had to be feeling every second of pain as his blood pumped from his body.

Cain knew what those gunshot wounds felt like. He'd been killed that way a time or two.

Eve kept pushing on the wounds. *"Call help."*

Cain shrugged and bent toward the man. "Guessing your own team shot you, huh? Shot you, and left you to die . . ." He shook his head. "Why'd they do that? From what I can tell, you're just a human. Not Wyatt's usual paranormal target at all."

"Am . . . human . . ." Damon rasped.

Cain studied the scene before him. Eve was checking the guy's wounds, swearing, getting her fingers covered in blood. They'd have to talk about that, later. "So why'd they turn on you?" Cain asked him.

The man's gaze, heavy, pain-filled, darted to Eve.

Cain's hands knotted into fists. "You didn't like what they did to her." And he remembered . . . when he'd rushed in to save Eve, this man had been there, banging on the door of her holding room. Screaming.

Help her . . . There's a woman in there—he's fucking burning her alive . . .

His screams had done no good.

"That your first time to see the dirty work your boss does?" Cain wanted to know. "Got a little too up-close and personal, didn't you?"

Damon tried to lift his head. Eve pushed him right back down. "I'm trying to keep you alive. *So will you stop moving?*"

"I'm not trying," Cain told the guy with a grim smile. "But if you tell me what I want to know, maybe I'll help put you out of your misery."

Eve gasped and jumped up. She grabbed for the phone. Cain moved at the same time. He wrapped his arms around her and snatched the phone away. Her eyes, shocked, wide, found his.

"Cain?"

He pushed her behind him and turned to stare back down at Damon. "That pool of blood is just getting deeper."

Damon wasn't trying to rise any longer.

"Your own men shot you. Wyatt betrayed you. What the hell kind of loyalty do you owe him?" Cain demanded.

"Please," Eve's soft voice. "Wyatt has other test subjects, Damon. He's going to hurt them, the way he tried to hurt me. We just want to save them."

She wanted to save people. Cain wanted to kill. Why couldn't they both get what they wanted?

We can.

"Where is he?" Eve asked the human, her voice so light and gentle. "Don't die without helping those others. *Tell us, please.*"

"B-Beaumont . . ." The word seemed torn from Damon. Probably because it was. "He's got . . . second lab . . ."

Cain waited.

"In . . . Beaumont."

Cain had heard of the city. A small town, just inside the North Carolina border, nestled in the mountains. "Thanks for the information. Now you can die happy." Or maybe with a semi-clean conscience.

"Cain!" Eve shoved at his back.

Sighing, he stepped out of her way. She immediately fell beside Damon. Her blood-smeared fingers reached for the man's cheek. She leaned in close and told him, "You aren't dying."

His eyes narrowed.

"Yeah, it hurts like a bitch, I know, but the bullet missed your heart, and that second wound's just a graze."

While she was talking Cain was calling nine-one-one . . . and keeping a close watch on Eve.

"No vital organs were damaged."

The woman sounded like a doctor. Fitting, since she'd played one back at Genesis. Cain wondered . . . how much of that role had been pretend?

"You get stitched up, get some good drugs in you, and you'll be just fine." Eve gave Damon a light tap on the cheek. "Sorry I had to press down so hard on your wounds, but I needed you to hurt a little bit more."

"Pain can make people talk," Cain murmured. The nine-one-one dispatcher answered in his ear and Cain told her to send an ambulance. "We've got a human down."

Eve looked back at him with a frown.

Cain tossed the phone onto the countertop. "You make one fine bad cop." He could admit when he was wrong.

The left side of her mouth hitched into a half-smile. "Told you that I have my moments."

Yes, she did.

"But your bad cop . . . was better," she admitted.

Because he hadn't been playing.

Eve glanced back at the groaning man on the floor. "Just

stay still until the ambulance gets here. You really will be okay."

Anger tightened Damon's face. Anger and pain.

Eve rose and went to the sink. Cain shadowed her moves—just in case Damon wanted to attack. She washed the blood away from her fingers. The water turned red as it poured down the drain.

Cain took Eve's arm and began to lead her from the kitchen.

"You'll . . . stop him . . ." Damon's voice. Weak. Growling.

Cain glanced back. "I will." A promise.

Damon nodded. "Good. He's . . . sick . . ."

"A real monster," Eve whispered. She cleared her throat and told Damon, "When the doctors sew you back up, get out of that hospital as soon as you can. Wyatt tried to kill you once, and when he finds out he didn't succeed, he'll come after you again."

When you worked with the devil, you had to expect to feel the fire. "And if you try to warn him that we're coming," Cain said, voice sharp and hard when Eve's had been soft, "I *will* be back for you."

Damon's breath heaved out. "Won't . . . tell . . ."

He'd better not.

But just in case, Cain planned to attack the lab in Beaumont as soon as he could.

The distant wail of an ambulance's siren reached him. Help. Coming quickly for the human.

They hurried back to their vehicle. Left the blood behind. Didn't look back.

By the time the ambulance turned onto Branchline, Cain was already heading in the opposite direction. He watched the ambulance's flickering lights in his rearview mirror.

"They'll save him," Eve said, sounding so certain. "The wound was all gore, but nothing vital had been hit."

He glanced her way.

"Two years of med school," she explained with a sigh. Her eyes closed as if she were tired. "I know what death looks like."

She also knew how to be one fine actress.

She'd just bluffed her way into getting them the information they needed.

How fucking perfect.

Beaumont.

Now, to just find a safe place to leave Eve while he turned Wyatt's new playground into ashes.

CHAPTER THIRTEEN

"It's not happening," Eve said into the silence that filled the car. She knew exactly what Cain was planning, and the guy needed to think the hell again.

He shot her a fast glance from the corner of his eye.

"You're not dumping me and going after Wyatt on your own." Right, like she hadn't seen that one coming from a freaking mile away. This was not her first ball game, not by a long shot. "We're in this together, remember? I'm not about to sit on the sidelines now." Not when things were finally coming to a head.

The road had passed in a blur of yellow and white lines and asphalt, but she'd known exactly what Cain had been thinking. She'd seen him try to slow at a few motels during their road trip.

Looking for the right spot to dump me? Not happening.

"You go with me," Cain said, "and you die."

Trying to scare her. He didn't get it. She was already plenty scared, and the fear changed nothing. "I've been dodging death since I was four years old." Maybe it was easier to confess because of the darkness that filled the car. "That's when my parents died. When vampires killed my father and a fire took my mother away from me."

"Eve . . ."

"The fire spread through my house. Burning everything

but me. I remember screaming and crying, but the flames wouldn't stop. I couldn't do anything but watch them . . ."

Mommy. Daddy!

She choked back the memory and tasted ash. "I hated fire after that." Her gaze slid to him. *Still do.* But she'd stayed next to Cain anyway.

What did that say about her? Drawn, pulled, to the one thing she hated most.

"I'm . . . sorry." His words seemed rusty.

"So am I." Her whisper. "Vampires took my family away. They took *everything* from me, but I didn't let that stop me." Not during all those long years she'd spent alone. Bouncing from one foster home to the next. They'd said she couldn't connect with the families. That she didn't know how to bond. That had been bull, and she'd known it even as a kid.

I just didn't want to risk loving someone and losing them again. Sometimes, it was better, safer, to just not care at all.

"You've helped. Done your part." He seemed to be gritting out the words. "There's no need for you to face more danger."

"Trace is my friend." For a while, the only friend she'd had. "I have to—"

"I'll get the wolf out for you." The car sped faster. "Don't worry about him."

Anger? She frowned, not expecting that. "Trace . . . he's a good guy, Cain." Once you looked past the snarling surface. "He helped me, I helped him." So many times.

"You . . . care for him."

"Yes."

His jaw locked.

"But we're not lovers." She should have put that out there sooner. A vein flexed in Cain's jaw. *A lot* sooner. "We never have been. Never will be."

The fast look he fired her way was full of surprise.

"He's my friend. That's all." *You're my lover.* She'd gotten too close with Cain, too quickly. After only a few days, he didn't know what she was really like. How could he? Maybe he thought she just made a habit of jumping into bed and having really hot sex.

She could straighten him out easily. "Cain, I've had four lovers in my life." Eve frowned. *"You're* the fourth. This thing with us"—the wild, hot sex, the need that couldn't ever seem to be filled—"hasn't happened to me before." It was important that he understood that.

He pulled off the main road. Headed toward the no-tell motel nestled near the edge of the woods.

Dropping me off?

Her jaw clenched. "I can make my own way to Beaumont, you know. Leaving me here—it won't stop me."

He stopped the car. Turned off the lights.

"I'll be right on your tail. I'm not going to just—"

In an instant, he had her in his arms. His mouth was a breath from hers. "I'm glad there were only four . . . though I'm damn tempted to hunt down the first three."

Wait. What?

"I want you, Eve, the way I haven't wanted anyone or anything ever before."

Her lips wanted to tremble into a smile, but the harsh look in his eyes had her holding still. The gearshift pressed into her leg.

He held her tightly against his chest. "You can make me weak," he growled in the dark interior of the vehicle.

The car seemed too small then. Maybe he was too big. Her hands were on his chest between them, but Eve wasn't pushing him away.

She was trying to understand him. "You're leaving me again."

At least it wasn't a truck stop this time. . . .

"No, I'm stopping the asshole who's been trailing us."

Trailing us . . . Her head whipped around just as a pair of headlights cut into the parking lot around them. Darkness had fallen as they traveled, and she hadn't been aware of anyone on the lonely road behind them.

She realized that Cain hadn't parked their vehicle right in front of the motel. He was on the side in the shadows with his lights off.

As soon as the other car pulled to a stop, Cain jerked away from her and rushed toward the other vehicle.

She could just see Cain's powerful form with the aid of the moon and the dim glow of a fluorescent light from the motel. The other car's windows were dark, tinted so that they looked black in the night.

Cain yanked open the driver's side door, nearly ripping it right off the vehicle. Sometimes, she forgot just how strong he could be.

He reached inside and yanked out a man. Tall. Big. Wide shoulders.

In the moonlight, she saw the flash of his fangs. *Ryder.* The vampire sank his teeth into Cain's throat.

Eve shoved open the car door and raced for them. *"Cain!"*

But Cain had already broken free of the vamp's hold and shoved the vampire back. Ryder's body dented the side of his car.

"Bad mistake, vampire," Cain growled. "I *was* going to let you live . . ."

"Can't live . . . without her . . ."

The pain in Ryder's voice made Eve's heart ache. The vamp seemed to really care about his phoenix.

Ryder rose to his full height, baring his fangs. The two men circled each other. Going in closer, closer . . .

One will die.

"Where are you heading in such a hurry?" Ryder demanded. "You talked to the human, then you swept out of town." Blood dripped down his chin. "What did he tell you?"

Cain just smiled. "Why didn't you ask him yourself?"

Ryder's face tightened, but his arms stayed loose at his sides. "The other humans got there before I could make him tell me." Ryder's gaze cut to Eve. "But I know you found Wyatt. I *know*, and I can help you."

With his enhanced strength and speed, he just might be a strong ally.

If they could trust him.

We can't.

"I can taste the fire in your blood," Ryder said as he swept the back of his hand over his chin. *"Just like hers . . ."*

The vampire was on a dangerous edge of obsession, and Eve knew he'd turn on them in an instant, if it meant he could get to his phoenix.

"I gave you the chance to walk away," Cain growled, voice low and cutting. The parking area was deserted. The whole place looked deserted, except for the faint glow that shone from inside the motel's office. "You should have just kept going."

"Tell me where she is!" The vampire leaped toward Cain.

"No." Cain punched the vampire in the chest, a pounding blow that crunched bones.

The two men were a twist of bodies. Punching. Kicking. Brutal fighting that was silent and vicious.

Since Cain's fire wouldn't work on the vampire, it looked like Cain was going to kill the guy the old-fashioned way.

By tearing him apart.

"Stop!" Eve yelled.

Neither man even looked her way.

I can taste the fire in your blood.

Cain kept swinging. Eve glanced around. The railing

near the motel's office was old and sagging . . . and made of wood.

Yes. She raced toward it. Saw the sleeping form of an old man inside the office. Ignoring him for the moment, Eve shoved her hips against the railing, then she yanked hard on the loose wood. Once, twice . . .

A chunk of wood broke off in her hands.

There was another way to kill the vampire.

She ran back to the two fighting men just as Cain tossed Ryder onto the ground. The vampire landed on his ass. He began to lunge up.

"Don't!" Eve jumped near him. The stake hovered over his chest.

Ryder froze.

Good. Looked like she had finally gotten his attention.

Cain came up behind her. She could feel his strength all around her. He wasn't going to like this part, but there wasn't a choice.

Eve kept one hand wrapped tightly around the stake. Maybe it was sliding into Ryder's flesh, just a little, but she needed the guy to understand she meant business. She lifted her other hand and turned it, wrist first, toward Ryder's mouth. "Bite me."

Cain's hands closed over her shoulders. "Are you insane?"

Ryder wasn't biting her. He'd tilted his head to the side, and, sure enough, he was looking at her like she was the crazy one.

Takes one to know one . . .

"He can taste the fire in your blood. He said so. He said you tasted like the other phoenix." She pushed her wrist toward the vamp's mouth. Since when did a vampire turn away from a bite? "If I'm like you, he'll know with one taste, Cain."

She wasn't going to let Cain kill the vampire, not when

he could give her so much valuable information. *Tell me what I am.*

If she was like Cain, like the other phoenix, then she wasn't alone. She wasn't the freak in the world.

"Bite her and you die," Cain promised.

"Don't bite me," Eve snapped right back, "and I'll shove this stake in your heart."

"I can take it away," Cain whispered in her ear. "By the time you can even blink, I can have that stake in *my* hand and in the vamp's heart."

He could, she knew it. But . . . "Don't." Her head turned just a few inches, so she could meet his stare. "I need to know this."

She gasped at the sting of pain in her wrist. The vampire had sunk his teeth into her. The skin broke beneath his fangs, and she felt his tongue against her flesh. She jerked her hand, wanting to recoil, but forced herself to freeze.

Have to know. I want to—

"Enough." Cain's snarl.

Ryder lifted his head and licked the blood from his lips. His eyes seemed to glow a bit as he stared at Eve. "Lot of power . . . so much . . ."

She swallowed. She'd heard talk that some vampires could drink the power right from the blood of their prey. Power . . . life.

"But you're no phoenix." Ryder gave a brief negative shake of his head. "You're something"—another swipe of his tongue over his lips—"altogether different."

Of course she was. Her skin chilled. Eve stared down at the vamp. "You truly want to save her?"

He nodded.

"Beaumont," she told him. "Damon said Wyatt had a lab in—"

But the vampire was already gone. His kind could move so quickly.

Kill so easily.

"Why?" Cain demanded, voice cutting like a knife.

Eve tossed the stake to the ground. "If Wyatt kills me, I want to know if I could rise again." *Like you.*

But she wasn't like him.

Wasn't like anyone else that she knew. Even among the paranormals, she stuck out like the freak she'd always been.

He caught her hand. There were two small puncture wounds on her wrist. He cradled the flesh, lightly running his fingers over her hand. "Why'd you tell him about Beaumont?"

"Because we need all the help we can get." Did he hear all that emphasis on *we*? She sure hoped so. "If the vamp wants to attack, let him." Her head tilted as she studied Cain under the moonlight. "That'll give us the distraction we need in order to get inside and get to Wyatt."

One brow rose even as he kept stroking her flesh. "You've got a devious mind."

Yes, she did.

His head bent toward her. His lips were bare inches from hers. "If a vampire ever tries to bite you again . . ."

She shivered at the lethal sound of his voice.

"I swear I'll kill him before his teeth ever touch your flesh."

Her wrist seemed to throb. She gazed into his eyes and saw the certainty of that dark promise. "If a vamp ever tries to bite me again"—she brought her lips closer to his—"I swear I'll kill him myself."

She kissed Cain, pressing her lips tight against his. Eve needed his taste. Wanted him so much.

The ache inside her never seemed to stop. She couldn't remember ever wanting anything as much as she wanted him.

His tongue brushed over hers. Thrust into her mouth. She rose onto her toes, holding him tighter. She wanted to get closer to him. Skin to skin—only that would be good enough.

He lifted her up. Pushed her back against the cold, metal body of the car that Ryder had left behind. His mouth didn't leave hers. Her hands were on his shoulders. His hands bit into her waist.

His tongue . . .

A moan built in her throat. It had to be wrong to want someone so much.

But . . . being wrong . . . oh, it could feel good.

Cain's head lifted. His gaze, simmering with dark fire, met hers. Eve's breath came out in a low rush. She couldn't look away from him.

Not even when she heard the shuffle of footsteps heading toward them. When she heard the cocking of a rifle, it was Cain who turned to face the new attack, not her.

"What the hell are you doin' to that girl?" a fierce voice demanded.

Eve knew the voice had to belong to the old man, the one who'd been sleeping in the motel's office.

"Nothing she doesn't want done," Cain murmured back.

I'd definitely wanted it. She still did. The threat of a rifle wasn't cooling her lust.

"Either get a room and *pay* me," the guy snapped, "or get off my property."

Eve caught Cain's hand. "We're leaving." They were so close to Beaumont. They'd be safe only after they took down Wyatt, after they ended the twisted manhunt that he had launched on them.

The man, hands trembling a bit, lowered his rifle. As Eve and Cain walked by him, his gaze swept over them. Seemed to linger a bit on her face.

It's dark. He won't see much.

"You—you sure you don't want a room?"

Eve frowned. The guy was trying to get them to stay?

"Just forget you ever saw us," Cain advised him, opening the passenger door for Eve and ushering her inside their borrowed ride. "It'll be better that way for you."

When they pulled away from that little motel, Eve glanced back. The old man was still standing in the middle of the parking lot, watching them.

James Andrews didn't move until the red taillights had disappeared. But as soon as that car vanished, he sucked in a deep breath.

That man's eyes had glowed with fire.

James pulled his phone from his pocket. Dialed the number he'd called a dozen times before . . . ever since he'd started working with Doctor Richard Wyatt.

His motel didn't get a lot of business. Too old. Too hidden. But the supernaturals, hell, they loved to stop by his motel.

Maybe because it *was* hidden. Maybe they thought they'd be safe, nestled in the little rooms that were surrounded by mountains.

They thought wrong.

On the third ring, his call was answered. The person didn't speak to him, but James knew the drill. "A man and a woman were just at my place, " he said, "and the guy . . . his eyes were on fire." The damnedest thing he'd ever seen.

James heard the swift inhalation of air on the other end of the line.

"Why didn't you keep them there?" Wyatt demanded. "You know what you're supposed to do when the paranormals come to you."

James was supposed to do the usual routine. The one that brought him cash, and made the freaks disappear. Normally, he gave them one of the special rooms. When they slept, he pumped the place full of gas—some brew Wyatt had made. The supernaturals didn't wake up, not even when Wyatt's men came to haul them away.

And James got a nice bit of money for his trouble.

It was the perfect deal for him. Hell, he hadn't even needed to install the vents in the rooms. Wyatt's men had taken care of everything. Set up the ventilation system, got the drugs all in place for him.

All I have to do is give the supernaturals the right room key.

It was a perfect deal for him.

"They wouldn't take a room." His mistake. He'd come off too aggressive. At first, he'd thought he was dealing with humans. He'd heard their voices as they argued, though, and he knew . . . "But they're coming your way. I heard 'em mention Beaumont."

He didn't want to know how those two had found out about Beaumont. He sure as hell would never go there. If he did, James knew he'd find too many supernaturals gunning for him.

"Thanks for the tip." A brief pause. "You'll be getting your payment soon."

James smiled. He was getting close to retirement. A few more grand, and he'd kiss these mountains good-bye.

The call ended. James took his rifle and his phone and headed back toward the motel. Dead leaves crunched beneath his feet.

"Bad mistake . . ." The words seemed to drift on the wind.

James spun around. But no one was there.

"I remember you . . ." That voice again. Dark. Angry.

James dropped his phone and clutched his rifle tighter. He started to back up, heading toward the office.

He backed right into something. Someone.

James spun around, lifting his gun.

The gun was snatched from him. Tossed away.

A man stood before him. No, not a man. The bastard before him had fangs. "Do you remember me?" the vampire asked.

Blond hair. Tall. Big. With death in his eyes.

Gulping, shaking, James shook his head.

"Maybe you've drugged so many of us that you just can't remember. . . ."

He couldn't. He tried not to remember. But sometimes, those faces still slipped into his nightmares. "P-please . . ."

"Please make it quick?" the vampire finished.

No, that hadn't been—

The blond grabbed James's throat and yanked him forward. "I will because, you see, I have other business tonight."

James tried to break free, but the vamp was too strong.

"You sent me to hell," the vampire told him. "Now guess where you're going."

James couldn't scream. The pressure on his throat was too much. Then the fingers lifted. He sucked in air.

The vampire plunged his teeth into James's neck. The bite was brutal. A burning pain that ripped and tore and he could hear the vampire gulping and drinking and . . .

James hit the ground. Everything was even darker. He tried to speak, but couldn't. He could hear the drumming of his heartbeat. So loud, but growing . . . slower.

"Now I've got to go." The vampire's voice. The guy was walking away. Leaving him to die alone on the dirt. "You know how it is . . . places to go, more people to eat . . ."

CHAPTER FOURTEEN

Eve hunched down beside Cain as they studied the Beaumont facility. It hadn't been too hard to find the place. They'd spotted a black SUV as soon as they entered the small town, seen the two men driving, and tagged them for military. Since the rest of the town consisted of boarded-up old buildings, the shiny SUV had instantly caught their attention.

From what she could tell, Beaumont was a ghost town—the perfect place for Wyatt to conduct more of his experiments.

Once they'd spotted the SUV, it had just been a matter of following those guys back to Wyatt and his facility.

Another lab. A tall, chain-link fence surrounded the facility. The fence was topped with barbed wire. Eve counted four guards patrolling near the gate—and there was only one gate. They were armed. *Very* armed. Rifles in their hands. Two guns strapped to each hip. *Overkill.*

"Guess they don't want any visitors," she said, voice soft. So much for being a big, old *voluntary* facility.

She couldn't tell much about the building. It was big, made of heavy stone, and the back of the place seemed to sink into the side of the mountain. Eve was willing to bet that they were looking at the top layer of the lab.

With Wyatt, what you saw wasn't what you got.

"How many layers?" Eve muttered, frowning. Just how many levels were there in that place? How far down would they have to go?

"No sign of the vampire," Cain said, his own eyes sweeping over the facility. "Or if he's been here, he didn't leave any blood in his wake."

Eve swallowed. "There are cameras stationed every five feet on the building." They could take out the guards, but they'd be monitored on-screen. Unless . . . "Think you could raise some fire?" The fire and smoke could block out their image. With that distraction and smoke cover, they could get inside the gate.

Cain gave her a smile with a wicked edge. "Always." The flames flickered in his eyes. "But I'll need a charge . . ."

What?

He had her in his arms. Crushed against his chest. His lips took hers. So wild and hot. His hands were in her hair and she found her nails digging into his shoulders.

Heat built between them. She could actually feel the rise of the fire. Burning, *burning* . . .

Then he was gone. Pulling away from her and moving so fast, he'd already knocked out the four guards before she could even lift her fist. Then a wall of fire and smoke surrounded the building.

So much for the cameras.

Eve bent down and scooped up one of the guards' weapons. The gun, a Glock, felt heavy in her grip. She took a deep breath, one full of smoke and fear, and headed after Cain.

She saw another gun just a foot away. Why take just one weapon . . . ?

Cain had already yanked open the main door. She could hear sirens blaring. *Fire alarms.* The fire would cause confusion. Chaos. There wasn't a better time to slip inside.

"Stand down." Wyatt's voice blasted through the intercom system.

Eve's fingers tightened around the gun. "Let's go." There was a stairwell to the left.

A guard rushed at them.

Cain threw him back. The guy slammed into the wall.

Cain kicked open the stairwell door. The area was small inside, cramped. They hurried down. Opened another door—

"I told you to stand down," Wyatt said.

There he was. Just waiting in the middle of the hallway.

Only he wasn't alone. A dozen armed guards were behind him, and Trace was in front of him. The werewolf was on his knees, and Wyatt had a gun shoved against Trace's temple.

"Silver bullets, of course," Wyatt told them with a small smile. "Since silver is the only thing that keeps his kind down."

Cain lunged forward, but Eve shoved her left hand against his chest. "Stop." Cain was fast, but was he fast enough to beat Wyatt? One squeeze of that trigger, and Trace would die right in front of her eyes.

"I thought you might feel a certain . . . affection for the wolf." Wyatt's smirk was so knowing it sickened her. No, *he* sickened her. "Now toss away the gun, Eve."

She tossed it. Good thing she'd taken the liberty of grabbing *two* guns. The other one was tucked in the back of her jeans, hidden below her shirt. Wyatt probably hadn't seen her grab the other gun, thanks to the smoke and fire. She just had to get close enough to use her backup weapon.

Close enough to blow that smirk off his face.

"Come toward me, Eve," Wyatt said.

She could get close enough. She took one step.

Cain grabbed her arm, freezing her. His hold was tight

enough to bruise. "You don't move." Then he was in front of her. "I'll give you five seconds to let the werewolf go. To let your men get the hell out of here."

Eve's hand began to inch toward her second weapon. Cain was so big, a perfect wall to shield her movements.

"Five seconds," Cain said again and she could smell the scent of smoke. She knew the scent was coming from him. "Or I'll burn this whole bitch of a facility down around us all."

The fire wouldn't hurt him. Or her.

But it would kill Wyatt and the humans. And Trace.

Her hand froze. "Cain?" Okay, she'd known that he planned to torch the place, but she'd thought he'd do that *after* they got all the prisoners out.

"You're not caging me again," Cain told Wyatt, his voice dark. Deadly. "You're not caging *anyone*."

Murmurs came from the guards. The shuffle of feet as they no doubt started to back the hell up.

"Five." Cain's voice cut through the room.

"You won't burn me!" Wyatt's shout.

Eve was sure he would.

"Four." Cain hadn't moved. His legs were braced apart, his hands up at his sides. Eve shifted to the left, and she could see fire swirling above his open palms.

"Eve!" Wyatt was sounding desperate. "Stop him, Eve, or you'll never know what you are."

Was he really going to toss that at her? Like he knew anything about her. Eve's eyes narrowed. She wouldn't fall for his tricks.

"Three."

But she couldn't let Trace die. Could Cain control his flames? Send them out to attack a specific target? She tried to edge around Cain to see Trace. She was sweating and her hands were shaking.

"I know what you are, Eve!" Wyatt was sweating, too.

But he still had his gun to Trace's temple. Trace just stared forward, eyes glassy. *Drugged.*

"You don't know," she whispered. This was her moment. She'd pull up her gun, shoot Wyatt.

What if he shot Trace?

"Two." Cain's determined voice. The flames flared higher.

"She was just like you!" Wyatt yelled. The gun lifted one inch from Trace's head. "The fire couldn't hurt her, because of what she was!"

No. "My mother died in a fire."

Wyatt's gun rose more. Eased away from Trace's head. "That's what the world was supposed to think. The vamps killed her long before the fire ever touched her. Fire never could hurt her." Wyatt's eyes were on Eve. "Want to know the truth? I can tell you! I can—"

"One." Cain's hands lifted.

"I don't want the truth. I want you to get the hell away from my friend." She yanked up her gun and fired.

The bullet caught Wyatt in the shoulder and he staggered back. All the guards with him immediately lifted their weapons to fire, but Cain sent a giant ball of fire rolling toward them. The men yelled and most dropped to the floor. One shot his weapon, but the bullet missed her and—

Wyatt was laughing.

Eve lunged forward and grabbed Trace's hand. "Come with me." She yanked him toward her and they fell to the floor.

Wyatt was still laughing.

She looked up. He'd yanked open his shirt to stare down at the bullet wound. Only . . . the wound was closing. Wyatt's eyes were bright and wild and he was lifting his gun to aim it at her.

Richard Wyatt wasn't human. Or, at least, he wasn't any-

more. Eve realized the scientist had been playing Frankenstein with his own body. Just what had he become?

Eve targeted her own weapon on him. So the first shot
hadn't done any good. Maybe the next would.

She fired the gun, even as he did. But his bullets didn't
hit her. Trace had lunged up. The silver bullets thudded
into his chest. He grunted and fell back. Wyatt kept firing,
until his empty gun clicked.

"One protector down," Wyatt muttered. He didn't seem
fazed by the growing fire. The guards had backed up, getting away from the fire, but they had their weapons ready.
The sprinklers burst on from overhead, drenching everyone in the hallway. Eve stayed crouched on the floor, but
Cain stalked forward.

Her bullets had hit Wyatt, but the man was still on his
feet.

"Science can beat the supernatural," Wyatt said, sounding perfectly normal, as if he hadn't been shot multiple
times. "What we can do is amazing, really."

Cain reached through the flames and grabbed Wyatt. As
she watched, Cain snapped the man's neck. Wyatt fell to
the floor.

Her breath choked out. *Over.* Just like that, Wyatt was
dead.

"Come on!" Cain grabbed Eve's hand and pulled her to
her feet as he sent a rush of fire at the remaining guards.
"Get the hell out of here!" he yelled at them.

They scrambled. Didn't even try to fight. With the fire
raging, how could she blame them?

Snap.

Eve stiffened. Even over the flames, she'd heard that
sound. Bones snapping. Popping.

She glanced over her shoulder. Wyatt was standing up
again. Tilting his head from side to side as he popped the
bones of his neck back in place.

"Nice try," he murmured, his eyes on Cain. "Now it's my turn."

But instead of coming at them, he jumped back.

Just as all the guards were heading back. Carefully moving away from them.

Trap. Eve knew it, too late.

The floor began to tremble beneath them. No, not just tremble. *Move.*

No wonder the guards were backing up. She glanced over her shoulder. The stairwell had been sealed off. Armed guards stood in front of the door. The floor beneath them, holy hell, the floor was opening, opening . . .

Cain grabbed Eve and hauled her toward the nearest wall. There was only darkness in that growing hole. The hole that had once been the floor.

"Trace!" She screamed his name as she saw his body fall into that black pit.

The entire floor seemed to break loose. She and Cain fell, tumbling down into the darkness below. He held her as they dropped, wrapping his body around hers. When they hit the bottom, she felt the thud of the impact vibrate through their bodies.

They'd fallen into darkness. Complete and total darkness. Cain's head and back had slammed into the floor, but he didn't ease his grip on her. His hands tightened.

Eve's hands slid around him. She could feel . . . stone beneath them, and she heard the sound of breathing. Rough. Raspy breathing.

Something grated overhead. She looked up. "No!"

The light above her vanished as the area closed off once more. Wyatt had sealed them in.

Cain groaned beneath her. Something . . . else groaned from the darkness.

They were locked in, but they weren't alone.

"F-fire, Cain," she whispered into his ear. He was hurt

beneath her. She knew it. The fall had been brutal. Too long. At least three stories. They'd fallen straight down.

Her hands found his face. Smoothed over his cheek. Pushed into his hair. She felt the sticky wetness of his blood. *No.*

The breaths around her grew stronger. "T-Trace?" He hadn't been moving when he'd fallen. Hadn't appeared to even be alive. Could that breathing be him?

More groans. No, growls. Coming from the left. The right.

Not Trace. Eve's own breath choked out. "Please, Cain," she whispered, holding him tight, "I need the fire." She needed to see. Had to see what was coming for them in the dark.

Something touched her hair. Eve whirled. She still had her gun. "Get back!"

Pain sliced across her back. Eve screamed. Something had . . . clawed her. "Stay away from us!" Cain wasn't moving. Still breathing, but she knew he was hurt badly. Was he dying? "Cain?"

She felt the tightness of his muscles beneath her hand. He was trying to move, but he couldn't. "Just a little fire," Eve whispered. Begged. "I need to see . . ."

What's coming for me.

She found his hand. Turned it over. Then, in the dark, her lips met his. She tasted blood on his lips. And he felt— cold.

Cain *never* felt cold.

"The fire," she whispered against his mouth. "I need . . ."

A small spark sputtered to life in his hand. Like a weak candle lighting the room.

And revealing the monsters that waited for them.

Eve's gaze swept to the left. To the right. She saw the fangs. The claws. The monsters coming. Just a few feet away. Waiting to pounce on her.

Too many.

Vampires.

These didn't look like others she'd seen. They didn't just have sharp canines—*all* of their teeth were razor sharp. And the nails breaking from their fingertips looked like long, black knives.

What the hell? This wasn't the way vamps were supposed to look. This was something totally foreign to her.

"K-kill . . ." Cain rasped.

She lifted her gun. The bullets she had left might slow the vampires down, but it wasn't going to stop them all.

She could still hear what she'd told Cain earlier. *If a vamp ever tries to bite me again, I swear I'll kill him myself.* Eve had meant those words.

There were too many to kill. She wouldn't be able to take them all out, no matter how hard she tried.

The vamps were ignoring Trace's body. *Because he's already dead?* They were focused only on her and Cain.

And on Cain's blood. There was so much blood. She could feel it beneath her fingertips. With that faint light from Cain's fire, she could see the broken bones in his arm. His twisted legs . . .

"Kill . . . me . . ." Cain whispered.

Her gaze flew to his face. "No!"

Another slice over her back. Eve screamed and turned back, firing her gun. A vampire cried out, the sound like an animal's shrill cry of pain and rage.

She'd made a hit. How many bullets did she have left? *Not enough.*

"Come . . . back . . ." Cain's voice. So low. Pain-filled. "I can . . . stop . . . them . . ."

Yes, the fire could burn through the vampires, she knew that. *But I don't want to be the one to kill Cain.* She couldn't be the one.

Another swipe of claws over her skin. Eve fired the gun.

Caught another vampire and heard that same high-pitched cry.

"*Eat . . .*" A whisper from the darkness. From the vampires that were shuffling closer.

Her hands were shaking. "Stay away from us!"

"Kill me . . . Eve . . ." Cain's voice. So weak. Broken. "Kill . . . me . . ."

But she couldn't. She couldn't look into Cain's eyes and pull the trigger.

He'll come back.

Cain's body jerked. His breath rushed out.

Gulping. Slurping.

A vampire was drinking from Cain's leg. Eve fired again. "Stay away from him!"

That feeding vampire fell back with a screech. But the others inched closer.

"My . . . fire . . ." Cain's voice was weakening even more. He was hurt too badly. She knew he wasn't going to survive much longer. Either her bullets took him out or he kept suffering. He kept facing agony as the vamps tried to drain him.

Her cheeks were wet. From blood or tears? *Both.* "I'm . . . sorry . . ." She couldn't let the vampires eat his flesh. Not during these last desperate moments. She couldn't do that to him.

"Come . . . back . . ." His words were a bare whisper. One she had to strain to hear as she leaned over him. "You . . . run . . ."

She nodded.

"Don't want to . . . hurt . . . you . . ."

But he wanted her to shoot him.

She lifted the gun to his heart. The fire in Cain's hands was flickering, fading, and the vamps were closing in as the darkness spread once more.

Their claws reached her, tearing into her skin. Cain's body jerked and shuddered, and Eve knew they were attacking him, too.

"I'm sorry," she told him, crying hard, unable to stop her tears. Eve pulled the trigger.

"Remarkable," Richard said as he watched Eve kill her lover. The gray images played before him on the screen, the gritty, night-vision surveillance cams making the forms of the vampires look like long, desperate shadows.

Shadows with glowing eyes. Shadows that were grabbing Eve. Poor Eve. She'd used her last bullet on Cain. She was still trying to fight back, but she couldn't seem to summon any fire on her own.

Not like her mother.

How disappointing.

Flames began to flicker around Cain's body. The regeneration process had begun, but the phoenix had better hurry. If he didn't rise soon, Eve would be dead long before Cain was able to draw breath again.

"Taste . . . sweet . . ." Fangs tore into Eve's shoulder, digging deep. She screamed at the pain and shoved the vampire back. She punched and she kicked, and the vampires still kept coming.

Since the gun was out of bullets, she used it like a club to hit them.

They weren't near Cain anymore. The minute he'd died, they'd left his body, and come after her. She figured the bastards must like fresh meat. The kind of meat that was still *alive.*

Hurry, Cain, please, hurry . . .

"Drain you dry . . ." the vampire who'd bit her rasped as he came at her again.

Drain you dry . . .

Eve stiffened. Another vampire had said those words to her. So long ago. The night her parents had died.

The scent of smoke teased her nose. *Yes.* Smoke meant flames and flames meant . . . Cain was coming back to her.

Fire lit up the area, flashing as it consumed Cain's body. The vampires jumped back, screaming.

Eve got a good look at the vampire who'd been trying so hard to make a meal of her.

All teeth. Giant eyes. Deadly claws. But . . . but there was something about his face, the curve of his jaw, the stark lines of his cheeks. She stared at him, heart racing, and realized—

I know him.

A girl never forgot the face of her nightmare.

The vampires were backing away from the fire, giving off screams that felt like they were going to shatter her eardrums.

"You wanted a bite?" Eve snarled to the vamp she remembered. The one who'd always haunted her. "Come and get it." She grabbed him and fell back toward Cain—and the fire.

The vampire's flesh ignited instantly, like dry leaves in a flash fire. The skin burned, the muscle . . . all melted away in an instant.

Eve was left holding ash in her hand as the fire burned brighter.

Some of the vampires were running down a long, dark tunnel on the left. *So much damn darkness.* Others were frozen, staring with gaping mouths and wide eyes at the orange and red flames.

The fire raged. Bigger. Brighter.

Cain stood up. He went right for the vampires who'd stayed behind. Touched them with his hands and they melted before him. One. Two. Three. They went down so quickly. Burned, *burned*.

Eve wanted to close her eyes. She hated to see the carnage and the smell . . .

It was choking her.

But she kept her eyes open. The vampires died quickly, but their screams seemed to linger in the air around her.

Then Cain turned to her.

Fire was at his feet, seeming to sputter out and fade away. He stared at her, and she could see the flames flickering in his eyes.

"Do you know me?" she whispered. On his last rising, he'd seemed so confused. Lost.

He stared at her. Stalked toward her. Eve's back was pressed to the wall. The tunnel was a few feet away. But some of the vamps had escaped down that tunnel. If she ran that way, they could be waiting for her.

Cain's eyes were locked on her, too bright with the flames that he stirred. "You . . ." His voice was dark, rumbling.

He recognized her. Eve's breath left her in a rush. He knew who she was. He knew—

"You"—a muscle jerked in his jaw—"*killed* me."

There was fury in his stare. So much dark rage. And deadly intent.

Eve glanced toward the dark tunnel once more. Cain had tried to warn her. She should have listened when he'd told her to run.

He reached for her.

I'm listening now.

She ducked under his arm and raced down the tunnel, but she could hear the thud of his footsteps as he followed her and she knew . . .

There'd be no escape.

★ ★ ★

"Run," Richard whispered as he watched Eve flee.

Cain followed right after her. The phoenix didn't bother running. He just slowly stalked his prey.

Why should he run? He'd track Eve down easily enough. It wasn't like the tunnel had an exit. Eve would hit a dead end soon enough.

"Sir . . ." From the guard on Richard's right. "Do we need to go down and follow them?"

Richard shook his head. "No need. There's no way out of that tunnel." It was why the vampires were trapped there. The area had proven to be the perfect prison for a particular failed experiment.

Richard glanced over at the guard. His eyes narrowed. The guy was sweating. Had it been the first time the man had seen a vamp get fried? If he stayed around Genesis, it sure wouldn't be the last time he saw such a sight.

Richard was glad those particular vamps were gone. He'd figured that once Cain was tossed in their midst, the vamps wouldn't last long.

That breed of vampires had proven to be a disappointment. An unfortunate experiment that had gone wrong. His father had made those beings. Tried to transform soldiers into an enhanced breed of vampires.

At first, the transformation had seemed to work. The soldiers who'd volunteered for the program had become stronger, bigger, and faster. Their senses had been better than any shifter. They'd been such great hunters. Perfect killers.

At first . . .

The genetic splicing had been flawed, though. The humans hadn't been able to maintain the transformation, not at an optimum level.

The speakers on Richard's right picked up the sound of a scream. Not the high-pitched cry of the vamps in that hole, but a woman's cry. Eve.

His fingers tapped lightly over the keyboard. He'd counted on Cain to protect Eve when he'd dropped her into that hole. Cain had already risen once—all alone with Eve—and not attacked her, so Richard had thought Eve would be safe with him.

Maybe he'd thought wrong.

He glanced back at the monitor. "Send a team in. Bring the female out." He needed her, and he couldn't afford a miscalculation with her life.

"Yes, sir." the guard replied readily enough, but then he hesitated. "Ah sir, just how far does that tunnel stretch into the mountain?"

Richard kept staring at the screen. He'd been in that tunnel once, a lifetime ago. Been trapped with the vampires. *Another experiment.* His father had always enjoyed those experiments.

Richard had hated the darkness. Hated the vampires all around him.

He'd been seven years old.

And *he'd* been the experiment then.

Don't worry, son. They don't want your blood. I'm sure of it. His father's voice. And then he had just . . . pushed him into the dark. Pushed him into that pit with the vampires. *I just have to test them.* His father had left him with the monsters.

How long was I down there?

Richard swallowed back the memory. Shoved it back deep inside.

This lab, all of it, had been created by Jeremiah. The first Genesis lab. The original. The place that still housed so many secrets.

And plenty of failures. Failures that were hard to kill. Failures that had to be contained.

"The vamps made that tunnel," Richard said. They'd clawed it, hacking their way through the dirt and rock over the years. Searching for a freedom they'd never find. "It ends in a wall of stone." His father had made sure of that. No getting out, not for the pet project that had gone so horribly wrong.

Vampires who could never satisfy their hunger. More beast than man, their intelligence had begun to plummet just weeks after their transformation. His father had wanted to make a super soldier, a human with a vampire's strengths and none of the creature's weaknesses.

Instead, the soldiers had broken down. Their bodies and minds hadn't been strong enough to survive the change for long. After a few months, they'd had all the vamps' weaknesses.

And very few strengths.

They'd been such a disappointment to his father.

"My vamps are better," Richard said, the words a dark growl. *So much better.*

"Uh, sir?"

Richard stiffened and glanced back. "Didn't I tell you to get a team in there?"

"But . . . the phoenix, the vampire—"

"Use the tranqs on them and bring the girl out." Cain could rot in that dark pit for a while longer, but Richard wanted to start harvesting eggs from Eve before the phoenix decided to kill her.

If he hasn't already . . .

Eve wasn't screaming anymore.

CHAPTER FIFTEEN

H*unt.*
  Cain rushed through the darkness, striking out at the beings that were foolish enough to attack him. He touched them, the fire flared, and the beasts turned to ash.

The tunnel smelled of death. Blood. Rot.

And . . . *her.*

Sweetness inside the gaping mouth of hell. A light scent that pulled him forward. One image was burned into his head, the image he'd had as soon as the fire brought him back.

A gun, pressing into his heart. Her. Dark hair streaming around her, shadows slipping over her body. Tears glistening in her eyes. "I'm . . . sorry . . ."

Then the thunder of a gun. The white-hot agony as a bullet ripped into his heart.

She'd shot him.

Killed him.

Now *his* beast wanted vengeance. The fire burned inside him, so hot that when he breathed, a puff of smoke appeared before his mouth.

Deeper he went into the tunnel. He could hear the shuffle of footsteps. To his right.

He reached out—another vampire died by his hand.

Then he heard her scream. A wild, terrified cry. He rushed after the sound, running as quickly as he could.

Mine. She was his to punish. No one else could hurt her. No one else should fucking dare to hurt her.

Mine.

The beast knew it. Even death couldn't change that truth for him.

He saw them. Eve, struggling in the arms of a vampire. She was holding him off, pushing him away from her neck, but the vamp's teeth were mere inches from her.

He lunged forward and grabbed the vampire. The man tried to scream, but couldn't. Cain didn't give him a chance.

The vamp died instantly.

She ran. She lurched away and tried to escape into the darkness once more. Didn't she realize? There was no escape.

He sent his fire out, letting it lick the ground on either side of her body. The fire showed that there truly was no way out. A wall of giant rocks waited just ahead.

She stumbled to a stop. After a moment, she spun around, facing him again. He kept advancing on her. One step at a time. The flames were low on the ground, burning softly, but he could make them rise with a thought.

Or he could let them die.

He saw her eyes and knew she didn't fear his flames. *Just the darkness.*

He smiled at her and let the flames die. The darkness took him—and her—once more.

But while she couldn't see in the dark, he had no such trouble. He could see her perfectly. From the top of her tousled head, all the way down the slender length of her body.

She was all alone with him in the dark. No one to save her. No one to hear her screams.

Did she realize how close he was to her? He could see her head turning as she strained to see in the darkness.

I see you. He lifted his hand and let the back of his fingers trail down her cheek.

She jerked back, gasping. Then softly, "Cain?"

The name pierced through him.

"Cain, please tell me that you have control right now." Her voice was breathy, husky. Sexy.

His cock began to swell as he inhaled her sweet scent. He slid closer to her and touched her again.

"It *is* you." Relief had her words shaking.

If he'd been a vamp, would he have bothered with touches? No, he would have attacked with teeth and fangs.

She'd been attacked. He could smell her blood, and that coppery scent pissed him off.

No one else hurts her.

She stood before him. Her small body was trembling, but she wasn't trying to flee. Probably because there was no place for her to go.

His hand drifted down her cheek. Eased over her chin. Then his fingers wrapped around her throat. Her pulse raced beneath his fingers, drumming so quickly.

"Say my name, Cain."

He frowned at her.

"Who am I?" she whispered to him.

She was the woman who'd shot him. His fingers began to tighten around her.

"Who. Am. I?" she rasped.

"Mine." It almost hurt to say the word, but it was the truth. He knew that with all his being. This woman—small, deadly—was *his.*

And she'd betrayed him. Killed him. It was his turn to punish her.

He pushed her back against the rocky wall of the tunnel. Kept one hand around her throat.

"Cain—"

His mouth took hers. He was rough, he knew it, couldn't stop it—didn't even care to try. He thrust his tongue into her mouth, and he took what he wanted.

Her.

He'd died for her. He figured he deserved her. She owed him.

His cock was stretching, aching with arousal. His clothes were gone. They never survived the fire. His flesh pressed against her, but it wasn't good enough. He wanted more.

He began to push her down to the ground.

Her eyes were so big in the darkness. Wide. Afraid.

For some reason, her fear stirred the rage that was always so close to the surface for him. His hand fell away from her throat.

Instead of pushing her down, he lifted her up, caging her against the rocks with his body. Her hands lifted and wrapped around his shoulders as she fought to find her balance.

But she wasn't fighting *him.*

He put his mouth on her throat. Licked her. Sucked her delicate skin. Let her feel his teeth.

The vampires had thought they'd mark her.

No. He'd be the only one to mark her.

"Cain . . . come back to me," she whispered. Emotion filled her words.

He growled and his fingers went to the snap of her jeans. He yanked the jeans open. Shoved his hand inside and pushed past the silk of her panties.

She was smooth. Soft.

But not wet. He was hungry for her, ripping apart with his lust, but . . .

She didn't want him.

"I'll make you want me," he promised. She had to want

him. She was the only thing the beast wanted. Without her . . .

Fire. Madness. Hell.

"Say my name," she told him again, her voice that husky purr that had his cock jerking eagerly against her. "My name, *say it.* Let me know that you're back with me again, Cain."

But there was a wall of fire and fury in his mind. He looked at her and knew only that she was his.

She'd killed him.

She'd made him burn.

He fucking needed her . . .

His hand rested between her legs. He pushed a finger inside her. She gasped beneath him. Her hips arched.

She likes it when I lick her neck.

The knowledge whispered through him as his mouth settled on the column of her throat. He touched her with his lips. His tongue.

She shuddered against him.

His fingers pushed into her a little more.

He nipped her flesh.

Another shudder and . . . he could feel the wet heat of her arousal beginning to moisten his fingers.

His thumb pressed over her clit. She gasped at the move, and her hips arched again, the move almost helpless. Not trying to get away, she was pushing closer to him.

He pulled back his hand. Put his fingers in his mouth. Tasted her.

Yes.

He was the one to fall to his knees. His hands grabbed her jeans and the thin slip of her panties. Yanked them down. Tossed them away.

Her hands curled over his shoulders. "W-what are you—"

His hands wrapped around her hips. He pushed her back,

just a step, then lifted her up. "Spread your legs." A guttural order, but he had to taste more of her. Was desperate for more.

All he knew was a haze of lust and need. *Want her. Take her.*

Slowly, she spread her legs.

He lifted her higher. Positioned her so that his mouth hovered right over her sex.

Then he took her. His tongue thrust into her sex and she jerked against him. *Good.* Her taste filled his mouth. Cream. Woman. Sweet and rich and perfect on his tongue.

He tasted her. Took from her. His tongue licked over her skin, over her clit, and then thrust into her sex. She whispered his name. Her nails sank into his shoulders.

When she came, he felt the climax against his mouth. It made him hungry for more.

Another lick. Another taste. Then he surged to his feet. His body was tight, aching, his heart beating too fast and his blood seeming to burn his veins. He needed release. The explosion of climax. He needed—

"Cain." She sighed his name as her arms wrapped around him.

He needed her. The witch who'd killed him. The woman that he knew belonged only to him.

His cock pushed between her legs. He didn't hold back. Couldn't. He thrust into her as hard and as deep as he could go. He wanted to take everything from her.

Because he was hungry for everything.

Her gasps filled his ears. His body drove into hers. Over and over. The fire filled him, burning him from the inside out. She jerked at the feel of his hands, and he tore them from her. They were too hot—

She can handle the fire. A whisper from inside. An instinctive response. *My fire won't hurt her.*

He slammed his fists into the wall behind her head.

Rocks and dirt rained onto his shoulders. Fire sputtered from his hands.

And still he took. Too fast. Too hard. She couldn't match his rhythm. He couldn't stop.

"Cain." His name. Breathed this time as she held him close.

His name. His woman.

His thrusts grew even wilder. Her legs were locked around his hips. Holding tight. Her hands braced on his chest as she drove her hips back down against his. Again. Again.

He erupted inside her, driving into her and shuddering with the force of a release that gutted him. A pleasure that ripped past the fire and the hell and touched the man caged inside him.

"Eve." Her name broke from him.

She came around him, shuddering, her sex gripping him and greedily taking the last of his orgasm.

She was Eve . . . *his* Eve. His memories flooded back to him. Vampires had been attacking. They'd been coming for her. Clawing her. Biting him. He'd told her to kill him.

She had.

His fingers rose from the rock wall. Slowly, carefully, he pushed back the curtain of hair that had fallen to conceal her face from his view. His fingers curved under her chin, and he tilted her head back so she had to meet his gaze.

"Eve," he said her name again, almost tasting it. He could still taste her.

Her lips quivered, then curved into a slow smile. "You're . . . coming back to me."

He was. But he was still fighting the beast inside. A beast that wanted only to destroy. To burn.

Not her.

Even in the midst of his fury, the beast didn't ever want to hurt her. Neither did the man.

"Yes," he said slowly and his voice didn't sound quite right. Too rough. Too raw.

Her legs slid down his body, her smooth skin brushing over him. He pulled out of her, hating to leave her body. He was still aroused. Not close to being satisfied, but . . .

His sanity was back . . . for the damn moment. Shame burned through him.

A fucking tunnel? Against a dirt wall? With dead vamps yards away?

Had he really taken her there? Why the hell wasn't she attacking him?

"I'm sorry," she told him. "I didn't want to shoot you. But they were coming. They were biting you and—"

He saw her eyes close and kissed her. Not with the wild roughness of before . . . softer. "I know." He'd already been dying. Slowly. Moment by moment. He'd been watching her suffer. Helpless, his spine broken, he hadn't been able to fight back against the monsters coming for them. "I was dead anyway." He'd just lost the memories for a time. Lost everything—to the greedy claws of the fire.

He could never tell how he'd rise. If he'd be sane. If he'd remember . . .

Or if the fire and beast would strip his memories away.

I remembered her. He had, dammit.

Mine. He'd remembered Eve before, too. Even back at Genesis, when he rose, he'd thought of . . .

Her.

He knew what that meant. Knew how dangerous such a connection was. For him. For her.

Before he could speak, Cain heard the thud of approaching footsteps. He caught the stench of fear and sweat. Humans. Racing through the tunnel.

Coming after them.

He grabbed Eve's clothes. "Get dressed." He needed to

tell her how sorry he was, but the beast was still too close to the surface. And with those men coming . . .

Kill.

Burn.

He wasn't exactly battling the most gentle of instincts.

"We just want the woman!" a man's voice called out. "Send her to us! We want to make sure she's safe."

Now they came to save her? Where had the fools been when the vampires were attacking?

When I was attacking?

He couldn't look in her eyes.

Her hand brushed over his arm. "I wanted you, Cain. I've always wanted you."

His breath was ragged. His chest aching.

Cain pushed her behind him. Heard the rustle of her clothing as she dressed. "Come any closer," he yelled to the humans, "and you die." Fair warning. The only warning they'd get before he let his fire end them.

"The tunnel's already falling in . . ." a voice shouted back. Not Wyatt. Another male. One with a death wish.

I can grant that wish.

More rocks and rubble fell onto him. Onto Eve.

"It's not stable. The vampires dug this hole, but it just kept falling on them. With your fire . . ." The voice was coming closer. So were the footsteps. Six, seven men? *Eight.* "If you blast again, the whole place will collapse."

Their shouts weren't exactly helping to stabilize the tunnel. Did the assholes know that? He bet they did—and that they didn't care.

A light shone in the darkness. A bright light that caught him and Eve in its illumination. "You'll just die and come back," the male voice said, "but what about her? You really think she'll survive a cave-in?"

No, she wouldn't.

Ryder had said Eve didn't have the blood of a phoenix. Why would he have lied about that?

Why would he have told the truth?

Never trust a vampire.

Cain didn't trust anyone. Except . . . Eve. Somehow, some way, she'd gotten beneath his skin. Beneath the fire.

"I couldn't find a way out," she said, rising to whisper in his ear. "Just stones. Dirt."

A dead end.

That bright light kept shining right on him.

"I've got a better idea," the voice told him. It wasn't sounding so afraid any longer. More like cocky.

A bad mistake. Cain had never been able to tolerate cocky jerks.

"Why don't you send the woman over here . . ."

Behind that light, Cain saw the man's gun point toward the top of the tunnel.

That bastard was going to shoot the tunnel at its weak points and force a cave-in.

The fire began to rage inside Cain. The beast hadn't been calmed, not appeased nearly enough. This jerkoff was tempting him. All but begging for death.

"Send her here, or *I'll* send this whole damn place crashing down on you both."

The men behind the leader lifted their weapons. They pointed them not at Eve and Cain, but at the tunnel's top, its sides.

When they fired, Cain knew the tunnel could collapse. Eve would die. She'd suffocate or be crushed.

And he'd rise to find her broken body.

"Go," he forced out to Eve.

She didn't move. "And what happens to Cain?" Eve asked.

Silence, then . . . "Nothing," the lying human told her. "We'll leave him just where he is."

Such bullshit. Cain caught Eve's hand. So soft. His gaze

stared into hers. "They can't kill me." Well, not for long, anyway. "They'll just piss me off."

She shook her head. "But when you rise"—her voice was so soft that it barely whispered in his ears—"you come back . . . different, Cain."

Each time, he did. Darker. More lost. But he'd been fighting to hold his sanity.

For her.

What would happen if he rose and she wasn't there?

He forced himself to release her hand. "If you stay with me, they'll kill you." He couldn't allow that.

He couldn't protect her, not there. Too much fire could destroy the place, and then he'd be the one to destroy her.

Not gonna happen.

"Wyatt wants her alive." The leader's hard voice came again. His weapon was still pointed at the ceiling. "So just send her over, and we'll get her out of here."

But they wouldn't do the same for him. He knew what would happen next, even if Eve didn't.

He wanted to kiss her. Taste her. But time was running out. So he stepped away from her. Let all emotion wash from his face. "Go."

Eve still hesitated.

"Shoot the wall!" the leader barked.

"No!" Cain screamed right back. He caught Eve's shoulders and pushed her away from him—and right at the guards. "Get her the hell out of here."

"Cain!" Arms reached for her. Eve fought them, glancing back. *"Cain!"*

He stood frozen. There wasn't another option. Didn't she see that?

Cain stared at the leader of those guards. Memorized him. The receding hairline. The thick neck. The beady eyes. "I'll kill you first," he promised. He saw the gun's barrel tremble. His gaze swept around, learning the faces of all the men. The shadows didn't hide their identities from him. The darkness hid nothing. "Then I'll come for the rest of you if any man so much as bruises her skin."

Some of the smarter humans immediately eased away from Eve. Maybe they'd get to keep living.

But there was always at least one dumbass in any group. The lead guard appeared to be that one. The man scurried back like a rat running in the dark. "Oh, Wyatt's gonna do more than bruise her." The taunt was tossed out after the guy had backed up about five feet. Did he think Cain couldn't see his smile? "He's gonna cut her open. Dissect her"—he fired his gun, a fast blast at the tunnel's ceiling— "and you can't stop him!"

As if on cue, the others began to fire their weapons. Dirt and rocks fell down, burying him. Cain had expected this.

Eve hadn't.

The guards weren't holding her. They were too busy firing and backing away. They must have thought she was afraid of the cave-in. He'd learned Eve wasn't afraid of much.

She lunged toward him.

No, Eve!

But she ran through the falling debris. Ran straight for Cain and threw herself into his arms. They tumbled back, back, and he rolled them away from the collapsing edge of the tunnel. As the dirt rained down, as the rocks hit him, he covered her with his body and hoped that he'd be able to keep her alive.

"Open your eyes."

His voice slipped through her mind. So deep. Rumbling. She loved the sound of Cain's voice.

"Dammit, Eve, don't do this . . . *open your eyes.*" He shook her. Hard.

She opened her eyes, but saw only darkness. A total and

perfect black. Eve opened her mouth to speak and choked. What the hell? She spat out dirt.

Cave-in.

She tried to sit up, but strong hands held her down. "Breathe, Eve."

There wouldn't be much to breathe, not for long. Those bastards had sealed them inside the tunnel. *They buried us alive.* If she weren't already choking on dirt, she'd be whimpering.

Cain's hands slid over her body. She jerked at the touch. She couldn't see anything in that darkness, but she could feel his body surrounding her. Eve spat out more dirt and managed to rasp, "Cain . . . light." She needed his fire. She hated this darkness. It was suffocating her.

No, that would be the dirt and rocks.

"Can't." His voice was grim. "The fire would burn up the oxygen in here. You need it too much."

Her heart seemed to stop at those words. "We're trapped." Not a question. She'd realized it could happen as soon as those jackasses with guns had started firing. But she hadn't been able to leave Cain.

He didn't respond, but then, he didn't have to. His fingers brushed over her face. She turned in to his touch.

"You should have gone with them."

"So Wyatt could slice me open?" At least she could talk easily now. "No, thanks."

Cain's hand left her. She missed his touch instantly in the dark.

"You'd rather die slowly here with me?" Anger hummed in his voice.

It felt like she couldn't get in a full breath. Her imagination? Her fear? Or was there just no damn air in there? "I'd rather not die at all." She reached out in the darkness and her hands clutched him. "But I wasn't going to leave you trapped in this hole alone."

Her hands were on his chest. His heart raced beneath her touch. "If I'd been alone," he growled, "then I could have used the fire to blast my way out."

"You still can. You know the fire doesn't—"

"We could run out of oxygen before the fire gets us free. Or the whole fucking mountain could just fall on us. I'll keep coming back, again and again, keep burning . . . but you won't."

Brutal words. Cold. The truth?

Eve pushed away from him. Surprisingly, there was enough room for her to rise to her feet. Her movements were slow, mincing, careful. Once she was at her full height, she stepped forward in an attempt to explore their small space.

Almost instantly, Cain's hands wrapped around her shoulders and pulled her back against him. "You're heading toward the cave-in."

She turned and lifted her hands right out in front of her face. She waved them, and saw nothing. Dammit. "You can see perfectly, can't you?"

"Yes."

She touched the rocky wall that had been at the end of the tunnel. So heavy. "Someone put these here. . . ."

"Probably because they didn't want those vamps ever getting loose."

She didn't want to think about the vampires. Or the memories they'd stirred up in her mind. *One thing at a time.* The only thing she was thinking about was survival. She touched the rocks.

Cain grabbed her hand. "Baby, why do you have a death wish?"

Eve tried to snatch her hand back. She couldn't. He was too strong. "I don't."

"Then why did you stay with me?" In the darkness, his

words were more snarls than anything else. So much anger. No, *fury*.

She had fury of her own. "Why are you so pissed off at me?" Eve demanded. "Because I didn't want to get my body sliced open by that freak? Or because I'd rather die in the dark with you than—"

He whirled her around and pulled her against him. "You're supposed to live." He backed her up two steps. "We're running out of air. No one is going to come for us. *You were supposed to live!*"

His eyes started to burn in the dark. Finally. She could see the fire blazing at her. The only light in the blackness.

Was there madness in that light? Maybe. But she had her own madness, too. "I wasn't going to leave you alone." Her words sounded calm. How was that even possible? She could see Cain walking that fine line between reason and fury. She had to keep him from crossing over, so she told him the truth. "I knew I'd be safe with you."

His hands bit into her shoulders. "You're going to be dead with me."

"Then you'd better hurry and find a way to save us both"—she said the words with confidence—"before I run out of air."

He jerked away from her so quickly that she stumbled and slipped to the ground.

"Eve—" His hands reached for her, but she shoved him back.

"Eve, I didn't mean—"

She crawled on the ground. Rushed toward the rocks. Lifted her hand, not touching them, just *feeling*.

"I'll get you out," he swore. "I will. I'll find a way."

"You don't have to." Her hand moved to the left. "Cain, I-I found it! I can feel air . . ." The lightest breeze was blowing through the heavy rocks.

No wonder Genesis had walled up this end of the tunnel. The vamps had been close to freedom.

They just hadn't been strong enough to break free once the rocks blocked that freedom.

Cain was beside her in an instant. His hand pressed forward. *"Hell, yes."*

Eve started to smile. They were going to make it out of there. They'd be safe.

But then Cain's fiery eyes turned back to her. Why was there no relief in his gaze?

"Eve . . ."

"Get us through the rocks," she told him, knotting her fingers into fists. "Do whatever you have to do, but get us out."

The rest of the mountain might collapse on them. She got that. But if they didn't try, if they just sat in the dark and did nothing, she was guaranteed a slow death. "Get us out," she said again.

Cain rose. Pulled her to his feet. Then he wrapped his arms around her and tucked her chin against his chest. "Keep your head down."

She nodded against him. His heart thundered beneath her ear.

His body grew warmer against hers. His bare flesh heated, warming like a furnace.

She saw the flash of fire that seemed to come straight from his body—a flash that ripped around her and circled them, twining like a snake.

The fire revealed her prison. Barely five feet. A wall of earth where the tunnel had been. Destruction. Decay.

Buried alive.

The fire swelled around her. Swelled, focused.

"Close your eyes," Cain said.

She didn't. She wanted to see every moment.

Her head tilted, and her gaze cut toward those heavy

rocks. The fire lunged at the rock wall, a snake striking. Again and again.

The rocks began to shake. Dirt fell from above.

The fire swelled higher. Burned so bright.

The mountain trembled around them. The ground rocked. The walls shook. And the dirt kept tumbling down. *Cave-in.* She knew it was happening, but there wasn't a thing they could do to stop it.

Cain shoved more of his fire out, blasting at those rocks. Blasting . . .

And the mountain seemed to explode.

Eve sucked in a gasp of air, but choked on dirt. The thick dirt was everywhere, showering on her, smothering her. She tried to push against it, but couldn't.

Then she was being pulled, yanked from the dirt, still held tight against Cain's hard body. He pulled her, heaved her through the falling earth even as he pushed her toward the fire.

Into the fire.

Eve felt the whisper of the flames around her. Heard the crackle as it smothered out the rush of falling earth. Her hands grabbed onto Cain and she held him as tightly as she could.

She was tumbling, rolling, and he was with her. His body twisted around hers as they thudded onto the ground.

Eve opened her mouth. Sucked in a desperate gulp of air. The earth shook around her.

Cain scooped her into his arms. Raced away. She looked back over his shoulder and saw the small opening that he'd carved into the mountain. An opening that barely looked a foot wide. How had they gotten out of there?

The opening closed. The ground kept shaking.

And Cain kept running. He ran and ran with her—until they fell into the icy cold water of a lake.

★ ★ ★

"You . . . left her down there." Richard stared at the guard. Stuart Montgomery. Ex-Marine. Ex-police detective. A guy who should have known how to carry out a simple order without screwing everything to hell and back.

The alarm was beeping, a constant shriek. It had started beeping as soon as the facility trembled.

"We were trapping him, sir," Montgomery told him. Sweat beaded the guy's forehead. "We didn't know she'd run back to his side."

"Your mistake," Richard snapped out. Those trembles had been constant for the last five minutes. How long could Eve last in that hole without air?

Not long enough.

"Hand me your gun," Richard ordered.

Montgomery stiffened. "The phoenix did not escape, sir. He's still down there. . . ."

"And he'll stay there until he manages to dig himself out." Which he would do, Richard had no doubt about that. "But she can't survive that long." He'd given a simple order. How hard was that to follow? Retrieve Eve Bradley.

Not *kill* her.

"Give me your weapon." The commanded was snapped from between Richard's gritted teeth.

Two other guards stood behind Montgomery, waiting tensely, with their eyes on Richard.

Slowly, Montgomery lifted his gun from his holster and handed it over.

"Thank you." Richard stared at Montgomery, wondering what to do with the man before him. Shooting him instantly was so tempting, but what purpose would it serve?

His father had always taught him that life and death had purpose—meaning that nothing was to be wasted in this world. "Take Mr. Montgomery down to the main lab for holding," he told the other guards.

They immediately stepped forward.

Montgomery stiffened. "The lab?" He gave a rough laugh. "Throw my ass out of here. Fire me, whatever. But I'm not going to the damn lab—"

"Yes, you are." Richard nodded to the guards.

They grabbed Montgomery's arms. He tried to struggle against them. How annoying.

Richard put the gun on the desk and picked up a syringe. While Montgomery snarled and fought, Richard walked right up to him and plunged the needle into the man's throat.

Montgomery's eyes rolled back into his head. The guards dragged him toward the door.

The man would make a good addition to the new supersoldier program. His body was the right size. He was in top shape. He might be able to survive the transformation.

And if he didn't . . .

No death is a waste.

Richard reached for the intercom. "Unit Twelve, report to the east side of the mountain." The side just beyond the rocks. When Cain broke free, that was where he'd be.

And maybe, just maybe Richard would get lucky. Maybe the phoenix would manage to drag Eve from the rubble.

Life and death . . . both always had a purpose.

CHAPTER SIXTEEN

Cain's head broke from the icy water. He gasped, sucking in a deep gulp of air. His arms were around Eve, and her breath heaved out as they made their way from the lake.

Sodden and exhausted, they fell onto the earth. The stars stared down at them, too bright after the darkness of the cave.

Eve's hands slid over his chest. "Are you all right?" She pushed up to study him. Her wet hair clung to her neck and shoulders.

Cain nodded. He was the one who should be asking about her. He hadn't been sure that he'd succeed in getting her out of there alive.

Her lips trembled into a small smile. "How about we don't do that again, huh?"

In spite of the hell they'd just faced, Cain found himself laughing. He didn't know how she did it, but Eve could get to him. As no one else ever had. He reached for her, sinking his fingers into her wet hair. "How about we don't," he agreed. Then he kissed her. A light, soft kiss that wasn't about the rough lust between them. The desperate hunger. It was just about . . . her.

Eve pulled back from the kiss as if startled. Her gaze

searched his, but he had no idea what she was looking for in his eyes.

"Isn't this fucking lovely," a dark voice drawled from the right. "In the middle of hell, you two are taking time to screw."

Cain leaped to his feet. He knew that annoying voice. It belonged to a vampire that was long overdue for death. "Ryder."

The vamp gave a little salute. "As impressive as it was watching you two leap out from the inside of that mountain, why the hell were you running away from Wyatt? You were supposed to be taking him down."

Eve rose and came to Cain's side. "Sorry. We were a little busy fighting to stay alive."

Ryder just laughed. "Like that matters to *him*."

There were plenty of trees around them. Easy enough to make a stake. Cain figured he could have a stake in that vamp's heart in about, oh, thirty seconds or less.

"Did you see her?" Ryder demanded, stepping forward. Cain could all but smell the guy's desperation. "Did you see my—"

"All we saw were more fanged assholes like you," Cain told him and offered his own smile. "Only they burned fast enough." Actually, they'd burned faster than any vamp Cain had ever seen.

Ryder shrugged. "What? Am I supposed to care that you killed some vamps? You think I *wanted* to be this way? A bastard turned me . . . and I staked him as soon as I could."

Why didn't Cain buy that story?

The vamp shook his head. "Do you have to be naked out here? Damn man. Seriously, you don't go to war naked."

Cain's teeth ground together. "After I kill you, I'll be sure to take your clothing."

"Come and try," Ryder taunted.

Fine. Cain rushed forward in an instant and shattered the closest tree. He turned back with his makeshift stake, ready to drive it into Ryder's heart.

Ryder had moved. He stood behind Eve. Not touching her. Just smirking as he gazed at Cain over Eve's delicate shoulder. "Do you think you could go through her," he asked Cain, "in order to kill me?"

Cain advanced. He could push Eve aside before the vampire would have a chance to attack. He could—

"They weren't like you." Eve turned away from Cain as she faced the vampire. "The vampires in that mountain didn't look like you. They didn't smell like you, and they didn't attack like you."

She'd caught Ryder's attention. "What are you talking about?"

Eve's mouth tightened, then she said, "The vampires that Wyatt kept locked in that hole, they weren't . . . normal."

Cain frowned at her. There was a normal for vampires? Not likely. Supernaturals were abnormal by their very natures.

"Their claws were black, and their fangs . . ." Her hand reached up to Ryder's mouth.

If that prick nipped her fingers . . .

Eve let her hand fall away before she ever touched Ryder. "It wasn't just their canines that were sharp. Every tooth was long and curved. They had a mouth full of fangs."

Ryder stared down at her with wide eyes. After a moment, he shook his head. "That's not . . . possible."

"Sure it is," she said as she glanced back over her shoulder at Cain. "With Wyatt, *anything* is possible."

Then she stepped to the side.

Cain sprang forward, but he didn't drive the stake into Ryder's heart. He just shoved the tip into the vamp's chest. Let the bastard know that if Cain had truly wanted . . .

You'd be dead on the ground.

That wasn't what he wanted . . . yet.

"I knew one of them." Eve's voice pulled Cain's gaze to her.

Ryder yanked the stake from his chest. "Asshole."

Cain ignored him.

"I remembered him," Eve said. "His voice, what he said—*I remembered him.*"

Cain could hardly recall those vampires at all. When he'd fallen into the pit, his spine had broken. Blood had choked him. He'd heard the vampires. Smelled them. Felt them bite into his flesh.

But then he'd burned. When he'd risen, he'd barely seen the vampires at all. They'd just been prey.

Eve looked so pale in the starlight. "He was there when my parents died."

Cain advanced slowly and touched her shoulder. "Are you sure?" She'd told him that her parents died when she'd just been a child.

A slow nod. "I couldn't ever forget his face. It's starred in too many of my nightmares, but . . . his eyes had changed. Gotten bigger. Darker." She swallowed and Cain saw the small, painful movement of her throat. "And I think he remembered me."

Well, hell.

He glanced back over at the mountain.

"They're coming," Ryder muttered but Cain had already heard the thud of approaching footsteps. Wyatt had sent out his human minions to make sure Cain didn't make it out of the mountain.

Too bad, asshole. I'm already free. The guy would have to learn to move faster.

"Time to get some clothes," Cain said as he turned toward the approaching threat rounding the mountain.

Eve glanced at him, eyes wide.

"I could go for a bite," Ryder added, voice mild.

Cain nodded—and they attacked.

"We've got a wounded man!" Cain called out as he lifted Eve over his shoulder. They'd taken the liberty of borrowing some clothing—perfect camouflage—from the guards who didn't need the uniforms anymore. They were unconscious and would be for a long time to come. It wasn't like they'd miss the clothes.

"Hurry up!" Ryder snapped. He kept his head down. Anyone looking at him would see only the green uniform he wore and his issued weapon.

Eve's head was covered by one of the hats that a guard had been wearing. She'd slipped the uniform over her own clothing, helping the loose outfit fit a bit better. But since she was the one playing injured, the guards wouldn't get much of a look at her.

Not before they were taken out.

The guards near the building's entrance rushed toward them. "Need a medic," one said into his mike. "We need—"

Cain knocked him out with one punch.

Ryder's fangs flashed as he took care of the other man.

Too easy.

Cain lowered Eve to her feet. She cut her eyes toward him, not saying a word.

Wyatt would never expect them to storm right back after their failed attack last time. And Cain always loved to do the unexpected.

Ryder took the guard's key card and swiped it across the entrance. The door slid open and he bared his teeth at Cain and Eve. "This is where we part ways."

Cain had been itching to ditch the vamp.

"Whichever one of us finds Wyatt first," Ryder said, "well, then that lucky bastard gets the pleasure of gutting him."

With that, the vampire slipped down the hallway, easing perfectly into the darkness.

Cain headed left, but Eve's light touch on his arm stopped him.

"I didn't come back to kill Wyatt," she said.

That sure was the reason he'd come back to this hell. He glanced at her and saw the tension and worry etched onto her lovely face.

"I came back for Trace."

Shit. Cain's body tensed. The werewolf was dead. Cain remembered seeing him get shot. Not once, but over and over. No way would Trace be coming back.

Eve saw the thoughts in his eyes. Her lips firmed and she shook her head. "No. Trace is strong. If anyone could survive, it would be him."

Cain heard footsteps approaching. He stepped into the shadows, pressing his back to the wall. Eve mirrored his movements perfectly.

The footsteps grew closer. Closer . . .

Cain grabbed the guard, wrapping his fingers around the man's neck and jerking him into the air. The human never even had the chance to scream.

Cain tightened his hold.

"Stop." Eve's whisper.

Teeth clenching, he did, but he didn't let the guard go.

Eve leaned toward the terrified human. "The werewolf that was brought in earlier . . . where is he?"

Cain eased his hold, just enough to let a whisper slip from the man's throat. "How . . . the . . . fuck . . . should I . . . know?"

The human thought he could play tough. He thought wrong.

Still keeping one arm around the fool's throat, Cain grabbed the man's left hand—and broke it.

The color bleached from the guard's face.

"Try again," Cain urged.

"D-dead . . ."

It was the answer that he'd expected. A werewolf wasn't built to survive that kind of silver impact.

"F-failed . . . experiment . . ."

Ah, now wasn't the guard turning into a talker.

"Where's his body?" Eve demanded and Cain realized that she had a gun shoved into the man's side. He knew that she'd taken that weapon from the hands of a fallen guard back near the lake. The woman liked to be armed. Cain could respect that.

"Furnace room . . . gonna . . . burn him . . ."

Eve stabbed her gun harder into the human's side. "Tell me where to find that room."

"Go . . . left . . . all the way . . ." He tried to point with his broken hand.

Someone was being useful. "And Wyatt?" Cain wanted to know as he flipped the guy around to face him. "Where is he?"

The guard stared at Cain. Yeah, that was fear blazing in the man's eyes. Cain knew that look well.

"His office . . ." the guy muttered. "Basement, sub-level one . . ."

Definitely useful info. Cain slammed the guy's head back into the wall.

Now someone was unconscious.

Cain had caught sight of an elevator on his first trip into the fun house. He shoved the guard's body into the corner then turned right, heading for that elevator.

He'd taken two steps when he realized Eve wasn't coming with him. He froze. They only had so much time. . . .

Cain glanced back at her.

"I have to see him for myself." Eve's chin lifted. "I'm not leaving until I make sure that Trace is dead."

Morbid. And a pain that she didn't have to experience. "They've probably already burned his body."

She flinched. But Eve turned away, heading back down the hallway that would take her to the furnace room.

Guessing Wyatt burned plenty of bodies in there.

Cain looked back at the elevator. This was his chance. He'd slipped in, and now he could get to Wyatt. The bastard still thought he was buried under all those rocks.

The perfect opportunity . . . Cain stalked toward the elevator.

This was what he'd wanted. What he'd fought for. Vengeance. Wyatt deserved every minute of torment that he was about to get.

Cain's fingers lifted toward the elevator button. He heard Eve's footsteps slip away.

Eve kept her back pressed to the wall as she eased down the steps and headed toward the furnace room. Just the name of that place had her stomach tightening. Trace didn't deserve this end.

My fault. He'd been trying to help her, and he'd wound up here. How the hell was that fair?

She wasn't going to leave him there, even if all she could do was drag his body away from this hellhole. Trace had been her friend. She wouldn't just leave him without a backward glance.

Two guards headed toward her. Even though she had a weapon, Eve didn't leap forward and fight them. Stealth and surprise were her tools, and if she could avoid some bloodshed, then yes, please, that was what she'd like to do. She hunched into the shadows and didn't make so much as a sound.

The guards marched by her. Didn't even glance her way. Once they were gone, she started breathing again.

And after a few moments, she started walking. Now that she was on the right floor, it wasn't hard to find the furnace room. There was just one big, heavy metal door at the end of the hallway. All the other doors were made of normal wood. She was guessing the metal entrance led to the flames.

To Trace.

There was a lever in front of the metal door, no doorknob. So she spun the lever. Once. Twice. The third time, she heard the grind of gears and the door slid open with a clang. She stepped inside.

"What the hell are you doing here?" a sharp voice demanded.

Crap. Eve whipped out her gun and pointed it at the guy in the white lab coat.

He gulped and his eyes doubled behind the lenses of his glasses. "Guard, what's happening?"

Right. She was supposed to be a guard. "Th-there's a change in plans. I'm here for the werewolf."

His gaze darted to the table on his left. To the body that was covered by a white sheet. "I'm disposing of him now."

"The hell you are."

He blinked, then his gaze swept over her. "You're not one of the normal guards. This isn't your floor."

Seriously, the dude was slow on the uptake. Didn't he realize she had a gun pointed on him? Was that normal guard behavior?

In this place, maybe it is.

Eve smiled at him. "No one has to get hurt here. I'm just going to take that wolf off your hands."

But the man put his too-thin body between her and that table. "He has to be destroyed. He's infected."

Infected?

"I told Wyatt the experiment was dangerous, but the

fool wouldn't listen. They never listen to me here." Sweat beaded his high forehead. "I have to burn the body before the wolf wakes up."

Before the wolf wakes up . . . Her heart slammed into her chest. "He's still alive?" Hope had her feeling light-headed. Yes! Trace was—

The man lunged for her. His fingers wrapped around the barrel of the gun and he tried to yank the weapon right out of her hand.

He was lucky she didn't shoot his idiotic self right in the heart. Instead, Eve jerked the weapon back even as she kicked the guy in the groin. He groaned and staggered away a few steps, almost ramming into Trace's body.

"Are you crazy?" she snapped at him. "You don't charge at someone holding a gun." That was a pretty clear rule.

Well, you didn't charge when you were just a human, anyway. And this guy seemed to shout, "Human!" from every pore.

But he wasn't looking at her. He'd grabbed the table— no, not a table, a gurney—that held Trace's body, and he was shoving that body right toward the open furnace. A big, giant furnace with a gaping mouth and flames burning inside. The thing looked like what she'd seen inside a crematorium once.

Not the nicest memory.

"Stop!" Eve screamed, lifting her gun. "I don't want to hurt you."

He ignored her. He was too busy panting and shoving that gurney. Trying to dump Trace's body in the fire. "Have to . . . destroy . . . before . . . monster wakes . . ."

No. Eve lunged for him and swung the butt of the gun at the man's head. There was a loud thud as the weapon made contact.

The guy fell to the ground, his body sprawling in a limp heap.

Eve stepped around him and yanked the gurney away from those dancing flames. She grabbed the sheet and tossed it aside. "Trace?" Bullet holes covered his chest. So much silver. She could smell it all around him. Silver and blood.

Holding her breath, Eve put her fingers to his throat. Was there a pulse there? Or was it just her imagination? Her gaze flew around the room. There—a tray of instruments. She rushed to them, dropping her gun on the nearest countertop. She'd get the gleaming tweezers and pull out the silver bullets, or what was left of them. Werewolves always healed better once the silver left their bodies.

She curled her fingers over the tweezers, sent the other instruments scattering, then heard a screech of sound behind her.

Eve spun around. The gurney had flown across the room and crashed into the wall and Trace—Trace was on his feet. Still bloody, but standing on trembling legs.

"Trace!"

His head snapped up at her call, and his eyes locked right on her.

She'd never seen such fury in his stare before. So much blind rage and hate. It all seemed to be directed right at her. "Trace, I'm sorry," Eve whispered.

There was no recognition in his eyes. Just more fury. He charged for her, and claws burst from his fingertips.

Eve leaped back from his attack. Her fingers flew over the instruments. She grabbed a scalpel. The gun was too far away. "Trace?" Her fingers curled tightly around the weapon, but Eve didn't think she could use it. He had been hurt so much already because of her, she didn't want to do anything else to him.

His hand closed around her throat. He lifted her into the air, and her feet kicked uselessly.

Then he smiled at her, a cold, cruel smile that flashed his fangs, and fear iced her heart.

★ ★ ★

Wyatt hunched over his desk. It was only a matter of time, just a few more moments.

And his prey would be coming to him.

He couldn't look eager. Couldn't even look aware. But he was ready. So were the guards who waited in the next room. As soon as the sensor alarm was triggered in his office, those guards would leap out and attack.

He wasn't stupid. He knew Cain wouldn't be held back for long. He also knew the phoenix wasn't just going to run away with his tail between his legs. No, the phoenix would be coming right inside the lab.

I'm ready.

He didn't need Cain any longer. The man was a threat that had to be eliminated. Luckily, Wyatt knew just how to reach the phoenix's vulnerable spot. Eve was the key, a weapon that, with time and care, could be molded and used most effectively.

But he didn't have time for her training. Not then. He did have a backup plan. Another who could kill Cain. Another who *would* . . . for the promise of freedom.

Wyatt kept his back to the door as he pulled a small mask over his nose and mouth. Anyone coming from behind wouldn't see that mask. A fatal mistake.

Cain's mistake.

The door hissed open behind him. Such a soft, silent sound. If he'd been a normal human, he would have missed that telling noise. Thanks to his father, Wyatt was far from normal.

And I've got the scars to prove it.

The floor creaked beneath his would-be attacker's feet. He let himself smile. Just a little closer . . . just a little closer . . .

Wyatt pushed the button under his desk, and the door to his office slid closed, sealing the attacker inside with him.

He raised his hand to hold the mask in place and spun to face Cain. "Your mistake, phoenix—"

Cain wasn't there.

Ryder stood a few feet away, his fangs out.

"W-what—"

No, that wasn't the plan. Gas fell through the slats in the ceiling, but it had never affected Ryder. The vampire was too old, far too powerful, and only a stake or fire could take him out.

We'd thought he was just a changed human. When Ryder had first been targeted, their intel had been off. Ryder wasn't easy prey. Far from it.

He was the fucking king of the vampires. Maybe the first one ever born.

The door to the right slid open. Wyatt's guards rushed out, just as he'd planned.

Ryder killed all five of them instantly, then dropped their bodies to the ground. Their blood covered his shirt, his hands, his chin.

The gas continued to leak into the room.

Taking his time, Ryder closed in. "You have something of mine, Wyatt" he said, snapping his teeth together, "and I want her *back.*"

She couldn't breathe. Eve clawed at Trace's fingers with her left hand even as she used her right hand to stab him with the scalpel—*sorry, Trace, sorry!*—but he wouldn't let her go. Dark spots danced before her eyes. His claws were cutting into her skin. She couldn't suck in a breath. As she fought him, Eve could hear the pounding of her own blood, echoing and throbbing in her ears.

I'm dying. At the hands of the last man she'd ever expected to hurt her.

"Let her go."

That couldn't be Cain's voice. Cain was gone. He'd headed off to fight Wyatt. That *wasn't* Cain's voice.

And Trace wasn't letting her go.

"I said . . . *let her the fuck go!*"

Eve couldn't see anyone. The room had gone black but she smelled . . . burning flesh.

Then she was on the floor. Her hands and knees slapped into the hard tile as she sucked in as much air as she could. The air seemed to sting her lungs, but she didn't care, she just wanted to breathe.

After she managed to get in a few breaths, Eve pushed the hair out of her eyes and lifted her head. She could still smell that horrible, acrid scent—and it was coming from Trace.

He was on the floor, rolling around to smother the flames that licked along his body.

Cain grabbed Eve's arms and pulled her to her feet.

Cain. "What—you came back."

His gaze blazed at her. "Something's wrong with your werewolf."

Um, other than him being on *fire*?

Rising onto her toes, Eve glanced around Cain's shoulder. Trace was back on his feet. He was . . . smoldering. He stared at her and Cain like he couldn't wait to rip them apart.

"Trace?" Her whisper. "Don't you know me?"

That blind gaze said he didn't.

"Animals fear fire," Cain said, and Eve realized he was keeping his body and his flames between her and Trace. "Right now, he's far more animal than man."

Yes, he was. Eve could see it. She didn't know why this was happening. Trace always had such control over his beast, and he would never, *never* hurt her.

The bruised flesh on her throat told a different story.

The females in Trace's pack had been hunted long ago,

picked as easy targets by their enemies. They'd been attacked, slaughtered, all to send a message to Trace's father.

We're taking over.

Trace had found the broken body of his mother. His sister.

And he'd been the one to go out and kill the other alpha to get his vengeance. Trace had one rule in the world, one rule that he always followed . . . Trace *never* hurt a woman.

But he just hurt me.

Cain sent a burst of fire toward Trace. Trace snarled and backed up. Eve realized then, Trace hadn't spoken. He hadn't said a word since he'd climbed off that gurney.

More animal than man.

Only he hadn't shifted into the form of a wolf. His claws were out. His body looked *bigger* than before, but he wasn't shifting.

The experiment didn't work. The words whispered through her mind and made her heart ache. Wyatt. He'd done something to Trace. Changed him.

"I told you!" The scream had Eve's head snapping to the right and finding the guy in the white lab coat. He'd staggered to his feet. "We should have killed the monster before he woke up!"

Killing Trace hadn't been an option for her. It still wasn't. Her friend was in there, somewhere. The same way that Cain was there when he rose from the fire. They just had to find a way to reach Trace—

Trace leaped across the room and slit the human's throat.

Eve's jaw dropped. *Not Trace.* He'd never killed so coldly. Never attacked a human like that. "Trace?"

But he wasn't looking back at her. He was running away from the fire. Racing from the room and leaving her behind.

The flames continued to sputter.

Cain turned to face her. "He's dead."

She shook her head. "No, he's just—" *Broken.* Eve swallowed. "Wyatt got to him. Experimented. We have to find out what he did so we can change Trace back."

The words sounded hollow to her own ears. She knew, better than most, that people couldn't always go back.

Cain tilted up her chin, and she saw his eyes narrow as he took in the bruises marring her throat. "I can see his fucking fingers and the *claw* marks."

Eve caught his hands. "It wasn't him." Not really. Not the man she knew him to be, but it had been the beast he kept so carefully chained inside.

Cain twined his fingers with hers. "Stay with me." The words were an order. "I won't let anyone take another hit at you."

She grabbed the gun with her left hand. She wouldn't be caught off guard again. Eve climbed over the human's dead body. Swallowing, she forced herself to bend down and close his eyes. No man should die with such terror stamped on his face. When Trace realized what he'd done . . .

Eve looked away from the blood. She stepped away from the body. Her heart *hurt,* but there was nothing she could do for the guy. And if they didn't move, more guards would come.

Put one foot in front of the other. She followed Cain, feeling hollow inside. She ignored the pain in her throat and kept walking down the hallway.

When a guard rounded the corner and almost slammed right into Cain, he reacted instantly. One hit took the guard down. They kept walking. Climbing the stairs. Moving soundlessly as Cain tracked their prey.

When they reached the third floor, Eve heard a soft hissing. She frowned at that sound and glanced around.

"Gas," Cain whispered.

Because, of course, nothing could be *easy.*

But then that low hissing stopped. Glass shattered.

Cain rushed forward, with Eve following right behind him. But Cain threw up his arm and stopped her before she could enter the room with the smashed door. "Wait, you can't breathe the—"

But the gas—the familiar, faint white smoke—was dispersing. The windows in the room had been smashed and fresh air was sliding inside the office.

Wyatt's office.

And Wyatt was the one who hung, with his hands and face bloody, half-out of the nearest window.

Cain leaped across the room and grabbed him.

Eve didn't move. Her gaze swept around the area. Lingered on the pile of dead guards. Their heads hung, twisted the *wrong* way. Blood covered them. Such brutal kills.

Nausea rose in her, and Eve glanced away. Her gaze found the files scattered on Wyatt's desk. There. That was what she needed. *Proof.* Data for her story, but more . . . maybe the answer to helping Trace was in those files.

She rushed forward. Started flipping through the pages. Tables. Charts. Her eyes scanned down the text. Read about the experiments. The drugs.

Vampire blood.

Evolution.

Rebirth.

Her breath heaved out. She grabbed the flash drive nearby and hooked it to Wyatt's computer. Then she started scrolling through the files, copying as much as she could and—

"You can't kill me." Wyatt's too-calm voice chilled Eve and had her glancing back over her shoulder.

Cain had yanked the guy away from the broken glass. There were slashes all over Wyatt's face and arms, and what looked like bite marks on his neck.

Ryder.

Her gaze searched the room, but there was no sign of the vampire.

"I bet I can kill you," Cain promised, and he let his fire out.

Wyatt's eyes widened in fear, and when the flames licked at his legs, he screamed.

"No!" Eve jumped forward and grabbed Cain's shoulders. "Stop it!"

Cain turned on her with fury. "You're trying to save *him*?"

No. She shook her head and glanced at Wyatt. He was slapping at the flames, trying to put them out. He looked . . . scared. "I want to save the others." Trace. The humans who were still alive in the building. The other paranormals who were trapped there. She swallowed and, focusing on Wyatt, Eve demanded, "Tell me how to fix Trace." Because when something—someone—was broken, it could damn well be fixed.

Wyatt rubbed his hand over his neck. It looked like the slashes and bite marks on his skin were already starting to close.

Bullets hadn't killed him. The guy had enhanced healing.

What the hell is he?

Wyatt was just smiling at her, cocky once more now that he thought death wasn't coming for him. "There is no fixing your werewolf. The beast is out, and he'll kill and destroy until there's nothing left."

Cain snarled and tried to lunge forward. Eve tightened her hold on him. "We need him." Cain couldn't kill Wyatt. Not yet. Wyatt was the only one who could tell them what had been done to Trace. Trace . . . and probably so many others.

Wyatt laughed, then his voice was mocking as he said,

"Yes, yes, you *need* me. You can't kill me. No one can. If I die, I take all my secrets to the grave." His gaze found Eve's. "Like your secrets. I know them, every . . . single . . . one."

Goose bumps rose on her arms.

Wyatt's calculating gaze slid between her and Cain. "Maybe there is a way to save your wolf . . . *Maybe.*"

Eve tensed. "Tell me!"

"The cure's right beside you. Your phoenix."

"He's bullshitting," Cain growled. "Trying to save his sorry hide."

Wyatt just shrugged. "Your kind . . . so rare, so powerful. Too powerful for even death to contain. You can survive anything, and just rise from the ashes."

"Trace isn't a phoenix!" Sweat slickened Eve's hands. "He can't survive. Tell me how to help him!"

Wyatt's focus was on Cain. "His tears. The tears of a phoenix. Legend has it that they can heal."

What the hell was the guy going on about now?

"But I can't get him to cry. No matter how much pain I give him." Wyatt's lips twisted. "Can you even cry? Maybe it takes a soul to cry . . . and monsters like you don't have souls."

"*You're* the one who doesn't have a soul," Eve fired back at him. "You're the one who's dead inside." Cain had been right. The guy was just bullshitting them.

Wyatt's gaze came back to her. His smile chilled Eve. "The phoenix has a connection with you. Maybe when you die . . . perhaps he'll break then. Maybe then we'll get him to shed a tear and save your wolf."

"*She's not dying!*" Cain's roar.

Wyatt acted as if he didn't even hear him. "Poor little girl," he said, his accent thickening as his eyes swept over Eve. "Unlike Cain, you never had a problem with shedding tears. I read the report. Heard the stories about how you cried so long and hard when your mother died. When your father bled out before you . . ."

Eve's heart slammed into her chest.

Cain's hand curled around Eve's. "He's just screwing with you."

No, he was torturing her. "Those vampires . . ."

The ones that had been in the pit, the ones they'd killed . . .

Wyatt's smile widened. The bites had almost faded completely from his neck. He lifted a brow. "Remembered them, did you? One of my father's . . . experiments. Unfortunately, those soldiers weren't strong enough to adjust to the vampire DNA running through their bodies. They mutated. Became rabid feeding machines within just a few months of their transformation." His smile faded. For an instant, he almost looked sad, but Eve knew that fleeting expression had to be just another one of his tricks. Wyatt didn't care about anyone or anything.

"Your father transformed those men?" Eve held her body carefully still. Beside her, she could feel the leashed power vibrating within Cain.

Wyatt nodded. "A failed experiment. One of the few my father had." Wyatt lifted his hands and stared down at them with narrowed eyes. "One of the few," he said again, voice softer.

Why weren't guards storming into the room? Swarming them? Eve glanced back toward the door. Everything was off about this place. But . . .

He knows what happened to my family. Cain was wrong. Wyatt wasn't just toying with her. The guy actually knew about her parents. After so many years of wanting the truth, Eve couldn't just walk away. "Why did they die?"

Cain wasn't attacking. Wyatt was talking. She'd keep him talking for as long as she could.

Wyatt's gaze flickered to her. "If your mother couldn't be contained, she had to be killed." Said so coldly. "My father—Jeremiah—believed it was too risky to keep her alive."

Eve shook her head. She felt as if someone were ripping into her heart. Not just someone—Wyatt. "My mother—why her? Why was she picked for the experiments?"

The slashes on Wyatt's arms had closed. Blood still pooled around his feet, but the guy no longer showed any sign of injury. "Because she was a dragon shifter," he said, voice tight. "Jeremiah knew a dragon shifter was too dangerous to run free. Left on her own, she would have killed too many. She had to be stopped." It sounded like he was reciting a story he'd heard many times before.

Maybe he was, but every word was new for Eve.

Dragon shifter. Her gaze fell to her own hands. She'd never shifted a day in her life.

"Even with her last breath, she was saving you," he said. "Her fire stopped those vampires from killing you."

The fire that she'd feared for so long? It had been to protect her? *Her mother's flames.*

"Eve . . ." Cain's growl.

"The fire doesn't hurt you!" Wyatt rushed out, breaking over Cain's voice. "It can't. Your skin may look all soft and silken, but you've got dragon scales hidden beneath that surface. You *can't* burn."

She was having trouble breathing.

Looking too satisfied, Wyatt crossed his arms over his chest. "I've got so many secrets. Secrets you can't even guess at," he muttered with a hard glare at Cain. "That's why you can't kill me. Why the vampire couldn't kill me. If I die"—his eyes came back to Eve—"those secrets die with me."

He was right. They couldn't kill him. They needed him too—

"Too damn bad," Cain snarled and fire exploded from his fingertips—fire that raced for Wyatt. Wrapped around him. Wyatt screamed and fell to the ground. He was trying to put out the flames, but he couldn't. The fire was too hot.

"Stop!" Eve screamed. She lunged forward, but Cain's arms wrapped around her, and he hauled her back against his chest. "Dammit, Cain, *stop!*"

"He has to die." Flat. Hard.

But her past was dying with him. Trace was dying. All the others he'd hurt and experimented on could be dying. *"No, please!"*

His hold wouldn't break. Wyatt's screams filled her ears, and she barely heard Cain whisper, "I'm sorry."

CHAPTER SEVENTEEN

Eve was twisting and fighting in his hands, but Cain wasn't letting her go. Didn't she understand? If Wyatt survived, he'd just continue to torture. To kill. They couldn't let that happen.

He had to be stopped.

Eve's nails dug into Cain's skin. "You're killing Trace!"

The werewolf was already dead. Cain had known that with one look. The beast had taken over. "The man is gone. Only his animal remains."

"And when you come back from the fire, only the phoenix remains in you!"

Her words had him tensing, mostly because he knew how true they were. But, so far after his risings, he'd still managed to cling to the barest edges of his sanity.

Because of her.

She was looking at him with desperation in her gaze. "I haven't given up on you when you stare at me with a stranger's eyes, and I won't give up on him!"

An alarm was sounding in the distance. A shrill beep that wouldn't stop. Help would be coming for Wyatt, too late. The flames had burned so bright, Cain knew there was no chance of survival for Wyatt.

"When I stare into the eyes of the phoenix"—Eve snarled

and her fist slammed into his chest—"I don't give up on *you*. I fight to get you back. I fight for *you*."

And he was fighting to protect her. Wyatt would use her. Abuse her. Lock her in a lab and slice her open. Cain wasn't going to let that happen. Even if she hated him for what he had to do.

Better her alive, free, and full of rage than having her stone cold dead.

She pressed the barrel of her gun against his heart. "Stop it," she ordered, voice trembling.

He didn't stop the fire. It was too late. Didn't she see that? "Shoot me if you must."

"Damn you." Eve jerked free of his arms, and spun to face the flames.

Then she jumped into the fire.

Instinctively, he killed the flames. He knew the fire wouldn't hurt her, of course, but . . . he stopped the flames before he could even think.

He heard the low rasp of breathing. The fire had savaged Wyatt's body, but the guy—he was still alive? *How in the hell?*

Hurt, in agony no doubt, but still breathing.

Eve glanced up at Cain with tears in her eyes. "He's an experiment, too," she whispered.

Cain had thought nothing else could surprise him. "He experimented on his own damn self?"

Eve's hand hovered over Wyatt's burned flesh. Flesh that was slowly starting to heal as Cain watched. "I don't know."

The alarm was louder. Shriller. But no guards had stormed inside yet to rescue Wyatt. Why the hell not? Wyatt had to be their first priority in this place, but no one was coming to save his ass.

Cain stared at Eve. Wyatt wasn't a threat. Not then. But he still said, "If he comes at you, shoot him."

With the gun cradled in her hands, Eve nodded.

But would a bullet stop him? Bullets hadn't slowed Wyatt down before.

The guy's breath rasped out as his body shuddered.

Cain heard a scream echoing up from the hallway, a long, pain-filled cry. He rushed out of the room. Looked to the left, the right—

A woman stood in the middle of the hallway. Flames danced around her. Her long, blond hair twisted around her shoulders, and her eyes were as red as the flames that surrounded her.

Phoenix.

He'd found Ryder's lost lady, and she sure looked pissed.

She stared at him, not advancing, just watching. "Am I supposed to kill you, too?" Her voice was soft, barely rising over the fire, and completely without emotion.

Cain shook his head. "I'm not here to hurt you."

She laughed at that. "Of course, you are. They're all here to do that. To kill me, again and again." Her chin lifted. "I'm tired of dying. Maybe it's your turn now." She sent a line of flames right at him.

Cain lifted his hand. The fire stopped. He knew the red flames had filled his eyes when the woman staggered back. "You're not the only one who's tired of dying."

Her lips trembled. Then she turned and ran from him. More screams echoed up the hallway. Yells. Growls. Snarls.

Wyatt's "subjects" were loose. And from the sound of things, they were tearing down the place. Good. He hoped they ripped it all apart, brick by freaking brick.

As he watched the phoenix flee, Cain saw a dark shadow step away from the wall. *Ryder.* The vampire lunged forward and grabbed the woman, pulling her against him.

He got blasted with fire for that little move. Before Ryder could grab her again, a roar shook the hallway.

Trace burst from the stairwell. His claws slashed across Ryder's neck and the vampire's blood flowed.

Hell. Cain hadn't wanted to kill that werewolf. He knew Eve wouldn't forgive his death easily, even though the bastard had hurt her.

Trace turned to look at Cain. Bared his fangs and rushed toward him.

No, he hadn't wanted to kill him . . .

But it looks like I don't have a choice.

"In . . . jection . . ."

Eve frowned down at Wyatt. His chest was wheezing, his breath barely choking out. It looked like his body was trying to heal, but she wasn't sure if he was strong enough to come back from . . . this.

The sight of his body had nausea rolling in her stomach. Even after all he'd done, she hated to see him suffering like this. She hated to see anyone suffer.

"Wasn't . . . always . . ." Wyatt's eyes squeezed closed. "Like . . . this . . ."

She heard screams from outside.

Wyatt's breath whispered out. "They're . . . free . . ."

Who was? The supernaturals he'd caged and then played God with?

"Father . . . changed . . . me . . ."

Eve had to lean close to hear his words. But she wasn't stupid. She kept that gun pressed to his temple.

"Only . . . six. He *made* me . . ."

More burns and blisters faded. The savaged skin lightened.

She realized that Wyatt was part of the Genesis experiments, too. Another lab rat, one who'd been brought into the program by his own father.

"I hope that bastard's rotting in a grave somewhere."

The words burst from her. To experiment on his own child? Talk about being a monster.

"He's . . . not. Wants the world to think so . . . just pulling the damn strings . . ."

Eve's blood iced.

Wyatt's cracked lips formed a twisted smile. "Who do you . . . think . . . funded . . . Genesis?" Blood bubbled from his lips.

Eve frowned at him. His skin might be healing, but the guy sure seemed to be close to death.

"Need . . . injection!" His body shuddered. "Give it . . . to me . . ." He tried to point behind her, to his desk, but his hand fell back limply to the floor.

"I'm supposed to help you?" Eve asked, throat desert dry. But the truth was . . . hadn't she already? She'd stopped Cain. "After everything you've done?"

Wyatt couldn't talk any longer. It looked like he was having a seizure. Blood dripped from his lips. His eyes had rolled back into his head, and he shuddered, jerking convulsively.

"Dammit!" Eve jumped to her feet. "If I do this, you'd better tell me how to save Trace, got that? You'd better—"

She spun away and started searching through the desk drawers. Just paperwork in the top drawers. Files in the second. In the third . . .

Two syringes. One with a green label. One with a red. "Which one?" she demanded.

Eve swung back around and saw that Wyatt was on his feet. Not convulsing any longer. Not bleeding from the mouth.

An act. A very, very good one.

She dropped the syringes and lifted her gun. "Nice try, asshole."

A roar echoed through the room. Eve tensed. There were more screams. More yells.

"Sounds like Trace is here," Wyatt said with a little nod. Was he weaving on his feet? Maybe he hadn't been acting after all. "Now we'll have a real bloodbath."

"Is that what you want?" she demanded. "More death? For more people to suffer?"

He stared back at her.

"Weren't you ever human?" Eve threw at him.

He shook his head. "That part of me died a long time ago . . . when a boy was tossed into a pit of vampires and left alone in the dark."

He'd been tossed into that pit? The same way he'd dropped her and Cain into that hell? Her fingers wanted to tremble, but she tried to keep her grip steady on the gun. "Yeah, well, every part of you is about to die unless you tell me how to fix Trace." Fire hadn't worked—but it had sure come close to killing Wyatt. Another few minutes, and the guy would have been ash. The bullets had made him bleed when they'd hit his chest. He'd just healed too fast for the bullet wounds to slow him down. But maybe if she just aimed somewhere else, a more vulnerable spot . . .

Eve lifted the gun and aimed at his forehead. Wyatt tensed, and she saw the fear flash across his face. "Tell me how to fix him."

More roars. Eve swallowed. *"Tell me!"*

"There is no fixing him. He's only beast now. Not man. He knows only hunting and killing. There's nothing more for him. To him. He's a failed experiment."

"So are you," she whispered.

His body stiffened. "I'm not a failure. I'm the best experiment my father ever created."

Did the guy even hear what he was saying?

Wyatt kept talking. "I'm human, with the strength of a shifter, the healing ability of a demon, and the speed"—he moved in a blur, coming right in front of her—"of a fucking vampire."

He reached for her. But Eve had her gun dead center against his forehead. "Unfortunately for you," she whispered, "I know how to kill them all."

He grabbed for the gun.

I'm sorry, Trace.

Eve pulled the trigger.

The thunder of the gun froze Cain. He tossed the werewolf aside and raced back down the hallway. *"Eve!"*

He couldn't hear anything from Wyatt's office. Just silence. Thick and dark and total.

He shoved aside the remains of the door. Saw Eve and breathed again. She was standing near Wyatt's desk, holding a gun. Wyatt was on the ground with a giant hole in his forehead. A pool of blood was forming around his body.

"Want to hand me a piece of that wood?" Eve asked, inclining her head toward Cain and the smashed chair near his feet. "As a precaution, I really think we need to stake this bastard."

He grabbed the wood and tossed it lightly in his hand. Rushing forward, he shoved the stake into Wyatt's chest. The not-so-good doctor didn't move.

"And that's how you die," Eve whispered as she pushed back her hair. "Even if you are the *best experiment* out there."

Cain grabbed her hand. "Time to go." The mad scientist was dead, and they needed to get to safety.

But Eve shook her head. "It doesn't end with him, don't you see that? More scientists will just come along. They'll use his research. Genesis will continue."

He knew that. There were always monsters out there. Some of those monsters just happened to wear the bodies of men and white lab coats.

Eve pulled away from him. "I'm taking proof." She snatched up what looked like syringes from the desk and grabbed a black briefcase. She shoved the syringes in the case and yanked files from Wyatt's desk. "I am blowing this story wide open." She grabbed for a flash drive—

The howl from the hallway froze them both. Eve's shoulders stiffened. "Trace," she whispered.

What was left of him.

"Stay here," Cain told her. He actually thought Trace was trying to get to Eve. The beast had been fighting viciously to get down that hallway.

To Eve?

Not on his watch.

He ran back into the hallway. Trace was facing off against the other phoenix. His claws were up. He leaped forward.

Ryder grabbed his feet and sent the werewolf tumbling to the ground.

The phoenix let her fire out. Ryder jumped back and the flames circled Trace, closing in. He howled and swiped out, seeming to be confused. Lost.

"No," Eve's shout came from beside Cain. "You can't do this to him!"

She tried to shove by Cain, but he grabbed her arm, holding her back. "It's not my fire."

Trace's head jerked toward them. His face was human, but the eyes that locked on them were pure beast. He snarled and charged at the fire.

Leaped over the fire.

The werewolf was coming right at them.

Ryder screamed for the other female—the phoenix—to get out of the way. Trace kept charging, rushing with his claws up and his fangs bared.

Cain shoved Eve behind his back, then put up a wall of

flames in front of them. He hadn't wanted to do this, not with Eve watching, but there wasn't a choice. . . .

The werewolf wasn't stopping, so Cain had to stop him. He pushed out with his fire. The flames bit into Trace's arm. Another howl. More cries and . . . the werewolf turned away. He ran toward the far end of the hallway and jumped through the window. Glass shattered.

Eve shoved Cain aside as she tried to race toward that window. But Cain was with her every step of the way. He knew they'd find the werewolf's broken body below, and he hated for her to witness that sight.

She beat him to the window. There was no shielding her.

There was also no werewolf below.

Just broken glass. Guards swarming. No, guards fighting for their lives. The supernaturals were definitely out. Someone had opened the cages and let the monsters out.

Cain glanced back over his shoulder and tensed. The female phoenix had been cut by the werewolf's claws. He could see the dark blood staining her shirt and the wounds that ripped into her stomach. Ryder had her in his arms, holding her tight.

But Cain could tell she wouldn't survive those wounds. Death would come for her, then a rising. "Can you handle her?" he demanded.

He knew how dangerous a rising could be.

Ryder simply turned away and began carrying his phoenix toward the stairs. "Always."

The vampire shouldn't be so certain of that, but the guy had his own choices to make. *Your funeral, vamp.*

Cain had his priorities. Priority one—getting Eve to safety. The paranormals were wild, some could be on their side, some . . . could just be like the vampires they'd had to slaughter in the basement. Out of control. Rabid.

"Everyone's out," Eve said as if realizing how dangerous that situation was. "How?"

He glanced back down the hallway. Ryder was gone. *Ryder.* "I think they had a little vamp help." The vampire had wanted his phoenix, and Cain was betting he'd freed everyone in order to get to her.

"Cain . . ." Eve's gaze was on the madness below. "What happens to them now?"

Below them, a demon had just broken a guard's neck. Another guard fired and shot the demon in the back. Eve flinched.

"They get the hell out of here," Cain said. It was what most of the supernaturals were doing. Running into the forest. Fighting only when they were pursued. They wanted freedom. He understood that. It was what he wanted, too. "Come on." He grabbed her right hand. She had the briefcase in her left. The files, her proof.

It looked as if they'd both gotten what they wanted. All they had to do was live long enough to get away from the remains of Genesis.

And back to the lives they'd known.

The subjects were gone. The rooms remained empty and hollow. The guards had scattered. They'd been running for their fucking lives.

Jeremiah Wyatt leaned heavily on his cane as he made his way down the long hallway that led to his son's office. He knew Richard still had to be at the facility. His son hadn't contacted him, so . . .

You have to be here.

But unlike the guards and some of the supernaturals that he'd found left behind, Jeremiah knew that his son would still be alive. He'd made sure of it.

His experiments had paid off. Sure, Richard had begged

and pleaded, crying for him to stop the pain, but his son had been just a child then.

The boy hadn't understood just what sort of gift he was being given.

I made him strong.

No, Richard hadn't understood, not until Jeremiah had tossed him into the hole with the vampires. His son had been screaming, so sure that he was going to die.

He hadn't died.

I made you stronger.

His son's blood was poison to vampires. The fools had realized that soon enough. They'd stayed away from him. Poison blood. Fast-healing skin. Super strength. And his own God-given intelligence.

Richard was perfect. His best creation, by far.

He had to find him. . . .

His cane thudded lightly over the floor. Blood stained the tiles. Ash. Lights swayed drunkenly from overhead. It had taken him almost a full day to reach the facility. He'd been in Washington when he'd gotten the call from one of the fleeing guards, and he'd come to Beaumont as quickly as he could.

When you were already supposed to be dead, it was hard to move fast.

His men crowded in behind him, and when he reached Richard's office, one of them actually tried to go in first.

Fool. Jeremiah shoved his cane into the guy's gut. He could handle this scene on his own. If Richard wasn't there, trying to salvage their research, then his son would have left some sign showing where he'd—

Richard was there.

Jeremiah frowned and his cane hit against the floor.

Thud.

Thud.

Richard's eyes were closed and his arms were spread wide, looking almost like an angel's wings.

There was a giant bullet hole in his son's forehead.

And a wooden stake had been shoved into his heart.

Thud.

Thud.

Jeremiah's eyes burned. No, no, not his experiment. It wasn't supposed to end like this.

He bent, his knees creaking, and his hand closed around that stake. His fingers were slippery with sweat and twisted with arthritis, but he grabbed that stake and yanked it from his son's chest.

Maybe he'll come back. The boy could heal so well, maybe . . .

He wasn't healing. Richard wasn't breathing. His body was icy to the touch.

Please, Daddy, don't!

The boy had cried so much when the experiments started. So damn much. But the pain had been necessary. He'd transformed the boy. Made sure that he could survive anything that came his way.

Please, Daddy . . .

He hadn't survived. "Someone knew his weakness." A weakness that only Richard himself could have revealed. Jeremiah's hand tightened around the cane as he levered himself up. He hated to see his son like this. Such a pitiful waste. All of that time. All of that research.

Now I have nothing.

Jeremiah's gaze swept the room, rising to the tall bookcase on the right. The office had once been his, so he knew exactly where all the video surveillance equipment was hidden. "Get the feed," he said, pointing one finger at the camera he knew was there. "I want to know who killed my boy."

He'd make that person pay. His legacy had just been destroyed. His best experiment.

His son.

The cane slammed into the floor as he turned away.

He'd find his son's killer, and *make him pay.*

CHAPTER EIGHTEEN

When she slept, Eve looked so peaceful. Always beautiful, but sleep made her appear . . . innocent, too.

Cain leaned over her and brushed the back of his knuckles over her smooth cheek. He'd gotten them away from the nightmare in the mountains. Taken her to Charlotte. Booked a room in the fanciest hotel he could find.

Then they'd both crashed.

The silk sheets were soft beneath him. But they weren't even close to being as soft as her skin.

His lips pressed over the curve of her shoulder.

Eve stirred beneath his touch, and her eyes opened. "Cain."

He smiled. He liked the way she said his name when she woke. The husky whisper. The purr of sound. The hint of sex.

Her arms rose and wrapped around his shoulders. "Is it really over?"

He didn't let his expression change. "Almost."

She licked her lips. "They'll be here soon, won't they?"

He nodded, though he knew the words weren't a question.

She glanced over at the bedside table, at the glowing face of the small clock. "How much time do we have?"

"Just enough," he told her, but the words were a lie.

They wouldn't have enough time. Soon, he'd have to leave her.

Their lives were waiting for them. Time to get back to the way things had been.

So why did his chest feel so hollow when he thought of being without her?

"I called the reporters," he told her, "just like you asked." An anonymous call. To the press . . . and to the cops. "We probably have about ten minutes before our company arrives."

Her lashes lowered. "I want longer with you."

He pushed back the covers. Slid his body over hers. "And I want you." Cain kissed her, putting his mouth against hers and letting his tongue drive deep. Every instinct within him screamed for him to *take, take, take* . . .

But for this time, this last time, he forced himself to be gentle. He *could* be gentle, for her.

Her legs parted, and he slid between them. His cock pushed at the entrance to her sex, but he didn't thrust inside her. He kept kissing her. He stroked her with his hands.

Her moan teased his ears. Her hips arched against him.

His fingers slid over her breasts. Caressed the sweet flesh. He had to taste her there. A long lick, a kiss on her tight nipple.

"Cain . . ." A demand. He knew she wanted more than the soft caresses. He'd learned that Eve liked the sex hard, demanding. Normally, so did he.

But he wouldn't go harder. Wouldn't be rough with the passion that wanted to rage inside him. When she remembered him, Cain wanted her to remember more than just fire and fury.

He wanted her to remember the man he could be, too.

His fingers slid over her sex. His thumb pressed against

her clit. Her gasp told him how much she liked that touch, and when one finger slid into her, her sex was warm and tight around him. Ready.

But . . . not yet.

His head lifted. Cain stared down at her. There was so much he wanted to say to her, but all that came out was, "I won't forget you."

Her eyelids flickered. Her chin lifted just a bit. "No, you won't." Her nails scraped down his back. "You never will."

Cain thrust inside her. Her sex was paradise. Clasping him tightly, squeezing all along his length. He wanted to thrust and thrust, to drive in as deeply as he could go, but Cain kept a stranglehold on his control.

Hold back. For her.

He didn't want Eve to forget him, either. He wanted her to remember the pleasure he'd given her.

He kept the rhythm slow. Steady.

He heard footsteps coming in the hallway.

But he kept thrusting. Her eyes were on him. Only him.

Another thrust. Withdrawal. His thumb pressed over her clit even as he pushed into her creamy sex.

He saw the pleasure flash in her eyes when she came. Felt the ripple of her inner muscles around his length. Only then, *then,* did he thrust harder. Deeper.

He took. Her hips arched, and he went inside her as far as he could go. *Mine.*

The pleasure lashed through him. Strong enough to make him go blind. Strong enough to make him wish that he was someone else.

Someone who didn't have to leave.

Someone who could love.

His heartbeat thundered in his ears.

No, that wasn't just his heartbeat. That was a hard knock at the door.

"Mr. Smith?" a thin voice called out. Probably the hotel manager. "Mr. Smith . . . there are . . . people here to see you."

Cain stared down at Eve for a moment longer. "Don't mention my name."

It was what he'd told her before.

Her lashes lowered.

He wanted to *stay*. But staying—that would mean more danger for Eve. She had a chance now. A chance to do what she'd wanted all along.

She didn't need him.

I need her.

He pulled away from her. Yanked on his clothes and headed for the adjoining room. One jerk, and he broke the lock. There wasn't anyone else in that room, he'd already checked and—

"I've never seen someone so good at walking away."

He glanced back at her words. Eve stood beside the bed, pulling on her clothes. Had that been an echo of pain in her voice?

He didn't want Eve to hurt. Not ever. Not her.

And that's why I'm leaving.

Eve didn't understand, but he still had to hunt. There was something—*someone*—who would be coming for her.

The werewolf hadn't died. But he'd sure been hell-bent on his target.

Eve.

I'll find him. I'll stop him. Before the wolf could go after her. Cain couldn't afford to be caught in the bright light of the press. Not when he needed to stay in the shadows in order to hunt.

And to keep surviving.

"I'm not going far," he told her, wondering if she realized the words were a promise. Maybe she couldn't tell. He knew they sounded like a threat.

Her lips parted. "Cain?"

"Not far," he repeated. The beast inside him wouldn't allow him to leave her, not for long.

"Mr. Smith?" That nasal voice called again. "I-I . . . they want me to let them inside."

"See you soon, baby," Cain told Eve and watched as she turned away.

He shut the door and strolled through the connecting room. He unlocked the room's main door and headed into the hallway, appearing right behind the pack of reporters and cops who'd closed in on Eve when she opened her own hotel room door.

For a moment, he hesitated, but then he heard her say, voice clear and commanding, "My name is Eve Bradley, and I have proof that not only did Richard Wyatt set me up for a series of crimes, but Wyatt *and* Genesis Corporation have been abducting and experimenting on supernaturals . . ."

The reporters were filming. The story would be hitting televisions all across the state within minutes. The networks wouldn't miss out on a juicy story like this one— they'd want in on the action.

Eve's tale wouldn't be hushed up. The cops wouldn't be able to block the reporters.

The truth would get out.

Cain began to whistle as he walked toward the elevator. She'd get her headlines.

Eventually, he'd be back to get *her.*

"All charges are being dropped, Ms. Bradley," Detective Jason Roberts told Eve as he leaned across the table and pinned his baby blues on her. "By this afternoon, you'll be a free woman."

Her lawyer, an attorney sent by the local Channel Seven news team, leaned forward with an intent look on her face. "I want my client free within the hour."

Detective Roberts glanced her way. Those blue eyes—Eve was sure the guy used them to lull suspects into a false sense of security every single day—hardened a bit. "Then you need to go out and take that up with the judge, Ms. Hancock."

With a sniff, the lawyer rose. Janice Hancock stared down at him from her five-foot-three height and gave a smile that could have frozen Hawaii. "I will." She leveled her stare at Eve. "Don't say anything else to these cops, understand?"

Eve nodded. But talking wasn't a problem. Her whole bit was that she *was* talking. Sharing everything she'd learned about Genesis and Richard Wyatt.

It turned out that Uncle Sam wasn't exactly thrilled to be caught in the PR nightmare. Humans were outraged that supernaturals had been held captive and killed for genetic experiments.

When the public got outraged, the government took note—and started playing very, very nicely.

Eve waited until the door shut behind her lawyer. She liked Janice well enough—the woman was a shark, and sharks were always great creatures to behold—but she was planning to ask the detective a few questions of her own while she had the chance. "Did they recover Wyatt's body?" She knew the detective had gone back to Genesis in order to see for himself what waited in Beaumont.

She also knew . . . Roberts wasn't human. She'd caught the flash of fang when he'd been reviewing some of her evidence. The pictures of the mutilated shifters she'd taken from Wyatt's desk—those had *really* pissed off the cop.

"We found him," Roberts said with a shake of his head. "He was just where you said, lying with the stake next to his body and—"

Eve held up her hand. "Wait. Where was the stake?"

Roberts picked up a manila folder and thumbed through the notes. "Next to Wyatt's left hand."

Goose bumps rose on her arms. "When I left him, that stake was in his heart." She'd made sure of it.

Someone else had gone back in that room. Someone who'd taken the stake out—why? To try and help Wyatt?

She looked up and found Roberts staring at her. "Maybe the . . . Subject Thirteen that you mentioned? Perhaps he pulled the stake out?"

No, he'd been the one to shove it into Wyatt's chest . . . but Eve had claimed responsibility for that desperate act. She knew Cain wanted his anonymity, and she was trying to give it to him. *Trying to protect him, as much as I can.* Eve shook her head. "Maybe a guard, maybe someone else . . ." She exhaled. What did it matter? Wyatt was still dead. Genesis was a pile of rubble. Uncle Sam was cleaning up the mess.

"I want to put protection on you."

Eve stilled. After a heartbeat of time, her palms curled around the sides of her chair. "This protection had better not involve me being locked up someplace."

"A safe house—"

Eve shook her head, cutting through his words. "No." Simple, flat. "I'm finishing my story, I can't—"

"Every media outlet in the country is running with your story."

Yes, she knew it. And that was pretty damn awesome.

"While most humans are coming out as being on our side"—Roberts rolled his shoulders and the faint lines bracketing his mouth deepened—"there are others who still think we're just monsters who need to be put down. Those guys aren't going to like all this attention and support you're raising."

"And I'm supposed to do—what?" Eve asked him, lifting her brows. "Cower somewhere because I might get some threats? I was nearly killed—over and over—in the last few days. I'm tough, detective. I can handle whatever comes my way."

"Like you handled Subject Thirteen?"

She hadn't seen that hit coming.

Roberts cocked his head to the side. "We found more files on him in that lab, you know. Wyatt believed that Thirteen had a sociopathic personality and that he was an extreme menace to the human population."

"Yeah, well, Wyatt was also a lying sack of—"

The door opened. Another detective stood there. A balding guy with tired brown eyes. "She's clear. Her lawyer just raised hell with the captain. Bradley gets to walk out now."

Perfect.

Roberts swore. "You need *protection*."

Eve leaned toward him. "What aren't you telling me?"

The other detective turned away.

Eve wasn't about to let this drop. "You found something else at that lab, didn't you?"

A muscle jerked in Roberts's jaw and he gave a grim nod.

"Tell me."

"It's confidential. Can't be leaked to the press and you—you're the most famous reporter in the whole state right now."

She stared back at him. "This might shock the hell out of you, Detective, but I've managed to keep some secrets in my time." But if he didn't want to tell her what had him so all-fired determined that she needed guards, fine.

Eve pushed away from the table and headed for the door.

"Like you kept the wolf's secrets?"

Her breath burned in her lungs. Eve didn't go out that

door. She slammed it shut then spun to face the detective. "What do you know about him?"

"I saw Wyatt's files on him."

And? What? Was she going to have to pull the truth from the detective?

"Wyatt was working on a drug that would amp up a shifter's physical strength."

Yeah, Trace had sure looked like he'd been amped up. His muscles had bulged.

"Wyatt didn't want shifters to transform into animals in order to get that power boost." Roberts's voice was low. "He wanted them to have that power, twenty-four seven."

Eve waited.

Roberts jerked a hand through his hair. "When he first started working with the werewolves, Wyatt used a mix of adrenaline and a drug called Lycan-69, some brew he'd made. It was supposed to blend the animal and man within the shifter. To *always* make them one."

She remembered the way Trace had looked. Not just a man. Bigger. Stronger. With claws and fangs. But he hadn't been able to shift into the form of a wolf, not even when he attacked her and Cain.

Because he *couldn't* change?

"He'd given that dose to two other werewolves, but according to Wyatt, those test subjects had to be terminated."

Terminated. "Why?"

"Because their beasts took over. They lost the ability to reason as men. They had only one desire—to hunt and to kill."

Wyatt had better be burning in hell. "And he gave that same dose to Trace?"

Roberts shook his head. "He was adjusting his formula. Experimenting. Your wolf got Lycan-70."

So maybe the results wouldn't be the same. Maybe—

"Wyatt's report indicated that within five minutes of injection, your friend Trace killed three guards. He couldn't speak. Only growl and snarl. There was no sign of humanity in him. He was just . . ." Robert's voice trailed off.

A monster? A wolf in the body of a man.

She swallowed and hoped she kept the emotion from her face. "So that's why they had his body ready to be burned." Wyatt had been attempting to cover up his failed experiment.

The detective gave a slow nod as his gaze seemed to weigh her. Those deceptive eyes of his had to be seeing far too much. "There's a drugged werewolf out there, Ms. Bradley. One who only wants to kill. You sure that you feel safe being out in the open with him?"

She bared her teeth at him in a brittle smile. "Trace isn't coming for me. If he's functioning only on animal instinct, the last thing he is gonna do is follow me all the way to the city and—"

"I know a lot about animal instinct," Roberts drawled. "Far more than most."

She just bet he did.

"You said that he saw you when he woke up in that furnace room, that he tracked you up the stairs and to Wyatt's office."

She didn't like where this was going.

"His animal had your scent, ma'am. The guy probably doesn't know what the hell is happening to him, but he has *your scent.*" Roberts's hands dropped to his sides. "So trust me when I say, that wolf isn't gonna be forgetting you. Wolves don't forget scents."

No, they didn't. "Thank you for the warning, Detective." She turned away again and reached for the door.

He swore behind her. "You're still refusing protection, aren't you?"

"Yes." Because if she was surrounded by cops and Trace should happen to come for her, they'd kill him.

Maybe I can save him.

She opened the door and walked away from the detective. She could hear noise outside the precinct. Sounded like a roar. But it wasn't an animal, not this time.

Her lawyer sidled over to her. "You ready for this?"

Of course, Janice would know exactly what waited for her. "Always," Eve lied.

Two officers opened the front door of the precinct, and, for the first time in two weeks, Eve got a taste of freedom.

That freedom included being met by a swarm of reporters. Their voices blended together, roaring in her ears.

He followed her when she left the police station. He watched as she talked to the reporters. As she answered their endless questions with a tired smile.

There were shadows under her eyes.

He followed her to a news station. Eve didn't know he was there. No one seemed to pay him any attention.

All eyes were on her.

Her voice was strong and certain as she talked about Genesis. About the supernaturals and the humans who'd lost their lives in experiments gone horribly wrong.

She never glanced his way as the cameras rolled.

He knew she'd talked to government officials. The FBI had been with her for days. She'd cooperated with the agents. They'd helped get the charges against her dropped.

Justice could move swiftly in the paranormal world.

An escort took her back to her hotel. She slipped inside, wearing a ball cap over her head as she eased inside the elevator.

Just before the doors closed, he reached out his hand. The sensors reacted, and the doors slid back open.

He stepped into the elevator. They were alone. Finally, her eyes met his.

"Hello, Eve."

"Cain."

He hadn't been able to stay away.

The doors closed with a ding, and the elevator began to rise.

She took a step forward, then stopped. "I didn't—I didn't expect to see you."

He'd been desperate to see her. So damn desperate that if she hadn't gotten out of that precinct today, he would have ripped the place apart to get to her.

"The cops kept you too long." His fault. He'd let her go in alone. He lifted a hand and traced the shadows under her eyes.

Her smile seemed to squeeze his heart. "Considering the crimes I was wanted for, getting out this fast is pretty much a miracle."

She seemed so delicate to him. He wanted to pull her into his arms but—

The elevator doors opened. *Too soon.* Cain spared a glance over his shoulder. "Get the next fucking ride."

The guy wisely jumped back.

The doors slid closed, and Cain was alone with her again.

Eve shook her head. Did her lips lift into the faintest smile? He'd missed her smile. He'd missed . . . her.

"This isn't smart, Cain," Eve told him as her gaze held his. "I didn't tell the cops your name, but they found videos of you at that lab. They know what you look like." Her gaze searched his. "And I'm pretty sure the FBI is tailing me. They can get to you, through me."

Because he was a threat. Always would be. Cain knew that.

He also knew just where all the FBI tails were. The guys were so obvious. They needed to work on that whole secrecy bit. The paranormals could help them out with that problem. No one did secrecy quite like paranormals, those who preferred to stay under the radar, anyway. *We hadn't all wanted the humans to know about us.*

But there was no changing what had been done, thanks to a few asshole vamps.

Cain gazed back at Eve and asked, "Worried about me?"

"I got you out of one prison." She shook her head. "I don't want to have to drag your hide out of another."

But she would. He knew that. He bent and brushed his lips over hers. How could she taste even sweeter than before? Her mouth was open. Her tongue slid over his. Soft. Sensuous.

"I dreamed about you." His confession. When he'd slept, Cain hadn't seen the fire. Not death. Just her.

He'd known that he had to go back to her.

Her hands pushed against his chest. "Did you find Trace?"

Cain shook his head. He'd gone back to Beaumont. Hunted in the woods. Came up with nothing. There had been no sign of the wolf.

The elevator was slowing as they reached Eve's floor, but he didn't let her go.

He wanted to keep her. Why the hell couldn't he?

Mine.

She was the only thing that made him feel sane. Without her, he'd been . . . lost.

"You have to protect yourself," she told him, pulling away.

Cain stepped toward the back wall of the elevator. When the doors opened, she was the one who exited, and he watched her leave.

She didn't talk to him. Didn't glance back. Probably too worried that others were watching. On this floor, they were. The FBI had four agents stationed on Eve's floor.

But he had another way of getting to Eve. Without all

the eyes seeing him. Night had fallen in the city. Night was his time.

Just as she was *his*.

Everything was gone. The research. The facilities. The funding.

His son.

Gone.

And that bitch was on the news. Spouting her nonsense about truth and torture. He could show her real torture.

The same way he'd shown her mother.

Jeremiah stared at the TV screen. He knew Eve Bradley's face so well. It was the face he'd seen on the video at the Beaumont facility, the video that showed his son's last, desperate moments.

Eve had shot Richard in the head, then she'd ordered her lover to stake him.

Did she actually think there would be no punishment for her crime? The police had *let* her go. Just let the woman walk away.

Jeremiah wouldn't make the same mistake.

He already knew where she was. And where Eve was . . . the phoenix would be close by.

A phoenix could never stay away from his mate. The need to see her, the yearning, would be too much.

Eve had been sequestered by the police for days. That time must have driven the phoenix crazy. He'd be willing to risk anything to get close to her again.

Jeremiah smiled. He might not be able to kill the phoenix—damn immortal beast—but he could sure take care of the woman.

And without her, the phoenix's life wouldn't be worth living.

CHAPTER NINETEEN

Eve was in bed when she heard the rap on her balcony door. She sat up, heart racing, sure that she must be dreaming. Then the rap came again.

She was on the fourteenth floor. How the hell could someone be *knocking* at her balcony door?

Sucking in a deep gulp of air, Eve grabbed for her gun. Yeah, she had one. Courtesy of her lawyer. She was also more than ready to use the weapon if she needed to do so.

A late-night visitor, one who came by way of the *balcony* . . .

"Eve." Just her name, but she knew that voice.

Eve put the gun back on the nightstand and hurried across the room. Before she could reach for the lock, the balcony door slid open.

Cain stood there, his hair wet from the light rain that had begun to fall.

Eve shook her head. How had the guy gotten out there?

"I didn't want to scare you."

Wait. Did he smile? *He did.*

"So I knocked first."

Fourteenth freaking floor. "How did you get out here?"

Cain glanced up with raised brows.

Oh no, the guy had better not be telling her that he'd just dropped from the floor above her. But that wicked smile on his lips said . . .

Eve grabbed his arm and yanked him fully inside her room. "You're crazy!"

His eyes flickered. "Yes."

Not exactly the response she'd expected. Eve backed away from him.

"I should probably be staying the hell away from you," he said, his voice low and growling, "but I *can't*." His gaze raked her. "Sometimes, I feel like I need you more than I need fucking air."

The words were dark. No, *he* was dark. A big, dangerous shadow who stalked her across the room.

Eve was too conscious of the rumpled bed that waited behind her—and of her own need. Whenever Cain was around, she *needed*.

"I can't leave you again." The words held a ragged edge. "I think you might be the only thing keeping me sane."

That scared the hell out of her. But when he advanced on her, Eve didn't retreat. Not that time. She put her hand on his chest. "What happens to you?"

His head tilted to the side. His body was warm. So big. *Fire.*

"When you burn, Cain, what happens?" She'd wanted to ask before, but now nothing held her back. She wanted to know everything about him. Good. Bad.

Just as he knew everything about her.

His gaze slid over her and she felt it like a touch of his hands. "There are some things that you're better off not knowing."

Not this. "Where do you go?" The twist in her gut already told her.

"Hell."

The shake of her head was an instinctive denial. Not him. *No.*

"The flames from hell are the only ones strong enough to bring me back. So I die, the beast within me flies to hell, then that fire gives me the strength to come back."

"What is—" *It like?*

"More pain that you can ever imagine. Screams that don't stop. Agony that rips me apart."

He did this every time he burned? His heart pounded in a strong, steady beat beneath her fingertips. "Is that why, when you come back, you don't seem to know me?" She hated when he looked at her with only fury and fire in his eyes.

Just as she hated that Trace's eyes now showed only the beast.

As Cain stared at her, there was a tenderness in his gaze. A sadness. "Sometimes, I don't know my own damn self. I only know hate. Fury. The fire."

He was . . . darker each time. She'd felt that darkness growing.

"I have to fight to find myself again." He exhaled slowly. "But the last time, the last *two* times, I knew you when I came back. Not your name, just . . . *you.*"

Eve wasn't sure what that meant.

"You kept me in control."

Uh-oh. *That* had been control? If that had been a controlled Cain, Eve didn't want to see him without his restraint.

"Because you're mine."

Her heart lurched at that. "Cain . . ."

He stood before her. The back of her knees hit the bed.

"I climbed out of hell for you. To come back to you. When I rose, I wanted to kill everyone around me—anyone who stood between us." His words were so fierce.

"I'm not . . . safe, Eve. I've known that my whole life. Each time I die, I always know I could be a rising away from insanity. From not ever remembering who I am and letting the beast loose to kill and burn."

"You haven't hurt me." He hadn't. Not even when he'd been in that cage at Genesis. Subject Thirteen. The man with the wild eyes and the leashed power.

"I can't." The words seemed dragged from him. "I need you too much. If anything happened to you . . ."

Eve tilted her head back. "Nothing is going to happen to me." They were safe now. The big, bad beast that was Genesis was gone.

"If you die, you *can't* rise. You can't come back to me."

She caught his hand and pressed it over her heart. "I won't leave you." Didn't he understand? She'd been trying to protect him for so long. The story, the press, the days with the cops—all of it had been to protect him.

But he'd come back. Even though he could have just vanished, he'd found her. He'd put himself at risk for her.

"You deserve better." His words were gritted out.

And Cain deserved more than hell and madness.

"I want you." As she stared into his eyes, she saw the wildness flare. Saw the struggle for him to hold on to his control.

Screw control. For them both. Maybe they should rely a little less on control and more on need. Lust.

Trust.

Love?

She pushed him back.

Cain's eyes widened and he began to shake his head. "Eve . . ."

Did he think she was telling him no? She'd never tell him no. Not Cain. Not her dark lover.

Not the man who'd walked through hell for her. Literally.

She dropped to her knees before him. She didn't fear his beast. Didn't fear the man.

He'd given her pleasure before, held himself back to make sure the wild rush was hers. Now, it was her turn.

Her hands reached for the snap of his jeans. The zipper eased down between her fingers.

No underwear. But then, Cain wasn't exactly the type for silk boxers.

His cock pushed toward her, fully erect, the head already gleaming with a drop of moisture. The width of his cock was easily bigger than her wrist. Wide, long.

She licked her lips—then she licked him.

His breath hissed out even as his hands lowered to wrap around her shoulders. "You don't have to—"

Another slow lick. Then she eased back, just enough to look up into his eyes. "I want to." Still meeting his eyes, she kissed his flesh again. Opened her lips. Her tongue tasted the moisture on the tip of his arousal.

Tangy. Masculine.

She'd be having more, please.

Her mouth widened even as her left hand circled the base of his erection. She took his cock between her lips, sucked lightly, and pumped with her hand.

His fingers tightened on her shoulders. His hips pushed toward her. So eager.

She liked him this way. Cain didn't need to worry about control. Right then, she had it.

It took Eve a moment to realize that her own hips were rocking up with each stroke of her tongue over his flesh.

Tasting him turned her on so much.

She took him deeper into her mouth. Learned where he liked for her to lick. To suck.

"Eve . . ." There was a warning note in his voice.

She ignored the warning. Story of her life.

She ignored the growl and the hard hands on her shoulders and she gave him pleasure—even as she pleasured herself. She took more, deeper, loving the feel of him within her mouth.

"No more!" Cain's hands pushed her back. "I . . . can't . . . wait . . ."

She didn't want him to wait. Eve reached for him again.

In a flash, Cain had her on the bed. Her robe, a loaner from the hotel, was tossed across the room. He had her flat on her back with her legs spread, his hands holding hers to the bed.

His cock pushed against her sex. "You're wet."

More like soaking, but she wasn't going to argue. Eve arched her hips. *"Now."* She could be demanding, too.

She'd sure missed him over the last two weeks.

Cain thrust into her. He groaned. She moaned. And it was wonderful. Perfect. He filled her core, stretched her, sent pulses of pleasure rushing through her.

Then he started to move. Thrusting and withdrawing. Her legs locked around his hips and she held on for that wild ride.

Control was long gone, for both of them. There was no restraint. Only need. A desperate passion driving them toward a release that couldn't wait.

Her nails dug into his skin. His mouth pressed against her throat.

"Mine." Cain's growl, but it could have been hers. She'd thought of him as hers for so long.

Eve stopped thinking in the next instant. Pleasure hit her. Not a ripple. Not a wave. A freaking avalanche of pleasure that had the air freezing in her lungs as her whole body seemed to explode.

Cain was with her. His hold tightened on her. He drove deeper into her and shuddered with his release.

A person could die from that much pleasure. So . . . *good.*

Eve held him, riding out the climax, knowing only the

strong feel of his body against hers and the frantic pounding of their heartbeats.

When Cain finally rose above her, Eve's hands tightened instinctively around him. She didn't want him going anywhere. Couldn't they just pretend the rest of the world didn't exist? For a little while? Was that too much to ask?

She blinked open her eyes and found him staring at her. Watching her with a look she'd never seen before. "Cain? What is it?"

His fingers trailed over her arm, even as he kept his cock within her. "I should have left you."

Well, damn. Her brows snapped together. "Dude, pillow talk does *not* start this way."

It was his turn to blink. When she began to squirm underneath him—*seriously, his timing was shit*—he tightened his hold on her and held her still. "That's not what I . . . dammit, I just don't want you hurt because of me!"

She stared at him. "You haven't hurt me." Not even when he came back from the fire.

"Genesis kept files on me. The government has copies of all those experiments. Do you think they're just gonna let me walk away?"

"If they're smart, yes, they will." She'd gotten the impression from the FBI agents who'd visited her that—well, they were *afraid* of Subject Thirteen.

They hadn't exactly looked eager to walk into Cain's fire. They could be smarter than Wyatt.

Cain's gaze was so deep. "I don't want you hurt."

"I won't be." The promise seemed easy enough to give. Especially when she was wrapped in his arms. "Look, I might not be able to die and come back like you, but I'm strong, Cain." He should have seen that.

"I know." His lips brushed over hers. "That's why I want you so much."

Want. Need. Lust. There was plenty of that between them. Did she dare mention that for her, there was more?

Love.

Eve wasn't sure when the phoenix had burned his way into her heart. He had, though. She thought about him all the time. Wanted to protect him. Wanted to make love with him, of course, but she also just wanted . . .

"I want to go to the beach." The words were silly, but they came out anyway.

Cain frowned down at her.

"I want to see you in the sunlight," she told him and smiled at the image in her mind. "I want to see you in the sand. Without fire. Without danger. Without anything but us." He'd smile then, she was sure of it. She'd get to hear him laugh.

They could just be a man and a woman.

She wanted to see what Cain looked like when he was happy. "Can't we just be normal?" she whispered to him.

His gaze held hers. There was a flash in his eyes. Longing. She knew that look.

Pain.

No, wait. She hadn't meant that she *wanted* him to be normal. She loved him as he was. Fire and all. She'd just wanted—

The phone rang. They both tensed and glanced at the bedside table.

"Probably more reporters," Cain said, voice rumbling.

Eve shook her head. No, there were only a few people who knew she'd be there. She reached for the phone, even as she stayed in Cain's arms.

"Hello?"

"Ms. Bradley?"

Detective Roberts. She recognized his voice instantly. "What's happened?" If he was calling her, there had to be a problem.

"There was a werewolf attack in the club district a few minutes ago."

Hell. Her fingers clamped around the phone as she stared back at Cain. He was so close he had to have heard the cop's words. "You're sure it was Trace?" There were other werewolves out there, even ones who attacked. They could get pissed off, just like anyone else. Actually, they got pissed *more* than most folks.

Werewolves weren't exactly known for their peaceful natures.

"Witness described a white male, said he was about six foot five . . ."

When she'd seen Trace in that lab, he *had* been that big. Before, he'd been skirting six feet.

"Fangs, claws bursting from his fingers—"

Still, that could be—

"And he was shouting your name."

Okay, that narrowed it down. "I'm coming."

"No, you aren't. I'm giving you this call as a warning. The guy is here in the city, and he's hunting you. I *told* you that you needed protection."

Eve's eyes were on Cain. He reached for the phone. "She has protection."

"Who is this?" Roberts demanded.

"Her protection."

"Leave that job to the cops, buddy."

"If I do that, you'll all just die." Brutal words. True words. "I'm coming for the wolf."

Eve straightened her shoulders. No, *they* were coming.

Cain hung up the phone.

Her heart was still beating too fast.

"Eve . . ."

"I want to try and save him." She didn't know how yet. She just had to *try.* "Cain, I was alone my whole life, okay? After my parents died . . ." *Because of Genesis and Wyatt's twisted father* ". . . I never felt like I had any family. Until Trace."

Cain's jaw tightened. He eased from her body. Dressed in silence.

So did she. "He was the closest thing to a brother I ever had. Trace always had my back. He watched out for me, and I watched out for him."

Cain was staring at her. Just . . . waiting.

"I can't give up on him." She wouldn't. "We *can* help him." Someway. If some toxic mix of drugs had made him like this, there had to be a drug combination that could pull him back.

"We'll help him," Cain agreed.

Yes.

"We'll contain him and make sure that he doesn't hurt any humans."

Right. Containment, then cure. They could *do this.*

"But if he turns on you, Eve, if he tries to kill you . . ."

She shook her head. "It's not coming to that." Even she knew the words were a lie. He'd already tried to kill her twice.

But she still saw him as the seventeen-year-old boy she'd found on the side of the road. Alone. Just as lost as she was.

They'd needed each other.

They'd become a family.

You didn't turn your back on family.

Because of that, because she had to have hope for Trace, Eve asked, "Do the tears of a phoenix . . . can they really heal?"

Cain glanced up at her. His gaze was hooded.

"Wyatt . . . said that he wasn't able to make you cry." No matter what torture the sick freak had used. "But he thought your tears could heal . . ."

Maybe they could heal Trace. Maybe they wouldn't need drugs to bring the werewolf back to them.

Cain shook his head, and the hope of a swift healing died within Eve. "Those stories have always been out there, the whispers that my kind can heal." His lips twisted. "But the thing is . . . those tales are freaking bull. We *can't* cry."

Eve stared at him.

"Wyatt tried, all right. Every trick he could think of. No matter how much pain he gave me, it didn't work. The bastard even came up with some scientific shit about my tear ducts being abnormal, non-functioning. Hell yeah, they're non-functioning . . . my eyes *burn* with my power. My body doesn't work like a human's 'cause I'm not. Never will be."

She nodded. "I figured he was wrong. I just . . ." *Hoped.* "We'll find another way." There had to be another way.

"I can't shed tears. There's no healing power in me. There's just the beast I carry, Eve. The one who lives for fire and destruction." Cain stalked toward her, his steps slow and heavy. "There are some other things you need to understand."

She waited, body full of nervous energy.

"*You* are my priority. If Trace comes at you with his claws and fangs, I'll take the werewolf out."

She'd have to make sure that didn't happen. Just as she'd have to make sure that she *did* find a way to cure Trace. A way that didn't involve a phoenix's magic.

Eve turned away, grabbing for her bag, but Cain's fingers closed around her arm. "You aren't alone." The words were gruff. "No matter what happens, you won't be alone." His lips brushed over hers.

When he stepped back to release her, Eve grabbed his hand. She didn't know what would happen, but she needed to tell him how she felt. "Cain, I love you."

He just stared back at her.

She'd been hoping for a better reaction.

Her chin lifted. "And you aren't alone, either, understand?"

She wasn't sure he did. The guy looked pretty shellshocked. Eve smiled at him. Her phoenix. He'd understand, soon enough. She'd make him. "One day, I'm getting you on that beach . . ."

Not today. Today, they had a werewolf to catch.

Eve turned away and headed for the door.

"Why?" His voice was raspy.

"Because you'll love the sand between your toes." She got the feeling Cain hadn't enjoyed many free, fun moments in his life. That was going to change. She'd change it for him.

"No . . . why would you say you loved me?"

She glanced back at him.

"You don't." His words seemed so certain. "You *can't*."

It was her turn to ask. "Why not?"

"Because I'm a monster, Eve. I destroy everything around me."

She kept her face expressionless. He said he was a monster, but he sounded like a lost little boy. He should have known love before this moment.

He'd always know it now.

"You haven't destroyed me," she told him softly, swallowing the lump in her throat. "And you won't." Then, because she thought he needed to hear the words again and because the guy had *better* start getting used to the fact, she repeated, "I love you."

The pain that flashed on his face hurt her heart. It hurt even more when he whispered, *"Don't."*

Didn't he realize that he deserved to be loved? Everyone did. Once Trace was safe, she'd prove that truth to Cain.

She headed into the hallway. Before she could leave the

room, Cain grabbed her hand. "I know another way. A way unwanted guests won't see."

Frowning, Eve hesitated.

"I got in without being seen," Cain said, "and I'll get out that way, too. We don't want the Feds following us."

Or taking a shot at Trace.

"Trust me?" he asked, as he shut the door.

Her breath whispered out, but Eve nodded.

Cain led her back through the balcony door. The wind blew against her, carrying a faint chill. Eve looked down at the steep drop.

I can't rise.

"No one's on the floor below you. I made sure of it." His lips twisted. "I booked the room under an assumed name."

The room above her and the room below . . . the guy had been prepared.

He wrapped his arms around her. "Just hold on to me." She did.

He lifted her up. Stood on the edge of the railing. They fell. The wind whipped past them. One instant—

His body jerked, turning quickly, twisting impossibly in midair.

Then they were on solid ground. On the balcony just below her room. Eve could only shake her head. The man just kept being full of surprises.

"My reflexes aren't exactly human . . ."

Nothing about him was . . . and she loved him for that. Eve didn't want an average guy. She wanted Cain.

He led the way through the dark to the room's main door. The door clicked open. Cain and Eve eased into the hallway. Instead of heading for the big elevator on the right, Cain guided her to the staff elevator nestled just a few feet away. He pulled a key card from his pocket and swiped it over the access pad. The door slid open.

"You're a handy guy," she told him, impressed. Cain had definitely thought of everything.

He'd make for a fantastic reporter . . . or a criminal.

One brow rose. "This elevator will take us to the hotel's back entrance. Staff only. We should be able to leave without anyone seeing us."

One problem solved. Now, if they could just stop a raging werewolf, well, then they'd be set.

Getting to the club district was easy enough. Finding the cops—yeah, another easy task. They just looked for the flashing blue lights and the crowd of people.

There were no bodies on the ground, but Eve saw two men getting bandaged and loaded into the back of an ambulance. Another ambulance had already left—they'd passed it when they arrived.

There was still blood in the street.

Eve and Cain hung back, blending into the crowd of spectators. She wished she had a shifter's sense of smell so that she could find Trace but—

Cain inhaled. *"That way."*

She had something better. Her own personal phoenix.

They slid back through the crowd, heading for the alley on the left. She felt like dozens of eyes were on her and tensed, glancing back.

But she just saw the crowd. So many faces. They were focused on the blood. The chaos. Not her.

So why was she so sure that she was being watched?

Trace.

Cain's arm brushed against hers, and Eve almost jumped.

"There." He pointed into the darkness because, of course, where else would he point? Not like a werewolf would be hiding in the light.

Eve followed him. They headed into the crack between

the buildings. Moved away from the crowd. One block. Two. Then . . .

Eve saw the smashed window on the old building that slumped near the corner. Anyone could have smashed that window, though. A vagrant, someone wanting some shelter from the night.

A werewolf.

"He's inside." Cain had tilted his head to the right.

She'd been wondering just how good the guy's hearing was. Now she knew. They were at least twenty yards away from that building.

"Sounds like he's tearing the place apart."

Eve sucked in a breath and they headed for the rundown building. Cain knocked the rest of the window's glass out of the way and climbed through the opening first. Then he reached for her, holding her carefully to make sure she didn't get cut.

And he thinks he's a monster?

She heard the sounds of destruction as soon as her feet touched down inside the building. A crash. The shattering of glass. A wolf's howl.

She spun around, and through the darkness, she saw his eyes. Far too bright. Trace's eyes had never been that shade of green. Not while he'd been in human form. But as a wolf, his eyes had always glowed with power.

Part of her—a very big part—expected him to charge through the darkness and attack her. Cain must have expected that, too, because he positioned his body in front of her.

But Trace didn't attack. Instead, she heard the scrape of claws over metal, and Trace growled out, *"Help . . . me . . ."*

Tears stung her eyes. He'd finally spoken again. The words had been hoarse, rusty, but *he'd spoken*. Trace was coming back to her. Slowly, but he was fighting. "We'll help you," she promised as she stepped around Cain.

He tensed.

Eve made no move to approach Trace. She knew better than to charge at a wounded animal, and that was exactly what Trace was. "Do you know me?"

"*Eve . . .*"

Good. "Then you know I'd never hurt you. We're family."

Silence. Then more of that horrible scraping. She didn't flinch, but goose bumps rose on her arms. "Trust me, Trace. Cain and I can help you." They'd find a way to help him. They wouldn't give up.

He came from the shadows. Too big. Too strong. Muscled. A man's body but a beast's eyes and claws and fangs. His steps were so slow. Tortured. "*Help me . . .*" he said again.

"I will, Trace," Eve promised at once as Cain remained silent. "I will—"

"*Kill me,*" Trace's words cut through hers.

She could only shake her head. No, that was the last thing she'd ever do.

"*Or I'll kill . . . you . . .*" he rasped.

"The hell you will." Cain was talking. "You better dig fucking deep inside, wolf. Get your control. Because you aren't hurting her."

Trace's shoulders shook as he sucked in heaving gulps of air, but then he tensed. His gaze flew behind them to that broken window. He leaped forward.

Cain was turning then, too. Whirling around to face the threat they both had sensed.

When Eve turned, she saw Detective Roberts coming inside. His gaze found hers, then flew to the werewolf coming at him. He lifted his gun to fire.

"No!" Eve screamed.

He emptied his gun in Trace. Kept firing until Cain grabbed him and yanked the weapon away from the cop.

Trace had fallen to the ground. Eve rushed to his side. His eyes were open and the smell around him—

Silver bullets.

Not just normal silver. Some sort of liquid silver that was leaking out of Trace. Where had the cop gotten bullets like that?

Cain had hurried back to Trace's side. Jaw locking, he glanced up at Eve. She knew he thought Trace was dead.

Because I think he is, too.

Gut twisting, she whirled back to confront the detective.

"I'm sorry," he told her, shoulders slumping, "but I didn't have a choice."

She didn't think he was just talking about Trace.

"The bullets won't kill him. They'll just keep the werewolf immobile until all the silver drains out of him." The detective's hand reached under his coat, and Eve wasn't surprised to see him produce a second weapon.

Or to find that weapon aimed at her.

"Bad mistake," Cain told him.

Roberts frowned and shot a glance his way. "Let me guess . . . Subject Thirteen?"

Cain flashed a vicious smile. "The last man who called me that wound up with a stake in his heart."

"Yeah, and his old man's real pissed about that."

Cain tensed and his gaze flickered to the broken window. Eve frowned. A few moments later, she heard the thud of approaching footsteps.

His old man's real pissed about that . . .

Her mouth had gone bone dry. "According to my sources, Jeremiah Wyatt is dead." She threw the words out deliberately, looking for a reaction. Richard Wyatt had said otherwise, back in that nightmare at Beaumont. He'd *told* her that his father was alive. So the news stories about his death? *Faked*. "So it doesn't really matter how pissed he is in hell."

"If only."

That had been the reaction she'd expected. More confirmation—Jeremiah Wyatt *was* still alive, and the detective knew it.

"There's a cure, you know"—Roberts straightened his shoulders—"for whatever the hell they did to him." A jerk of his gun toward Trace's prone body. "They have some kind of injection that can make him right again." Softer, "Make *her* right again."

"They're coming for us," Cain said.

Eve looked at him and saw he'd already begun to stir fire near his palms.

Roberts shook his head. "No, they're only coming for you, Thirteen. Only for you."

The doors of the building opened with a long creak. Armed men raced inside.

A trap.

"I knew you'd come for the werewolf," Roberts said. "Well, actually, *he* knew."

Thud.

Thud.

Thud.

That wasn't her heartbeat.

About five men had entered the building. Not cops. Not even guys in military uniforms. Men in battered jeans, thick coats—all holding guns.

Like the guns would do them much good against Cain's fire.

"You're making a mistake," Eve told them. "I'm clear of all charges. The FBI is backing me up. The media is—"

Thud.

Thud.

One of the armed men stepped back. When he moved,

Eve saw an older guy with stooped shoulders, gray hair, and—and Wyatt's green eyes. "The government might have cleared you, Ms. Bradley. *I* haven't."

She was staring at a ghost. "Jeremiah Wyatt. You're supposed to be dead."

"So I am." His lips pursed as he studied her. "But it's your mother who's really dead. Your father. I know—I sent the men who killed them both."

Pain stabbed into her, but before she could speak, Cain attacked.

His fire flashed out. One man down. He ripped the gun from another. Aimed and shot at a third. Before that guy had even fallen, Cain had hit a fourth in the leg with a bullet. The men were falling like flies around Jeremiah Wyatt as he just stood there, smiling, while they screamed.

A big coat covered most of his body. From his neck to his feet. "You and your fire . . ." Jeremiah whispered. "Richard thought he could control you. Such a foolish mistake."

The guards were on the ground. Some were crawling away. None were trying to fight.

"That the best you got?" Cain demanded.

Jeremiah shook his head. "No."

No? Eve rocked back on her heels. Roberts was still there, sweating. When the fire had started flashing, the guy had looked so scared.

But he stepped forward, pale but determined. "I got them here—I did what you wanted—now give me the cure!"

Frowning, Jeremiah turned his focus to the cop. "Ah, yes . . . your *sister*, wasn't it? Richard had thought she'd be such a prime candidate for the program."

Eve got a crystal-clear picture of just why the cop had sold her out.

Family. She'd been right. It *was* hard to turn your back on them.

"The cure," Roberts snapped, his gun aimed at Jeremiah Wyatt.

How is that bastard still alive? He'd reportedly died of a heart attack ten years before. After Richard's snarled words at Beaumont, she'd dug up pictures of Jeremiah Wyatt on her computer at the hotel. Grainy photos had showed his funeral.

His casket must have been empty.

And the man should be pushing ninety, but . . . he looked about seventy. Maybe sixty-five.

Experiments.

"You want the cure?" Jeremiah drawled. He didn't seem concerned that his men had abandoned him. That he was pretty much *the* sitting duck right then. A phoenix to his left. A gun carrying cop to his right.

And a pissed-off reporter glaring dead center at him.

This was the man who'd ruined her life. Taken away her family. Left her lost and alone.

She'd never known so much hate.

"Kill her," Jeremiah said, shrugging.

At first, she thought Jeremiah was giving Roberts an order. *My execution.* Cain must have thought the same thing because he lunged for the cop.

But Roberts wasn't aiming the gun at Eve. He still had the barrel pointed at Jeremiah. "What?"

"There is no cure. Your sister's rabid. Just like him." A wave of Jeremiah's hand toward Trace's prone body. But Trace wasn't exactly prone right then. He was trying to roll over. To crawl toward Wyatt.

"You said—you told me there was a serum! A drug she needed!" Roberts was shaking. The barrel of his gun trembled. "You told me to lure Eve here, to get her inside this warehouse, and you'd give me the cure!" His teeth snapped together. *"Give me the damn cure!"*

"I did." Jeremiah's voice was calm and easy. "Kill her.

Cut off her head or burn her. That's the only way you'll ever free her. Once the wolves go rabid, they don't come back."

"You're a sick freak," Cain snapped.

Jeremiah's gaze turned toward him. That green stare narrowed to slits of ice. "You killed my son. He was such a good experiment, and you killed him."

"Richard Wyatt wasn't an experiment!" Eve yelled at him. "He was a person. A twisted psycho of a person, but he wasn't just an experiment!"

Jeremiah's lips tightened. "We're all experiments."

The guy was deranged. No big shock. Not considering the way Richard had turned out. Like father . . .

Jeremiah's lips relaxed. Eased into the twisted semblance of a smile. "I made Richard stronger. I made him better. When I started my work, the boy actually wanted me to stop. Told me I was hurting him."

Thud.

The cane pounded onto the floor.

"There is no growth without pain. No life without suffering." That faint smile was still on his lips when he pointed his finger at Cain. "You're about to suffer."

"Old man, I'm not scared of you." Cain turned away from him. He reached for Eve, but she pulled back.

"Get Trace." They'd take him to a hospital. He'd get help. Did Jeremiah really think he was the only one who worked in the field of shifter genetics? There were other experts out there. Others who didn't torture and kill.

Maybe there wasn't a cure yet. But there damn well could be one.

Cain hefted Trace over his shoulder.

Roberts hadn't moved. "You son of a bitch," he said to Jeremiah. "I risked my badge for you . . . I want my sister back!"

"That bitch is as good as dead." The words were snarled,

and before Eve could even blink, Jeremiah had lunged across the room. He opened his mouth—

And sank his teeth into the cop's throat.

Vampire.

No wonder the man didn't look ninety. He'd stopped aging. Maybe that had been him pictured in that coffin after all. Still and pale . . . a newly transformed vampire.

Eve grabbed Jeremiah's arms and yanked him away from Roberts—even as Roberts fired his gun.

Bang. Bang. Bang.

Two bullets blasted into Jeremiah's chest.

One went right through his body and hit Eve.

A roar filled the building as Eve staggered back. She lifted her hand to her chest, and blood soaked her fingers.

Roberts stared at her with wide, shocked eyes. "I didn't mean—"

She tried to nod. Managed to stagger back. Cain grabbed her. Wait. Where was Trace? Where— *"Trace."*

"Screw Trace. I'm getting you out of here." Cain's gaze was burning, flickering with flames. He pulled her into his arms. "It's all right, you're going to be all right . . ."

"No, she's not." Jeremiah's cold voice. He was still standing? "Because she's not getting out of here alive." He laughed, even as he swiped away the dripping blood on his chin. "I thought I'd slowly drain Ms. Bradley and kill her, make her suffer for what she did to my boy, but she's already dead . . ."

No, she wasn't. Eve wanted to scream at him, but she couldn't talk.

"Only a few moments left, then that heart of hers will stop. That bullet—*it killed her.*"

"I'm so sorry . . ." The detective's voice. Eve couldn't see him.

Cain was running toward the door with her in his arms, but then he staggered to a stop.

"You aren't leaving," Jeremiah snarled. "Not yet."

Eve forced her eyelids to stay open. Jeremiah had dropped his act. Ditched his cane, and moved with that super vampire speed. And . . . as she watched, he reached into his big overcoat and pulled out a small, black box.

Her breath choked out. She'd seen a box like that before. On another story that she'd worked on. A box like that had been found in the aftermath . . .

"I taught my son so much," Jeremiah said as he lifted the box in his bloodstained hands. "About genetics. About life. About the possibilities before us . . ."

In the aftermath of an explosion that had wiped out a home. A family.

"I also taught him about destruction. About how easy it can be to kill." His fingers hovered over the small switch on the side of the box. "With just one . . . touch . . . of a finger . . ."

He'd wired the building. Eve could only shake her head. He'd wired this place, the same way that his son had wired the chocolate shop.

No wonder Jeremiah had wanted Roberts to lure them to *this* warehouse. Get them in . . .

Then watch us explode.

"Bombs are all around us," Jeremiah said. "This is the end."

"Get the fuck out of the way!" Cain snarled, but he wasn't sending out his fire to blast Jeremiah. If he did, Jeremiah might hit that switch.

The whole building could explode then. *Would* explode, because she didn't think the guy was bluffing. Eve didn't even know how powerful the explosion could be. There were humans close by. How many would be hurt?

The pain in her chest was easing. Numbing. She could barely feel anything. Even her fingertips.

Her hands slumped down, dangling uselessly, but she made her eyes stay open. *Open.*

"They'll think your fire destroyed this place," Jeremiah said as his fingertips caressed the small, black case. "Subject Thirteen strikes again. He just couldn't let the woman he loved go—obsession drove him." His hand lifted, his fingers curling around the detonator. "And he killed . . ."

"You'll kill yourself!" Cain yelled at him. "The fire won't kill me. It won't kill her! Just you, bastard!"

"I'm ready to die." But he wasn't pushing the detonator.

Eve tried to pull in a deep breath. Couldn't.

"The vampire blood should have made me younger, given the years back to me." Jeremiah shook his head. "Not trapped me like this! And now that you've taken Richard . . ."

Thud. Thud.

It sounded like the old man's cane. But he wasn't using it. That too-slow thud was Eve's heartbeat. "Cain . . ."

He spun away from Jeremiah and raced for the other side of the building.

"Now I'm ready for death." Jeremiah's voice followed them.

So did the explosion. A fast, driving blast that lifted Cain and Eve into the air even as a furnace of heat swept over them.

The walls and the roof shattered. Debris rained down on them. The hungry flames consumed everything in sight.

CHAPTER TWENTY

Cain crawled from beneath the rubble. A slab of concrete had broken his leg. Gritting his teeth, he shoved the heavy stone aside. He was bleeding. Pain swept through him in driving waves of agony.

Internal injuries.

The fire hadn't killed him, but he'd be dead soon—the impact of the explosion was too much for his body to handle. His right arm was shattered. His head concussed. And inside . . .

His organs were fucking mush.

Focus on her.

Eve was in his arms. He'd used his body to protect her as best he could. He'd taken the hits, the full force of the explosion, for her.

But she wasn't moving.

He couldn't walk, so he dragged her with him. Cradled her as best he could. "Help!" He screamed out at the night not because he wanted to be saved, but because he needed someone to come and help her.

Eve couldn't die. If she did . . . *she won't come back to me.*

His body was shutting down. He felt it. Felt the surge of the fire inside him. *No.* He couldn't leave her yet. She needed him.

He put his hand on her chest, trying to stop that blood

flow. The bullet had torn through her delicate body. So much blood. It soaked her shirt. Poured through his fingers.

Beautiful Eve. She looked broken. A cut sliced across her forehead. Her eyes were closed, her lashes casting heavy shadows on her cheeks. She was so . . . still.

"Don't do . . . this," he grated out as he kept dragging her. They were almost clear of the wreckage, and he could hear sirens in the distance. Help was coming for her. She just had to hold on for him. A few more moments . . .

But she didn't stir at his words.

Another few desperate inches. Glass cut into his legs. Dammit. He hadn't just broken one leg. He'd fucking nearly lost the second leg.

Jeremiah had known what he was doing after all. It hadn't been the fire that hurt Cain. It had been the destruction. The heavy blasts that had sent walls tumbling onto him.

At least that bastard is dead. Blown into a thousand pieces. No vampire could come back from that.

Now if Cain could just save Eve.

He couldn't feel her heartbeat beneath his fingers. "Eve?" He pressed harder against her chest. Had that been a heartbeat? A weak flutter? "Eve, don't you do this to me!"

She didn't respond.

The fire burned within him, raging higher as the fear spiked within his blood.

I'm losing her.

He couldn't. He didn't want to be without her.

Cain shook Eve. "Open your eyes." She had to open her eyes. He had to see that she was okay. Before he left, before the fire took him, he had to be sure . . .

He choked on blood. Death wanted him. Death was fucking coming.

Wait.

He wasn't ready for death.

"Open your eyes!"

Eve couldn't die. She'd said—she'd said she loved him. No one had ever said that to him before. And . . . and he'd wanted to tell her that he loved her, too.

How could he not love her? The woman had obsessed him from the first. Addicted him. Damn near broken him with lust and need and then . . .

Then it had become more. Not just a physical need. He'd wanted to touch her all the time. To see her smile. To protect her. To make her happy.

Love. He hadn't been given a whole lot of it in his life, but he'd recognized the emotion for what it was.

She was the only thing he'd ever loved in all his days. How was he supposed to lose her now?

He shook her harder. "Open your eyes!"

But she wasn't. She was so cold, and even the heat from his skin didn't seem to warm her.

Cain hunched over Eve's body. "Please, don't do this to me." He hadn't begged for anything before. Yet for Eve, he'd beg. For Eve, he would do anything.

Her lips parted. Her breath whispered out so softly.

"Eve?"

He bent his head over her. She was talking. She was still alive!

Her words were whisper quiet. Even with his enhanced hearing, he almost couldn't hear them. Was almost afraid he'd imagined them.

"Love . . ." More a breath than a word.

His chest burned. Not from the fire swirling within him. But because Eve was ripping his heart out. "I love you," he told her. He pressed a kiss to her cheek. His blood stained her face. "Eve, did you hear me? I said . . . I loved you. *I. Love.You."* Don't leave me.

"No . . . walk . . ."

What the hell was she talking about?

"On . . . *beach* . . ."

He lifted her against his chest. The sirens were coming closer. *They won't make it in time.* He knew it, damn it. "We'll walk on the beach," he told her as he buried his face in the curve of her neck. His eyes burned, but not just from the fire. From tears.

He'd never shed tears before.

For her.

"We'll walk on the beach," he whispered, willing to promise her anything. "We'll walk in the waves. I'll hold you in the water. You'll be so beautiful . . ."

She'd always been beautiful to him. Strong.

Perfect.

"I'll hold your hand," he whispered and pressed a kiss to her neck. *Losing her.* He tasted the salt on her skin. His tears. "And I'll kiss you as the waves crash."

Her heart wasn't beating. She wasn't speaking. Wasn't moving at all. Her body was there, but he didn't feel Eve any longer.

Gone.

His head lifted. Cain saw an ambulance and fire truck race toward them and come to a screeching halt. Help, finally arriving.

Humans were often too late.

He eased Eve's head back and let it rest on the ground. He stared down at her face. When he rose from the flames, she'd be gone.

He'd be broken.

The humans were running toward them, but Cain shook his head. *"Stay back."*

They couldn't help Eve. Not now. If they came closer, they'd just die, too.

Wasn't that all his life was about? Death? Destruction?

With her, there'd been more. Without her . . .

Flames began to burn along his body. The fire wasn't even waiting for death to take him.

Maybe death had already taken him.

Through the flames, he saw the humans freeze. They stumbled back, raising their hands into the air. His own hands were on Eve. He had to keep touching her, even though she was gone.

Gone.

The fire erupted, consuming him, and when hell reached for him with greedy claws, Cain didn't fight.

The flames raced over her skin. Eve felt them, a warm touch along her body. Not pain.

She didn't feel any pain, not anymore.

Her eyes opened. Fire was around her. Such chaos. A slow drumming began, shaking her chest, then growing faster, harder, filling her whole body.

She gasped, sucking in air, near starved for breath. She tasted flames. Smoke.

There were raised voices. Screaming for her. Telling her that *help was there.*

Where?

She sat up and saw the flames. The building—the building they'd been in had been destroyed, but she was just outside of the broken shell that remained. On the ground. Eve glanced down at her clothes. Even in the darkness she could see the blood that soaked her shirt.

Her blood. She'd been shot. The detective—he'd hit her accidentally. She'd been trying to help him and—

Her hand touched her chest. There was no wound. She started to shake. There should have been a wound. The bullet had ripped into her. There was a hole in her shirt from the impact.

And there was a bullet next to her on the ground.

She touched it carefully. Confused, lost, body trembling.

"Cain." His name slipped from her. Cain would tell her what had happened. He'd help her. He'd—

He was burning. Just a few feet away from her. She could see his body through the flames. Big, strong.

Eve rose to her feet. Hands were reaching for her, trying to pull her away from the fire and wreckage. She looked to the right. Saw a firefighter. An EMT was with him. They were walking, but she couldn't hear them, not over the rush of the flames and the frantic beat of her own heart.

She was alive when she should be dead. And Cain— Cain . . .

"Come back to me," she whispered.

Through the flames, she saw his head jerk.

"Come back to me!" Eve screamed even as the fire-fighter dragged her away from the blaze. No, he didn't understand. The flames wouldn't hurt her. Cain wouldn't hurt her.

He'd saved her. Somehow, he had . . .

The tears of a phoenix . . .

The memory of Wyatt's words whispered through her mind.

Holy hell. Had Cain . . . had he cried for her?

Her breath choked in her lungs. Eve shook her head, tried to surge up—and couldn't move. She was being strapped down on a gurney.

"Relax, ma'am, you're safe." A woman gazed down at her. Blond, with big, wide brown eyes. "We're getting you to a hospital. Okay? Just stop fighting us."

But Eve couldn't stop fighting. She had to get back to Cain.

Someone was cutting open her shirt. Another EMT.

"So much blood . . . but where's the wound?" he demanded.

There wasn't a wound. Not anymore. Richard Wyatt had been right. The bastard had actually been right . . .

I can't get him to cry. No matter how much pain I give him.

Wyatt had never been able to break Cain, so there'd been no way to see if the phoenix had healing powers.

Maybe when you die . . . perhaps he'll break then.

Had she died? Had Cain somehow brought her back?

His tears . . . legend has it that they can heal.

They had. Her breath choked out. The tears of a phoenix could cheat death. Only his physical pain hadn't brought forth those tears. Something . . . else . . . had.

Love?

She tried to push up and look back at Cain, but the straps held her back. She could just make out the fire around him . . .

The firefighters were racing toward him.

And he—

Can he see me?

The ambulance doors slammed shut.

They were taking her from him.

Her heart still beats.

The beats called to him, the faintest whispers. She'd been alive. Watching him. Asking . . .

Come back to me.

Men in heavy masks were in his path. Trying to stop him from reaching her? Nothing could stop him.

No one.

He sent his fire at them. They ran back, screaming.

But the ambulance took her. Its sirens echoed in the night as it raced down the road.

No. *Not getting away.*

He wasn't losing her.

The beast was out, and the man within only knew grief and desperation.

Get her. Need her.

He leaped into the air. Moved faster than he'd ever

moved in his life. The fire gave him power. The beast gave him speed. When he hit the ground, the road buckled beneath him. He wasn't behind the ambulance any longer. He was in front of it. The vehicle hurtled toward him, coming with lights flashing.

He lifted his hand.

Destroy.

It was what the beast wanted. The ambulance wasn't slowing. *Attacking me?*

The fire flickered around his fingers, but from inside, buried so deep, the man's thoughts pushed through the rage.

Eve. Inside. Get her.

The ambulance driver braked the vehicle. A squeal of tires. The scent of burning rubber.

The driver stared at Cain in horror. Saw the flames around him. Then the man leaped from the ambulance and ran away.

Cain stalked forward.

Get her.

He reached the back of the ambulance. Yanked open the door. *Eve.* She was strapped down. A man was shoving a needle into her arm.

No.

A roar filled his ears. A roar that came from within. He reached for that man. *Kill.* The flames licked on the man's skin. He screamed. Begged.

"Stop!" Eve's voice.

The flames flickered.

The human scrambled back.

Cain jumped into the ambulance. Tore away the bonds that held her down and yanked her into his arms.

"Let her go!" A woman's voice. He didn't know that voice. Didn't know that woman.

He only knew Eve.

The other woman was reaching for him. Trying to take Eve back.

He needed Eve. There was too much darkness. He could barely breathe. Barely think.

Need.

"Stay away from us," Eve said. "Just stay away!"

The words drove into his skull. Pain exploded inside him and—

Eve put her arms around him. Her shirt was ripped open. Cut open? Her warm, soft skin pressed against him. "Just stay away. He isn't going to hurt me."

She was alive. Her words—they hadn't been for him. She wanted to be with him.

He carried her from the ambulance. Carried her down the street. Past the cops and the ambulances.

While most were smart enough to stay the hell back, one man came racing toward them.

"Not now!" Eve yelled at him.

The man—ash-stained clothing, desperate eyes, the stench of wolf on him . . .

He'd shot Eve. The memory whispered through Cain's mind.

"Keep everyone back," Eve called out. "His control . . . it's too weak now. *Keep them back.*"

Cain wanted that man to come closer. *Come taste the fire.* "That one will burn," he promised, voice a rasp. "So slowly."

Eve's arms tightened around him. "No. You aren't hurting him. You aren't hurting anyone."

He would. He'd make that bastard scream in agony and—

Eve caught the back of his head. Forced his lips down to hers. She kissed him.

He could taste the tears on her lips.

Tears? Eve was crying?

I almost lost her.

He remembered the taste of salt on her skin. Remembered being broken. Ready for hell.

Then . . .

I heard her heartbeat.

She'd come back, so he'd fought hell to get to her.

His mouth opened on hers. Desperate. So hungry. He kissed her. Again and again. Deep. Hard. Consuming.

The roar in his ears—that was the pounding of his blood. The beast fighting the man. But Eve was in his arms. Eve was kissing him. Eve was *alive.*

He pushed back the darkness. He held her tighter. Her body slid down against his. Flesh pressed to flesh. He didn't care about the others around him.

Only her.

She was the only thing that had ever mattered.

Eve pulled her mouth from his. She stared up at him with eyes so wide. What did she see?

Flames in his gaze?

A beast and a man?

Eve smiled at him. "Let's get out of here," she told him, voice soft and tender.

Maybe it was to protect the humans. Maybe she wanted him away from innocents. Right then, he didn't care. He just needed to be with her.

Had to be with her.

"Eve!" The detective's voice. Rage built in Cain, *grew.*

But the cop tossed her a pair of keys. Eve caught then in her left hand and closed her fingers into a fist around them. The cop pointed to a black truck on the right.

Other cops tried to move forward, but Roberts lifted his hand. "Bad fucking plan, trust me. Let him go for now, if you want to keep living."

The cops stopped advancing. Cain lowered Eve to the

ground, and she led him to the truck. Fire trailed in his wake.

They fled the chaos. Driving fast and hard. Eve's hand was in his. Her body pressed against his. He could hold onto his sanity for just a little longer. Until they were away from the humans . . .

For just a little longer.

He could fight the darkness. As long as Eve was at his side, he could fight any damn thing.

Silken skin. Moans. The press of her lips against his.

Cain felt the sensations on his body. They soothed him. *She* soothed him. Sanity was coming back. Moment by moment. Memories. Needs. Emotions.

Everything centered around Eve. He knew everything always would.

He'd driven them for hours. He'd had one destination in mind. Just one . . .

The beach.

He'd had to get her there. Had to be with her. So he'd driven until he'd smelled the ocean air. The salt water. Until he'd heard the cry of seagulls.

They were the only ones on the beach. The sun was rising. Eve was naked, pressing her body against his.

Her eyes were on him, and she stared at him with such a gentle gaze. No fear. She should have been afraid.

Had she ever feared him?

He'd feared her. He'd known that without her . . .

"I'm not going anywhere." She kissed him again. Her hips were over his. Her knees digging into the sand. "Not . . . anywhere." She took him inside her in one long, slow glide. Her hands were against his, pushing them back onto the sand. The sky above her was shot with red and gold. Just like fire.

She began to move on him, lifting her body, then pushing down against him. His cock was heavy, aching, and each movement made him even harder for her.

He could think again. Could focus past the rage and desperation. She was alive. Some way—*alive.*

His hips drove into her. Maybe too hard, but she didn't pull away. She smiled. Arched back against him. Took him deeper.

His groan filled the air, merging with the crashing waves. She lowered her chest against his. Her nipples slid over him, tight peaks, and her mouth took his.

Cain took control. He rolled her beneath him, letting the sand cushion her back. His tongue pushed into her mouth and the strokes of his body within hers pounded faster. He couldn't hold back. Not now.

With her, maybe not ever.

He wanted her to feel the pleasure first. His fingers stroked between her thighs. Stroked over the center of her need. He pumped into her. Thrust his tongue into her mouth.

Her sex clenched around him, and she stiffened.

Yes.

He knew her so well. Could tell every sweet move of her body. Loved the ripple of her release.

"Cain."

His name whispered from her lips. She did that to him— made him a man, not a beast.

The pleasure hit him, brutal, total, consuming. He held on to her even as he pounded into her core.

Eve.

His breath was ragged, his body weak, but he lifted his head and stared down at her.

She was smiling.

She made him want to smile, too.

"I love you, Cain," Eve said.

He kissed her. Tasted the truth on her lips. Somehow, someway, she actually did love him.

Only fair, considering that she was his whole fucking world. "I love you," he told her, but wondered if the words were a lie. Love—too tame a word for the way he felt about her. Too easy. His feelings for her were wild, intense, damn near terrifying.

Not just love. It felt like *more*.

Her fingers curled around his neck. "You saved me."

No. Not even close. Cain shook his head.

Her smile widened. "You did, Cain. You cried for me, didn't you?"

The taste of salt on her neck.

"The tears of a phoenix *can* heal. Wyatt was right about that." A sad sigh eased from her. "Just wrong about everything else."

Wrong. Twisted. So desperate for his experiments . . . even though he'd been tortured by those same experiments when he'd been just a boy.

He hadn't been the only Wyatt to make a monster. It looked like his dear old father had been the first to start the business.

You made your own son into a killer. A true monster.

When he'd been just a kid.

Cain would never do that to his own child. *If* he ever had a child, if Eve ever wanted . . . *I'd be better.* He could protect, not just destroy.

Did Eve know that?

He gazed down at her, saw the trust shining in her eyes, and understood that she did.

Cain realized that he liked the way he looked—from her eyes.

"What happens now?" he asked her.

A shadow of pain slid across her face. "Did you see—did Trace make it out?"

He didn't know. Couldn't remember what had become of the werewolf after the explosion. His focus had been on her. "The cop got out. Maybe Trace did, too." He'd offer her hope, always.

Eve nodded.

"They'll be looking for me now."

They. Not Genesis. That organization was dead. Jeremiah Wyatt had blown it—and himself—to hell. *And you don't get a ticket back, bastard.*

But the humans who'd been on that scene, they'd all gotten a clear look at him. Seen the fury and power that lurked inside him.

Subject Thirteen had a face. A face they would fear.

"You don't have to hide," Eve told him. "Not from me. Not from them."

He'd never hide from her. But as for the others . . .

"They'll want me dead."

"Then it's a good thing you can't die."

Her words caught him off guard. He'd expected a plan, not—not her fast, caustic reply.

Cain laughed. The sound was rusty, old, but the laughter built inside him.

Eve blinked, then her eyes widened. "This is what I wanted," she whispered.

The laughter faded slowly. *This is what happiness feels like.* No wonder humans went around smiling all the freaking time.

It felt good.

"*You* are what I want," he told her. "When I thought that I'd lost you . . ."

No, he didn't want to go back there. To the hopeless moments. He'd known only fury. Agony. *Can't lose her.*

Won't.

"Don't *ever* get hurt again," he ordered. He didn't think

he could stand it. And any humans around at the time of her pain . . . well, they might not be able to stand it, either.

"I'll try not to," she said softly, with a hint of a smile playing around her lips. "But, ah, can you do me a favor, too? Maybe . . . stop dying on me."

Cain wasn't sure how many more deaths he could survive. How much more darkness he could take.

Not true.

The knowledge sank inside him. He could die a hundred more times, he knew that. Die and come back—as long as she waited for him. "Stay with me,"

"There's nowhere else I'd rather be."

There *was* no other place for him. He only wanted to be at her side. Always. He brought her hand to his lips. Kissed her knuckles.

He rose. Pulled her to her feet. He was aware of the darkness, lurking in the back of his mind, but with Eve's hand in his, that darkness stayed in the background.

There wasn't any death on the beach. No fear. No rage. Just Eve.

Just . . . *hope.*

For more.

Her fingers twined with his as they walked toward the ocean. His feet sank into the sand. Eve's shoulder brushed against his arm.

There would be no more hiding in the shadows. Not for him. But the more he thought about it, the more Cain realized that he didn't care. He'd find a way to deal with the humans.

He had something better than anonymity. He had life.

He had Eve.

Cain kissed her and the passion stirred once more between them.

How he did love that sweet burn.

Eve.

Finally, he'd found someone who could look past the fire. Someone who wasn't afraid of the heat. Someone who'd always been meant to be—

Mine.

Just as he'd been meant to be hers.

Together, through fire, through death.

Through life.

EPILOGUE

Humans feared him. That was nothing new. His story filled the televisions. The newspapers. The Internet chat sites.

A phoenix. Myth. Man.

What the hell ever.

He didn't care what people said. Their gossip and their fears didn't matter to him.

She mattered.

Cain watched Eve walk toward him. She was coming from their house. The house he'd bought for her. Right on the beach, nestled high so the waves and the storms wouldn't hurt it.

Their home.

It had been just a few months, but he felt like he'd always been there with her.

Maybe Eve was his real home.

"I've found a specialist who works with wolves . . ."

Ah, he could hear the excitement in her voice.

Cain reached for her hand. "You mean *werewolves.*"

Eve nodded quickly. "She's been doing genetic research for years. I think—I think she might be able to help Trace."

Cain didn't point out that they hadn't seen the wolf since the explosion. His body had never been recovered. Not that much *would* have been left for recovery . . .

But Eve had hope. And if she believed the guy was alive, then he would believe, too.

"We can talk to her and find a cure." She was so certain.

And sexy. His lips skimmed over hers. "When do we leave?" He knew Eve. Always fighting. Always pushing.

That was fine—as long as she remembered who was by her side.

Her smile lit up her face. "I've already booked the plane tickets."

Of course she had.

"This will work," she told him, "Trust me."

He did trust her. He'd let her reveal his full story to the press. He'd worked with the FBI, *for her.* He'd bled, he'd died—all for her.

Trust? That was the least he'd given to her.

She turned away, pulling his hand so that he had no choice but to follow her. *Always.*

"Oh, and I'm pregnant . . ." she tossed back at him in a rush.

For a minute there, Cain wondered if his heart had stopped.

Eve glanced back. A flicker of worry had her eyes scanning his face. "I thought . . . um, you're still good with that plan, right?"

That plan. Marrying her. Having a home. Having a family.

"I know it's sooner than we'd thought," she said, the words coming fast, the way they always did when she was nervous, "and I didn't expect—but I'm glad and I hope you—"

Cain kissed her. Her lips were open, so perfect, and his mouth pressed against her.

This is happiness.

The thought whispered through his mind. The same thought he'd had months before, right on the same beach.

Then another followed it, a vow he'd made to himself. *I will be better.*

He'd protect the child, cherish him or her . . . just as much as he cherished Eve.

In the distance, Cain heard the faintest echo of a wolf's howl. His head lifted.

"Cain?" Eve questioned softly. "Your eyes . . ."

He knew the fire lit them. But the fire wasn't just about rage. Not anymore. He smiled at her and said, "I'm good with the plan."

More than good. The plan was pretty fucking perfect to him.

Eve hugged him, squeezing tight.

Over her shoulder, he stared off into the distance. The howl was gone. Pulled away by the crash of the surf. But he'd heard it, and Cain knew what would make the perfect wedding gift for his bride.

He just had to track that wolf . . . maybe he'd call in a blood debt for that job. That vamp Ryder *did* still owe him.

Cain smiled . . . and began to plan.

Keep reading for excerpts from

the next two books in

Cynthia Eden's

Phoenix Fire series

Once Bitten, Twice Burned

Available Summer 2014

and

Playing With Fire

Available Fall 2014

There was nowhere for her to run. She was pinned to the thick stone behind her and trapped with him in front of her. She shoved her head back against the stone as she tried to put a feeble distance between them, and unfortunately for her, that move had the effect of exposing more of her throat to him.

"You can't be real," she whispered. "Your teeth . . . your eyes . . . *none* of this is real. They drugged me. I'm hallucinating."

If only. Poor lady. She'd had no clue about the monsters that walked in this world, not until Wyatt had tossed her into hell. "Just . . . hold still. It'll be . . . over soon."

Just a few sips.

"No!" She screamed then rammed against him, a blow that was surprisingly powerful. Powerful enough to send him stumbling back five feet.

His ass hit the floor because he'd never expected that kind of attack from her. Humans weren't strong enough to toss vamps around like that.

The intercom crackled. "Ah now, Sabine, that wasn't part of the deal. I told you that if you provided nourishment for my guest, then we'd discuss your freedom."

Her chest heaved. A nice chest, he noticed, even through the rage and hunger. Full breasts.

"I'm not nourishment!" she yelled as she glared into the two-way mirror. "You can't do this to me! I have rights!"

"Your rights don't exactly apply here." Wyatt didn't sound concerned. Why would he? The guy had the might of the U.S. military backing his little "experiments."

The worst fucking mistake the paranormals had ever made was coming out of the closet. But some idiots just couldn't keep quiet. They'd shown themselves to humans. Gotten tired of living by the old ways—or hell, maybe even technology had been to blame. Too much advancement. Cameras everywhere. Eyes always watching.

It was hard to hide the beast inside when big brother was *always* spying on you.

So they'd come out, and freaks like Wyatt thought they could harness their paranormal power. Use science to make magic into their weapon of choice.

"If you aren't cooperating, Ms. Acadia, we can always take you back to your cell." Wyatt's voice lowered. "Guard, retrieve—"

"I don't want my cell! I want to go home! I want—"

Ryder pounced. In an instant, he had her in his arms. He twisted her hands and secured them behind her body. She was struggling, definitely using more than just human strength, but he was prepared for her. She wasn't getting away.

"I won't hurt you," he told her, hoping the words weren't a lie. Sometimes, the bite could bring a woman pleasure. A better release than sex.

Sometimes, the bite could bring pain. Worse than torture.

He didn't want her to hurt.

His mouth was desert dry. His fangs fully extended and aching. He could already taste her.

I just want her.

His tongue swept over her neck. Sampled, then he sank his teeth into her throat.

The woman—Sabine—gasped against him. Her body

arched into his as the first tender drops of her blood spilled onto his tongue.

"Make sure the recording is operational." Wyatt's voice seemed to come from so far away. "I want to get every bit of this."

But Wyatt and what he wanted didn't matter. Sabine's blood was on Ryder's tongue, and her blood . . .

Her blood.

It was like nothing he'd ever tasted in all of his four hundred years of existence. Not just warm—the blood was hot. Spicy. Rich with flavor. He wanted to lap it up, to savor it.

To gorge on it.

His hands hardened on her. He'd meant to take just a few drops.

He wanted to lift his head away. Wanted to so badly but . . .

Her blood was too good.

He drank more, greedy. Desperate. Her blood flowed through him, heating his body from the inside out and sending tendrils of power pulsing through him. Some humans tasted of wine. Some of the euphoria that came from drugs.

No one had ever tasted like her. Life. Sex. Pleasure. Everything he wanted was right there in her blood.

He drank deeper.

"S-stop." Her voice was weaker than before.

He didn't want to stop. He'd looked for this—he'd always wanted this taste. Craved it, when he hadn't even known what he was missing. His body seemed to be growing stronger, the muscles expanding with every drop of her blood that he took.

She sagged against him, and Ryder scooped her into his arms, holding her even when her head fell to the side and her breath rattled in her chest.

More.

More.

At first, he thought the urging was just inside him, but then he realized that bastard Wyatt was the one urging him on.

And the woman . . . Sabine wasn't fighting him any longer. She barely seemed to be breathing.

He jerked his head away. Stared down at her in disbelief. He hadn't taken that much, had he?

But he couldn't remember how long he'd been drinking. He only knew—

I still want more.

He lifted her higher against his chest. Held her cradled in his arms. There was no more weakness for him. Only strength. But she . . .

Her lashes were closed.

A fear unlike any he'd known before had his whole body tensing. He'd just found her. Ryder knew he couldn't lose her so soon. *Not. Now.*

And sure as fuck not by his own hand. Or teeth.

He brought his wrist to his mouth. Slashed open the flesh. He knew what she needed. "Drink for me." She'd be all right once she drank his blood.

"No!" Wyatt's voice thundered out. "Stop! Put Sabine down and back away."

"Fuck off." Ryder lowered them both to the floor so he could better tend her. But he kept her close as he put his wrist to her mouth. "Drink." She'd just need a little of his blood, and she'd heal.

If she'd just drink . . .

An alarm began to sound. Voices shouted over the intercom. Then footsteps rushed outside his door. The guards were finally coming in to face him.

It was the perfect time to kill them. But if he moved

away from Sabine, she'd die. She needed more of his blood. She needed him to survive.

His eyes narrowed on her face. *What are you?*

She'd been afraid. She'd fought him. She'd stared at a monster and had asked to go home.

Now she was almost at death's broken door.

"Get away from her!" Wyatt was shrieking.

She wasn't drinking. Ryder pried open her mouth. Forced drops of blood onto her tongue and then massaged her neck, trying to make her swallow. *Live.*

The guards grabbed him, trying to yank him away from her. *Hell, no.* He threw them back. Heard thuds when they hit the walls.

"You have to swallow the blood," he told her, voice dark and rumbling with command. "Come on . . ." *I didn't mean . . . to do this.* She'd been so afraid. He'd told her that he'd hold on to his control.

But the beast that he was hadn't been able to hold on. The beast . . . Ryder . . . destroyed. That was his life. All he knew. And he'd destroyed her, too.

His vision seemed to blacken. She was the only thing he could see in that growing darkness. Beautiful, so still.

His head sagged over her. *"Please."* He was the one to beg. He'd tasted heaven, and he'd tossed her to hell, all in one instant of time.

"Get away from her!" Wyatt's voice wasn't on the loud-speaker any longer. It was right there. In the room with him.

Kill him.

Ryder's head flew up. He bared his fangs.

And . . . and felt her mouth move lightly against his wrist. She was trying to drink, to take his blood.

Sabine was fighting to live. *Yes.*

His gaze snapped back to her. "That's it! Come on, just drink some—"

Gunshots blasted. Bullets drove into his chest. One. Two. Three. The force of the hits had him falling back even as his blood sprayed the wall behind him.

"I *told* you," Wyatt raged as he lifted his weapon. *Wyatt had fired?* "Back away from the female subject!"

Ryder ignored the pain and reached for her again.

"Stop him," Wyatt ordered.

Ryder realized the guards were back on their feet.

"Shoot him until he stops moving. The bullets won't kill him, but they can put him down for a time."

Bullets exploded, popping like firecrackers over and over again as they sank into Ryder's body. His chest. His arms.

He hit the floor. Blood seeped from his wounds. Pooled around him on the stone floor.

"Enough!" Wyatt lifted his hand. His eyes went from Ryder to Sabine.

She wasn't moving. Her head had turned and her eyes— wide open, still alive—were on Ryder. He could see the life in her gaze. She was trying to come back to him. *Trying.* She just needed more of his blood. Her hand lifted.

Was she reaching for him? Ryder gathered every single ounce of strength that he had. "My . . . blood . . ." Only a little more, and she'd be fine. He could save her. Her death—unlike all the others—wouldn't be on him. He started crawling to her through the blood.

"She's gonna live," one of the guards muttered. "I thought he was supposed to kill her."

He could be more than a killer. She could be more than a victim. Blood soaked his clothes. The power he'd gotten from her rich blood was gone, stolen away by a hail of bullets.

"He did kill her," Wyatt's voice was flat. "We just have to wait for her to die."

No! "Can . . . help . . ." Ryder was almost to her side.

"Chain him," Wyatt ordered. "He's too weak to fight you. Chain the vampire and let him watch."

Their arms grabbed him. Jerked him away from her. But he wasn't as weak as they thought, not even with the bullets lodged in his organs. Ryder fought then, clawing and snapping with his fangs. Half a dozen guards had to jump on him and yank him back to the far wall. Then they locked thick chains around his wrists, trapping him. The guards hurried back as soon as those locks snapped in place. They were bloody—from the wounds he'd given them.

When they moved away, he saw her again. Her chest was struggling to rise. Her eyes were still open.

"Don't . . . do this," he growled as he strained to break free.

Wyatt walked around her, staring down at Sabine as she sprawled on the floor. "Why do you even care? Shouldn't she just be food to you?"

Ryder didn't speak. He wouldn't tell the bastard anything about himself.

"I think one of the bullets must have ripped into your heart." Wyatt didn't sound particularly concerned. "You're bleeding far too much. Hmmm . . . I should have considered . . . will that wound to the heart kill you?"

No. It wouldn't. Ryder was healing already.

"I didn't intend for them to shoot you in the heart." Wyatt frowned at the guards. "Errors like that cannot be tolerated here."

The guy was fucking psycho.

A bullet to the heart wasn't normally an error. It was murder.

"You're just . . . gonna watch . . . her die?" Ryder yanked at the chains and didn't care when they cut into his wrists. He'd heal. He always healed.

She won't.

"Yes." Wyatt nodded and offered an almost absent smile. "Yes, I am."

Her eyes were on Ryder—her eyes . . .

He saw the life leave them. Actually saw a veil of nothing sweep into her stare. *"No!"* He yanked at the chains, twisting his hands, breaking his wrists as he fought to get free. He smashed his fingers as he tried to jerk his hand through the ring that bound his wrist. He didn't feel the pain as he struggled.

Dead.

"Exit," Wyatt snapped. *"Now."*

The guards started hauling ass. They were leaving her like that? Just sprawled on the floor like a broken doll?

Maybe there was still time. His right wrist shattered. *Maybe.*

"If I were you, I wouldn't move," Wyatt advised Ryder with a quick frown as he paused by the door. "This is her first change. I have no idea how powerful it will be."

Ryder didn't understand the bastard. He was moving, all right. *Won't give up.* Won't—

The door slammed shut behind Wyatt and his men. And . . . the scent of smoke teased Ryder's nose.

What the hell?

His gaze snapped back to Sabine. Her eyes were still open, only her eyes weren't dark brown any longer. The brown was changing, turning to a gold; then they seemed to burn red.

Red like fire.

The scent of smoke deepened around him. Ryder pulled his broken right hand free. The other—

Her body began to burn.

He yelled then, roaring her name, but the fire didn't stop. It blazed hotter, higher, and swept over Sabine's slender form. The white-hot heat from the blaze rushed over his skin, almost singeing him. Sprinklers erupted with a powerful spray from overhead, and the water drenched him, but did nothing to stop the blaze that consumed Sabine.

His breath heaved out. Ryder stopped fighting for his freedom. There was nothing to be done. No one could come back from those flames.

So there was nothing for him to do in the end but watch the fire burn, to hate himself for the monster that he was, and to wish that Sabine Acadia had never had the misfortune to walk into his prison.

As he watched, something began to move within those flames. *She* moved, and Ryder realized that Wyatt's experiments were just getting started.

Even though she'd died right in front of him, even though Sabine was burning, it sure looked like she was trying to rise from the fire.

Cassie shoved her way through the crowd, muttering apologies as she bumped into various paranormal beings—and humans—who filled Taboo. Since the paranormals had stopped pretending they didn't exist—and gotten wild with their coming-out party—clubs like Taboo had popped up in all the major cities in the U.S. and around the world.

Dante stood against the back wall. The vampire, a woman with long red hair and a way too short skirt, had her hands all over him. Bloodred nails, of course. Typical. The redhead was arching up on her toes and putting her mouth close to Dante's neck.

"Okay. You're just going to need to get away from him," Cassie snapped as she closed in on them.

The vampire froze.

Dante tilted his head to the side and glanced curiously over at Cassie. Was there any recognition in his dark gaze?

Of course not.

To him, she could have been any stranger off the street.

Don't let it hurt. Don't. Dante couldn't help what he was. But he could get the hell away from that trashy vamp.

The vampire spun toward Cassie and hissed. Wait. Hissed, really?

Cassie barely controlled an eye roll.

"Get lost," the vamp told her, baring her fangs. "He's mine."

Think again.

Cassie's hands were clenched into fists, and it took all her self-control not to swing out at the chick. "No, he's not." Said definitely. She looked past the vampire. "Dante, we need to leave."

He stiffened.

That's right. I know your name. Why, oh, why can't you know something about me? Anything?

But that was the way it always was for them.

She kept holding Dante's gaze. "Trust me on this," Cassie said. "You don't want her sinking those fangs into you." Dante's blood was special, and rather addictive to vampires. If the redhead got one sip, she wouldn't be backing away from him anytime soon.

Then I'd have to stake her. Oh, what a pity.

"Dante, we can—" Cassie's words ended in a gasp.

The vampire had lunged forward and wrapped her hand around Cassie's throat. With that one hand, she lifted Cassie off her feet. "Maybe I'll just sink my fangs into you, bitch." She leaned her head in close to Cassie and whispered, "Because no one gets between me and my meal."

"Y-you . . . don't . . . want—" Cassie tried to choke out the words but it was hard to speak, um, what with the vamp actually *choking* her and all. She was trying to tell the redhead . . . *You don't want to put your fangs in me. That would be a huge mistake.*

But the vamp wasn't giving her the time to talk.

"Let her go." Dante's voice. Cold. Flat. And as deliciously deep as Cassie remembered.

The vampire's eyes narrowed as she stared at her with a mix of disgust and rage. "You're right. We don't need her. We don't—"

"I said . . . *let her go.*" The threat in Dante's voice had goose bumps rising on Cassie's arms. "And I meant do it *now.*"

The vamp dropped her.

Cassie landed on her ass. Figured. She'd never been the graceful type.

The redhead turned toward Dante. "Ready to leave?" she purred to him.

Purring. Hissing. The vamp was so annoying.

"You leave." Dante sent her a look that could have frozen a desert. "I'm not done here."

"But—"

"And I'm not your fucking meal," he added, a touch of heat whipping through his words.

Ah, so he had heard that part. Cassie rather thought his enhanced hearing would pick it up.

The redhead glared at Dante, then at Cassie. A promise of retribution was in the vamp's eyes.

Ah yes, another day, another enemy. Cassie swallowed and rose slowly to her feet.

"I'll see you again," the vampire murmured. The words were directed at Cassie, and they sure sounded like a threat.

Wonderful. As if she needed any more threats in her life.

Then the vampire was gone. Probably off to find another meal.

"Who are you?" His voice was a low rumble of sound, one that sent a few more shivers dancing over her skin. Maybe some people—okay, *most* people—would find that deep rumble scary.

To her, it was sexy. Because of Dante, she'd always had thing for men with deep voices.

She squared her shoulders and stared up at him. "Did you burn again?" She'd seen him just a few months before in New Orleans.

He'd saved her life then. Had actually seemed to remember her . . .

But now there was no recognition on his face.

She stared up at him. Those high cheekbones, that square jaw. The firm lips that she'd never seen smile, despite all her attempts to make him happy.

His eyes were dark, so dark that they appeared almost as black as the thick hair that hung a little too long and grazed the back of his shirt.

His eyes were watchful, guarded as they swept over her.

"Burn?" Dante repeated carefully.

In the next second, he lunged forward—his move faster than the vamp's had been. His hand—big, strong, hot— wrapped around Carrie's arm and pulled her close against his chest. "Now just how the hell would you know about that?"

Cassie wasn't as tall as the redhead. Not even close. She was barely skirting five foot five, so she had to tilt her head back to hold his gaze. Dante was at least six foot three, and the guy was built along some very muscled dimensions.

His hold tightened. "Answer me."

His fingers seemed to heat up, and she knew his power was coursing through his blood. If she wasn't careful, he might burn her. Just how much control did he have?

"Please," Cassie kept her voice even with an extreme effort. "I'm not here to hurt you." No, she was there to beg for his help. If he'd remembered her, even a little, that begging would have gone over much better.

She cleared her throat. "The burn must be fresh. Your memory usually comes back within a week or so after your rising."

His face seemed to turn to stone.

Usually was the keyword. Dante had been through so much in the last few years. His memory was a very brittle thing. So was his sanity, a situation that made him a walking, talking nightmare for many.

"You must have been attacked," she whispered. Attacked . . . and killed. Because death was the only way—

He lifted her up and tossed her over his shoulder.

Cassie yelped, totally not expecting that move. She shoved her hands against his ass—um, a very nice ass—and pushed herself up so she could see around her.

Some of the club's patrons were looking at her, amusement on their faces. They weren't exactly the kind to help a lady in distress. The redheaded vampire was staring her way. *Glaring* her way, rather. And Dante was stalking away with her, his grip on her legs unbreakable.

Okay, so that was one way to get his attention.

She heard the sound of shattering wood. Had he just smashed a door? Sounded like he had. Cassie tried to crane around and see where they were going. It looked like they were headed inside some kind of back room. Stacks of boxes and bottles of alcohol lined the shelves.

"Get the hell out of here!" Dante's snarled order.

Three bodies ran past her, fast.

Then the world spun a bit, and Cassie found herself sprawled on top of a wooden table. Dante held one of her wrists in each of his hands, and he stood between her legs.

Oh, wow.

"Who are you?" he demanded.

"My name won't matter to you." She barely breathed the words. "If you rose recently—"

"Your name!"

"C-Cassie Armstrong. Cassandra . . ."

His eyelids flickered. "Cassandra." He said her name as if he were tasting it.

Please, remember me. So many times over the years she was sure that he did remember her, but then the tortures would start again. Torture and death.

He'd lose the memory of her, and she'd have to try so hard to get close to him again. To *make* him remember.

An endless cycle that left her hurting inside.

"I've dreamed about you," he whispered. His hold was an unbreakable grip on her wrists.

At his confession, her heartbeat picked up and hope blossomed inside her. Finally, finally, he'd—

"In my dreams"—a muscle flexed along his jaw—"you kill me, Cassie Armstrong."

Oh, hell. "I told you. I'm not here to hurt you."

"But you *have* killed me before, haven't you?"

Cassie knew she had to be careful. She wasn't like him. Dante could die, again and again, but he would just come back from each death.

He'd rise from the ashes and be born again.

While she would just—well, die. There would be no coming back for her.

With a thought, he could incinerate her. The heat that warmed her skin beneath his fingers could turn into a blazing inferno at any second.

"Last night, I dreamed about you." His words were a low growl as he leaned closer to her. The noise from the bar drifted into the room. The blaring beat of music. The scents of sex, blood, and booze. "You stared right at me, then you stabbed me."

His bad memories weren't going to make things any easier.

"Maybe you should tell me why I shouldn't just pay you back for that right now." His breath blew lightly over the sensitive skin of her neck. "And end *you.*"

She shook her head, sending her long hair sliding over her shoulders. "Please . . ."

"Oh, I like it when you beg."

Actually, he did. But that was another story.

"So you've had dreams . . ." Cassie started talking fast. She had seen him incinerate a man before. She didn't want that same fate. "Well, I'm your key. I know you. Every dark spot in your mind? I can shine the light and show you—"

He leaned over her even more. His mouth was just inches from hers. Inches? More like *an* inch. "What are you going to show me?"

"Everything," she whispered, promised. "I can tell you the secrets of your life. I can tell you *who* you are, if you'll just trust me."

His gaze searched hers. Some people thought that his eyes were just dark—mirroring his black soul, but they were wrong. There were flecks of gold hidden in his eyes. A person just had to look hard and deep enough to see them.

"Why should I trust a woman who's killed me before?"

"Because I've saved you, too." She'd risked so much to save him. "Believe it or not, you actually *owe* me."

"I don't believe it."

Her lips trembled.

His gaze dropped once more to her mouth.

"Dante . . ."

He kissed her.

She hadn't been expecting the move, and when his lips closed over hers, shock froze her for a moment. Then she realized—*Dante.*

Her lips parted eagerly for him, and the wall that she'd built to hold back her need for him started to fracture. His tongue pushed into her mouth. Not sampling, but taking, and it was just like she remembered. He kissed her, she wanted. Lust tore through her, and her wrists twisted in his grip because she needed to touch him.

She wanted—

His head lifted. His eyes blazed down at her, the gold starting to heat. "I remember . . . your mouth. Your taste."

She'd never be able to forget his kiss. He'd been the first

man that she ever kissed. The first to make her feel like she belonged to someone.

A someone who sometimes seemed to hate her.

"You can trust me," she whispered to him, desperate to make him believe her.

He gave a hard shake of his head. "No, that's the last thing I can do." Then he was moving away from her, leaping back.

For an instant, she didn't move. His eyes were on her, sweeping from the top of her hair down to her small sandals. He seemed confused. Yeah, well, so was she.

Don't kiss me and jerk away. She didn't have the damn plague.

"I woke up a week ago," he told her quietly, his voice still making her ache. "In an alley that had been scorched. I was naked, and there were ashes all around me."

Her heart beat faster as she straightened on the table.

"What happened to me?" he demanded.

"Dante, I—"

"Is that my name?" The memory loss seemed more severe than it had been in the past.

"Y-yes. That's what you told me to call you." But was it really his name? She wasn't sure. He'd never confessed too much about his life—at least, not his life before he'd come to be a prisoner.

"What happened to me in the alley?"

Okay. If she was going to get his trust, then she was obviously going to have to share with him. "I think you died."

He laughed. The sound was bitter and hard, just like the laughter she'd heard from him a dozen times. She'd tried for years to get a real laugh from him. That hadn't happened.

"If I died," he asked, "then how am I breathing now?"

That was the tricky-to-explain part. "Look, Dante—"

Shouts erupted from the other room. High-pitched, desperate screams that were immediately followed by the rat-a-tat of gunfire.

They found me.

Cassie's heartbeat froze in her chest. Then she was the one leaping forward and grabbing Dante's hand. "We have to go. *Now.*"